PRAISE FOR FIONA M

'McCallum shifts effortlessly from the relatable to the aspirational, from everyday domestic scenes to those big, life-altering moments we all experience. *Looking Out* is no exception ... Part of McCallum's charm is the way she treats her readers with such care, providing just the right balance of page-turning intrigue, escapism and down-to-earth relatability.'

—*Better Reading*

'This is a story which has much to remind us about regarding inter family relationships and the importance of long-lasting strong connections with others outside the family circle.'

—*Queensland Reviewers Collective* on *Looking Out*

'Always brilliant.'

—*The Australian Women's Weekly* on *Sunrise Over Mercy Court*

'A beautiful, unique and wonderful tale about love, loss, friendship, honesty, family, growing old and feeling unseen by writer extraordinaire Fiona McCallum.'

—*Happy Valley Books Read* on *Sunrise Over Mercy Court*

'A heart-warming and humorous story about rediscovering the small pleasures that make life worthwhile, from one of Australia's most loved storytellers ... A lovely meditation on reclaiming ourselves and our hope ... We can't recommend this enough.'

—*Better Reading* on *Sunrise Over Mercy Court*

'Fiona McCallum draws on her favourite topics to write about – human nature, care of animals and life itself. *Sunrise Over Mercy Court* is a tale of human relationships, connection, loss and renewed hope. It is another tender tale … Fiona McCallum is a heartfelt and sensitive storyteller … If you are seeking an in touch and personal novel about life, it is time to pick up *Sunrise Over Mercy Court*.'
—*Mrs B's Book Reviews*

'Fiona McCallum is one of Australia's favourite authors, and *Her Time to Shine* is another inspiring tale about finding strength and overcoming obstacles.'
—*Canberra Weekly*

'A master storyteller.'
—*Good Reading Magazine*

'A heart-warming book that deals sensitively with issues of loss, financial uncertainty and emotional repair.'
—*Canberra Weekly* on *Trick of the Light*

'A deeply moving story about loss and the unexpected benefits of having to find your feet when the whole world seems to be conspiring to knock you off them.'
—*Australian Country* on *Trick of the Light*

'*The Long Road Home* is a lovely read that transported me away for the day … this story was as comforting as it is entertaining.'
—*Better Reading*

'It's an inspiring tale about finding hope.'
—*Daily Telegraph* on *The Long Road Home*

'Fiona McCallum is one of Australia's most popular authors and *The Long Road Home* is another inspiring tale about rebuilding your life and taking chances ... a heart-warming and timely book.'
—*Canberra Weekly*

'This is a story for readers on a quest to find their wings and fly.'
—*Townsville Bulletin* on *A Life of Her Own*

'Her central character is usually a woman to whom the reader immediately warms ... you stay loyal to her despite everything.'
—*Country Style* on *A Life of Her Own*

'McCallum has a keen eye for fine detail and writes about raw emotion better than any other contemporary writer.'
—*WarCry Magazine* on *Making Peace*

'Fiona McCallum writes *Finding Hannah* with tenderness and insight ... will leave no reader with a dry eye.'
—*The Weekly Times*

'I am not ashamed to say I cried in places for the heartbreak was real and the everyday situations easy to relate to ... This is a wonderful story of recovery.'
—*Books at 60* on *Finding Hannah*

'McCallum writes to inspire her readers to find their true meaning in life and *Standing Strong* is certain to do this.'
—*The Weekly Times*

'*Standing Strong* considers duty, how to do what you know is right even when it's emotionally challenging. With its relatable

characters, dialogue and issues, this is a novel that will ring true for many readers.'
—*Better Reading*

'This is a very fine story, well-handled, and does not avoid the hard issues.'
—*Weekly Times* on *Wattle Creek*

'If ever there was a farm-lit book designed for competitive horse riders, this has to be it.' —*Newcastle Herald* on *Leap of Faith*

'Fiona McCallum wears her literary heart on her dustcovers and with her stories swirling through towns we know and live in, she turns next-door-neighbours into larger-than-life characters – plus a little horse with a big heart.'
—*Riverine Herald* on *Leap of Faith*

'A beautiful novel filled with romance, inner strength and above all, friendship.'
—*That Book You Like* on *Time Will Tell*

'*Saving Grace* is a must-read.'
—*Woman's Day*

'McCallum captures the nuances of a country town and the personalities of the characters that live there.'
—*The Big Book Club* on *Saving Grace*

'A moving melodrama.'
—*Courier-Mail* on *Nowhere Else*

Fiona McCallum was raised on a cereal and wool farm near Cleve on South Australia's Eyre Peninsula and remained in the area until her mid-twenties. Having lived in Melbourne and Sydney, she currently resides in Adelaide. Fiona is the author of more than a dozen bestselling novels that draw on her rich and contrasting life experiences, love of animals and fascination with human nature. *Right Way Up* is Fiona's seventeenth novel. For more information about Fiona and her books, visit her website at fionamccallum.com. She can also be found on Facebook at facebook.com/fionamccallum.author.

Also by Fiona McCallum

Paycheque
Nowhere Else
Leap of Faith
Sunrise Over Mercy Court
Looking Out

The Wattle Creek series
Wattle Creek
Standing Strong

The Button Jar series
Saving Grace
Time Will Tell
Meant To Be

The Finding Hannah series
Finding Hannah
Making Peace

The Ballarat series
A Life of Her Own
The Long Road Home

The Trick of the Light series
Trick of the Light
Her Time to Shine

Right Way Up

FIONA McCALLUM

RIGHT WAY UP
© 2025 by Fiona McCallum
ISBN 9781038921468

First published on Gadigal Country in Australia in 2025
by HQ Fiction
an imprint of HQBooks (ABN 47 001 180 918), a subsidiary of HarperCollins Publishers Australia Pty Limited (ABN 36 009 913 517).

HarperCollins acknowledges the Traditional Custodians of the lands upon which we live and work, and pays respect to Elders past and present.

The right of Fiona McCallum to be identified as the author of this work has been asserted by her in accordance with the *Copyright Amendment (Moral Rights) Act 2000*.

This work is copyright. Apart from any use as permitted under the *Copyright Act 1968*, no part may be reproduced, copied, scanned, stored in a retrieval system, recorded, or transmitted, in any form or by any means, without the prior written permission of the publisher. Without limiting the author's and publisher's exclusive rights, any unauthorised use of this publication to train generative artificial intelligence (AI) technologies is expressly prohibited.

This is a work of fiction. Names, characters, places, and incidents are either the product of the author's imagination or are used fictitiously, and any resemblance to actual persons, living or dead, business establishments, events, or locales is entirely coincidental.

A catalogue record for this book is available from the National Library of Australia
www.librariesaustralia.nla.gov.au

Printed and bound in Australia by McPherson's Printing Group

For Phillip, the best man I know.

*In memory of my beloved feline friend, Whisky,
who gave me thirteen wonderful years of companionship
and unconditional love.*

Chapter One

Colin checked the clock again despite having looked at it barely two minutes ago. He was a little tetchy after his previous session. As usual, his relationship counselling regulars, Julia and David, hadn't seemed at all interested in anything he had to say and had spent the whole of the allocated time arguing and talking over each other. He was always surprised when he saw their names on his appointment list. After each session he was sure they'd realise going their separate ways was the only logical solution to their ill-suited match and inability to effectively communicate. He couldn't see what, but they must think they got something useful out of their sessions, otherwise why would they waste their money in this fashion?

Oh well, that couldn't be his concern. Right now, what was of concern was that his last client for the day was already five minutes late. Was Andrea Carlton coming or not? He didn't know if this was the usual MO of the young woman or if something unusual had happened to delay her. This was her first appointment with him. He found himself sighing. It would perhaps be best if she didn't turn up – he was meant to be winding down his practice and retiring.

Colin didn't like to let anyone down. He was pretty sure he wasn't the most competent psychologist going around, but he loved his job and did his best. The country was in the grip of a mental health crisis, so it might be he was considered better than nobody when other places had longer waiting lists. A lot of his work was for organisations recruiting and taking care of employees, but he liked to think it was a testament to him being at least appreciated by a reasonable number of individual clients – both long term and new arrivals – that the spots available for private clients were constantly booked out. He'd never needed to do any advertising beyond having a Facebook page and a website.

Suddenly rain was drumming on the roof above him. He glanced out the window of the soulless rented room at the carpark outside the equally dull brick health centre. Water poured down the glass from the overflowing gutters. Lucky he hadn't already given up on this Andrea Carlton woman or he'd have been caught in the storm on his fifteen-minute walk home.

He glanced at the corner of the room where a collection of umbrellas usually stood in the tall ceramic vase beside the coatrack. Empty. Damn it. Umbrellas came and went. He didn't keep track of them. Clients left theirs behind, others took one. It was a revolving collection that replenished and emptied organically, with the numbers largely dependent on the season. A bit like his practice, really … Scarves tended to do a similar thing, though he always advised clients of them – left them with the office manager for collection. Scarves were more personal and revered than umbrellas, Joyce, his wife of forty-eight years, had told him.

There was a bold knock on the door he'd left open after having checked outside it for Andrea's presence just before. He stood up to greet her. She appeared a little sodden – wet hair, beads of water on her face and in her eyelashes, darker patches to her clothes.

'I'm so sorry I'm late! I ...' The woman's voice trailed off as she shrugged a little helplessly and proceeded to twist herself out from under her handbag draped across her body by a long strap, sending a few glistening droplets flying.

'It's quite all right.'

'God, I must look a sight. Got caught in a heavy downpour. Bloody spring! If it's not the allergies it's the random spontaneous downpours. They're never just a light shower, are they – always big fat drops this time of year. Sorry, I'm babbling.'

Colin closing the door seemed to act as a circuit breaker. She stopped talking and moving at the same time and stood looking at him, his desk between them. Then she put her hand to her hair.

'Shit. Sorry, I'm dripping all over the place too. Um ...' She looked around helplessly, frowning slightly at the box of tissues on the corner of the desk. Colin pulled a carefully folded and pressed handkerchief from his pocket and handed it to her.

He watched while she quickly mopped her face and then opened up the large square of linen and dragged it over her hair, front to back and then around. She then folded up the handkerchief and handed it back to him.

'Thanks,' she said. 'Right. I um ...' She looked from the two chairs on the other side of his desk to the couch against the wall.

'Sit wherever you like. Whatever makes you feel most comfortable.'

'Sorry. I'm a bit tense,' she offered with a cringe.

How many utterances of the word sorry is that now? Colin made a mental note, which he'd write down on the client file card waiting on his desk when they got going: *Appears very unsure of herself. Apologises profusely. Conscious or not?*

'And I say sorry *a lot*! It's a … a *thing*, apparently.'

Ahh, I see. He mentally adjusted his note: *yes, is aware.*

'That's perfectly understandable. There's no rush. Take your time to get settled.'

'I need to just get my shit together. Stop being so …' Colin watched as she shook her head as if to banish the unspoken, unfinished thought. 'Sorry, I'll stop babbling. I'm going to sit over here.' She indicated the couch.

Colin smiled to himself as she threw herself onto the couch longways and then linked her hands behind her head. People always thought the couch was for lying on, but it was there more for seating couples. You could tell a lot about how two people sat together on a couch – how far apart and at what angle. That was often more useful than what they said during several sessions. But thanks to every TV show and movie involving therapists, everyone thought the couch was for lying along. It obviously was for that, too – Colin used it for his daily afternoon nap – but for clients, lying down meant looking at the wall rather than him, or turning one's head.

Colin felt as if he'd been standing for ages, but in reality it was probably only a couple of seconds. He sat down at his desk.

'I'm really tense,' Andrea said, turning to look over at him.

'Just take a few moments to catch your breath. There's no rush,' he added again. 'And then you can tell me why you're here and what I can help with.'

'Actually, I think I'll sit up,' Andrea said, struggling to sit upright again. 'Sorry, I'm probably driving you mad with all this fidgeting. Oh. Sorry, mad probably isn't a word one should use in here, is it? Oh my god. Sorry.'

'It's fine. Please don't feel the need to filter or censor yourself on my account. This is your session. And you fidget as much as you need to.'

'Thanks. Sit still, Andrea! For goodness' sake, Andrea! You're too ... this, too that.' Colin noted the change in tone to her voice, as if she was now mimicking someone, complete with slight smirk and downturn to the edges of her mouth. He recognised the mannerism. And the fact she had it down pat hinted at an issue he was increasingly being engaged in for advice, and one that was a very big problem ...

'How do I get someone to like me? That's why I'm here. That's what I need help with.'

'Okay. I see.' He didn't. It was a how long's a piece of string type question. And not quite the one he'd been expecting, given the couple of other observations he'd made. He needed to unpack this. 'Is this about a new friend, boyfriend, girlfriend, partner, workplace issue?'

'Yeah, sorry. It's a bit complicated, huh?'

'Maybe a little.' He returned her slightly sheepish smile. She sighed loudly. Her whole being seemed to shrug, and her shoulders sagged forward. She appeared to deflate before him.

'I guess the first question is why the person's approval – which is what I suspect we're really talking about – matters to you.'

'My mother.'

Ahh. Is this going to be what I think it is?

'She hates me and I don't know how to fix it.' Colin was surprised to see her wipe a tear away. All the bluster seemed to have disappeared. She reached for the tissue sticking out of the box on the little table beside the arm of the couch. 'Sorry. I was so determined not to get emotional. I'm too emotional.'

'It's okay. It's an emotional topic. And big.'

'Yes. I don't know where to start, really.'

'How about beginning by telling me why you think your mother hates you.'

'She's critical of everything I do.'

Tick, Colin thought, marking an imaginary box in his mind.

'Nothing is ever good enough.'

Tick.

'I'm mainly a freelance photographer – weddings, corporate gigs, pretty much anything and everything. It's tough, but I'm doing okay. Well, I'm surviving. But apparently my work is only a "hobby" and success is a "pipedream".' Colin watched as she rolled her eyes and shook her head slowly. When she didn't continue after a significant amount of time, he prompted her.

'So, are you living at home?' he asked. 'Is that why you think she's so critical?'

'She's critical because she is. About everything. I'm a disappointment. And, no, I'm living with my partner – though I'm not sure how much longer that's going to last. I'm … Oh god. That's too big a can of worms. I need to deal with one thing at a time. I'll probably be here for the next forty years. I'm such a mess.' She tried to laugh but it was more a strangled sort of gulp that reached Colin's ears.

'What do you think your mother would rather you be doing, as a career?' Colin asked, trying to bring things back into focus, aware he needed to have at least given her something useful before she left.

'That's the point – nothing's ever good enough or okay. I'm an embarrassment, apparently.'

Oh dear. The signs are adding up.

'She tells all her friends. I've overheard her on the phone and in person. She even told an uncle I couldn't go to his birthday because I couldn't afford the airfare, which wasn't true at all. Yes, she tells lies – to suit whatever narrative she's trying to get across.'

Tick. This time the box marked in his mind was on a second list – the one for the mother.

'For the record, I had a wedding the day of my uncle's party, which she knew because I told her. More than once. It's as if she refuses to believe anything I say. I do weddings – I'm a photographer. Freelance. I can't remember if I said that already.'

'Okay. Great.' The problem here was as obvious to Colin as if it were being projected across the wall.

'It's not easy,' she went on. 'But I love it. And I'd like to think I'm good at it. I don't know anything, really. Honestly, I'm close to – well, at least, would love to, well, the idea of anyway – moving overseas where I don't have to see her. But then that would hurt my stepdad. Christ knows what he sees in her. And anyway, she'd most likely just rock up to stay for a few weeks for a free overseas holiday. She's completely incapable of adhering to any boundaries. It's easier to just give in. But it's exhausting. And it's affecting my relationship with my partner. They gang up on me, and I … As I say, I'm a mess. That's pretty much all I know.'

Colin made more notes, taking down Andrea's words and his observations, nodding as he did. Out of the corner of his eye he noticed she was wringing her hands.

'How long have you felt she, your mother, doesn't think you're good enough? Is it recent? Did something happen?'

'My whole life. I feel like I've spent forever trying to get her approval. And nothing has worked. I've made myself miserable trying to be what I think she wants, personality wise and with my career. I hated every job I had before photography. It's the only thing I've ever liked, well, except for the constant criticism, and since nothing is okay with her, I thought why not please myself? But I've come to realise her criticism is always changing anyway. So, I guess I'm here to get your permission to stop being so, so compliant. Or something. I don't mean write me a note or something. Although …' She looked up at him. 'Maybe she'd listen to a professional. No, actually, scrap that. She's perfect. She'd never entertain the idea she has any flaws, let alone seek help for anything.'

Of course not, if I'm right in my deductions.

'I can just hear her. "I'll go if it will help you, Andrea, but I'm not the one with the problem".' Again, Colin noted the change in tone. He watched as Andrea gave another exaggerated eye-roll.

After a long pause, he spoke. 'For the record, you don't seem a mess to me. Perhaps you're not the problem.'

'Ha. You try telling my mother that. Could you put *that* in a note? No, on second thoughts, she'd go ballistic knowing I'm talking to someone else about her.' Colin went to open his mouth. But Andrea held up her hand. 'I know, it's all confidential in here, isn't it?'

'It is.'

'But she'd be furious if she knew. We don't talk about anything remotely deep. Problems are a weakness. We're a sweep-things-under-the-carpet type family. If she knew, I'd get the silent treatment–'

Tick, tick, tick, for column two.

'–which, given what I've said, might on the surface sound like a good thing. But, trust me, it's not. It's horrible. And childish. It's weird saying your mother's behaviour is childish, isn't it? But it is. She throws tantrums, too, if she doesn't get her way on things – in private. In public she's oh so very controlled! Oh god. It's exhausting. Mothers and daughters, eh? I bet you get a lot of this stuff. Every one of my friends has mother issues; not to the same degree as me, but still. I just want to run away and hide from her. It's all just too claustrophobic. It's like drowning, I guess.'

'I understand. And, yes, I have seen plenty of people with similar issues.' Far too many and with devastatingly increasing frequency. But at least people were becoming aware and seeking help. *These damned people! They carry on as they please, leaving a trail of destruction in their wake – lives in ruins!* He paused for a beat as he reeled in his exasperation. 'Firstly, you don't have to have anyone in your life you don't want to. You're an adult. I would hope you wouldn't put up with a friend treating you badly or making you feel uncomfortable.'

'No, I wouldn't.'

'Being related by blood shouldn't make a difference.'

'But …' Andrea stopped. She nibbled on the inside of her bottom lip, seeming to chew over his words. 'But what if she needs me – like in a medical sense, or whatever? Family is everything – that's what I've been raised to believe.'

'Well, only you can decide what you're prepared to put up with. But remember, you owe it to yourself to protect your mental and emotional health. Parents can't assume having children will ensure they have an automatic carer, should they need it at any point. None of us is owed anything.'

'Oh. Wow. I know this. Well, I should. Thank you for saying it out loud. I needed the reminder.'

Colin watched while she took several deep breaths and then seemed to unfurl, as if the tension she'd been holding onto was seeping away.

'This isn't just run-of-the-mill mother-daughter personality clash issues, is it?'

'I don't think so, no.'

'So ...?'

'Have you heard the term narcissist? Or narcissism?'

'I have in relation to the former US president, Trump. You know, some of the things I've read about him and seen on TV remind me of my mother. I know that sounds bonkers because ... well, anyway ... Sorry, what were you going to say?' She flapped a hand to indicate for him to go on.

'I was just going to say, Google the term as well as find a checklist. I could run through it with you, but I think in the quiet privacy of your home in your own time would work better. It might give you a lot to think about.

'There's also a wonderful American psychotherapist who has lots of info online on the subject. I'll write her details down for you. She has actual lived experience due to having had a narcissist mother, and is therefore much better equipped to shed light than I am. If reading books on the topic is more your speed of things, she has several out. I believe her practice centres around helping clients navigate and deal with the fallout of having been raised by a narcissist parent. I know the signs, of course, and I can help. But mother-daughter relationships really are quite unique. And the family dynamic pertaining to narcissists adds a whole other complexity. There'll be a lot to digest. But if there's anything you wish to discuss, I'll be here.'

'Okay. Thanks. And then should I come back and discuss it with you?'

'If you like. That's entirely up to you.'

'We've finished for today, haven't we?'

'I think that's a reasonable place to finish up. What do you think?'

'Um. Yes. I've got something to focus on. Some homework to do. Thank you for listening.'

'It's what I'm here for. I hope you feel better than when you arrived?'

'Yes, I think I do.'

Colin didn't like how unsure she sounded. 'I've probably given you a lot to think about and more might come up. Just sit with it and note down any questions or thoughts you have for next time.'

'Okay. I do feel a little bamboozled, but it might be that I need to sit quietly and not think too much. I'm an overthinker. And overly sensitive. Apparently, according to my mother and my partner,' she added sadly.

'Well, maybe they're not sensitive enough,' Colin said kindly. *Understatement of the century!* Oh, how he longed to lay it all out. But Andrea, like all his clients, needed to come to things herself in her own time. He couldn't influence too blatantly, should only guide, provide food for thought. But he could see as clearly as the glass of water on his desk what the problem with Andrea was, and it wasn't her. Or certainly hadn't begun with her. Again, he silently cursed the havoc narcissists wreaked. The poor kid had a lot to unpack and deal with. He knew he shouldn't think of a thirty-two-year-old woman as a kid, but there it was. It wasn't just their age difference, though. Yes, he was entering his late seventies, but it was more her lack of confidence and fragile demeanour that caused her to seem much younger to him.

'I'll book when I've looked at my schedule,' she said, as she tapped her credit card on his machine. 'And, again, I'm so sorry I was late.'

'It's okay. Honestly.' He really wanted to ask if she'd like to begin to try to break her habit of profusely apologising. It was somewhere to start for giving her back her power. But she hadn't made that request of him. 'Here you are,' he said, handing her the receipt that had just come out of the printer.

'Thank you,' she said.

'My pleasure. Take care.' He stood up, walked to the door and opened it for her.

He glanced along the corridor in case any of the other inhabitants of the rented space, 'colleagues' who offered a variety of allied health services, were within the appropriate distance where one ought to acknowledge them with a nod and a smile. But there were none, so he headed back into his office, shut the door, and slumped into his plush chair to finish his notes on Andrea Carlton.

Poor kid, he again thought as he closed down his computer and turned off his desk lamp. He looked out the window before closing the blinds. The carpark was bathed in the subdued light of late afternoon, wet asphalt glistening. He pulled his coat on, grabbed his leather satchel and shrugged the strap over his shoulder, switched off his main light, then turned back to check all was in order, made sure the lock was engaged and pulled the door to behind him.

Chapter Two

Colin was grateful the rain had ceased and the sky was clear of storm clouds, though a brisk wind had started up. He paused and did his coat up to ward off the chill, before settling into his walk home. Regardless of the weather, he always reminded himself to appreciate being inside and not out on a building site in the mud, or in the heat, dealing with flies all day every day, and everything that went along with being a builder's labourer. Though, even after all these years, he did sometimes miss the feeling of sheer exhaustion in his muscles that rendered thought impossible upon bedtime, and the type of sleep that brought on. These days he sometimes didn't sleep due to his brain refusing to turn off, and worse than that was the fact he was meant to have all the answers for such a problem! He knew many techniques for tricking the brain into relaxing and going into neutral.

Sometimes he felt a right fraud, sitting opposite someone issuing his suggestions. Lots of people these days struggled to get a decent night's sleep – more so than when he'd started his practice. He didn't know if it was because people had more problems to keep them up at night or if they were more likely to seek help now the stigma of therapy was sliding to the wayside.

And it wasn't just confined to older clients – the young ones were a large proportion of insomnia sufferers too. He felt for them. He was sure life had been so much simpler once and, with that, less stressful. He'd heard the term 'life admin' – the amount of it being problematic – and how it related to people saying they didn't have enough 'spoons' or 'bandwidth'. But short of making lists and ticking off the small items one by one when energy or inclination allowed, there wasn't much else to be done.

The world's folk seemed generally tired – not the sort of tired a week's rest or a string of perfect eight or nine hours of sleep would fix. Much of life seemed to be a treadmill people were often too scared to step off of lest they be left behind. As far as Colin could see, the constant busyness of people, which stole their physical and mental energy, wasn't just confined to all the things requiring doing. It was also, he reckoned, something to do with all the noise in the form of actual electricity being used and the energy from all the stress radiating off everyone. Of course, most people would benefit from just stopping for a while – sitting on a beach, living in the present. But there was so much humans felt the need to worry about. And he was no exception.

He and Joyce were planning their retirement. He was meant to be stopping. A part of him was a bit scared. Mainly about the change of routine and whether they would have enough money. But he was also a little excited – though, if he was being honest, his excitement lay more in the feeling of accomplishment in getting to retirement age than all the time he'd have on his hands.

Joyce seemed to be loving it. Her employer had closed the boutique she'd worked at – retiring himself – so she'd gone a little earlier.

Colin envied her not having to make the decision to retire herself. He had to admit he loved coming home to her already there. The whole house had a different, better vibe these days. Usually she could be found pottering around in the kitchen or sitting at the table, engrossed in her phone or tablet, or down in her sewing room – humming away as she toiled. There hadn't been much sewing being done recently, though she'd always been prone to fits and starts. Sometimes he wondered if all the time she was spending on her phone was verging on the unhealthy, but he wasn't the sort to poke or pry. What was available for entertainment and connecting with like-minded people, far and wide, at the mere tap of a finger, these days was really quite marvellous, if a little disconcerting.

Colin paused, noticing a new sign up on a temporary fence outside one of the rows of plain red brick 1950s houses and sighed. Another property was going to be knocked down and the block carved up and several townhouses erected. Even worse, it was a house he'd done an extension on, back in the day. Soon there'd probably be no buildings left that he'd worked on in his former career. He really objected to the identical square boxes without eaves popping up everywhere. And the tiny blocks they sat on.

No doubt the lack of opportunities for children to get a decent run up or kick a ball a reasonable distance in their own yard with their friends, by themselves, or with a parent or two, was contributing to the general misery society seemed to be plagued by these days. Town planners, developers and all crowed about the nearby parks with their latest and greatest amenities. But Colin would put money on the fact most families would venture there once, if that, and realise it was too hard. Even just making the decision to go, packing up stuff to take, getting everyone there at the same time, would be nigh on impossible, he figured. So the kids, and the adults, for that matter, would stay at home on their devices and outdoor activity would be confined to occasional moments of *we should* ... and grunts and nods in response.

Sometimes he was really glad he and Joyce wouldn't be having grandkids. The whole world was in a hopeless situation. No, he shouldn't be so pessimistic, but it was pretty dire. In so many ways. People were the problem. The wrong ones were in charge – the loudest, the most arrogant, the generally least kind and considerate – which meant everything was pretty much screwed. This was a conversation he and Joyce had regularly. They often tried to pinpoint a solution and always came up short. Always ending with 'People! Damned people!'

Joyce often said she wondered how Colin dealt with his clients discussing their problems, day in day out, especially those who weren't really there to listen and learn, but rather to have their own views ratified. And he'd always laugh and say he was amazed she'd done customer service all those years. Sometimes Colin thought Joyce would have made a better psychologist or counsellor than him. She'd been so interested and helpful during his years of study – and since, with helping in the background – he thought she might have followed in his footsteps soon after.

He was grateful she hadn't, and it did feel a selfish thing to think, but he did like her steadfastness, and the fact that she didn't bring work home in her mind left her available to debrief with. Of course, he was very discreet about his clients – only dealt in generalisations, never specifics. Or if he did, only ever first names or initials. Never full names.

He trudged on, feeling a little heavier than when he'd left the office building. One day they'd return after a long trip to find their suburb unrecognisable. He was determined their own house and block would be decimated only over his dead body. Every month they seemed to get leaflets from one of the circling organisations. What boiled his blood were the ones that read as if they were from an individual couple needing a home. Several times Joyce had done some googling and found the names of the signatories were actually directors of a development company. He loathed underhandedness, preferred people to be straight up. Though very few were these days.

He put his key in the lock on his and Joyce's front door and opened it, calling, 'Darling, I'm home,' as he entered. He turned his head to listen for her response as he closed the door carefully.

'In the kitchen,' came her call.

As he unloaded his belongings into the hall – lunchbox out of his bag, which was then placed on the floor beside the hallstand where he hung his coat and hat before emptying his pockets of wallet, keys and phone into the bowl below. He made his way down the hall, carrying his lunchbox, and smiling at the very pleasant waft of cooking meat as he went.

'Something smells good,' he said, beaming as he went over to Joyce who was standing at the sink. He placed his lunchbox down. She turned and wiped her hands down her apron – oh, how he loved her ever-reliable idiosyncrasies and dependability – and wrapped her arms around his neck. After a quick hug and peck on the lips, they stepped apart.

'Rissoles.'

'Yum.' Friday evening's meal was always based around beef mince – rissoles, meatloaf or spaghetti bolognaise.

'I hope so. I'm putting paprika in. Just for a change. Apparently, it has many health benefits. And, it'll give it a little kick of spice. My mother would turn in her grave with me deviating from the family recipe, but there we are.'

'Oh you contrary woman, you. But you're my contrary woman.' Despite his light-hearted tone, he found himself frowning a little.

'Ha ha. Cuppa? I've just made myself one.'

'What brought about the sudden change, might I ask? Not that I'm objecting.'

'It was a suggestion by a woman in one of my online groups. There was a big discussion about changing up, or, er, modernising, older recipes. And paprika is apparently good for eyes and inflammation. I tell you, there's a wealth of information on all sorts of matters available at barely a blink!'

'I see.' He shook aside his consternation. 'I'll get the tea. You sit. I had a new client who was a little delayed, which is why I'm a bit late.'

'I thought you were meant to be winding down,' she said, eyebrows raised.

'Hmm.' He lifted the kettle to check its contents.

'You're too good to everyone,' Joyce said, sipping her tea while Colin got a mug out of the cupboard and put a tea bag into it. 'Young? Older?'

'Young. Thirty-two. A woman. Mother issues.'

'Oh, that old chestnut.'

'Hmm.'

'Narcissist?'

'Yep. It's early days, but it seems that way.'

'Poor thing. She's got some unravelling ahead of her, I suppose.'

'We'll see. I suggested she do some googling. So I wasn't completely soft.'

'Married?'

'At least partnered up.'

'To an abuser, I suppose?'

'Most likely. If my instincts are correct – about the mother, that is. I know the answer to this is ego, the need to prove blah, blah, blah, but I do still feel compelled to say, why do these people even have children in the first place?! Rhetorical. Obviously.'

'Yes. Quite. It does make you wonder, doesn't it, how ours would have fared if they'd grown up, and all of us together.'

'I sometimes shudder to think, given all we now know of the anecdotal evidence – or at least urban myths – about the kids of psychologists being very screwed up.'

'Well, yes, there's that.'

'Though, in my defence, I did come to this career later. That might have made all the difference.' Colin smiled, finished making his tea, then took his mug over to the table and sat down heavily. He was so appreciative of the fact they could openly talk about their loss, even joke at times about their kids. So many clients came to him to deal with grief who couldn't mention their loved ones or talk about them – sometimes even a decade on. Grief really was a difficult journey. He'd always be grateful their experience had bonded them even more. All too often such an event tore families apart. 'Anyway, enough about me. Tell me about your day. How was it?'

'I've had a good day, thank you. I've got through the last of the hall cupboard – even taken the bags to the op shop.'

'Well done.' Bags of donation items usually sat in the car for weeks, even sometimes months, before being delivered to their final destination.

'Yes. I've awarded myself a gold star!' Joyce grinned. 'I also finished the head scarves and dropped them off.'

Colin returned her open smile. He loved that they'd never lost their playfulness.

'You have been busy.'

'Yes. And I think I might have narrowed down the caravans a bit. Shall we go and look tomorrow?'

'Sure.' Colin wished he could feel more excited.

'And don't forget we've got Jim's retirement party tomorrow night.'

'Oh, yes. I had forgotten that. What would I do without you?'

'Not go anywhere, I should imagine,' Joyce said with a weary sigh.

Sounds good to me. Am I entering a rut? 'Do we have to take a gift?'

'No. Instructions are no gifts. Just a celebration.'

Colin really didn't feel like going tomorrow night. Jim tended to dominate proceedings ordinarily, so he would be insufferable as the centre of attention, gloating about the size of his share and property portfolios and superannuation balance. While he'd never said so to Joyce, Colin suspected Jim to be full of hot air. Because why, if one was so wealthy, would one wait so long to give work away – especially given all the lamenting over how hard and stressful his job as financial planner had been.

Colin regularly scoffed to himself that it was really one of those all care, no responsibility jobs – not too dissimilar to his own, in that way. It wasn't as if they were brain surgeons or pilots or air traffic controllers, with life and death literally in their hands. They just gave their opinions or suggestions and then basically held up their hands and said 'but it's entirely up to you'. And Jim could always say, 'Oh, well, I've always made it clear there's no guarantee the stock market won't crash, or *correct*, or whatever'.

At least Joyce had agreed to go with another planner in their company, was able to see how easily their friendship could be ruined by mixing business with pleasure. Jim regularly made digs about how much more he could have made them if he'd been in charge of their money. Presumably he had access to their figures, too, which irked Colin. But that was another thing he couldn't dwell on.

On the other hand, Colin did also quite enjoy eating high-end canapes – and they surely would be. *That* he would look forward to. At home, he and Joyce tended to eat plain meals – meat and three veg – just like their parents had, so he particularly enjoyed fine dining when it was on offer. They didn't tend to eat out much of their own volition – being very sensible with their money as well as not so keen to be out at night with their dwindling vision.

After dinner undertaken in companionable silence punctuated by murmurs of enjoyment and appreciation – particularly of the addition of paprika – they tidied up the kitchen together and then retired to the lounge room in time for the ABC nightly news. After several conversations about the items, they retreated into their devices – Joyce on her phone and Colin on the tablet, which Joyce had handed to him with the words, 'Here, check out these vans.'

Colin scrolled and clicked and read, but despite his best efforts could not conjure any enthusiasm beyond appreciation for the bright shiny beasts with all the mod cons. It was kind of like art he didn't have the space for or desire to own.

Not that they were into art. Their walls were adorned with tapestries Joyce and her mother and grandmother had made, framed photos, and some framed prints of famous artworks.

What the vision of the caravans roused in Colin were thoughts of what an enormous outlay it was and how they'd better like being in small confines together twenty-four-seven and traipsing around the country. Personally, Colin liked the idea of simply driving places and staying in motels – had, in the early conversations, years ago, pointed out that one could do a lot of miles and nights of accommodation for the price of a caravan and a four-wheel drive to tow it, particularly as caravanning still required nightly site fees and significantly more fuel and maintenance. And that was all before the cost-of-living crisis was on the news each night and in every second Facebook post and article online. But he couldn't argue with the benefit of not having to pack and unpack and lug suitcases, and the comfort of being at home while away from the bricks and mortar one. They were both homebodies – though he suspected he was considerably more so than Joyce.

She and a bunch of friends had gone off travelling all over Australia picking fruit for a year or two after school. Sometimes Colin wondered if he might have stifled Joyce, but she'd had plenty of time to speak up on the matter. It wasn't as if he was possessive or prone to flying off the handle. They led an amicable, quiet existence. He couldn't imagine a better life partner than sensible, well-adjusted Joyce – a thought he was regularly reminded of during his work days, which often involved counselling married couples, the children of working parents, or people trying to put their lives back together after having their hearts trampled and crushed.

One type that intrigued him the most was those couples who seemed to enjoy sparring – those who appeared ill-suited and even seemed to dislike each other, yet came to him week after week, ostensibly for the purpose of improving their relationship. Sometimes he was left wondering if they simply enjoyed his company. Plenty of times he'd gently suggested they might spend their money and time better elsewhere, but the hints never took and they'd always book another appointment before leaving together amid snipes and curses.

Of course, he couldn't tell them they'd be better off calling it quits and getting on with their lives separately and stop making each other so unhappy. They had to come to that decision on their own. Meanwhile, he had a business to run, and fortunately or unfortunately, depending upon how you looked at it, these clients contributed significantly to his bottom line.

Instead of letting it get to him, he reminded himself he was being paid and tried to commit comments to memory to share with Joyce of an evening. Despite being the more tolerant of the two of them, she often marvelled aloud at the fact he hadn't lost his cool and told them what he really thought. And it was always upon these comments that Joyce would then say, 'See. And this is why you're the psychologist and not me – I'd have been hauled up before the board and suspended well before now!' And then they'd laugh heartily for a few moments. And Colin was usually left marvelling at his own ability at the time to be so tolerant. He'd always been a good listener, but he'd never thought he'd be able to nod and hold his tongue so much as was required by his profession, though he was finding it more difficult these days to retain his composure.

He'd embarked on his studies for two reasons all those years ago – one, in response to realising the pension age would be increased and that those in manual jobs likely wouldn't be taken into account. He shuddered at the thought of trying to lug bricks and other materials at an advanced age and what one would do if one couldn't. Building and labouring weren't like working in an office where you could just shift around to accommodate one's failing physical body. And back in the late nineties workplaces were a lot less forgiving than these days.

The other reason for his going back to university and ultimately settling on psychology was to deal with the death of the twins. He'd felt that by retreating into something he could get his teeth into while also hopefully gaining an understanding of what he and Joyce were experiencing, they might get through it okay. One of the biggest things he'd learnt was that there was no one size fits all for navigating the pain of losing one's only children and the adjustment of pretty much every aspect of one's life going forward. Far from it. He'd learnt, frustratingly, that even those who'd lost children were in no better position to understand the loss borne by others because every instance and circumstance was different; every relationship to grief unique. Thankfully, he and Joyce had somehow dragged themselves through.

'So, what do you think?' Joyce's voice poked through the meandering thoughts he'd become lost in.

It's expensive.

But Joyce didn't wait for his reply. 'Happy to go for a look?'

'Sounds good.' What harm would going to see do? Maybe it'd make him get his act together and properly get on board.

Chapter Three

'So, what do you think?' Joyce asked. They'd just got into the car after the third enormous yard filled with brand-new and nearly new caravans, campers and motor homes.

'About what?'

'The caravan, Colin. Keep up.'

'To be fair, we've seen about thirty.' He looked over at her.

'Are you deliberately being obtuse and annoying?'

Don't get your knickers in a twist. This is supposed to be fun!

He sighed and took an extra breath in order to collect himself and reel in his frustration, which wasn't really with Joyce, or rather, shouldn't be.

He could see all Joyce's points. He really wanted to like the idea of caravanning. *What's the worst that can happen?* And a litany of horrible scenarios flooded him: him stooped over, dealing with poo, car accidents, road-rage incidents, jack-knifing the damned thing, having to ask someone else to get it into, or out of, a tricky or tight spot, and getting stranded for weeks without food or other essential supplies due to flood or other natural or manmade calamities. The list was endless!

They both said how much they hated all the palaver of getting ready for a trip, which was one reason why they hadn't done much travelling and were planning on hitting the road and only organising everything once. But there was so much to do and to decide on. With everything.

How would he even go being away from his safe and comfortable base for long periods of time? They'd never been away for longer than two weeks. Joyce had got homesick even more than him on the fourteen-day cruise they'd taken – both declaring how much they yearned for simply the atmosphere – yes, the *vibe* – of home. Did Joyce really think she could have that same feeling of home in a compact version, a version that didn't have the solid brick walls and tiled roof above?

'Colin?'

How could it be that two people who had spent such a successful and happy life together be so misaligned now? They'd managed to navigate all the ups and downs, the negotiations, and made big decisions with relative ease along the way – always been able to see each other's points of view and agree to disagree on plenty of things without holding grudges. Of course, the bigger question was why couldn't he tell her of his misgivings? He kept hoping he'd come around, so in the interim kept his thoughts to himself on the matter. The last thing he wanted to do was burst Joyce's bubble if he didn't need to.

There was the issue of giving up his practice and letting down his clients – current and future. But bigger than that, he felt, was that helping people gave him meaning and a purpose. Even those he saw who he didn't get through to were aided by learning that he wasn't the therapist for them. He doubted any significant satisfaction could be found in lumping canisters or hoses of waste, or successfully backing a long vehicle into a tight space. But maybe he was wrong. And that remained possibly the biggest problem of all – the unknown. He almost laughed aloud. Well, duh. Fear of the unknown was at the heart of probably ninety per cent of the issues he dealt with in his working life.

He stared at the brochures and again tried to decide which sewage system he was keener on using – or rather less keen. Would it be one of those things that would turn out to be much better – or, in the case of the toilet conundrum, okay – once they'd got going? *Just pick one.*

'They're all that bit different,' he said. 'All lovely, but we really need to nail down the must-haves. We might have to forego some of the bells and whistles. Cull the wants. They're very expensive.'

'I know they are. But we've been saving for this. I don't want to scrimp, Colin. And the woman back at the place before did say it was probably best to have something custom made. Though that will mean a bit of a wait. Damn every man and his dog hitting the road.'

'Hmm.' Colin imagined a heap of calendar pages being turned in his mind like a flip book, representing the delays that would undoubtedly occur, and could all but hear the *ca-ching*, *ca-ching* of all the additional money they would have to spend for the privilege of specifying the finer details. Though he did like the idea that he'd have more time to mentally prepare. Except, of course, a sizeable non-refundable deposit would need to be paid upfront. He knew it was reasonable, but he felt rushed.

'Don't forget we'll also need the right vehicle to tow it – all the correct specs. Did they say get that first or after?' he asked.

'Either or. Remember the guy at the first place said vehicle first and the young woman just then said her parents got theirs afterwards. I think there's still a delay on the vehicles front. So, we might need to see what's available and when.'

'The last thing we want is a caravan stuck in the driveway without any way of moving it.'

'Well, it wouldn't be, dear, would it? How would it get there if we've got nothing to tow it, do you think?'

'Oh. Right. Good point.' He cringed. Normally they'd look at each other and then burst out laughing at their silliness. But Colin was too tired and, from Joyce's tone, she was clearly too tetchy. Colin put his hands on the steering wheel and stared out the windscreen.

'And just for the record …'

He knew from her tone that he was required to answer, or rather enquire. 'Yes?' He checked in his mirrors several times and began slowly reversing out from their parking spot.

'I'm not having a van without a toilet and a decent shower.'

'Right. Noted.' *Ca-ching, ca-ching.*

Honk!

Suddenly the grill of a small truck was inches from the back door.

'Careful!'

'I am! He came out of nowhere, Joyce.' Colin was shaking. The truck honked again.

'Well, go forward. He wants you to go back in.'

'Impatient bastard,' Colin muttered.

'Well, just do it!'

'Okay. Okay.' *Christ, Joyce, there's no need for you to snap at me too!* Despite having driven this small sedan for at least the last decade, Colin struggled to get it into first gear. It stalled. And then in his bumbling state he accidentally pushed the accelerator – giving it two pumps – before turning the key again. The car coughed and refused to start.

'Oh, Colin. For Christ's sake!'

Colin bit on his bottom lip in order to stop himself snapping back and making matters worse.

After managing to get the vehicle started next go, Colin found the right gear and then forward momentum, shooting back into the space and only just braking in time before launching onto the low barrier in front.

There was a roar behind him and Colin raised his hand in apology, glancing in the rear-vision mirror as he did, to see the middle finger the truck driver gave him in response.

'No need to get angry,' he muttered. 'It was barely thirty seconds out of your day.' Though in his mind it felt like they'd been a problem and at a standstill for hours.

'Well, the poor fellow probably has an impossibly tight schedule,' Joyce said, turning in her seat to look after the truck. 'Yes, he's a courier. Poor thing.'

'What about me?'

'Oh, for goodness' sake, Colin. How are you going to go in a big vehicle towing a van of considerably more length and weight?'

That's a very good point. A new layer of anxiety came in over the quiver of fear still humming from a moment ago. He'd always thought he'd like being in charge of a big rig, that it would make him feel bigger and more important than he was. Right then, the thought terrified him. If he hadn't had Joyce with him, he might have sat there and worked through it; come to the decision he really didn't want to go down this path after all. But they'd been talking about it and idly planning for it for years. *You'll be right. Plenty do it. And it's only money.*

'Don't worry. We can do a driving course. I've got a brochure about that here in my pile. I'll dig it out later.'

'No point until we have a vehicle and our whole setup.'

'No, that's right, I'm just trying to ease your obvious tension, dear.'

'I'm fine.'

'Well, I think the steering wheel currently being crushed by your death grip would say otherwise. Poor you. But poor Carolyn the Corolla!' Joyce said with amusement in her tone, stroking his thigh.

'Oh, yes. Goodness.' He looked at his cramping hands, clamped white-knuckled on the wheel and released them, cringing at Joyce. 'Carolyn, please forgive me,' he added, patting the steering wheel.

'I wouldn't mind popping into Target on our way past, if you're up for it,' Joyce said after they'd been driving in silence for a while, Colin thankful for the two ABC radio announcers presenting a scintillating discussion of the latest political furore.

'I'm not really, actually. Do you mind if we go up later, if it's that important? The traffic's rather heavy at present and I have to be honest but I am still feeling a little frazzled.'

'That's quite all right. Not that you're still frazzled, that is. Deep breaths, dear.'

Colin nodded.

They arrived home and Colin was pleased to get out of the car. All the way he'd been unable to shake the frightening reminder of all the driving – and not just ordinary driving in the small Corolla – he had ahead of him. But, disappointingly, his heavy mood followed him inside and hung around while they dumped everything on the small kitchen table, constructed their cold rissole sandwiches, and moved around each other getting glasses of water and cups of tea.

'A thought, dear, about the caravans. Well, rather, the driving aspect. I think we should both do the driving course. Just in case,' he said.

'I agree. There are all these stories in the online forums about people suddenly having to drive because their other half has been carted off by the RFDS after a heart attack or accident or whatever.'

'I very much hope this is not you having homicidal thoughts, Joyce!' *Wouldn't surprise me, given your crankiness of late.*

'Maybe! Only kidding. But, seriously, Colin, it's always the wife you hear about being stuck, and I refuse to join those ranks. I'm not going to be a clueless woman!'

'I can't imagine you ever being so, dear.' Colin brightened a little. Maybe he was overthinking it. Maybe when they did the driving course Joyce would decide she wanted to do *all* the driving. Sure, she hadn't in the last however many years – he always drove the two of them. But stranger things had happened. She might just find a whole new season, so to speak. But he was getting ahead of himself. They needed to nail down a van and vehicle first. And they might have another six to twelve months before it all came together.

'Right,' Joyce declared as she wiped her hands on the hand towel hanging on the oven's handle after they'd cleared the table and tidied up after lunch.

Colin looked up, waiting for whatever was coming next, his eyebrows raised in anticipation. But without another word, Joyce was striding purposefully from the room and thudding down the hall, leaving Colin standing where he was, gazing out the kitchen window. He filled the kettle again and put it back on its base and clicked the start button and went back to staring out the window as the kettle hissed to life. He'd better trim the hedge. But first he needed another fortifying cup of strong tea.

He'd just poured water onto the tea bag when Joyce's presence filled the kitchen doorway again.

'Another cuppa?' he enquired.

'No, thanks.' She put the tablet on the table, along with a document wallet labelled *Caravan/4WD* as she plonked herself back onto her chair.

'Oh. You mean now? You want to do a deep dive now?'

'I thought so. Do you have somewhere else to be?'

'Not really. Was just thinking the hedge out there needed some attention.' He nodded in the direction of the nearby window.

'Oh.'

To Colin there seemed to be a silent standoff going on. He didn't want to give in but couldn't exactly push the point. The average person would consider the hedge not in need of trimming. Oh well, it had been worth a shot. 'I'm sure it can wait an hour or two,' he conceded.

'All righty,' Joyce said. Colin went back and sank down onto his vinyl chair.

'This is supposed to be fun. *Is* fun, Colin.'

'I'm just a little worn out from this morning's excursion. It was a lot to take in.'

'Lunch was meant to provide the buffer on that score. Come on. Buck up. First, I think we need to check the balance in the account.'

'Okay.' Colin nodded. 'Go ahead,' he said. He knew exactly how much was there – checked it almost daily.

'Right.'

And there it was again. *Right*. That word was seriously grating on him – or, rather, the way Joyce was saying it.

'Don't say the numbers out loud when you put them in,' he said, peering at Joyce while she brought up the online banking.

'I know. God, Colin, what is with you?' she muttered.

Me? What's with you, more like!

Both of them had an agreement to not say the customer number, password or balance aloud in case the phones really were listening. They'd have preferred not to do online banking at all but had accepted it many years ago for its convenience. Joyce turned the tablet around to show the balance of the savings account titled *Travel and Special Projects*. Colin nodded and watched while Joyce noted it down on the lined pad beside her.

'Actually, come round here and sit so you're not reading upside down and I'm not having to turn everything around constantly.'

Colin nodded, vacated his chair, and dragged it around to beside Joyce.

'It's going to be a shame to not be getting all that monthly interest now the rates have finally gone up,' he said. He couldn't help it. They'd lamented their cash deposits doing stuff all for around a decade and, just when they were providing a return, it was going to be over.

'Stop being such a wet blanket, Colin. Anyone would think you had changed your mind.' He waited with bated breath for her to stop and look at him and ask sincerely, have you changed your mind?

And what would he say? Oh no, of course not? Actually, I think I have? Or at least confess he was feeling a bit pressured? Maybe. It was all well and good as a goal just beyond the horizon, a source of mere discussion. But now he was having doubts.

'I've worked too hard, and dreamed about this for too long, for you to stymie me now, my love. And it's okay. If it all goes wrong, we can always sell the house and/or subdivide or what have you,' Joyce muttered as she tapped and swiped away on the device.

The blood in Colin's veins seemed to stop. He looked at Joyce, unable to keep the incredulity and fear from his features. What was wrong with her? She knew that was his worst nightmare.

'Oh, lighten up, I was only kidding. Golly, you are tetchy today.'

He raised his eyebrows and looked at her, but she was busy on her screen.

'Just what we need,' she said, peering at the screen and looking intensely interested, or maybe perturbed. Colin couldn't quite tell which.

'What's up?'

'Just something on Facebook caught my attention.' She flapped a hand dismissively, but Colin could see she was still a little distracted.

'Would you rather not do this now?' he asked, mentally crossing his fingers.

'No. Best to at least look at things now while the visits are fresh in our minds, I think.'

'Okay.'

'Great. Well, I liked this one,' she said, bringing out the glossy brochure and tapping at it with her finger. 'I think it's the brand with the better reviews and comments in the Facebook groups and forums, but I'll double-check that. And it's not the biggest, so there'll be more flexibility for which vehicle we can have.'

'Hmm.' It was lovely, Colin thought, all fresh and shiny. 'Is that one we have to order and can custom a bit?'

'Um. Hang on. Yes. And it's made in Queensland. So, we could drive up and get it, rather than them shipping it down. Well, trucking it, I mean, that's the term, isn't it?'

'I assume so.' *Last thing on my mind.* He liked that they might have made a decision – or rather, that he might not have to look at caravans every night for the next six months. 'What vehicle, do you think?'

'Hang on a sec.' Joyce was tapping. 'Oh, damn. The one I want isn't available. This one.' She pointed – again adhering to their distrust of potentially spying devices. They didn't want to be bombarded with a heap of ads for cars going forward, as well as caravans and all the associated goods and services. 'I suppose one really oughtn't choose a car on colour, ought one?'

'As good a reason as any, I would have thought, provided it does the trick in terms of towing and weight and what have you. I like that colour.' Colin did have to admit he rather liked the idea of one he could sit up high in. With every second car on the road a four-wheel drive or SUV these days it was often a struggle to see past when out driving.

'There's still a six-month wait on it, by the looks. I suppose that'll blow out to nine or ten – that's what people are saying online. Oh well, it'll be worth waiting for.'

'Yes, I'm sure.'

'You don't sound sure, Colin. Are you okay about this?' She was now looking directly at him and her hand was on his thigh.

'I'm not *not* sure.'

'That's not very helpful.'

'I think I'm just feeling jittery. What if we don't like roaming about and being so confined? I have to admit, after this morning with that truck, I'm a bit concerned about how I'll go with the driving, the towing. It's not like I've even towed a little two by two trailer for a decade.'

'This morning was nothing and I don't know why you're dwelling on it. It was just some guy who was impatient. He honked twice, Colin. Really, what has got into you, I don't know.'

Exactly. If that has me so rattled, how am I going to be with towing a van? But Joyce had moved on. And while he was a proponent of listening to one's intuition, he wasn't sure that's what was making him so reluctant. He was just being a coward, most likely.

'We've already agreed we'll both do a driving course. Then maybe I'll do all the driving. How about that?'

'You're right. Let's not jump the gun on these decisions.'

'I'm sure you'll be fine as a passenger, car-sickness wise, in a four-wheel drive – people say that being up high makes the world of difference.'

Colin wasn't surprised that Joyce was effectively reading his mind – it happened quite often that she spoke aloud his very thoughts at the same time he was having them, or very soon afterwards.

'You know the other thing, of course …'

'What's that?'

'When are you actually retiring, winding up the practice and going to be available to hit the road?' Thankfully again Joyce didn't indicate she was really expecting an answer. 'You need to get onto it. I can't help you with that. Well, I can – I'll happily cancel all your appointments and shut down the online booking system and put a post up online and one on the website, if you want. I know, I know, you feel a certain loyalty to your existing clients …'

'We'll get there. It'll all fall into place,' Colin offered, unsure if he believed it or not.

'You know, we'd better start thinking about getting organised for tonight,' Joyce said.

'I'm a bit weary. I'm going to have a lie down on the couch.'

'Okay.'

'Don't worry, I'll set an alarm.'

'I thought you were going to trim the hedge.'

'It can wait. I've lost interest in it.' Colin got up, kissed Joyce on the forehead, rinsed his mug and put it in the sink and then left the room. He was very weary and in need of psyching up if he were to get through the evening's socialising.

Chapter Four

Colin woke from his nap feeling decidedly unsociable, but nonetheless dragged himself out into the kitchen where Joyce was still – or again, he couldn't be sure – poring over the morning's spoils of information and brochures and scrolling on the tablet. Well, that or trawling Facebook. He couldn't be sure. He sat down.

'Better?'

'Hmm.'

'We really don't have to go if you're not feeling up to it,' Joyce said, not looking up from the paper she was making notes on.

He wanted to say, *'Great, let's not go then'*. But from her tone he knew she was not really giving him the option of staying home.

'We don't have to stay late. And I would like to go. We never go anywhere much these days.'

And there it was. He knew it shouldn't but this felt like a dig to Colin – as if he were the one solely responsible for declining every invitation that came their way. The truth was that tonight *was* quite rare – especially since it was at a private home. They sometimes met up for breakfast or lunch, and less often dinner, at cafes and restaurants. They all grumbled that they were too tired and didn't have time to cook. Perhaps that might change now they were all starting to retire and had days to prepare and then recover from a bout of socialising. God only knew how they'd done all they had with young kids. Ageing and stages of life had a lot to answer for.

He could sort of see why the young ones might forego saving money in lieu of enjoying themselves with travel and experiences while they had the energy. It really was true you could have it all but not all at the same time. Especially when the world was finally waking up to what a raw deal many women got with carrying the load of domestic tasks and child rearing and then ending up with less funds in retirement. Even if she was married to a fiscally responsible bloke. Or other half, he corrected.

His thoughts went to his married clients Julia and David, from yesterday. Several times he had longed to take Julia aside and point out that when they split up – and they would, he was sure of it – she'd better have some level of financial independence in place.

He didn't go into their finances, just listened to them complaining about each other and carefully tried to get them to see that their disrespect for each other and constant nitpicking was not okay. Particularly for the kids at home, who he knew were a twelve-year-old and a fourteen-year-old. Oh well, at least they might have time to carve out a half decent life, given they were only in their early forties. Women in Colin's age group were at seriously high risk of homelessness, a shocking statistic.

'I've made an executive decision,' Joyce announced.

'Yes ...?'

'I'm going to email the caravan company about putting a deposit down and ordering.'

'I see.'

'It's okay. I'm being sensible. The smaller one is fine. I agree, going too big might make it unmanageable, plus the outlay and cost in fuel for towing et cetera et cetera. It'll give us options with vehicles, too. We can go looking at them next weekend. Okay?'

'Okay.'

'A little enthusiasm, dear, would be nice.'

'I'm just a bit slow after my nap. It is indeed exciting news. We can celebrate tonight.' He rubbed his hands across his face and ignored the quick quiver and momentary tightness in his chest, telling himself it was reasonable to be a little jittery at this juncture. He thought he was excited too, and grateful for Joyce taking charge.

'So, you really are going to have to try to start pulling back a bit on the work front. You've got six months, tops. And that's not the sort of six months you've been dilly dallying over for the past twelve. I'm serious, Colin. I don't want the van sitting in the driveway for aeons. I'll be wanting to hit the road when it arrives.'

'Right, yes, dear.' He raised his hand in a salute.

'Exactly. Well, someone has to take the helm.'

'And I very much appreciate that you are.'

'Thank you for saying, Colin. Right, so am I pressing send on my email to the caravan people enquiring about the van availability and so forth?'

'Oh. You're that far along?'

'Yes. I just said I'd made an executive decision. Keep up, Colin.'

'Yes. Oh, why not – do it!' *High time you took a risk, old man, and dipped a toe off the safety of the jetty, or whatever analogy we're going with.*

It would be fine. Joyce had his back – their backs. They were both quite tight with money and sensible – though he was generally more so – and there was no reason why that should change. The reason they worked so well was that on things that mattered, they were always in the same chapter if not on the same page.

'Right. That's sent. Wow, we're really doing this.'

'Yes, we are. Well done.'

Joyce looked at him, her eyes shining with slight surprise. He got up and went over and wrapped his arms around her shoulders and kissed her on the top of her head.

'Oh, and I was looking at your business Facebook page,' she said. 'I've scheduled posts for World Mental Health Day and for Carer's Week.'

'Perfect. Thanks.'

'Do you think I should put something on the website about the business winding up?'

'No. Not yet.' Colin wasn't sure how he was going to handle that. It had to be done carefully. He struggled with the fact he'd be letting people down who he knew didn't have much other support. But he could also see he needed to let go for Joyce, and himself too. He couldn't work forever.

'I suppose we'd better get ready,' Joyce said, breaking into his thoughts.

'Yes. I really hope that insufferable Roger fellow won't be there. Though I suppose I've just jinxed us in saying that.'

'Probably. Anyway, of course he will be – he's our hosts' brother-in-law or cousin-in-law or something. I can't quite remember, but I do know he's not just a random colleague or old school friend or whatever.'

'Oh, yes, that's right.'

'Anyway, he'll be your problem as there always ends up being a segregation of men and women,' she said cheerfully.

Yes, don't remind me. Fabulous.

'Do you think we should have our own retirement do?' Joyce said, pausing at the end of the hall.

'If so, we'd have to have two. And we're a bit late for yours.'

'Yes, that's true, on both counts. Maybe we should pull our fingers out and at least have people around, just because – it's been ages since we did that.'

'Hmm. We could do it as sort of a smashing a bottle over the caravan type launch party – like they do with boats.'

'That always gives me anxiety – feeling the bottle will hit the wrong bit and damage something. Boats, by all accounts, are so fragile. And I bet it'd be like breaking a mirror – I think I've heard that somewhere. That if something goes wrong upon launch, the vessel is plagued forever more.'

'That's just a silly superstition, dear, like rain on a wedding dooming a marriage.'

'Oh no, it's not. Every single wedding we've gone to where it's rained hasn't lasted,' Joyce said.

'Really? Are you sure?'

'Completely. You can think about it while I go through the shower,' Joyce said, getting up from her chair and kissing Colin on the cheek. 'I'm glad it was sunny on our day,' she added, tapping a finger on his nose.

'It wouldn't have mattered because we're not superstitious.'

'Ah, yes, but the stats don't lie,' she said, and left the room.

Colin, rather than running through the list of people they knew who'd divorced and trying to remember if their weddings had been dreary on account of the weather, became stuck on the fact Joyce had surprised him with her apparent sudden superstitious mindset. She was usually as level-headed as he was on these things. Oh well, she was allowed to have different thoughts.

'At least we'll have something interesting to impart tonight,' Joyce muttered as Colin drove them, concentrating, having memorised the route after studying the map on his phone. He preferred not to have the device in view while driving – he'd heard too many stories of overzealous police officers pulling people over and either insisting they had a phone in hand when they didn't and/or claiming distraction via the passenger holding the phone. He preferred to pull over if necessary. Memorising the journey – or trying to – helped stretch his brain cells too, he thought, which was a good thing to do. Personally, he couldn't see how reading a map on a phone was any more dangerous than consulting a street directory on one's lap, but the law was the law, strange and incongruous as it was at times.

'What's that, dear?' Colin said, having just negotiated a turn.

'The caravan. Our plans. I said, at least we'll have something interesting to talk about for a change.'

'What do you mean, for a change? You always keep people enthralled with your hilarious stories about your work encounters.' *Well, you used to. Of late, you've been rather less fun.*

'You're too kind. That may have been the case. But I'm retired now so there's no more interesting stories to tell.'

Colin detected a slight harrumph of lament from beside him. *Hmm.* 'You're not having regrets about retiring, are you?'

'No. Well, not really. It's just I'd rather have gone out on my own terms.'

'I know.' He put his hand on her thigh. 'You can always try to get another job, if you miss it that much.'

'So says a member of the patriarchy who was never going to get put on the scrap heap as soon as their mouth drooped and their hair went grey.'

'Anyway, my point was meant to be that you'll always have stories to tell – you make a good tale out of the most seemingly innocuous interaction and have people hanging on your every word. You always have and you always will.'

'Thanks for saying, dear.'

Colin nibbled on his bottom lip, wondering if Joyce's mood was something to do with apprehensions over the significant step towards their massive change of life to come. Maybe they were both tired from all the thoughts and overload from the day's excursion. He really liked that they wouldn't have to be traipsing through caravans and yards of them again. They'd only done it a few days here and there – and thankfully he hadn't had to do the legwork – but still it felt good to not have to be doing that anymore.

He was also at the point, despite being the main driver, of thinking he'd be happy for Joyce to select a new car and he would adapt, rather than going through the whole choosing process again like they just had with the caravan; discern which was the most comfortable, with the best vision from one's particular seating position et cetera. He did have a tendency to quite easily become bamboozled. At least Joyce seemed to be enjoying managing the whole process.

'Hello, welcome,' Helen called from the open door as Colin and Joyce made their way up the path. She and the guest of honour, her husband, Jim, were standing in the doorway, the well-lit hallway stretching out behind them like an airport runway.

'For you,' Colin said, holding out the wrapped bottle after the round of air kisses, handshakes and backslaps had been completed. 'Congrats on the retirement, Jim.'

'Oh, but we said no gifts,' Helen said.

'But thank you, all the same,' Jim said, clutching the package to his chest. 'Come in, come in. In typical fashion, the women are mingling in the house and the men are out the back. This way.'

Colin touched Joyce's hand as she turned off the hall to follow Helen and he carried on down the long carpeted hallway and out to the grand expanse of sandstone paving and immaculate landscaping beyond.

'Fellas, most of you must already know Colin Palmer,' Jim called. 'Colin, you know everyone, I think. If not, just introduce yourselves. Tom, can you please get Colin whatever he wants to drink?' A young lad, dressed in the wait staff garb of black pants and white pressed shirt, nodded and stepped forward.

'Just a light beer, thanks, Tom, whatever's on offer,' Colin said.

In the moments it had taken to procure his beverage and have the bottle of liquid poured into a glass, all the mingling men had gone back to their conversations. Colin stood sipping his drink, feeling awkward and wondering who might be the friendliest and welcoming to approach. He longed to go over and sit down on the low wall near the pool, but no one else was over there so it didn't feel the right thing to do. Maybe in a bit; he'd see how his integration went first. Colin really preferred one on one interactions to this type of socialising in small groups.

He'd just cringed to himself at spying annoying Roger, when the man in question had raised his glass and with his other hand beckoned to him. Seeing no other option, without appearing rude, Colin made his way over.

'Colin, great to see you.' Colin was surprised to find himself being greeted like a long-lost old friend. He looked around to see who else was there he knew that he might use as an escape and feign a desperate need to speak to. But really, everyone was on the same plane in terms of relationship status. 'How's things?' Roger asked.

'Good, good. How about with you?'

'Great. Do you know Al, Steve and Barry?' he said, nodding around the small group he'd just stepped away from in order to greet Colin.

'No, but good to meet you all,' he said, shaking hands.

'So, what do you do? Or are you retired?' asked one of the men, whose name had promptly left his mind.

'Ah, no. Not far off though. I'm a psychologist in private practice.'

'Brilliant. So, tell me, can people really detect guilt based on how someone reacts to, say, learning the dead body of their husband or wife, or whatever, has been found?'

'Oh. Um.'

'Oh, come on, Al, leave the poor bloke alone. He's off-duty,' Roger said.

Colin cringed.

'We've had this conversation a few times over the years. Book in and pay him for his time. And, no, I'm not giving you free financial advice, either,' Roger added, raising his eyebrows over his drink.

'Yeah, all right. Point taken. I'm just making conversation.'

'Anyway, don't forget those shows are always done after the fact – with the benefit of hindsight. So the interviewees are probably being prompted by producers to say stuff they possibly ordinarily wouldn't think or say, for the purposes of drama or keeping the piece interesting.'

'Hmm. Sounds like you should be in my line of work, Roger,' Colin said with a laugh. 'My apologies, but it's slipped my mind what exactly it is you do?'

'Stock broker.'

'So, are you retiring soon – people in your line do relatively early, don't they?' Colin said, feeling the need to contribute, if only as thanks to Roger for taking the heat off him.

'Yes, they do tend to – generally speaking. I'm meant to be winding down. Can't seem to let go. Should just pull the pin. But …' He shrugged.

'Same with me,' Colin said, feeling a wave of solidarity with Roger.

'Oh, you blokes should just pick a date and, bang, it's done. Like Jim did,' Barry said. 'That's what I'm doing – end of the semester and I'm done.'

'Well, it's all right for your sort of profession,' Roger said. 'Not quite that simple when you have clients to take care of. There's a certain amount of hand-holding to do – ease them onto someone else, make sure they're comfortable, right, Colin?'

'Yeah, whatever. You keep telling yourselves that. I need another drink. Catch you later,' Barry said, and moved away. The rest of the group wandered off after him, leaving Colin and Roger alone.

'I've meant to be easing back for a while now, but I can't seem to say no to existing clients or new ones.'

'Oh, I hear you. Finances isn't at all in the realm of what you do, in terms of dealing with potentially vulnerable people – though I do have some clients on my books who are trying to navigate terminal illness. And from what I read regularly, the mental health sector is in a right state in this country, by all accounts, and just getting worse,' Roger said.

'Yes, it's a worry,' Colin agreed.

'And makes it harder for you to walk away.'

'Exactly.'

'I'm glad there's so much discourse and recognition around mental health now. Too many of my peers have died by suicide. We just had to suck it up, keep it to ourselves and get on with things. I'm glad those blokes left when they did. Last time I was with them they went on about how soft the young ones are and how they won't work and how much they whinge about not being able to buy a house. And then, of course, we get the rant about interest rates of the eighties, blah, blah, blah. It got quite intense.'

'I can imagine. Hello there.' At that moment a golden Labrador appeared beside them and they both made a fuss of the dog.

'My favourite sort of fellow guest; present company excepted, of course,' Roger said.

'Mine too. I actually took you for a social butterfly, networking extraordinaire.'

'Once, maybe. All an act, I assure you – in the name of building the business. But one thing I'm looking forward to in retirement – if and when I ever find a way to let go – is no longer having to look out for potential clients to spruik and schmooze wherever I go.'

'I guess that's one good thing about the mental health crisis – I've never advertised and the books seem to go along okay. Honestly, I'm not sure how I'm going to tell them I can't see them anymore, especially when I can't seem to find anyone to put them onto. Not looking for a career change, are you, Roger?'

'Hell no. I couldn't sit and be as polite and patient as I'm assuming you'd need to be.' He laughed.

'It's a struggle at times, I can tell you.'

'But, seriously, I feel for you. I hope you're not under too much pressure to pack it in,' he said, a little ruefully. 'My Caroline. I get it – she's been stuck at home supporting me, raising kids and helping out with grandkids. She now wants to hit the road.'

'Hitting the road as in caravanning?'

'That's the one.'

'Same with us. We've only today decided on a van, actually.'

'Congratulations.'

'Thanks.'

'Am I sensing some reluctance on that front too? I mean in addition to giving up work.'

'Yes. A bit.'

'What's up?'

Oh, so many things.

'Um. Okay. This is up your alley. How did you get the numbers to add up? I'm struggling to justify the investment when we're finally getting some interest, particularly on a depreciating asset. And when you take the ongoing costs into account – the enormous fuel consumption, site fees et cetera – it makes sense to simply drive and stay in a motel or hotel.'

'In purely financial terms, I agree, it doesn't add up. But it's the emotional side of things that can't be accounted for and which is so important – especially to my Caroline. Having her own bed and knowing the bedding is clean, not packing and unpacking all the time …'

'Hmm.'

'I do see her point. And she really wants to do it, so I'm willing to put it aside.'

Colin nodded.

'There's always the option of taking shorter trips to start off with to get used to things. We might have to because of the issue with the insurance becoming null and void if the house is left empty for too long. Neither of us are keen on having strangers in the house, at this point.'

'Hmm. I've had the same concerns.'

'What else is bothering you?'

'Honestly, my biggest one is about one's ablutions.'

'What, about toilet facilities in the van?'

'Yes. We've gone canister over hose system, but I really don't want to think about human waste at all after I've flushed,' Colin said.

'Ah yes, canister versus hose – I've done a deep dive online. A part of me is curious to see if tales of hordes of people traipsing over to the ablutions blocks with buckets of pee first thing in the morning so they don't have to empty their van systems so often is an urban myth or not.'

'Sounds real enough from what Joyce tells me. She's doing all the research. The toilet system is probably actually my biggest fear about caravan life.'

'I admit I have my concerns too. But I'm telling myself it's just fear of the unknown and will be fine. Because can it really be that bad if so many are committed to the grey nomad lifestyle?'

'That's true.'

'Anyway, if it helps, we'll be going with the canister waste system too. I've had too many visions of a scene in a movie I saw ages ago where they're emptying with hoses and end up covered in excrement. Makes my stomach curl just thinking about it.'

'I know what you mean. I must have seen the same movie. Urgh.'

At that moment a waiter appeared with a tray of finger food in one hand and a stack of napkins in the other.

'Perfect timing, young man, thank you,' Roger said with a chuckle.

Colin wasn't sure he wanted to eat now, but also reached for an item from the tray, the identity of which was not immediately apparent to him.

'On a serious note, you might be overthinking it all, Colin, like I was in the beginning,' Roger said, with his mouth half-full.

'You could well be right.'

'Though, of course, it's fine for me to say all this. I'm yet to actually bring myself to pull the pin on work.'

'Hmm. Yes, there is that issue remaining for me too.'

'Good chat, as the young ones would say,' Roger said. They raised their glasses and clinked them together.

'Indeed,' Colin said, returning Roger's smile. Suddenly he felt much better about his future. There was something very fortifying about knowing you were not alone in what you were feeling. His practice, his profession, was based on it.

Chapter Five

Despite their later than usual time getting to bed after being out the night before, Joyce and Colin arose on Sunday around five minutes before their 7.30 daily alarm went off. They'd even managed to remember to change the time on their bedside clock to reflect the start of daylight saving. Despite his general ineptitude with, and mistrust of, many technological advancements, Colin couldn't help experiencing a little thrill of awe that his mobile phone did this without any intervention on his part. You woke up on the Sunday, looked at the screen, and voila! Neither spouse tended to linger in bed of a morning, but that day saw them groaning and muttering about the hour they'd lost and a desire for the current government to do away with it forthwith.

As he went through the house, pulling up the blinds and opening the curtains, per his usual morning schedule, Colin wondered if they'd change any part of their routine when they were both retired. He hoped not; he particularly liked that Joyce had kept up her end of things in the past three months.

One thing he loved was breakfast being prepared for him by Joyce. Yes, he knew he was possibly considered chauvinistic. But he would happily have been chief breakfast maker if Joyce had made that preference known in those early days. They were both nurturers and had settled into their established roles without complaint. Some things had changed over the years; they only had to communicate their desires and renegotiate. They'd always been good at that.

While he ran the electric razor over his face in the bathroom, Colin paused to think what things had been negotiated along the way, and came up empty. He'd always done the vacuuming. He smiled at hearing Joyce getting out the crockery and cutlery down in the kitchen for their poached eggs. Oh. He suddenly remembered. No, not quite a renegotiation, but their Sunday poached eggs used to be accompanied with sausages or bacon. But the revelation of his high cholesterol during a routine blood test – for both of them – had seen a substitution for baked beans. Not really as enjoyable as a treat for Sunday but not too bad either. Weekdays were two Weetbix and milk and a tiny sprinkle of sugar during the warmer weather months, and porridge during colder seasons. Saturdays were toast and vegemite or jam, or sometimes even half and half, if he couldn't decide. Saturdays were the only days they had to think about it. A well-honed structure made life easier. He'd been saying and living this motto his whole life, since it was instilled in him by his parents. His mother had been a nurse and his father a military man. He also had them to thank for his perfect hospital corners and always having shoes so shiny he could see his reflection in them, no matter their age.

Joyce had been raised around the chaos of poverty and alcoholism. Her upbringing, while dramatically opposed to his in terms of routine and order, had caused her to be a neat-nick, and as obsessed as he with things being just so. Colin found it fascinating that two such different backgrounds could create people with similar values when it came to household matters and very different views elsewhere.

Growing up in a family that had struggled to make ends meet saw Joyce become a little more frivolous than Colin, who was tight-fisted because of a more casual approach to finances by his parents. Joyce, when questioned, would always say she knew what it was like to go hungry so would eat when she could – for want of an analogy. It served the same purpose for being well clothed etc, too. Whereas Colin preferred to have a buffer. Still, despite their differences in this area, they still rubbed along okay. Most likely because Joyce saw Colin as the authority figure – had certainly done so many years ago. He really hoped she saw him as equal in a partnership, but didn't like to tempt fate by making queries. Colin was of the view that if it wasn't broken, it didn't need fixing or pulling apart or digging around in.

'Breakfast,' Colin heard Joyce call. Gosh, he'd really got caught up daydreaming this morning. It must be his tiredness, he thought, hurrying to finish his ablutions.

'If your eggs have gone hard, don't blame me,' Joyce said, hanging up her apron on the hook behind the door and then taking her seat at the table.

The day seemed to pass on fast forward, as Sundays did, and it was time to put the newspaper in the recycling bin and close the curtains and blinds while Joyce prepared their roast dinner, which always supplied meat for sandwiches for during the week that he ate in his office. This week would be cold roast lamb – Colin's personal favourite.

He didn't take food to heat up in the tiny kitchen at work because he suspected many of the other collection of small allied health businesses renting office space in the centre were vegan and would be highly bothered by any detectable scent of animal products, such was the vibe of the place these days. He also kept himself to himself generally. In the few brief interactions he'd had recently, everyone there seemed lacking in patience, which was ironic given their new-age type businesses, which all seemed to peddle some sort of remedy for serenity. It was actually probably only his advanced age and assumed impending retirement that hadn't seen him asked to vacate before now.

'Yum, it's smelling good,' Colin said, coming in from taking out the rubbish and emptying the kitchen organics caddy.

'Wash up, because it will be ready soon.'

'Right you are,' he said, making his way up to the bathroom. Afterwards he sharpened the knife ready for carving while Joyce poured in the liquid from steaming the greens and finished the gravy. After dinner they'd enjoy an alcoholic beverage – tonight, gin and tonic; sherry in the colder months – while watching the ABC news and then whatever came after it until bedtime at around nine-thirty.

Chapter Six

As Colin sat eating his breakfast, the fact Joyce was continually scrolling on her phone was irking him.

'What's going on in your world that has you transfixed?' he enquired.

'Um. One of the Facebook groups I'm in is rallying about the proposed drilling in the gulf. I'm thinking of joining them.'

'Actually going somewhere and meeting up, you mean, not just signing a petition and writing letters?'

'Yes. What's wrong with that?'

'But why drilling in the gulf, particularly? And do they even work — protests, I mean?' The words, along with his clearly sceptical tone, were out before he could stop them.

'The whole world is going to hell in a handbasket — the planet, the people, every damned thing!'

'Oh, I agree with that.'

'So, something has to be done about *something*, Colin. We have to at least try on one front or another. Small steps, remember? Trying to protect the gulf is at least somewhere to start. And now

I'm not working I can actually do more in a boots on the ground basis.'

'I suppose. But actual protesting? In person? It just seems so … so, futile.'

'It probably will be. But so is doing nothing – and you of all people should know how bad it is for people's mental health to feel completely insignificant and powerless.'

'Hmm. Yes. I didn't mean to imply it's a waste of time.' He tried to backpedal.

'Oh, come on, Colin, that's exactly what you were saying. We – I – have to care about something more than just myself – ourselves, for the betterment of things. Complacency has got us into this mess. Something has to be done.'

'Actually, I don't think it's complacency, rather greed, dear, that's …'

'Really, Colin? Now is not the time.'

Colin was a little shocked at Joyce's vehemence. They were usually so good at these sorts of discussions, coming to an agreement, even if that agreement was to agree to disagree. Joyce had vacated her chair and was thumping mugs on the bench, making their tea. She turned around.

'Anyway, if I get arrested, you'll post bail, won't you?'

He laughed. But then realised she was steely-gazed and serious. When had he last seen her so … so riled? Crikey, what was going on? He didn't like that their world felt like it was teetering. 'What are you and your friends planning?'

'They're not *technically* friends. More acquaintances at this point. It's a Facebook group.'

'Oh god, you're not going to glue yourselves to the road or windows of some corporate office, are you? That sort of behaviour only makes you look unhinged.'

'Thanks for that, Colin.'

'Where's all this coming from? You're not an activist – not in the sense of protests the likes of which could get you arrested.'

'Maybe I am. Maybe I've just been on hiatus and I'm tired of being sensible. And you're clearly forgetting the seventies and eighties. We've discussed before that we were both at the rally against the Vietnam War, well before we met. And we've done our fair share of turning up together. I can't believe you'd forget us going to that protest for nuclear disarmament, and the ones to stop those god-awful re-developments going on about the place. Is any of this ringing a bell, Colin? Honestly, sometimes I wonder at you.'

Of course! How could I have forgotten all that? She's right; we were really quite active back in the day from a social conscience perspective.

'That was a very long time ago. And look where it got us. Precisely nowhere. Anyway, it's not the same. These days everyone seems so highly strung. I think peaceful protest is a misnomer. You can't know when people you're mixing with might have been pushed too far and be looking for an ignition point, or are on that awful drug, ice.

'Seriously, Joyce, if you need an outlet in order to feel productive now you're retired, what about volunteering for one of the organisations actually doing something to help? Native animals, the homeless, domestic violence ... There's any number of causes to choose from – the world's a total mess all round.'

Colin wondered if what was really behind Joyce's outburst, or need for action, or whatever this morning was about, was some sort of guilt around their plans to buy the caravan and vehicle. She'd never been a fervent greenie – neither of them had. They'd often rolled their eyes and muttered between themselves about the lofty goals of the young ones being out raging against all the mining and environmental pollution with phones in hand with apparently no concept of what went into producing the devices they held and vehicles they moved around in – electric or otherwise. Not to mention the energy required for all the essentials – whether you opted out of fast fashion or not.

'Well …?' Joyce said, bringing his focus back into the room. Her arms were still folded across her chest.

'What's that, dear?'

'Bail? You'll bail me out, if it comes to it?'

'Sure. Why not.' *Humour her, old man. There's no way she'll do anything to get arrested when it comes to the crunch.* Joyce had too much respect for police and authority in general, as did he. They'd received nothing but compassion and respectful treatment from the police on their few interactions.

Colin was relieved to see Joyce nod, unfold her arms, and then go to the fridge and retrieve the tray of cold meat. At least things were normal enough that she was still going to prepare his sandwiches.

'You're probably right. So, anything interesting awaiting you today at your office?'

'Not really. One of my regular couples is back for counselling…' Colin tried not to sigh as an image of Darren and Michelle Peacock came to mind.

'Are they one of the lots that drive you a bit bonkers?'

'Oh, yes. And before I get to them, I think there's a couple of psychometric tests for employees to do. So not a very exciting day all round.' Colin wasn't a fan of that sort of testing and didn't really agree with the way organisations seemed to pick and choose people based on their ability to fit in, rather than accepting them for their individuality and appreciating what their unique qualities might bring to the table. But doing them did contribute significantly to his bottom line. He supposed dropping his corporate clients would be a way to start winding the practice back and perhaps feel less like he was abandoning those who really needed him ...

'That's Mondays for you! I thought the main system used in the early two thousands had been debunked as bunkum.'

'A view only accepted in some circles, it seems. There's been a run on them lately.'

'I think you're right,' Joyce said, placing his lunchbox on the table a few minutes later.

'Eh?'

'Yes, there are probably too many unknowns with protesting these days. People or organisations not sticking to the actual point – derailing things – or handcuff-happy cops. Best I find another hobby,' she added with a sigh.

'I wasn't aware you were bored.'

'I'm not really. Though I do want to be useful. And get out and about a bit more. I'll look into volunteering opportunities again.'

'Well, don't forget you're planning to email the caravan people today. And look at vehicles – unless you want to do that together? I have to say, I do feel a bit uneasy about the vehicle side of things, what with it feeling like we're on the cusp of EV being maybe affordable and fuel being so expensive.'

'Hmm. That's a point. I'm not convinced the infrastructure is advanced enough, nor that the vehicles have the towing capacity yet. But leave it with me. You're right, though, in that I do seem to have enough to keep me on my toes – today, at least. And, as it's Monday, chicken pasta or stir-fry for dinner?'

'Either or. Surprise me.'

'It's hardly a surprise, but as you wish,' Joyce said with a laugh.

And there she is, my dependable, predictable Joyce, Colin thought with relief as he drained his mug.

Chapter Seven

Colin was always a little annoyed that Darren and Michelle Peacock's sessions tended to be the last of his day. Just like David and Julia on Friday, they'd been coming to see him about their relationship for a long time, but never took on board anything he said – or didn't seem to – and, unsurprisingly, had made no progress that he was aware of.

Uh-oh, he thought as they each acknowledged him with a nod as they filed past and took their seats on the couch. They sat as far away from each other as was possible, which was normal for them, with their arms folded and displaying scowls. *There's at least something you have in common*, Colin thought, watching them carefully.

'How are you both today?' he asked, feigning brightness, instantly regretting his choice of greeting.

He thought the grunts he received might have been interpreted as, 'Okay, thanks,' but couldn't be entirely sure. *Brace yourself, Colin, we're in for a bumpy ride.*

'Right. So, how did you go with the exercises I set to work on being less abrasive with each other?'

'We tried. Well, *I* did,' Darren said.

'Really? Not from where I'm sitting,' Michelle said. 'You've been a prick all week.'

'Here we go. See, this is what I'm dealing with, Colin.'

'Perhaps it might be more helpful to start with the present, or, more specifically, what's particularly bothering you both today,' Colin said.

Darren sighed deeply. 'She's upset with me for almost running us late. And, for the record, we were right on time.'

'Yes, but not without considerable stress. He won't even listen to the woman on the sat nav, so what hope do I have? And, anyway, if you want to know, I'm still upset about last night.'

Here we go.

'What did I do last night?'

'You left your glass *and* mug on the sink after I'd cleaned up.'

'But I was planning to have another drink. Yes, of whisky *and* of tea. I changed my mind. The dishwasher was already running. I rinsed them and put them upside down. Where the hell else was I supposed to put them?'

'You could have dried them and put them in the cupboard.'

Colin shifted in his chair as his thoughts momentarily strayed to the mug currently sitting on his own sink back at home. *Is Joyce harbouring such irritations towards me? No, she'd say something if it bothered her.*

'Then you would have told me off because they weren't clean! See, Colin, I can't do anything right!'

Oh my god, you two, really? This is how you're going to spend your money and our time today? Now I'm *in need of a bloody whisky!* He began doodling hard straight lines on his pad of paper in an effort to quell or at least try to express his rising frustration.

'Um, guys, I think–' Colin tried, but he could see his words went unheard. At least they were looking at each other, but Michelle's expression could cut through a glacier. He felt a bit for Darren in that moment.

'And you could have at least told me you were upset,' Darren said, a little more quietly.

'I did! Are you being serious right now?'

'Well, clearly I didn't hear you.'

'For fuck's sake! And it was Sunday night. So why do you think we didn't have sex?'

'It's *making love*, Michelle. And, um, because you were asleep when I came in?'

'Was I, Darren? Really?'

Colin rubbed a hand across his face and took several deep breaths. *We're back at sex again, where you started with me months ago? Really? You two are doing my damned head in. You're draining, you suck the air right out of the room. I wonder how your friends fare being around you. Do you have any? Do you socialise? The way I feel, I can scarcely believe I had such a lovely nap earlier. Seriously, have you ever considered how ridiculous and petty you are? I shudder to think what you're like in the privacy of your own home if you're like this here. It's EVERY. SINGLE. TIME.*

'I think it's time you two considered separating,' Colin blurted out. As the words seemed to catch up with the two people sitting at each end of the couch, they looked at each other and then fixed their glares on Colin.

'What do you mean?' they said in unison.

'Well, you've clearly not made any headway here in the past six months.'

'But you're meant to help us stay together,' Michelle said.

'Yes. Exactly,' Darren said, nodding.

Colin almost laughed and threw his hands up and shouted aloud, *'Finally, something you agree on!'* Instead, he calmly said, 'Ah, now, not necessarily. You wanted to learn to communicate better. And look at you – you're still arguing about petty matters. Dishes on the sink? How and when to stack the dishwasher? Come on. How old are you?' Colin's fury began to take over. He felt his face begin to flame, but couldn't stop the words.

'But we were. This is how we communicate,' Darren said.

'Yes. We always have,' Michelle said. 'It's what works for us.'

'Yet here you are.' Colin spread his hands out, palms up. 'Week after week you come here, wasting all our time and your money, asking me this or that. And then apparently ignoring any and all advice I give. There's nothing more I can do for you. My advice is to separate. And not have children together. Because if you're anything like you are here, in your own home, your environment would be very toxic indeed, and most likely completely ruin a child. And now, you two need to pay and then leave.'

'We're not paying, we haven't had a full session,' Darren said.

'Yes. And you've not helped. At all,' Michelle said.

'I couldn't get a bloody word in. And when I do, you ignore my guidance. If you don't pay, you can answer to my solicitor and/or debt collector,' Colin added, a little breathlessly. He didn't know where this had even come from. He didn't have a lawyer or debt collection service, had never needed either before.

He stood up and pressed the details into the EFTPOS machine and then held it out towards his recalcitrant former clients. Suddenly the energy seemed to leave him like a retreating wave. He desperately wanted to put his hand behind him and make sure his chair was there to catch him and sink down into it. Thankfully, the bluster seemed to have also left Darren and Michelle who had also now stood. Their cheeks were red – from embarrassment or anger, Colin wasn't sure. Possibly both. Each was silent and looking a little pale. He felt bad at seeing Michelle was on the verge of tears. Tears he was used to, but it pained him to know he might be the cause. Michelle pulled a card from her wallet and tapped it on the machine.

Colin tried not to let his relief show. Yes, it was only money, but it was the principle.

'Right, well, um, thanks,' Michelle said, accepting the receipt that he'd just folded and handed over. It had seemed to take an inordinate amount of time to print.

'I do wish you all the very best,' Colin stammered, heading over to the door to let them out. 'But maybe some time apart would work for sorting out your true feelings.'

'You're probably right. Thanks,' Darren said quietly, as he passed through the open door.

'Really, Darren, do you mean that?' Michelle said, grabbing Darren's arm. 'Why didn't you say weeks ago, instead of ...'

Their words faded as the door Colin had just closed behind them clicked shut. *For Christ's sake*, he thought, slumping into his chair. He probably should feel worse about it than he did. But he was a little rattled. Where had that outburst come from? Was he losing the plot? Entering a late-in-life crisis or something? He rubbed his hands over his face. Oh well, at least he was rid of them, and someone hopefully more appreciative of his service would book their spot. He ran a wait list that would advise someone automatically via the app and email that there was now a place available.

Crikey, Colin thought as he prepared to head off home.

As he pulled his office door shut behind him, the centre's manager caught his eye and raised her eyebrows. *Great. I've woken the dragon too. No doubt there'll be a group email reminding us to be mindful of other tenants and their clients and to keep our voices down.* He acknowledged her by raising his hand and shrugging in what he hoped would convey a mix of ah, what can you do and expressing his apologies for the disruption.

As he walked home, he began feeling a little unsettled. He really was probably lucky Darren hadn't thumped him – punched him in the nose or jaw. Actually, Michelle too, for that matter. They were both gym junkies and participated in the weightlifting side of fitness. Perhaps they were on some sort of supplement that made them cranky. Oh well, he was rid of them.

The thought should have caused relief and contentment. But he was still a little shaky as he put his key in the front door of home. Maybe he was dehydrated or experiencing a touch of hypoglycaemia. He was a little hungry, now he thought about it.

'Hello, Joyce, I'm home,' he called. 'Are you here?' He paused and listened for signs of her presence. God, he really hoped she was there to debrief with. He felt in need of some coddling, he was a little ashamed to admit. A surge of relief hit as he heard her voice coming from far down the hall.

'Coming. There in a tick.'

'Oh my god. What a day. Or, rather, what an ending to the day. Am I glad to see you,' he said, sagging into her embrace.

'Yes, it seems you've had quite the interaction!'

'What do you mean?' He stepped back and scrutinised her, frowning. Her eyes twinkled with amusement and she was smiling. She led the way through to the kitchen where she tapped the screen of the tablet on the table so it lit up.

'Client by the name of Michelle Peacock?' Her eyebrows were raised.

'What about her?'

'She's left a review on the business Facebook page.'

Colin sat down.

'And, no, it's not a positive one,' Joyce said.

Uh-oh.

'And worse than that, people are responding to it. It's becoming a bit of a pile-on.'

He peered at the screen and then felt all the muscles in his face sag. 'Oh, dear.' He hadn't given any thought to the possibility of Darren and Michelle posting a negative review online. He tried to read the message, but couldn't seem to focus. He was tired. They'd been exhausting and he'd thought he was rid of them. Yet here they were. And, worse, they were now infiltrating his homelife and downtime.

'Did you really tell them to split up?'

Colin nodded. His stomach began to churn as another thought seeped in. 'Oh my god,' he said. 'What if they report me to the board?' The words of the long post were swimming, so much he couldn't read them.

'Well, they say they're going to.'

'Don't you sound so cheerful. It's not amusing, Joyce, this is a disaster.'

'Oh, come on. You're wanting to retire. What's the worst that can happen?'

'I certainly don't want to go out by being deregistered or anything embarrassing like that.'

'I bet they won't even file a complaint. Probably all bluster. They'll blow off their steam online and that'll be the end of it, most likely.'

'But ...' His vision cleared and he peered closer at the screen. 'But people are sharing it, reacting, commenting.'

'Well, what you've said has been said now; you can't take it back.'

'Should I? Do you think I should issue a response, an apology?'

'No, rule number one with these online things is, don't engage. Remember? I suggest you just ignore it. It'll blow over. You know the adage: today's news is tomorrow's fish and chip wrapping, or whatever it is.'

'But ...'

'No buts.'

'Oh god.' Colin, finally getting his eyes and brain to focus properly, clicked on the comments. 'It's not just their friends, or whoever, responding. Other clients appear to be joining in – past and current.' He recognised some of the names. So many times he'd wished to hear how clients he no longer saw were faring, how things had turned out for them – both the happy and less enjoyable clients. How infuriatingly ironic that they were doing that here now. Because, unfortunately, he knew enough about Facebook, thanks to Joyce telling him, to know that anything typed in that little box beneath kept on giving a post energy – like oxygen fuelling a fire. He sent silent thanks to those few people saying positive things and a double-dose to those who'd typed 'If you don't have anything nice to say, say nothing' and the like. He knew if he couldn't ignore the words entirely – and he couldn't – he should focus on the kind comments. But despite all his training and experience, he was still human. It hurt. And he wanted to get it to stop.

'What are they saying? I'll be back there in a sec.'

'"Colin Palmer should be called Colon because he's full of shit". Charming. Oh god, Joyce.'

'Actually, that's pretty funny. Clever.'

'Thank you, Joyce. Not helpful.'

'It is a bit funny.'

'Yes, okay. Well, this one will definitely tickle your fancy then: "Palmer. Yup, if he thinks he's helpful, he's got his hand on it".'

'Huh? I don't get it. What's amusing about that?'

'Palmer. Mrs Palmer and her five daughters. They're calling me a wanker.'

'Oh. I see. Look, there are some positive ones, too. Try and focus on those. Oh, but what's this symbol one? There's a few of them quite similar. I can't tell if it's good or bad. It looks like … a capital W and … what is that thing meant to be with the hooks? It's too small.'

They both peered at the screen and then tried squinting.

'Oh. I think that's an anchor,' Joyce said, leaning across the table to see.

'W and an anc … Oh Christ, again, it's wanker.' He sighed loudly.

'Oh dear. Look, just turn it over and stop looking.'

Colin ached to type in a defence. He looked plaintively at Joyce.

'Could you just put a …' He pointed to the device where comments rolled down the page.

'No. Absolutely not. Not even anonymously. It'd be too obvious if I set up a new name – Joyce Palmer is a bit of a giveaway – and post as someone with a brand-new profile and zero friends. I'm not sure but I think people can tell if you're not fully legitimate. And I think Facebook has cracked down on multiple profiles, in an effort to stop trolling.'

'Well, get them to stop this … um … trolling.'

'I don't think you can. Just turn it over and stop looking.'

'Can we delete it? The whole post. *Should* we delete it?'

'I don't know if that'll make it worse. I really think it might be best just to ignore it.'

'Oh god.' And then Colin had an idea. 'Why don't we just delete the whole page?'

'We could. Though that seems a bit drastic. You've got some lovely comments in the past, remember, including the occasional update via private message. People seem to prefer that as a medium to email, so you'd be losing that avenue. You have to take the good with the bad, remember.'

'That's true. You're right, it would be a shame to let one bad apple spoil the whole basket.'

'Put it out of your mind and leave it to me to keep an eye on it.'

'You're wonderful, Joyce. I really appreciate you taking the load.'

'I really am certain it'll blow over soon. Some celebrity will put their foot in it and all the keyboard warriors will flock to that like moths to a flame. Seriously, though, good on you for putting an end to the Darren and Michelle farce. By all accounts it was excruciating. I know they'd bothered you from the outset.'

'Christ, though.'

'I'm surprised it took you that long to react. You've more patience than me.'

'That was well established many moons ago, my dear.'

'And there's my darling husband,' Joyce said, reaching around and hugging him from behind. 'It'll blow over. You'll see.'

'And if I get hauled up before the board?'

'Then we'll deal with that then. You'll have a chance to plead your case, if you don't want to simply hand in your registration – depending when, if, it happens. And most likely you'd be fine. It's all very subjective, so bound to ruffle feathers. Maybe you should be more forthright more often and you won't have to make the decision to retire,' Joyce said cheerfully.

'Dear, that's really not a very helpful attitude. And it's the prin–'

'I know, the principle. They're very important. I'm just trying to adopt a glass half-full attitude. What's done is done. I'll make dinner. You go and have a shower. And stay away from all devices!'

Chapter Eight

Colin, a little bleary-eyed from a particularly good, and much needed, nap, and therefore in need of a bathroom visit to wash his face to revive him, was slightly startled to open his door to find his next booking, a woman by the name of Shirley Royal, already sitting there.

'I hope you don't mind me being a little early. I'm Shirley Royal,' the woman said, smiling broadly at him and leaping up while shoving what appeared to be a knitting project into a soft fabric bag with wooden handles. 'It's a failing of mine,' she added, most likely feeling the need to breach the silence before it could become awkward. Momentarily discombobulated, he gazed at the woman standing before him with her grey hair arranged in a bun and a jovial expression on her face that suggested she might break out into laughter or song at any moment. There was a sort of anticipation about her, he thought – a readiness to spring into some sort of action at any point.

'I'm happy to wait. If there's something you need to do first?' Shirley said.

'Oh no, that's quite okay. And, it's not a failure in my book. Being early.' He was already feeling much enlivened in her presence.

'There's not nearly as much punctuality as I would like.'

'Oh, I agree. Particularly with the young ones.'

'Sadly, across the board, in my experience. It's really quite tiresome.'

Colin smiled. Despite her words, Shirley remained cheerful. Colin felt instantly buoyed and, dare he even think it, joyful. *What could she possibly be wanting to see me about?*

'Come in,' he said, standing aside with his arm outstretched.

'Thank you.'

'Sit anywhere you like,' he said, noticing her looking around as he closed the door behind them. She chose one of the steel-armed chairs upholstered in black and sat, keeping her bag of knitting on her lap. Colin watched as she wrapped her arms tighter around it, pulling it to her stomach. He couldn't tell if she was using it for protection or protecting it from harm.

He settled into his own seat behind the desk and linked his hands in front of him in a loose way he hoped conveyed openness and warmth. Shirley Royal peered back at him and slowly blinked a couple of times.

'So, Shirley, how can I help you?'

'I'm here for some of this tough love I've been hearing you're so good at issuing. I looked you up and saw the cranky online review from the couple you apparently told to split up. Good for you, I say. In just their online post they sounded pretty bloody obnoxious!'

'Oh. Well, um.' *Thanks. I think.* He struggled to form a decent response. 'I'm not sure …'

'I don't want someone who'll just sit there nodding and asking me how I feel about this or that a million times …'

Well, I do do rather a lot of that, to be honest. And the Darren and Michelle Peacock situation was an anomaly that I'm not planning on repeating. Colin opened his mouth to speak, but found he couldn't get a word in without appearing rude and cutting the woman off.

'You'll not be for everyone – um, obviously – but none of us are. But, anyway, here I am.' She spread her hands out wide.

'Er.'

'I'm serious. I mean it. I want you to lay it on me. I need to get my shit together,' she said and let out a sigh, and then proceeded to purse her lips and shake her head slowly in a sign of consternation.

Colin frowned. His forthright approach had got him into enough strife as it was.

'Please,' she insisted.

'Well, at least tell me what the problem is.'

'Um, I'm being a bit vague, aren't I?'

Colin smiled as he waited for her to continue.

'My husband Norman died and I can't seem to get over it – as in, stop thinking about him. He's occupying far too much of my mind and I want it to stop.'

Colin struggled to keep his eyebrows from raising and his mouth from dropping open.

'Er …' he said.

'I've always been an overthinker, but, I mean, I didn't even like him. Oh, well, no, that's a bit harsh. Obviously, I liked him once. Or, well, perhaps there's no *obviously* about it, I suppose. There've been plenty of marriages throughout history made out of convenience or with strangers, thanks to cultural or religious arrangements or what have you.' She paused, the skin between her eyebrows puckered tightly, as if she was contemplating her words. 'But we were not like that at all. Although, looking back, it was sort of a marriage of convenience – for both of us, to escape our respective horrible families. And we did get along well – or at least okay – on the whole ...'

Colin was about to speak, but didn't get the chance.

'But seriously, he was a dreary fellow, didn't want to do anything. Absolute bore. He was a good man and I didn't dislike him. Even at the end. Or maybe then, a bit.' Again, she paused. This time to tap a finger to her lip.

'It wasn't his fault he got cancer, but, fuck – oops. I hope you don't mind people swearing ...'

Colin waved away her concern. He was struggling to hold back a grin.

'All that waiting around. Hence the knitting,' she said, patting the bag still on her lap.

Colin noticed it was now being held a little less tightly.

'I might have become somewhat obsessed,' she added, grinning and then cringing. 'And the damned wool is so bloody expensive. Did you know they send our fibre – from Australian sheep – over to China and then bring it back as yarn? What a ridiculous situation. It's no wonder the world and humanity is a complete f– um, disaster. Seriously, does everything seem upside down? Everything – peace, war, whichever way you look at that – environmental issues, waste. Climate change – does it even change, or is it just on a larger cycle that we don't yet have enough data for? I ask you. Anyway, that's what I reckon. It's all bloody whack-a-mole.'

Colin frowned. He was having trouble keeping up. And what was the last thing she'd just said? Whacka what?

His confusion must have registered because she said, 'Oh, you know. You must know. Whack-a-mole,' she enunciated slowly. 'It's a game. Maybe an idiom and most likely a million memes by now … But there's a wooden mallet and moles – you know – the animal; small furry thing, squinty eyes, long nose, small buck teeth …?'

Now Colin really nearly did lose his teetering composure because Shirley had just chosen that moment to scrunch her eyes shut and arrange her own mouth in such a pose. He forcibly swallowed his bubbling laughter to instead cough and then clear his throat. He wanted to shake his head in an effort to try and figure out where she was going with all this. And where she'd already been, for that matter.

'Anyway, it's a futile business because they keep on popping their little heads out of holes, despite being pounded with the mallet.'

'Surely not. It sounds a bit cruel.'

'Oh no, it's not based on real moles being hit, well, I bloody well hope not. I think it was originally an arcade game in the USA. Anyway, the point I was trying to make was all the carry-on in the world is like that – you deal with one issue, knock it on the head, and immediately another one pops up. As I say, *futile*.' She waved her hand and then sat back in her chair in sudden silence, as if her mouth was a tap that had been tightly turned off. She looked at him, again blinking a couple of times, and seemed to be waiting for him to speak.

'I'm not sure what you want from me – what I can do to help,' he finally admitted after mentally scrolling back through her words. There'd been something about climate change, her dead husband, cancer …

'I need your tough love to stop me thinking about my rather exasperating husband who has finally kicked the bucket. Tell me how to stop him infiltrating my thoughts,' she said with a decent amount of exasperation of her own.

'So you're wanting closure?' he ventured.

'Now, Colin, you don't get much more closed than dead. Death really is the most obvious form of closure, wouldn't you say?'

'Well, yes, I suppose so.' *Is she manic, bipolar, having an episode of euphoria?* He didn't think so, but every person's experience and symptoms were a little different. 'Do you think you might be depressed, or anxious?'

'No. Definitely not. I'm glad he's gone. No, rephrase that. Not *glad* ...' Again, she paused and tapped her lip with an index finger. 'Glad he's no longer suffering and I'm not having to sit for hours on end in those stark and dreadfully odorous rooms.

'And the out-of-pocket expenses! People have no idea. We're meant to be a first world country with this great medical system. But nobody talks about the cost of the privilege of dealing with a bout of cancer or other issue, and treatment requiring visits to specialists. Mind the fucking gap! Someone should talk about *that* gap. There should be a fucking uprising, I tell you. Anarchy. But oh no, we've got free health care. It's bullshit. There are next to no bulk-billing GPs anymore. And, of course, the system doesn't cover dentistry. But perhaps don't get me started on that!

'So, no, I don't dare get depressed or anxious in case I need to see a specialist! Oh no!' she added.

Colin was just thinking, *but here you are*, when she seemed to read his mind.

'Present company excepted, of course. From your Facebook page and online presence, I thought you might have been worth my time and money. But, Colin Palmer, quite frankly, I'm beginning to feel a little duped.'

'Perhaps if you were clearer and let me get my thoughts together and, better yet, allowed me to get a word in, I might have a chance of helping you!'

Colin was shocked at realising he'd said the words aloud.

'There you are!' Shirley sat up a little straighter. 'I admit, I tend to ramble, another failing. Please, impart your wisdom. I will be silent.' She clasped her hands in her lap and looked at him demurely.

'Well, grief takes all sorts of forms and it sounds to me as if you really were quite fond of your husband …'

'Really? I suppose so. There was a big turnout at his funeral, too. He would have loved that … Point taken,' she said in response to Colin's raised eyebrows. 'But I will just need to interject. I need a way to get over it, or through it, or whatever, without too much palaver. It bloody annoys me that he's still such a big presence in his absence. Like a lingering fart. If you know what I mean?'

'Yes. I do.' Again, he fought a bubble of laughter and had to swallow hard. 'Unfortunately, Shirley, it doesn't tend to work like that. It's something to work through and it's going to take as long as it's going to take. You might not think you're grieving, but you are. Think of it as recalibrating instead, if you like.'

'Ooh, that's an interesting word – I like that one.'

Colin ignored her and ploughed on, finally finding his footing. 'All sorts of things need to be grieved, any type of loss – even the smallest, most inconsequential thing needs to be given its time and to be released and moved on from. Just because you might be … um … glad he's gone, doesn't negate the other parts to be addressed. It's very normal to be relieved when someone passes – especially if they've been in pain. A cancer battle is a particular circumstance where it would be very apt to be grateful the person no longer suffers. But also remember to consider what an enormous hole or gulf has been left in your life. Your world is irrevocably altered. Now there's a gap you have to mind,' he added, offering a sympathetic, knowing smile.

'Ooh, you're clever.'

'So, in case I haven't made myself clear, Shirley, I can't give you any tough love on this,' he said, gently. 'Grief is not something to be trifled with. Go gently. And slowly. Be kind to yourself. Don't sweep it under the rug.'

'So, there's no quick fix?'

'I don't think so, no.'

'Well, I tried,' she said. 'Damn you, Norman,' she said, raising a fist and looking up at the ceiling.

'What exactly is it he, or rather your grief, is doing that you're trying to banish?' Colin ventured.

'Oh, I don't know. It's the empty house. I hate that it feels like he's still there – not in a ghost-like sense, I don't believe in spirits – but is clearly not there. It's hard to explain, really.'

'Maybe it's not what's there but what's not.'

'Perhaps you're right that I'm missing him. Oh god. Bloody hell. Maybe I am trying to avoid the unavoidable.'

'How long has he been gone for?'

'Three weeks.'

Three weeks! Colin struggled to keep his eyes from bugging and his mouth from gaping. He bought a beat of time by blinking and clearing his throat.

'Um. That's very soon, Shirley.'

'Is it? How long's about right?'

Sadness engulfed Colin. He shook his head slowly.

'That's rather a how long's a piece of string question, isn't it?'

'I'm afraid so. Some people never come to terms with their loss – grieve forever …'

'You'd better not do that to me. I'm telling you!' she said, again looking up, fist raised.

They sat in silence for a moment.

'Our time is up, isn't it?' Shirley suddenly said.

Oh. Colin checked the wall clock, surprised to find how much time had passed. 'Yes, it appears so.'

'Here we are.' Shirley held out a bank card. Colin felt guilty taking money from her, since he clearly hadn't helped her. He hesitated.

'You've been very helpful,' Shirley said.

'Really?'

'Oh yes.' She beamed.

'That's good to know.' He smiled as he handed back her card and receipt.

'I might even come back again. But for now, I think I need to go away and process things for a bit.'

'Okay. Fair enough.'

'Thanks again.'

'It's been my pleasure.' He walked Shirley to the door and opened it.

'And you keep ignoring the haters online and be yourself. The world needs some common sense dished out. It's a shitshow out there.'

'It sure is,' he said with a laugh. He wanted to say she'd been a wonderful client, had cheered him up, but that would be crossing the line.

Chapter Nine

Colin's step was lighter that evening as he made his way home from work. He was so intent on discussing his day with Joyce he almost didn't see the suitcase sitting just the other side of the hall table.

'I'm ho—' The words stopped in his throat. *What's she up to now?* Something told him the suitcase was packed and not sitting out of the way while she was tidying.

'Oh, there you are. Good. Perfect timing.' Colin raised his arms to reach out to Joyce for their customary greeting hug, but she bustled past to look in the hall mirror.

'What's going on? You look stressed.'

But Joyce was too busy carefully applying lipstick to answer. While he waited, he ran through the list of people they knew who might be unwell or injured or what have you, requiring a visit that was far enough away to necessitate an overnight stay, and came up empty. All family and friends living interstate had either dropped out of their orbit along the way, or died.

'Okay, phone, charger, wallet, ticket,' Joyce said.

It was all Colin could do to remain silent and still. He shoved his hands deep into his pockets to help.

'Right.' Joyce now stood facing him, a hand on each of his shoulders, trapping his arms by his side. 'I'm answering a callout online to go and wash birds near Perth. Some bloody fool let their boat run aground and oil has been spilled.'

'What? Wait. Hang on. What are you doing?'

'Colin, I don't have time to explain. I'm flying to Perth to help save water birds who've been covered in oil. They'd die if ... Anyway, you can read about it. It's all over the news. If it isn't, it should be. Bloody careless big business, environmental vandals.'

'But–'

'I managed to get your dinner done – zucchini slice. Just heat it up in the microwave or eat it cold. And I've taken the tablet computer so you'll have to remember to bring home the work laptop if you need a larger screen. I think that's all I need to tell you. Oh, and as I predicted, the online furore has ended. There's been no new comments, shares or reactions all day.'

'Oh, that's great news. Thank you. Per your advice, I haven't looked at it again.' *Fingers crossed they've vented sufficiently and I won't hear from anyone else on the matter.*

'I think that's a good policy for you. I'll let you know if there's anything you really need to know. Anyway, my ride's going to be here any–'

They turned their heads at the double-honk of a car horn out in the street.

'Okay. Sad but exciting times. Fingers crossed we get there in time and can make a real difference. See you.'

Colin was pecked on the cheek and released. As he was putting his hands out to hug his wife, she was already raising the handle of her small carry-on size suitcase and dragging it towards the front door.

'Well, um, good luck,' he said, raising a hand in a wave instead.

Regathering himself momentarily, he stood at the open door and watched as Joyce put her suitcase into the car's open boot. He could see several people were sitting inside the vehicle.

'Bye,' Joyce called, one hand on the open car door, the other waving to him.

'Keep your phone charged. And call me!' he shouted back. He waited until the car was out of sight before going back in and closing the door.

Wow, what the hell just happened?

Colin wandered from room to room, unable to settle, wondering what to do with himself. He wasn't sure how long he'd been moping for, and was a little surprised to find himself in Joyce's sewing room, staring into the tidy space, when her cranky voice in his mind suddenly snapped him out of his reverie as abruptly as if he'd been slapped: *Oh, for goodness sake, Colin, pull yourself together. Stop being a big baby!*

'You're quite right, dear.' He pictured her flushed face as she'd left. When had he last seen her so full of vigour? He should be happy and excited, at least for her – definitely not being an old misery guts. She'd been a bit tetchy lately, so this break and change of scenery might be just what she needed.

'Okay. So, let's make the most of having the place to ourselves,' he said aloud. God, he wished he had a dog or cat, bird even, for company. Though, no, he loathed the idea of birds being stuck in cages. *Hmm.* He tapped his lips with his finger. *Music! That's what's needed!*

With a more determined stride, he went back down the hall and through to the lounge where he opened the cupboard containing the records. Having chosen one at random, he slipped it out of its protective sleeve, gently popped it onto the turntable and set it going. When had they last put music on that was loud enough to waft out to other rooms? Once, the pair of them had danced around the space, music turned up loud, the speakers mounted high up on the walls working beautifully. It really was lovely – the perfect balance of sounds, he thought as the Beatles drifted through the room. Feeling a little better, he wandered through to the kitchen, humming to himself as he went. He opened the fridge and peered in. There was a plate with a domed plastic microwave cover concealing its contents. He lifted the edge with his finger.

'Yum. Thanks, dear. Much appreciated.' Though he momentarily wondered if he should fully embrace the bachelor life and order in a pizza. Again, he found himself wondering when they'd last done that. Had they ever? They must have done. Most likely, though, it was an activity confined to a time with kids – probably during a sleepover with friends staying. He tried to recall, conjure up images, but his mind refused to comply.

Sadness descended, not helped by the mournful tones of the accompanying music track. He closed the fridge and then opened it again, suddenly fancying a beer. But there wasn't any. Probably best. He'd have a gin and tonic later. Though he'd better be careful. He might get melancholy when drinking alone. Alcohol was not the answer. *It might help, though*, a little voice inside piped up. He shook it aside and went down the hall to take a shower.

Clean and fresh, but far from feeling content, Colin turned off the music in the lounge and went to the kitchen. He heated the zucchini slice, added a pile of salad, and put the meal down on the table in his usual spot. But he didn't take his seat. He didn't want to look across at Joyce's empty place. In fact, the whole space felt awkward due to Joyce's absence. It was as if the soul had been sucked right out of the room. He thought about taking his plate through to the lounge room and eating with it on his lap.

Joyce's voice immediately came to him, *'Really, Colin? Don't even think about it.'* He smiled, picturing her look of consternation and slow shake of her head. And then she'd turn back to the sink. Even being told off was better than this emptiness.

'Probably best to stay put,' Colin muttered, and pulled the chair out from the table and plonked himself down to eat. It was a good batch of zucchini slice, he thought and looked forward to telling Joyce when he spoke to her. He wondered when that would be and where exactly she was at that moment. Had she boarded the flight or was she still checking in? How many were going with her? He really hoped she hadn't been sucked into some elaborate catfishing, fraudulent scheme or other. *Oh.*

He got up to turn on the small radio that sat on the shelf and was tuned on low every morning for them to be across the day's news from the outset. Despite him not touching the volume button the ABC news reader's voice came into the room loudly, much louder than it did in the morning with the accompanying rattling of crockery and cutlery and hum of human activity. He hesitated, trying to decide if he needed to adjust the sound level, but left it. He didn't want Joyce coming home to all the little things changed. Silly, he knew. But they often said, 'Ah, it's the little things,' with great affection. And their radio at just the right volume for their morning preparations was one such thing.

He was just in time for the start of the bulletin and found himself pausing, his fork lowered as each item came and went. And then there it was: 'Volunteers are rallying to try and save hundreds of birds washing up on the Western Australian coast covered in oil while authorities try to get to the bottom of who has caused the devastating incident ...' Colin felt himself shift a little with relief. And then he scolded himself. Joyce was an intelligent woman. There was no way she'd go running off, jumping on planes without doing her due diligence. How very disrespectful of him to think otherwise.

But the next item caused a shiver of smugness to flicker. 'And an update on the latest corporate privacy breach ... Everyone is being reminded, whether they're directly involved or not, to remain vigilant where their banking and identity is concerned.'

God, it's a bloody runaway train. Every man and his dog has everyone's details. It was probably more to do with luck than good management that he and Joyce hadn't been caught out by anything nefarious. It was no longer enough to simply not click on links in emails. It was all around them, on a twenty-four-seven basis these days – exhausting just to think about.

Once upon a time you really only had to worry about being mugged outside at night and relieved of your funds and credentials in person. At least the authorities could try to do something about that. But this sort of situation was out of control. His mind boggled with the scantest thought of what was involved with staying safe and dealing with it all.

He really hoped the people Joyce was with were above board. Surely they must be if they cared about saving birds. A little surge of pride started up and then climbed over the top of what was slight envy that he wasn't off doing something so demonstrably important and selfless. Could he go and surprise her? Should he? No. He had his books full that week. And, anyway, he didn't want to be seen to be stomping all over Joyce's thing – raining on her parade.

They'd always been so independent. Well, he'd thought they had. Perhaps only in his mind. They did, after all, spend all their time together when not at their respective jobs.

Oh. My phone. He'd left it charging. *What if Joyce has tried to call?* He leapt up. And was then filled with an irrational sense of disappointment when he turned it over and saw no notification of either a missed call or text message. The feeling was so acute it was not unlike a painful soccer punch to the stomach. Phone still in hand, he returned to the table. Christ, he really had to get a grip. Joyce would be appalled, though also a little heartened – he'd like to hope.

Resuming his meal, his thoughts began to swirl again. Yes, he was annoyed at himself for his apparent disrespect for his smart, intelligent wife, but also, it was very much out of character for Joyce to run off and join a cause, especially one requiring hopping on a plane, and that concerned him. She'd never been a fan of flying, which was one of the reasons they never went anywhere, or hadn't, really, since their honeymoon to Tasmania.

If he were being honest, he was also a bit piqued that she hadn't discussed purchasing an airfare before the fact. Even during the fact – as she'd booked. How much was it, anyway?

He logged into the internet banking on his phone and was shocked to find the fare was seven hundred dollars, and that another thousand had been taken out at an ATM. He tried to tell himself that was fine. But it didn't help. Worse, he was even more annoyed now – particularly that she'd taken the funds from the joint account. Yes, it had travel in the title, but they had their own accounts. So why had she used that one?

His frustration released. *Oh, for god's sake, stop being an old grump. There's plenty of money. Since when have you been such a tyrant? And so bloody needy and insecure, for that matter?*

Colin recognised his reaction for what it was – he was feeling unsettled, jolted out of his safe little cocoon and was scrambling, desperately trying to grab hold of the parts of what felt like an unravelling reel to stop them. *Mate, you're miffed because you've been sidelined, left out.*

He could imagine having this conversation with a friend. But he didn't have any. Well, none he was that close with. Actually, you didn't need to be super close with someone to say, *'Hey, want to grab a beer and go and sit and have a chat?'* – no, just a quiet contemplative time in company. But all the people he knew would be very suspicious if he made such a request. And, anyway, Colin didn't like to impose. And wasn't spontaneous enough to anyway. And also, imagining the looks of pity at poor Colin not being able to cope with Joyce being gone for one day, was quite off-putting. Jesus. He really was quite pathetic, wasn't he? *We can do this, Colin. Okay, mate? It's going to be fun. If not fun, at least okay.*

While he still had the banking open, he thought about going into Joyce's account and transferring the money to cover what she'd taken to keep things tidy and in order.

But, just in time to stop himself, he realised that might be misconstrued, so shut it all down instead. No, they were not short of funds, but it did rankle that there was an anomaly in their well-established system. He idly thought about phoning or texting to ask her if there was a reason for her using that account. But now was not the time to bother her. He hoped she'd be safe. And that she had taken enough warm clothes. She'd travelled light. Should he offer to send anything else? Again, a quiver of envy rose in him at her being on an adventure.

Right. Dishes, tidy up, TV, bed, he told himself decidedly, and put both hands on the table to hoist himself up again.

'Thank you for dinner, dear,' he said, 'that was great.'

In the lounge with the TV on, Colin brought up the next episode of the series they were watching – *The Newsreader* on ABC. Dare he go on ahead without Joyce? He didn't know what else to watch. Joyce tended to choose their viewing since they liked many of the same shows. Oh well, he'd watch it again later with her, if it came to it – not the same, but still. He settled in with his phone on the coffee table in front of him where he could see the screen if it lit up with some activity.

Despite enjoying his show, unable to be ignored was the gaping absence beside him – Joyce's head on his lap with her own legs stretched out. He hugged one of the heavy feather cushions to him in an attempt to replicate the weight. Stirring inside was the nagging thought: *I really hope I've been adequately sympathetic to my clients when they've talked of being suddenly thrust into singledom through the loss of a partner due to death or separation.* He thought so. But he didn't really think he'd understood until now. And this was a tiny blip – mere hours.

Only four, in fact, he realised with a jolt. It was no different than if Joyce were tucked away down in the sewing room. Though the far-off sound of the gentle chug, chug of the sewing machine, the click up and snap down of the foot being lifted and dropped were a reassuring soundtrack. And the occasional curses when something went wrong. He smiled. A little sadly. He'd give up his left pinkie to hear Joyce's exclamation of, 'Oh, damn it!' While her ultimate creations showed her at her best, the activity really could bring out her worst.

Starting to yawn, Colin got up to get ready for bed, taking the phone with him.

Having cleaned his teeth, he slid into his side of the bed and lay on his back with his hands clasped behind his head, feeling a little uneasy. He needed to go to sleep to be ready for a full day tomorrow, but he also didn't want to miss a communication or update from Joyce.

Part of him didn't think she'd disturb him when he was meant to be asleep. But another part of him accepted that this was unknown territory. And, also, Joyce would understandably want to share all the excitement and quite possibly painful moments with him.

He typed out a text message: **Goodnight from me. I hope all is well there with you.** He deliberated over whether to say he missed her or not but then chose not to, unable to decide whether it would make him appear to be not coping, and thus pathetic, or add pressure to Joyce to come home – or perhaps even become annoyed with him. He added a love heart and pressed send.

Chapter Ten

Colin woke with a start and lay quietly in the dark listening to the sounds of the house, unsure what had awoken him. Something seemed off. His heart rate began to quicken. He held his breath in an effort to hear better. But the more he concentrated, the louder the whooshing in his ears seemed. He tried to detect which sounds were part of his imagination and those that were real, if any.

He rolled over, seeking comfort, a warm presence, and was jolted right back to reality at discovering Joyce's cold and empty side of the bed. Of course. She wasn't there. How could he have possibly forgotten? He'd just been dreaming about her – having a conversation on some subject or other. It had been so real.

Oh. The phone. He rolled back over to his side and began patting the top of the bedside cupboard in search of the device he was sure he'd left right there.

Thump.

Damn it. At least he knew it was now on the floor.

He turned the lamp on and blinked against its harshness. God, he loathed these new types of led energy-saving bulbs, even the warm white variety. And their electricity bill hadn't gone down as a result of their arrival on the scene, he thought cantankerously. He imagined having this conversation with Joyce, and being told he was a crotchety old git. And he'd agree. He was feeling decidedly put out. And where was the damned phone?

It had better be worth retrieving right now, he thought, carefully lowering himself out of bed and onto his hands and knees. *For Christ's sake.* He reached under the small cupboard towards the phone, stretching, stretching.

Bang.

'Ouch. Damn it.' He flopped onto his stomach and huffed from the exertion and his building annoyance. *What's the bloody time anyway?* He hadn't even checked the bedside clock radio, so intent was he on hearing from Joyce.

With phone finally in hand, he shuffled back and then sat upright against the bed. He'd stay put for a bit before trying the next phase in getting up. These things took time – stages – at his age.

His mind went to being out and about with people pushing past, him being jostled as if invisible, the accompanying mutterings of frustration at his daring to be out in public. Old age was not for the faint or weak of heart, or unsure of foot.

'You confounded thing,' he said to the phone which had a black screen. He pressed the button several times, and then shook it. It seemed to grunt at him and then go silent and blink again. *You're an idiot. You've forgotten to charge it, you old fool.* He thought he had over dinner, but perhaps he'd forgotten to switch the power point on. He did that more times than he cared to admit. Or maybe it had done an automatic update overnight and that had sucked it dry – it did that sometimes. *Oh well, doesn't matter. Let it go. The pertinent thing now is what if Joyce needs, or has needed, me?*

He scrambled onto his knees and then onto his feet with all the grace and speed of a drunk baby elephant, slipped his feet into his slippers and lumbered out into the kitchen where his charger was set up on the bench. At least it was alone, which meant Joyce hadn't forgotten hers, he thought, cursing silently as he struggled to connect the tiny end of the cable to the seemingly smaller hole on the bottom of his phone.

Colin leant forward over the bench watching the phone before reminding himself of their oft-used idiom: a watched kettle never boils.

Damn it, I'm wide awake now – may as well boil the kettle. At least its roar – insanely loud in the empty, night-engulfed house – wouldn't wake Joyce. As the water poured in, he almost let go of it as he let out a cry. It dropped into the sink with a loud bang that seemed to echo right around the room. *God, who's that out there?* His heart began to really race.

With a hand to his chest, and his face close to the cold glass, he peered out the window. Nothing. More movement caught his eye just as he shifted position. And then he realised. *It's your own bloody reflection, you old dill.* He hadn't pulled the blind down. How could he have forgotten to do that?

As he leant back and picked up the kettle, a slightly hysterical laugh bubbled up. He took several deep breaths in order to return to some sort of calm. Utterly ridiculous. *Get a grip.*

He made his tea and settled with his mug at the table to wait for the phone to charge.

After going over and trying to turn the phone on, he was finally met with success. He was perturbed to discover it was 4.14 am. But his heart soared at seeing the little icon advising of a new text message. He put in his code and then opened the app.

> Arrived safe and sound. Chaos here. Lots of dead birds. Lots to try and help. All very sad. Need to get to it. Might be off the air for a while. Limited coverage. No idea of accommodation yet. Will update you when I can. Lots of love, J

He tapped out a response, pausing, deleting, carefully choosing his words so he didn't add to her burden but also not neglecting to show his love. He settled on:

> Righto. Take care. All the best with it. Much love from me to you.
> Here if there is anything you need or I can do. Lots of love, C.

He then spent an inordinate amount of time searching for the right facial image. *What are those things called again, the little pictures?* he wondered as he searched. *Immys? No, that isn't right. Oh well.*

Even with his glasses on, he struggled to decipher their expressions. Finally, he chose one indicating blowing a kiss – the more formal looking of the two, well, he hoped. He didn't want to come across flippant or anything. He really struggled with those little pictures, so tended to avoid them. But these were unusual times that required him to step outside his comfort zone, he figured. Far too exasperated to look for any more appropriate ones, he pressed send.

He levered himself up, thought to ignore his empty mug and leave the table but didn't – couldn't let everything go to the dogs the moment Joyce turned her back – and then made his way back to bed.

Colin woke again, this time to the alarm, with gritty eyes and the heaviness of a very poor night's sleep.

He took on both his and Joyce's roles, turning on the radio and kitchen light and set about having breakfast and preparing for the day. *This I can do*, he thought, as he made cold meat, cheese and chutney sandwiches and then left the kitchen, having to return when he realised he needed to turn off the light again as Joyce wasn't there.

Chapter Eleven

Colin had been surprised to see Andrea on the day's list. He'd thought she'd get enough information and help from the online community and more experienced therapists on the matter via their books and blog posts and articles. Though he was very curious to know how she was faring. He was a little surprised at how much he was looking forward to seeing a familiar and friendly face today.

'Andrea, hello. Come in,' Colin said.

'Hi,' Andrea said, coming in like a fierce wind, throwing herself onto the couch, kicking her shoes off and putting her feet up over the arm and then turning towards Colin. 'Sorry, I'm all over the place.' She let out a loud huffing sigh. 'Okay, so …'

Colin watched as the young woman seemed to try to gather herself and her thoughts. She turned to study the image of a large tree on the other wall. He waited her out.

After a few more moments, she nodded decisively and then began to speak again. 'Firstly, thank you. Because oh. My. God! Everything makes so much sense now. *I* make so much sense.

And my choices – though it's more like being programmed than actual conscious decision-making on my part, isn't it?'

Colin nodded, he hoped encouragingly.

'Anyway. It's like my upbringing, my life, has been … growing up in a cult. But I haven't been. I thought I was part of a normal family and that my mother was just a control freak and a bully who didn't like me. But she ticks all the boxes on the online narcissism checklist, so it's worse than that. A whole lot worse. And after what I've read, I can see it's impacted everything about me. And leaving home and having a partner hasn't helped. That's actually made things worse because I've realised the guy I was with is one too. I've literally gone from the fat into the fire. Well, um, not *literally* literally, but … Well, you know.' She flapped a hand and then wiped some stray hairs from her face. 'I hate that I'm now considered a victim, a victim of childhood abuse, and most likely have complex post-traumatic stress disorder as a result. Fuck! Sorry for the swearing.'

'Don't be. It's a lot to deal with. How can I help?'

'I'm not sure you can, to be honest. From what I've read, I think it's like a thread I have to keep pulling and start unravelling everything. And then when it's all piled up on the floor, I'll have to start knitting – putting – myself back together, and then my life.'

'That's a good way of looking at it. Except, perhaps, it's not one whole piece – more like knitted bits, those granny squares, I think they're called, that you then put together to make a large project? It might be best to focus on one bit at a time. Otherwise, you run the risk of being overwhelmed.'

'Good point. It's going to be hard, isn't it?'

'Yes, I have no doubt. But not too hard.'

Andrea nodded. 'I've always wondered things about myself that don't seem to make sense. And now they do. Now I know I'm an extension of her – or that's how she sees me – which is why she's said so many times I can't be alone, I have to have a man. "You'll be lonely",' she mimicked. 'But, honestly, I love being on my own. It's her that hates it. I've actually just left my partner.'

'Oh. I see.' Colin pondered his own sudden enforced solitude at home. All told, he hadn't minded it and was doing his best to embrace it. Maybe in a few days he'd find himself loving it too. He couldn't see it, but stranger things had happened. Anyway, his situation wasn't the same as young Andrea's because it was temporary and he and Joyce were at a different stage in life.

'She'll be disappointed in me when she finds out, because he was "oh, such a good catch".' Andrea rolled her eyes. 'I'm living in a hovel of a flat, down the back of one of my friends' places – basically a shed, and probably technically not fit for habitation, legally, or whatever. But I feel like for the first time in my life I can breathe. Even the nasty voice – which I've realised sounds scarily similar to my mother's – telling me I'm useless and can't do this or that, is quietening.'

'That's great.'

'And guess what?'

'What?'

'I'm not lonely. Well, sometimes a bit, but I think that's due to the grief of the ending of my relationship, because while it wasn't good – downright abusive at times, I now realise – it did provide some certainty. And change is scary. So, that's well ...' She shrugged. 'A thing. But Mum's always told me I'm not capable of being alone. And you believe the person who knows you the best, or is at least meant to care about you the most, don't you? But I've come to realise – thanks to the online forum full of people with similar experiences – that the loneliest place to be is inside a toxic relationship. And for me that's been my family, my whole upbringing. And then with Todd, my partner. What an absolute clusterfuck.

'Thank goodness I had my grandmother and my dad before they died, because did you know …? Oh of course you do – you'd be right across all this. But that's the factor that has pretty much ensured I'm not a complete fuck-up, like an addict or whatever. It's so sad that there seems to be no middle ground on that.

'I've also realised how tired I am, how draining it's been trying to live up to expectations I'll never meet, being someone I'm not, in order to please those I never will and whose goal posts are constantly changing.'

She scrunched up her face and then put her hands over her eyes.

When it didn't appear that Andrea was going to continue, Colin spoke.

'Maybe you're relieved to know, comforted to finally understand and confused as to how to move forward and figure out where to go to from here?'

'Yes. All of that,' she said, turning towards Colin. 'I'm also glad I found you. Thank you. I literally owe you my life.'

She fixed her eyes on him and when she turned her lips in on themselves, Colin could see clearly what she meant – the point to which she'd got and dragged herself back from. He could see there were tears in her eyes. He felt his own throat tighten a little in response. He nodded.

'I was … I was … so close,' she said, and gulped.

'I'm glad to have helped. But this is all you. You're doing the work. I just shone the torch in the right direction for you to make your own way. And you don't owe me anything. Well ...' He smiled. 'There is my fee, which isn't insignificant.'

'And worth every cent. Oh, one other thing ...?'

'Yes?'

'I'm thinking of going no contact. Cutting ties. With my mother. Completely. Because I've been trying for so long to manage our relationship and protect myself as best I can, but nothing has worked. And nothing's going to change, is it? Like, it's true that these people will never seek help because they don't see anything wrong with how they are. Right? I mean, that's what everything I've read so far says.'

'That's my understanding and clinical experience, yes. I think some do agree to counselling in order to be seen to be fitting into society – in order to keep playing a role. They're often great mimics of the right behaviours, societal norms et cetera. It's well documented that while they don't experience empathy or love, like people without a borderline personality disorder do, and aren't capable of feeling it, they watch and learn and often display these behaviours. It's how they manage to achieve the detriment they do, and why so many who know them outside of their targets see someone different, someone diametrically opposite the lived experience of their victims.'

'Hmm. I read about flying monkeys and triangulation. Scary stuff! So, it's true, isn't it, that if I go no contact, I pretty much have to cut ties with everyone we have in common, or at least be very careful about what I say, and to whom?'

'I'm afraid that's often the situation. Each experience is unique. And I've not been through it myself.'

'There are so many bits to think about. And every bit is bloody exhausting!'

'I can imagine.'

'I feel really ripped off,' Andrea said sadly, causing Colin to ache inside. 'I've spent three decades wanting and needing and trying to get love from a mother who was never going to give it to me, isn't actually capable of it. It's fucking fucked up.'

'Yes, it is.'

'Why did she even have kids? Don't worry, I'm not expecting you to answer that. Anyway, I'm determined to finally, one day, feel good enough. That's my life goal.'

'Sounds like a good plan to me.' Colin's heart went out to her because he knew that it might just take the rest of her life to achieve, if she ever did at all.

'Now I know, and can see it all so clearly, I do feel like a bit of an idiot for not realising sooner.'

'Please, don't. They're very clever operators. Instead, perhaps try to find a way to be grateful for learning about it before it's too late to change yourself and your future. Thirty-two isn't old. It may feel like it, but trust me, it's not. I know of people my age who are only just starting out on the same journey you are.'

'That's sad.'

'It is. Just remember: knowledge is power, and power is healing.'

'That's so true. Thank goodness the disorder is being talked about so much now.'

'Yes. But I do fear it's potentially going too far the other way.'

'What do you mean?'

'Well, people are now casually throwing the words narcissism, narcissist and related terms around, often incorrectly, which dilutes their importance and potential danger.'

'Yes. That's true. Every second person is now a narcissist and people are being gaslit or gaslighting someone all over the place.'

'Exactly.'

'Humans: so complicated!'

'Oh yes, they are,' Colin said.

'I don't know how you deal with it all every day.'

'Sometimes I wonder the same thing,' he said with a smile. *Thankfully I have a wonderful wife to go home to. Usually.*

'I feel for her husband – not my father, obviously. He's a sweet guy. I'd love to enlighten him, but I think he's still too deep in the cult that is my mother for that,' she said. 'Maybe one day I can liberate him too, but for now I need to deal with my own stuff. Starting with liberally using the word no!'

'Good on you. And remember, because it's going to take some practice to stick to your resolve, "no" does not always require a follow-up explanation. "No" can be a full sentence if need be. But, as I said, it takes some tenacity. You'll be used to feeling the need to explain yourself and justifying your words, I imagine. So, start with taking little steps by adding a small explanation – less than you normally would, and resort to white lies if necessary. I know it's not ideal, but you are the most important one in this – your welfare is utmost, so take the attitude of "whatever it takes". White lies in some circumstances, if they are used for good, are perfectly fine.'

'Okay. Good to know. Thank you. You know, you're very wise.'

'I appreciate you saying.'

You'll be all right, he thought, *because you've managed to remain kind and with a sense of humour.* Well, he really hoped she'd be okay. At least she was on the right track of understanding it all and ultimately healing from the trauma. That was the main thing. But it was a genie you couldn't put back in the bottle.

Andrea must have caught him glancing at the clock, because she said, 'My time is up, isn't it?'

'I'm afraid so.'

'Don't be. I've really appreciated hashing all this out with you.'

'It's been my pleasure, Andrea. Take it slowly. Remember, bite-sized pieces. It's time for you to be good to Andrea and put her first.'

Chapter Twelve

Colin had just returned from having ducked out quickly between clients to use the toilet and upon checking his phone, realised he'd missed a call from Joyce. *Damn*, he cursed as he unlocked it and rang to check his voicemail.

'Just thought I'd try you as opportunities are slim and far between. All is as well as can be expected here. Not sure we're making much difference, but it feels good to at least be trying. Hope all is well there with you. Lots of love.'

He immediately rang back, prepared to go against his rule of not keeping clients waiting. He'd be quick, just say hello and hear Joyce's voice.

Well, I guess I heard her voice, he mused as her recorded voicemail message cut in.

'Just me returning your call,' he said. 'Hopefully we won't play phone tag for too long. Lots of love from me back to you. Oh, and I'm sure everyone appreciates what you're doing. Hang in there,' he added at the last moment before ending his call.

Everyone appreciates it except me, that is, he thought, as he sat contemplating his message. *I wish you were here. Needy much?*

Out of frustration with Joyce being away and uncontactable, and him having to fend for himself, and determined to not dwell on negatives and get on with making the best of things, Colin took a detour via the corner shop for a takeaway meal on his walk home. At the kerb, he turned left instead of right and headed towards the old-fashioned deli that he was sure must have some sort of offering of the convenient variety.

'Hello there,' he said, standing looking at the young lass behind the counter. He studied the enormous board above her head that had three columns of offerings. Being as it was Wednesday, he should have pork, but a glimmer of defiance saw him keen to buck the trend. But with what?

He was grateful the young woman busied herself – or at least pretended to – with something behind the counter and didn't just stand there staring at him or drumming her fingers impatiently.

'Um. What do you recommend for someone who never has takeaway?' he said.

'Our hamburger with the lot and regular chips is pretty popular. We actually won a local award,' she added, pointing to a small glass sculpture up on a shelf to her right.

'Oh, well, now that sounds good,' Colin said, beaming. 'Congratulations.'

'Thank you,' the kid said, flashing him a friendly, genuine-looking smile.

'I'll have one of those, thank you. Would you like me to pay now or when you're finished?' he asked, looking around to see if she was manning the place on her own or not. 'I'm out of practice.'

'No worries. When I'm done works. That way you can decide if you want a drink or anything else. Maybe something for dessert?'

'Oh, good idea.' They turned away from each other – the girl towards the fryer and grill and Colin to take in the rest of the store. *Dessert,* he mused. *Now there's a thought. Some chocolate for in front of the telly? An ice-cream?* Though he'd have to eat that first before it melted. *Go on, be a rebel, old man. Maybe another day.* Neither he nor Joyce really had much of a sweet tooth.

Colin wandered on. Ooh, but a ginger beer would hit the spot. He opened the fridge door and reached in.

After a full lap, taken slowly to kill time so he wouldn't have to loiter at the counter, and also to take in the inventory for future reference, he arrived back just as a wrapped round mound and cup of chips disappeared into a paper bag.

'There we go – cash or card?' the young woman said, placing the bag beside his elbow.

'Oh, you still take cash, do you?'

'Yes. Doesn't happen very often these days, but it's up to you.'

'Just curious. I'm happy to tap. Covid forced me onto that dark side of things,' he said, smiling and holding up his card. The girl nodded.

'Wasn't that all a weird time?' she said absently while pushing buttons on a chunky black EFTPOS machine.

'Oh yes. It certainly was.' He held his card against the device until it beeped and then tucked it back into his wallet.

'Well, enjoy your meal,' she said, holding up the paper handles of the bag for him.

'Thank you. I'm sure I will. Have a lovely evening,' he added, returning her beaming smile and touching the brim of his hat with two fingers.

His mood was so much more buoyant than it had been when he'd entered the shop, he found himself humming as he walked. But with each stride, the scent of fried food beckoned and eventually became too much to resist. He opened the bag and dug out a chip, idly wondering as he bit into it – magnificently crunchy outer, soft pillowy inside – how long Joyce would be away. *Goodness, what a fine chip.*

'That'll be the lard,' he could hear Joyce saying, with slight disapproval. They occasionally ate oven fries, which while also crinkly, didn't have the same indulgent taste. These reminded him of the hot chips eaten at showgrounds and markets and the footy back in the days when one didn't feel the need to watch one's waistline or cholesterol quite so closely.

Again, having decided eating in the lounge room wasn't worth the risk, Colin instead sat on Joyce's side of the table for a change.

He put his meal on a plate to catch the drips, and then tucked into his burger, which required two hands to hold, as he thought about how his different food and also change of seat felt a little refreshing. Apparently, a change was as good as a holiday, he mused. Maybe it was. But still he longed to have Joyce there to share the experience with and debrief about his day.

Chapter Thirteen

Two more nights had passed before Colin and Joyce finally managed to speak. He'd been a little concerned, but had seen her in her bright purple swimming top with long sleeves and almost fluorescent sunhat on news footage, though of course the footage could have been a few days old. Still, as he watched during the evenings, the mass of filthy birds had decreased. But so had the number of volunteers.

'Hello. Finally!' he said when Joyce's name appeared on his lit-up screen.

'Hello,' she said. 'Yes, it's been a … time.'

'You sound tired.'

'I am. Exhausted.'

'Well, well done. I've been following along on the news. It looks like you saved a lot of them.'

'But a lot of them died, dear. It's so sad.'

'Oh. But …'

'Don't believe all you see on the media, remember?'

'Yes. I know.'

'If you're not seeing the true extent of things over here then it's because the corporates have too big a finger in the pie or on the board or something. Damn it.'

'Well, you did your best. And you went all that way. That's an admirable effort, in my opinion, dear.'

'Thank you. How are things there?'

Colin's heart sank at hearing the defeat in her voice. He really hoped she was down due to exhaustion and would bounce back soon.

'Oh, much the same.'

'Have you been eating properly?'

'Um. Well, that depends on what you mean by properly,' he said, grinning in an effort to make light of things.

'Oh, Colin, whatever do you mean?'

'I've been patronising a few of the local takeaway establishments. I can vouch for the Indian and the Chinese places. And that deli around the corner from work does a mean burger and chips.' He was possibly becoming a little too fond of eating takeaway. And the cost was prohibitive in the longer term.

'Mean as in good, or mean for your arteries? Oh, whatever, I don't have the energy to quibble.'

'Don't worry, there's been plenty of fruit and veg involved. So, all good. Don't you worry about me. More to the point, how have *you* fared in the food department? You're the one out in the wilderness.'

'Well, that's true. But thankfully, one of the other volunteers managed to get a food truck involved, which provided a great range. Their vegetarian curry was particularly good. And then another one turned up – most likely for the publicity – serving coffee. I don't care why they were there; I might have died without my coffee fix the second morning! God, I am not sure I even know what day it is.'

'Friday evening,' Colin said. 'Where have you been sleeping? You *have* been sleeping, haven't you, not washing birds this whole time?'

'Oh, don't be ridiculous, Colin. Didn't you see the photos of the tent city up in the dunes?'

Colin found himself sighing with satisfaction, relief and slight bewilderment at hearing his dear beloved Joyce being herself from so far away. Oh, how he missed her and yearned for her return – cranky disposition notwithstanding, he thought, regretting his recent uncharitable ponderings about her cantankerousness.

'No. That didn't make the news. Or I didn't see it.'

'Aren't you following the Facebook page?'

'What Facebook page?'

'I sent you a link or invite or whatever it's called. Didn't I? I'm sure I did.'

'I must have missed that too.' But Colin didn't think so – he'd been watching the phone like a hawk.

'Don't worry about it, that particular crisis is over. Or, at least, we've done all we can for now.'

'So, what's next? When are you coming home?'

'Um. Well … I'm going to hang around for a bit. A few of us are going to stay at the holiday house of one of the others, in case more birds wash up.'

'Oh. Okay. Any idea how long for?'

'No, not at this stage. I can't get past the thought of a decent hot shower at this point. I pong something wicked, I'm sure.'

'I see.'

'There's nothing I need to get back for, is there? I mean, you're fine, aren't you?'

Colin's previous buoyancy ebbed away.

'Oh, I'll survive. You do what you need to do. And you're right, you're retired. At least you're getting some time away while you wait for me to get my act together.'

'Yes. Well, I'd better go. I can see everyone heading to the minibus taking us. I'll be in touch again soon. But be warned, it might be a while – we've been told mobile coverage is sketchy. Hit and miss, apparently. So don't worry.'

'Right. Noted.'

'Okay, then, you take good care.'

'You, too. Bye for now. Love you,' Colin added at the same time the call ended.

He now felt decidedly heavy and sad. And telling himself not to be so silly and needy did nothing to buck him up. A moment later a text came through, causing Colin to feel his low mood lift:

Love you.

He replied with a love heart. *Emoji! That's what they're called!* He experienced a welcome jolt of triumph.

Colin had just settled in to watch *MasterChef* when another text notification chimed. He turned the phone over, hope gripping him. And then he frowned at reading it was from Aileen Rodgers, inviting him for dinner the following evening – **just casual, no need to bring anything, just yourself.** When had Aileen ever texted him? And it was very short notice. Had Joyce coopted Aileen and John Rodgers to issue a pity-meal invite? Oh well, he'd take a free meal any day! But was it because Joyce was planning to stay away for quite some time yet, or because he'd sounded down on the phone earlier? Something had bugged him about Joyce's demeanour, but he couldn't put his finger on it. He told himself over and over that it could just be her voice sounding different across the miles and her no doubt exhausted, defeated state. But still, in the last few hours he hadn't been able to shake the feeling something was off.

Should he go over there? Maybe they could do with a counsellor on hand. But he couldn't just turn up like he was checking up on Joyce. How would that look?

And anyway, I don't even know where the hell she is, now they're not going to be where the birds were. Had she said where the holiday house was that she was going to stay in? No, he was sure she hadn't. *Let it go. She's a grown woman. She's probably having a ball without you.*

That thought did nothing to cheer Colin up. But it did go some way to shifting his thoughts back to the TV in front of him. It wasn't like the old days where you had to rely on public phone boxes. Joyce had a phone and a tablet and was with a heap of other people – how many, he had no idea – with all manner of communication devices. She'd be able to get a message to him one way or the other. Or get help from the local authorities if necessary. She hadn't sounded worried, just wrung out and needing a rest. And in need of a nice hot shower. She'd most likely be a different person next phone call.

Maybe he'd get onto the search for a four-wheel drive – that'd perk her up. Meanwhile, he'd thank Aileen for the offer of dinner. He was in! It was one less meal for him to find. He tapped out a short message and pressed send.

Chapter Fourteen

Colin had forgotten to bring the laptop from the office, so his vehicle research was hampered by the small phone screen, which he gave up on. He'd meant to get groceries but still hadn't managed to conjure up the necessary energy – though had checked the pantry and fridge and was satisfied there were plenty of eggs, baked beans, bread, milk, cheese and other staples. Instead of tackling the hedge, he'd dug around the roses and added fertiliser and pulled some weeds. He was a little weary as a result and would have preferred staying home. But, nonetheless, was grateful he didn't have to source his evening meal.

'Greetings. Welcome. Come on in,' Aileen Rodgers said, kissing Colin on the cheek, accepting the bottle of wine with thanks, and ushering him in before closing the front door behind him. Colin made his way through to the enormous open space where a small group was either seated on tall stools or standing around a large marble island bench picking at platters of dips and assorted culinary items and sipping from glasses.

'Here he is,' John Rodgers said, coming over to shake his hand. 'Beer?' he said, thrusting a bottle into Colin's hand.

'Er, yes. Thanks, and for having me,' Colin said.

'It's a pleasure. Now, I think you know everyone here?' Colin looked at all the faces – some were familiar-ish but others were not. He'd probably met each of them at some point along the way. 'You can introduce yourselves and save me the trouble.' He was glad when they all raised their glasses and called hi in various forms as a collective greeting and he was spared from further awkwardness. 'So, how's bachelorhood?' John said, jovially, clasping Colin's shoulder and ushering him closer to the others.

'Huh?'

'Joyce is away, isn't she? So, you're baching, living alone for a bit?'

'Oh. Yes. That's right. It's only for a few days. Week or so,' he revised, realising it was not far off being a week already. 'She's gone off to wash those oil-covered birds near Perth,' he added, sensing awkwardness looming and feeling uncomfortable under the scrutiny.

'Oh. Right.' Something in John's tone caught Colin's attention. *What does he know that I don't?* But the conversation moved on so swiftly he didn't have a chance to seek clarification or dwell on his thought.

'Wow. That's dedication for you,' a woman in a red skirt said.

'Yes, very noble,' said a man in a navy-striped shirt.

'How wonderful,' a woman all in black said. 'You're not into that sort of thing?'

'Oh no, Colin's still working,' Aileen chimed in.

'Ah, right.'

Colin was disappointed to find himself becoming a little crotchety. Overly sensitive most likely, but the word *working* seemed to have been uttered as if with a hint of distaste.

'Good for you,' someone else said. *Are they being patronising?* 'What do you do again?'

'Psychologist. Private practice,' Aileen cut in, further annoying Colin. Why wasn't he allowed to answer for himself? 'Hanging on by his fingertips, aren't you, Colin?' Colin fully expected her next words to be 'you naughty boy', such was her tone. *For goodness' sake!*

'I don't know how you do it,' John said. 'I couldn't listen to all those problems, all that *whining*. It's bad enough with an office full of staff and their endless inane dramas and gossip. Thankfully none of that to deal with now. Oh, the joys of retirement!' There was a collective muttering of agreement. Colin smiled politely and nodded.

'Mental health and self-care, and the like. It's all the rage now, isn't it?' another woman said, looking up at Colin. He became a little mesmerised by her enormous brown eyes that blinked often but slowly.

Um. Well. Where to start? What to say? Was he even expected to answer? Thankfully the woman's husband, or partner – certainly the man standing very close to her – spoke.

'Exactly,' he said. 'Every second person is depressed or suffering anxiety – or both these days. We all just got on with it, didn't we? It just wasn't in the vocabulary.'

'Exactly. These days, everyone seems so intent on being *happy*,' a woman with brunette shoulder-length hair said. 'But you can't be, can you? Not all the time.'

'No, that's right,' Colin said, feeling the need to say something in the growing silence. All eyes seemed to be boring into him. Oh, how he wished Joyce was there by his side. She always knew exactly what to say, and when and how he needed rescuing in these sorts of situations.

'So, what's that about, anyway?' brunette woman's partner, a man with a beard, said.

'What's that?' Colin said.

'Everyone going on about mental health and self-care,' bearded man said.

'Ah, which bit, exactly?'

'Well, you know. Everyone being *into* it. All the talk, all the therapy. I mean, I don't want to offend you personally ...'

'Not at all,' Colin said, plastering a pleasant expression on his face. He wanted to add, 'you pompous git'.

'Xavier, stop interrogating the poor man,' Aileen said, and laughed. She came over and linked her arm through Colin's bent elbow. 'Burying one's feelings is not the way to go these days, right, Colin?'

'Er, no. And, actually, a lot of people in all sorts of situations and points in their lives benefit from talking to someone impartial to nut stuff out,' Colin said, taking strength from Aileen standing beside him.

'You don't need to go the hard sell, mate. But, really,' Xavier persisted. 'It's not much different to sitting in the pub with a group of mates chewing the fat, is it?'

'Well, that depends, I guess.' Colin couldn't tell if the guy's tone was defensive or indicative of genuine curiosity. 'I will say it all depends on the depth of discussion and what the person in need, er, needs. And how equipped the friends are to adequately give the right support.'

'How to say something without saying anything. Come on, man, this is why I'd never go to a psychologist,' he scoffed. 'No offence, Colin old mate, but there it is.' He pointed to Colin. 'They don't help you, don't actually tell you. They use airy-fairy roundabout discussion where you basically arrive at the decision all on your own. Session after session.' He indicated spending money by raising a hand and rubbing his thumb and forefinger together.

'I'd better check on dinner,' Aileen said quietly, patting Colin's arm and slipping away from him.

'It's not for everyone. As I said, it depends what the person needs or wants to achieve,' Colin said.

'Well, the suicide rate is the highest it's ever been. So …' Xavier shrugged. 'Just saying. Just another industry preying on the vulnerable.'

'Come on, stop it, Xavier,' his partner, the brunette woman, said.

'Maybe that's because it's publicised more now,' the woman with the big brown eyes said. 'It never used to be talked about – was too taboo – even in quiet circles, full stop. Let alone in the media.'

'And I happen to think that was a good thing. You don't want to be giving people ideas. I mean, if it wasn't so in your face, as it is now, would that be something so many would decide as a course of action?'

Colin rubbed his face and longed for the ground beneath him to open up and for him to disappear. Or someone else – anything to distract the group away from him and change the track of the conversation.

'I'm in the business of empowering people so they don't get to that point,' Colin persisted. 'Sometimes all they need is a sympathetic ear, some empathy for what they're dealing with. If you've never been so down on your luck as to need that succour then that's great, but many in our society are suffering. And, personally, I think they're braver for seeking help than the alternative, the ramifications of which reverberate through the whole community. If you're so self-absorbed and arrogant that you can't see past your own privileged circumstances and needs then I pity you, because you clearly lack empathy.'

'Ooh la la, now that's me told. Good for you, sir. You could be right. I've been called an arsehole many times. Doesn't bother me. It's got me to where I am. And as you correctly point out, I have it good,' Xavier said.

Colin cleared his throat and looked a little sheepishly at his hostess, hovering nearby, who was staring at him with her mouth slightly open.

'Wow. It's good to see you finally arc up. Always so meek and mild, is our Colin,' John said, smirking, and draping an arm around Colin.

He resisted shaking John off. Instead, he raised his bottle, plastered a pleasant smile on his face and called out, 'Cheers, thanks for having me.'

They all muttered salutations in response and raised their drinks.

'Colin used to be a builder, you know,' Aileen said. *Now you think of a change of subject*, Colin thought sardonically.

'Oh, now there's a worthy career,' a guy in a bright orange floral shirt cried. *Uh-oh, maybe I thought it too soon*, Colin silently revised. *Oh god, here we go again.* It was clearly pick on Colin Palmer night tonight. He was beginning to think he might know how the fake rabbit being chased around the track by the greyhounds felt.

'I beg your pardon?' Colin said, trying not to give in to the sigh trying desperately to escape.

'You know. Oh, I mean *honest*. As in, you can directly see the fruits of your labour.'

'God, horrible time to be in the housing game, though,' navy-striped shirt said. 'Look at all the outfits that have gone belly-up in the last couple of years. I'm glad I retired when I did. The brush with cancer saved me. Now, you don't very often hear of someone being grateful for that sort of diagnosis, but here we are. Cheers to beating the bastard!'

Colin tried not to visibly frown as he wondered how these old, and he'd thought dear, friends of his and Joyce's – well, more Joyce's – were friends with such horrible people. Though he shouldn't judge. For all he knew, this guy was ordinarily very amiable. What Colin was sure of was his presence – either looks, demeanour, or both – seemed to be triggering something in this guy. God, he wanted so badly to go home. But he couldn't bear the thought of watching *Midsomer Murders* without Joyce beside him. They'd never missed an episode.

'Come on, you lot. Dinner's nearly ready. Take a seat in the dining room. Wherever you like – there's no set seating.'

'So, do you have grandchildren?' brunette woman asked quietly beside Colin as he made his way with the group to the dining table.

'No. You?'

'That's a shame. Oh yes, they're the lights of my life! Well, our lives, actually – me and Xavier.'

Colin looked to where she was indicating her husband, his gaze falling on the obnoxious fellow he'd silently renamed The A-hole. It took much of his resolve to not let the words on his mind slip out: *'Oh, he's with you. You poor woman. If you need therapy, here's my card.'* Colin was surprised at the cheekiness rising up in him, causing his fingers to itch to drag his wallet out of his pocket and actually offer a business card. He really hoped the guy was just playing up to the crowd. *Oh well, not my monkeys, not my circus*, he thought, pulling out a chair and sitting down.

The brunette woman beside him leant in close and whispered, 'For the record, I don't share Xavier's views on … well, most things, really. If we're being honest.'

'I see,' was all Colin could say. His brain was trapped on the question *well why are you with him then?*

'So, did you not have kids, then? Or what?' the woman said.

Colin was just about to explain about the twins, but Aileen cut in as she delivered a plate of roast chicken and vegetables in front of him. 'So, Joyce tells me you've ordered, or are ordering, your van? I can't quite recall what she said now. Anyway, you're progressing?'

'Um. Yes.' Colin hesitated. He wasn't quite ready to let go of his earlier interaction. He hated that the twins' absence was ignored or so quickly dispensed with. He got it. Aileen wanted to avoid any awkwardness. And he wouldn't intentionally introduce any. But sweeping away such an important part of his and Joyce's lives and pretending James and Thomas hadn't existed wasn't fair either.

He opened his mouth to speak, but accepting the moment was too far gone, he instead attacked his meal, which was delightful and almost worth having to sit and endure this insufferable company, he thought.

'Which caravan did you decide on?' his red-skirted neighbour said as she took a mouthful of food.

Colin swallowed and opened his mouth to answer, but didn't get a chance.

'Be careful. A couple of the companies are a bit roguish,' John said, appearing beside him holding a bottle of wine in each hand. 'Two or three up in Queensland have gone belly-up.'

'Oh, yes,' Xavier The A-hole's voice boomed from the other side and end of the table. 'That was …' Colin missed the names in the hubbub of John going around the table asking people whether they wanted red or white wine and filling or re-filling their glasses accordingly, but was unperturbed. Joyce would do the necessary due diligence.

Talk about which four-wheel drive vehicles everyone owned saw them through the remainder of the main meal, with Colin somehow managing to avoid being included in the conversation, much to his relief.

'Can I help clear?' Colin said, noticing Aileen was up and gathering the empty plates.

'Thanks, Colin, but stay put.'

'Okay. Next question for the table,' he said. 'May as well pick your brains since you're all so knowledgeable on the grey nomad subject. Best first trip to go on? Places to avoid?'

This sparked exuberant discourse and gentle debating, which Colin was pleased carried on even through the delivery and consumption of dessert – a scrumptious slice of cheesecake with some sort of berry sauce. Even the clatter of the collection of the next lot of plates and then the appearance of hot beverage paraphernalia on trays did nothing to quell the chatter, which, much to his relief and delight, Colin had managed to avoid being embroiled in. He got away with simply nodding along and appearing enraptured.

Once coffee and teas were consumed – eschewed by Colin – he began looking for an opportunity to excuse himself and head home without appearing to do so too early and thus be considered rude or unappreciative.

'Well, that was lovely,' he said, twice, over a reasonably long interval and slapped his hands on his thighs in the hope he might remind others of the advancing hour and wouldn't have to be the first to depart. But, alas, no. The others around the table barely registered his comment, so consumed were they in their chatter, the thread of which Colin had lost in his focus on how and when to make his move.

And then someone yawned. And someone else saw, and the action made its way seamlessly around the table. Colin almost cheered.

'Oh goodness. Is that the time? I've had such a lovely evening. I didn't realise how late it had got,' Colin said, struggling to rein in his enthusiasm to leave. Joyce always took the lead on these things, too – signalled when it was the right time to leave, in terms of politeness and their own desire. He was way out of practice with all this.

Suddenly a stack of takeaway containers appeared in front of him.

'Oh, wow,' he said, looking up at Aileen and then around the rest of the table, frowning slightly.

'Since you're baching. Lots of leftovers.'

'That's unnecessary, but very good of you. And much appreciated. Thank you.' Oh goodie, he thought, sizing up the amount. He might even get several meals out of it.

He said goodbye to everyone and they spilled out onto the concrete driveway in a haphazard mob, a little too loud in the suburbs, Colin thought, though unlikely to be considered so at ten pm on a Saturday evening. No doubt Aileen and John's neighbours were younger, though probably with kids trying to sleep. There weren't many of their age group still in their original homes.

He gave a final wave and held up the plastic containers as he got into his car at the kerb, a sudden feeling of loneliness sweeping through him. He was a little shocked at its ferocity.

Chapter Fifteen

Sunday felt strangely oppressive to Colin with the number of hours he had to pass alone. He tried to stay in bed but found he couldn't ignore his usual breakfast time, so got up and went down to the kitchen to get on with things and wait until an appropriate hour to head out and mow the lawn. With Western Australia being two and a half hours behind South Australia, it was far too early to try and call Joyce.

He'd done the lawn and just come in and finished washing his hands when his phone vibrated and chimed to life on the bench. His heart soared at seeing it was Joyce calling. *There you are!*

'Darling, hello!' he said. 'How's things?'

'Hello there. Good. I feel like a new woman after a decent night's sleep and soak. They have the most wonderful spa here. We all ended up with skin like prunes.'

'Good for you.' Colin thought Joyce still sounded tired. He hoped it was just because she was relaxed.

'So, what have you been up to? How was dinner last night at Aileen and John's?'

'Oh, so you know about that? Well, bang goes most of my news.'

'I haven't spoken to Aileen this morning, if that's what you mean. She called during the week to satisfy her curiosity as she was sure she'd seen me on the news.'

'Ahh, so it *was* a pity invite?'

'Oh, don't be so petulant, Colin. Be grateful you got invited and given a lovely meal.' *Wow, Joyce, ouch! You must be really tired.* Colin wanted to say the words but didn't want to ruin their conversation, or risk ending it early now they'd finally managed to connect.

'It was quite nice. The food was, anyway, and she sent me home with an armful of leftovers, so that was especially good.'

'Of course she did. That's very Aileen. So, tell me who all was there.'

Colin rattled off the names of those he could remember and the descriptions of those he couldn't. Joyce seemed to know them all except Xavier – aka The A-hole.

'God, he sounds like an insufferable fellow, that one,' she said after Colin had told her of the conversation he'd endured. 'I wish I'd been there to give him what for. Sounds like no one's ever put him in his place – would be about time.'

'Yes. You were needed. I rather let the side down, I think.'

'Well, confrontation was never your strong suit, dear, that's what you need me for.' *Oh, you've no idea.* There was his treasured Joyce. He sighed to himself with relief at feeling connected with her again, despite the miles between them.

'I miss you,' he said.

'Oh. I would have thought you'd be enjoying the peace and quiet. No clickety click of the sewing machine, no cursing the news and all the crap on Facebook I go on about …'

What is she talking about? When have I ever, even in jest, commented about any of her mannerisms or hobbies in the negative? 'Anyone would think you weren't missing me,' he said.

'Well, it's a little hard when I've been so busy. And now occupied here, in a different way. It's wonderful.'

'Right.'

'Oh, I didn't mean to …'

'It's okay. I'm just feeling sorry for myself. Being ridiculous.'

'You'll be right tomorrow when you go back to work and your routine. I imagine today's a bit of a wrench, being the weekend. What have you got planned? You have to do *something*, not just wallow, if you're feeling fragile, don't forget, dear?'

'*Yes, I'm the therapist, remember,*' he wanted to say, but kept the words to himself. Fat lot all his training was doing him now. He did need reminding. 'Yes, I've just done the lawns. Oh. And yesterday I spent some time online looking at vehicles – four-wheel drives. Haven't been out to test drive any … And luckily I went last night because really everyone there only seemed to rate Toyota, Mitsubishi and Nissan. So, there you go. Narrows things down a bit.'

'Right.' He expected her to be pleased, or at least show some gratitude in him having done what he had in that regard. Instead, he was experiencing silence from the other end of the phone.

'So, that's one step closer,' he added. 'Are you still there?'

'Yes. Hang on a sec. I'm just …' she said a couple of moments later. She seemed to Colin to be flustered.

'What's going on there?'

'Oh. Nothing. Just someone taking orders for coffee. I won't chat for too long. Our host is taking us for a drive to show us around in a bit.'

'You sound like you're having fun,' he said, and instantly regretted his mournful tone.

'Colin, it's not my fault if you're not making the most of your time. I'm not responsible for moderating your mood. And, yes, I am having fun, as it happens. It's been good to get away and meet some interesting people and do something for someone else for a change.'

'I see.' He frowned. What was she saying exactly? Her tone was decidedly tetchy. 'Well, you are missed very much by me.'

'You were saying, the vehicles?'

'Yes. I think the Nissan is the best bet. It's a little cheaper of the three. But I might look into it a bit more in case there's something better suited, as it's on backorder.'

'Okay. Great. That sounds like a plan. Good for you.' Colin could detect her waning interest, but before he could end the call, she did.

'I've got to go now – the others are waiting.'

He sat with the phone on the table, staring at the now-black screen, trying not to feel put out but failing miserably to perk himself up.

'Right, old fellow, let's go and pull some weeds,' he said aloud, again wishing he had a dog to talk to instead of the empty house. For a moment he paused. Dare he get a dog while Joyce was away? She'd told him to do something to occupy himself. That would do it. He was shocked at his almost spiteful and decidedly childish thought. Gosh. He hoped they were okay and could weather this new course.

Yes, he thought as he went out, *we'll be all right when we get back together.* This was what trying to have a relationship over distance was like – fraught with opportunities for misunderstandings when one couldn't observe the micro expressions and body language, and the other couldn't reassure when misunderstandings occurred or moods strayed.

One thing Joyce was right about was his need to feel a sense of purpose. Mowing the lawn hadn't really done that, or not well enough. He should be thinking about planning some meals for the week and actually get organised, rather than cobbling together whatever he could find in the fridge. As enjoyable as the takeaways had been, he couldn't keep on doing that. It was too expensive, for a start. But he couldn't find any impetus to go grocery shopping, either.

She'd only taken a small bag with her, so she wouldn't be gone for long, he reminded himself, and brightened. In fact, he was surprised she hadn't bemoaned travelling so light and asked him to send more things on to her. Not that he had the faintest idea of how to go about that, given he still didn't know exactly where she was. Though presumably in that case she'd furnish him with details.

Chapter Sixteen

Joyce had been gone almost two whole weeks, which felt like an eternity to Colin. He was surprised to find her on the doorstep when answering the door and momentarily stood there stunned and wondering why she hadn't used her key, or even let him know of her impending arrival.

Last he'd heard she was off having a fun time relaxing at the new friend's place and they'd had to rely on text messaging due to patchy reception. Several times Colin had teetered between being happy for Joyce to be enjoying her time and being a little miffed he seemed to have been all but forgotten as the texts had become shorter in duration and came in less and less often. He'd tried to tell himself it was natural that she'd be distracted and not missing him as much as he was her, but had remained a bit put out. But that all evaporated when he'd recovered from his surprise of seeing her standing there.

'Finally! You're home! Why didn't you tell me – I could have come and picked you up from the airport. And don't tell me you've lost your keys,' Colin said, dragging Joyce into a tight hug, which seemed to become slightly awkward. Since when had hugging his beloved Joyce been like this? Surely, they weren't that out of touch with each other after such a short amount of time?

Movement out on the street caught his eye. An SUV-style vehicle was parked at the kerb. It was idling – he could hear the engine purring. He released Joyce and stepped back. 'Do I need to pay the driver or something?' he said, nodding towards their driveway.

'Um. No.' Joyce turned. 'That's Carmel. She'll be ...'

'Oh, a fellow comrade. I'd love to meet her. Invite her in.'

'She, er, has somewhere she needs to be. Maybe later.'

'Okay.' Colin waved to the driver.

'What are you doing?'

'Waving. Being friendly. A friend of yours is a friend of mine. What's wrong?'

'Oh, Colin, honestly.'

'What?' Colin was genuinely mystified. What was up with Joyce? Did she not want to be home? *No, just a bit of awkwardness due to us resuming our lives after an interruption. Bound to be some getting back up to speed after being apart when we never have been before.* But he remained unsettled. 'Cup of tea?'

'Sure, sounds good.'

'When you've caught your breath, I want you to tell me everything. I'll even sit through every picture on your phone. That's how much I've missed you,' he said, draping an arm around her shoulders. He was stunned when she seemed to shrug him off, and then swiftly told himself he must have imagined it. Perhaps she was just feeling grimy from travelling.

'Feel free to have a shower first, if you like,' he added.

'What, do I smell or something?' Joyce said, turning her head to smell one arm pit and then the other.

'No. I was just ...' Colin gave up. *Jeez, Joyce, what's with you? In these instances, it was best just to be silent.*

'My apologies. I'm tired from travelling,' Joyce said, patting his shoulder. Relief swept through him.

'After you,' he said, waving his arms to usher her down the hall.

In the kitchen Joyce sat down, not on her usual chair, but on one of the two that usually remained unoccupied – James's. *What are you doing?!* Colin stared at her.

'What?'

'Nothing.' He shook his head. 'Would you prefer coffee? Or something else?'

'Since when have I ever drunk coffee in the afternoon or evening, Colin?'

'I don't know. But something's up. You seem different.' Colin tried not to frown as he scrutinised her, trying to figure out what had changed.

'Don't be silly, Colin. I've only been gone for two weeks.'

'Yes, and I've missed you for every second of it.'

'That's nice.'

'I take it you didn't miss me, then?'

'Stop being so needy and sensitive. I was busy. And exhausted most of the time. And we spoke and texted so much there wasn't a lot of opportunity to miss you.'

'I see. So, tea it is.' Colin sighed to himself quietly. What was wrong with them? They should be excitedly chatting about their experiences of being apart, since it was such an unusual state for them, and catching each other up with things. But maybe she was right about them staying in touch – it had kept them tied together enough that they now had nothing to talk about. But that couldn't be right. They'd always found something to ignite discussion, no matter how inconsequential. 'How was the flight?'

'Not bad, thanks.'

Oh. Colin suddenly realised what was different, not so much about her presence, but her arrival.

'Did they lose your luggage? I thought that particular crisis affecting air travel might be over now. How annoying for you. Do we need to do anything?'

'No. It's fine.'

'I suppose they have the system down pat since they've had so much practice with putting it to use,' Colin said with a laugh. He was disappointed Joyce didn't take his attempt at humour and run with it, as she usually would.

'Yes. So how are things with you? How's work? Managing to ease back any?'

'Hmm. Not really. Nothing exciting to report.' Colin was annoyed with himself for his curt, non-committal answers. He was being childish but he didn't want to share anything with Joyce now, didn't want to reward her rudeness. And, anyway, he was now too on edge. Something was definitely up. He could feel it. He delivered their mugs and sat down. Did they really just need time to readjust to being together? Or … Oh, no, maybe she'd found a cancer or something.

'Is something wrong, Joyce?' he asked, just as Joyce said, 'There's something we need to talk about.'

Oh no. He felt his features drag downwards, as if the muscles in his cheeks had failed. He reached a hand over to cover hers. But he was stunned to find her dragging hers out from underneath. God, how bad was it? Had she not been off washing birds at all? Had she been having tests and/or treatment in secret, trying to spare him the distress of knowing something until he really had to? But they'd always had the difficult conversations, had navigated several health scares and had gone together through every step, dissecting each piece of information. He frowned. Whatever it was, it was clearly big, difficult to talk about.

Joyce was wrapping and unwrapping her hands around her mug while staring down into it. He noticed her cheeks go in and out a couple of times. He waited her out. His hands were in his lap, fingers linked. He concentrated on being still. Waiting. He was sure he could hear the clock in the hall ticking, but it was battery operated and silent. Somewhere far away he heard several sirens ring out. Ambulance, police, fire? He had no idea which. He hoped whatever was going on would turn out okay. They rarely heard sirens out here – there were no fire stations or hospitals close enough for it to be a regular disturbance. But right then he was grateful for it because it served as a slight circuit breaker for their inert state.

Joyce looked up at him. She partially opened her mouth and then closed it again, and did so a couple more times. It seemed to take ages before she finally spoke again.

'I'm leaving.'

Colin blinked and shook his head slightly in an attempt to dislodge his confusion.

'Oh. Do you have another campaign to get to?' *Ah, that would explain the car outside.* Relief nudged him inside again. He hadn't checked if it had left or was still there. 'Do you want me to get the bigger suitcase out from the garage?' He went to rise, but his legs were uncooperative.

'I'm leaving *you*, Colin.' Everything seemed to catch up to him then, like cars colliding in a highway pileup, slow, hard, forceful.

'What? What do you mean?' Though a tiny voice deep back in his brain told him he knew exactly what she meant.

'I don't want to be married to you anymore.'

'Don't be ridiculous, Joyce.' A bubble of hysteria rose up and escaped as an incredulous burst of laughter. But Joyce didn't laugh. Or smile. Or say, *Just joking, come here, you great galoot, I've damn well missed you.* As if she would; they'd never really been that sort of gushy couple, had they? Suddenly Colin didn't think he knew what they'd been like at all, other than permanent, steadfastly loyal, together forever past, and forever future.

'If you want to do more travel, alone, that's fine with me. I can keep the home fires burning. I don't mind. If I'm too boring, too settled ... I've said I'll go in the caravan – when we get it, and ... Honestly.'

'Colin.' Now it was Joyce who had her hand over his.

He stared at their hands on the table. When had he even put his there? It didn't feel connected; it was behaving of its own accord. Joyce's felt cold and hard. And then he saw his own hand retreating, slowly dragged out from under Joyce's.

'It's not about you.'

Anger began to rise inside him. 'Not about me? We're married, Joyce. You and me are a *we*. If it's about you, then it's about me.' *Well, pretty much.* The fury started to slide away and he silently begged it to remain. That was better than the slow pain seeping in, intensifying now, pulling him in on himself. He fought it to stay upright and not sag and give in. Whatever was going on with Joyce, she was trying to protect him by pushing him away. He'd had plenty of clients who'd done this over the years, whether consciously or unconsciously. Humans, at times, could be a bit like animals that took themselves off alone to die. Some people withdrew, usually so their loved ones didn't have to see or share their fear and pain.

'It's okay. Whatever's going on, we can get through it together. Like everything else.'

'Not this, Colin,' Joyce said, shaking her head.

'Tell me. What is it?'

'I've met someone else.'

Of course she had, lots of someone elses. *What is she talking about?*

It wasn't the words but the tone that finally poked through into his consciousness. Of all the things Joyce could have come home and told him, he'd never have picked this. Not in a million years.

He knew of clients in their sixties and seventies, strangely more often now, who had exited marriages after the kids had left and they were staring down the barrel of a life stuck with the one person – usually a person who had verbally, mentally or physically abused them. Somehow it was the prospect of retirement – all that potentially empty time, just the two of them – that had seen the tide turn when they'd contemplated leaving before but couldn't find the necessary strength.

But that wasn't him and Joyce. They were happy. Or, at least, content in their little bubble of well-honed routine.

Really, what was happiness but an unsustainable long-term state? People striving for constant happiness were always disappointed and dissatisfied. Contentment was an achievable constant state of being. Happiness was not. People wanting that – lauded by all the marketers of lifestyles and all manner of products, pushing like drug dealers – were setting themselves up for constant disappointment. It was one of the greatest issues of current society, in his opinion.

He cursed his brain for wandering off in another direction. This was big; he needed to stay focussed. But he didn't want to. He forcibly reran her words through his mind, seeking further clarity. *I've met someone else?* That's what she'd said. If it was someone who wanted to travel constantly and was ready to leave, then he was probably a little relieved, if he were being honest.

He almost said the words. He came very close to saying, *'Actually, I've realised I don't want to do the grey nomad thing.'* But he couldn't. It would come out in the wrong tone. And he'd appear small-minded and petty, as if he was trying to play tit for tat and engage in one-upmanship.

'Are you going to say anything?' Joyce said.

'What can I say?' he said sadly. 'If you don't love me anymore, then …' He shrugged instead of finishing his sentence. 'I don't own you. It's a free country. No one owns anyone.' He was heavy. Every word took more effort to drag up than he thought he could manage. He could feel the tension in his chest from the building dam against tears. His face felt grey, devoid of flowing blood.

'I'll always love you, Colin.'

'That's not fair, Joyce. You can't say you've met someone else, that you're leaving me, and then say you still love me. Is there anything I can do to make you stay?'

If there was, right then Colin wasn't sure he had it in him to do it, no matter how small a task or movement.

'It's just that I want something different now.'

'What's that supposed to mean? You've found someone wealthier, younger, more energetic, what? I thought we rubbed along well, you and I.'

'We have. We did.'

'But? Joyce, I think some decent explanation is in order, not this beating around the bush claptrap. Otherwise it's impossible not to think of you as being anything other than very shallow and incredibly self-absorbed right now.' He welcomed the return of anger. 'You go away *one* time on your own and can't remain loyal? I can't help but wonder–'

'I'm not leaving you for another man, Colin,' Joyce said with a sigh. 'I've fallen in love with a woman. Carmel.'

'What?' The words and their meaning collided inside him again. 'You're a lesbian? You've suddenly decided you're a lesbian?' Colin wanted to laugh at the nonsensicality. But he was too shocked. And frustrated. And hurt. And feeling rejected.

'I haven't decided. I guess I must always have been, but perhaps I buried it. And, technically, I suppose I'd be considered bi-sexual. Please don't think I've hated sex with you forever, Colin.'

But that was exactly what he was thinking at that moment. In fact, going through his mind were images from years past – a long way back, if he were being honest – of them in various sexual positions. Enjoying sex. He felt like he'd been scammed, conned. He rubbed his hands over his face.

'But I don't think it's really necessary to put labels on it, is it?'

'I'm stuffed if I know anything right now, Joyce! Christ.' One word seeped in over the top of the heavy sludge occupying much of him. 'Carmel,' he said. 'She was here – that was her who just dropped you off.'

'Yes. Does that make a difference?'

'No. Oh, I don't know.' Colin couldn't explain that his interest was mainly down to the relief of having gripped some tiny sliver of clarity in all this. 'So, where to from here? I guess that's the question.'

And then more clarity dawned. Or rather, another image came to him: Joyce's missing small suitcase. 'You're leaving now, aren't you? Carmel – the woman in the car – is still out there, or coming back. You're just here to get more clothes.'

'Yes. I am, Colin. I can't exactly stay now, can I?' She offered him a grim smile.

'No. I suppose not.'

'Oh, and you're now in charge of any aspects of the business that I've been taking care of. So don't forget ...'

Colin knew Joyce had said something else, but her words were a distant muffle as he experienced another tumbling of thoughts, suggestions and bargaining. *Don't leave. Don't leave me. Stay. Live here with Carmel.* The notion and the intensity of its arrival shocked him. He was as conservative as they came, and here he was with the most ludicrous suggestions pushing at the edges of his lips. Who was being self-absorbed now? Who was trying to trap Joyce, if only by emotional machinations?

'Oh, Joyce,' he said instead. He had so many questions, but none of them useful or pertinent right now. 'I suppose we'd better discuss things going forward, in a rational, adult manner.'

'Well, we are adults and we're us; I'd expect nothing less.'

Colin wanted to rage – tell her she was wrong, that he was unpredictable, and would fight this all the way. But he didn't have the energy or the will. And, anyway, he *was* predictable and rational. He longed to behave out of character and shock Joyce. But to what end? She was leaving him. For a woman. Now was not the time for grand gestures. If there'd even been a time for that, he'd missed it. Had he dropped the ball back when they'd met? Had they become too settled too early? Had she needed more outward shows of passion all this time? God, he felt like a failure and as if he knew nothing about the human race. *Have I been failing every one of my clients along the way too? Am I a pathetic loser in all departments?*

'So, what's the plan?' he said, having to force the words out through his exhaustion and disappointment, like pushing partially set superglue from a tube.

'I'm going to pack the larger suitcase. Then, sometime soon, I'll come and get some more things. And when we've had time to digest what's gone on, and the reality of the future, then perhaps we can sit down to discuss and settle things?'

Colin nodded. 'What about the caravan on order?'

'Um. I cancelled it. So, that's something. And I didn't go any further with deciding on the vehicle.'

Fury tried to overcome Colin's tiredness again. He stared at her. *You lied to me?* Out of all he'd learnt just now, possibly the worst thing was the fact that she'd lied about the caravan. Though, actually, he realised, his heart thudding slowly with the magnitude of it, *you've really been lying to me the whole time. Even if only through denial or omission, it's still lying.*

He was really sad that she hadn't at least, during all their time together, mentioned that she had issues with or queries about sex and sexual preference. He'd thought they could discuss anything and everything – thought they had been all this time. Christ.

'Do you need me to make myself scarce – head out for a walk – so you can get your things together?'

'Well ... I don't want to drive you from your home ...'

'It's your home too, dear. *Joyce*,' he corrected.

'You can call me dear. I really am sorry.'

He got up. She did the same.

'I'll go for a walk. Call Carmel to come and get you. I'll go out for an hour. Will that be long enough?' He picked up his phone and studied the time.

'Yes, I think so. Thanks. Thank you for being so understanding.'

Again, Colin nodded. He wanted to shout that he wasn't being understanding – that he didn't understand this at all. As he moved past her, she reached out a hand, as if to placate him and/or offer reassurance. They'd always been a reasonably tactile couple – sometimes a touching of hands or weighty arm around a shoulder had said more than any number of words could. But right now, he needed to be far away from her. Her touch was like a red-hot branding iron. He needed air. He kept walking and gently shrugged her off.

Joyce opened her mouth as if to speak but sighed instead.

Out of habit, he dragged his casual coat from the hallstand on his way past and eased into it, popped his hat on his head. Having pulled the door to carefully behind him, he pushed his hands deep into his pockets and made his way down the path.

Chapter Seventeen

Colin was pleased to be out in the fresh air away from the cloying atmosphere inside. He was in an odd state of wanting to sink to the ground and stay put, and also run away from the house. But at his age, he couldn't run anywhere. Often, he couldn't be accused of even hurrying, when in his mind he was doing just that. Steps must be taken deliberately and one had to watch where one placed each foot. Just walking as an elderly person was a precarious business. The slightest trip could cause a tumble, the most innocuous tumble a broken hip, or worse. The young ones who rushed about their business, whooshing past – on foot or on scooters or skateboards or bikes – had no idea what lay ahead.

He paused to cross the street and checked each way twice. The late afternoon sun was surprisingly still bright, and he cursed having forgotten his sunglasses. He pulled his hat down a little at the front to provide better shading. He realised he was panting slightly. He bent over in an effort to catch his breath. His head began to spin with random thoughts, both rational and less so. *Why was Joyce doing this? Why did she have to go and upend their lives* like this? How could anyone fall in love so quickly — or even be sure that was the new future they wanted? And then he sighed. He'd known the moment he'd met Joyce that she was for him. *And back then she'd said the same. So, how, after all these years, could she have that feeling again? Would she know it when she saw it? Could it be she was just caught up in the frenzy of service?*

He stood back up. Being bent over really wasn't helping. He fought to breathe against his tight chest, and resist putting a hand to his heart as a few people walked towards him. He returned their smiles, but his was more of a grimace. He wanted to be back inside the house where it felt safe. Out here he felt lost, dazed; hot in the sun despite the chilly breeze that had seen him do up his buttons — which he had no memory of doing. He set about unfastening them, his fumbling fingers struggling. The more he struggled the tighter the coat seemed to become. It felt like the cuff of a blood pressure machine, except around his entire torso, being pumped up, tighter and tighter.

Somehow, he managed to get the buttons undone and began flapping his coat to create some airflow. He was sweating and could feel the air becoming even colder as it connected with damp patches under his armpits and across his chest and back. His forehead prickled.

Colin's thoughts went back to Joyce and one settled on him and rolled around: *Why make such a dramatic move so soon?* And then the avalanche of thoughts came over him again: How could she be so sure? Did she loathe him that much? Could it be some sort of test, some kind of cry for help? But no — they had always been able to share things.

He turned slightly back towards home, which was now well out of sight. Should he return and suggest they do a trial separation? He'd offer for her to go off and scratch whatever itch it was she was embarking on and if she wanted to come back in, say, a month or two, then she could. He loved her *that* much.

But of course, that was being very dismissive and patronising – suggesting she didn't know what she wanted. She'd made herself very clear. No, he was being the needy, self-centred one. He began to blame himself. For not encouraging her to go out and make female friends instead of it always being the two of them, or socialising with couples. Had he been too clingy? Was that why this was happening? Had she spent her whole life with him yearning for something else? Is it that she'd just got to the end of her tether? Was it about sex? It must be, because Joyce was actually leaving him for someone else, not just going on a holiday. So, it was more than a platonic meeting of minds. It must seem, at least to Joyce, to be the whole kit and caboodle. Sex must be involved. He wondered how it worked in a same-sex female couple?

Actually, he would rather not think about it at all.

But there it was, as plainly as having been presented on a platter on the table. Of course, sex wasn't only physical – or rather, intimacy wasn't only sexual. At the heart of sex that wasn't purely animalistic physical release, was intimacy. And intimacy relied on emotional connection. People connected on a level of shared vulnerability. Perhaps this Carmel woman had captured his darling, generous Joyce's heart through emotional pain – whether intentionally or less manipulatively.

She's left you, mate.

The words seemed to have been carried to him on the wind. He thought he'd heard them, even going so far as to turn around to see who had spoken. His stomach muscles lost their strength and his shoulders slumped. All the bargaining, blame, questions, wouldn't help, would they? He had to find a way through. Just like so many of his clients, he would have to learn to put one foot in front of him, then the next, and gradually piece a life back together.

He felt a renewed sense of appreciation and wonder for each of his clients he'd seen undertake the journey – beginning with fears, pain and sadness, confusion, barely a husk of a coping person, until weeks, months later, they were excitedly telling him about their plans for the future. And all the success stories relied upon the ability to take care of oneself, find one's own path, and search inside themselves for who they were. Because suddenly being alone after being part of a couple, or even a cosseted family unit, necessitated finding oneself – who you really were. So many thought they'd known, only to discover through solitude and being forced to search the depths of their soul that they'd pieced together a composite of other people's thoughts, ideals, wants and values. It was so easy to lose yourself as an individual when you wanted so badly to be liked, appreciated and considered to be successful. Human nature relied on some form of connection, even of simply being an amalgam to your true self and the hope that you'd be okay.

How many people had he encouraged in their gloomiest times? And of course that included himself. And Joyce. They'd managed to get through their darkest period together, intact, with neither falling apart at the same time. Each of them had taken turns holding the other up when one was weak and failing.

Colin became a little angry. *I need you, Joyce. How can you leave me now?*

But this was her doing – how could he want her?

Because she's my best friend. And I'm lost without her. He felt the cold wind against the corner of his eye where tears were forming. He tried to tell himself it was just the breeze. But it wasn't that cold, nor that fierce.

Turning away from the house again, he trudged on.

A few minutes later, Colin was almost surprised to see his brown office building in front of him. It was in darkness and lifeless, given it was Sunday. He unlocked the back main door and went in. The alarm let out a steady squeal, signalling his intrusion.

Damn. What's the code again? He'd used it plenty of times, as recently as Friday morning. And his brain was suddenly reluctant to reveal it to him. *Oh damn. Oh damn. No. Think, damn it, think!* It was only ever the four digits of the postcode, changed on the first of each month, with tenants advised via email. *What order is it for October? Damn it.*

Oh. Yes. He punched it in and let out a sigh of relief when the noise stopped.

He unlocked his office, went in, and closed the door behind him. He slumped onto the couch. He'd never felt so keen to be here and let out silent thanks to the ugly but comforting presence of the building. Being here, in a space that was both familiar and entirely his, gave him a renewed sense of calm and strength. This room was tainted neither with Joyce's presence nor her impending absence. Had she even ever set foot in here? He didn't think so. He'd always kept his office hours regular and never let his work bleed into his relationship or stray into his homelife beyond their discussions, which he'd always really appreciated.

Was that why Joyce was leaving? He'd thought she'd enjoyed sharing his work to that extent. She'd certainly given that impression. Or at least, she'd never complained. He felt the uneasy teetering of reality at acknowledging he really couldn't be sure of anything anymore, given the earlier revelations and occurrences. *At least I've got you,* he thought, looking around the room with a sense of fondness. Though, really, it was a pretty drab, nondescript space. Still, it was a safe place.

Well, here we are. At a cross-road. On the edge of a cliff. God, we've got all the cliches today. He tried to silently laugh it off, find some humour. But failed. He was just very, very sad. And lost. And bewildered. Shocked, too. The thought of Joyce not being in his life hurt physically inside him – right in his heart. He held his breath, willing the sharp pain to withdraw. When it didn't, he was forced to take short, shallow breaths.

Christ. Am I having a heart attack? He should have left the back door unlocked – despite it being against the rules – in case he needed to call an ambulance.

His eyesight seemed to cloud and the room began to spin and shrink around him. He was suddenly struggling to breathe. And he was clammy, with his coat too tight again, despite it still being unbuttoned. He tried to shrug it off but it held on like a straitjacket, pinning his arms behind him, aided by the fact he was sitting on it. He eased off the couch and then out of the garment, and tossed it on the floor.

Finally able to breathe a little easier, Colin tried to take an inventory to ascertain if he needed medical assistance. He was quivering as his physiology fought the conflicting flight-or-fight response. But with a lack of faculties or any idea of where to go in response, he remained frozen externally, with his insides churning. There was no pain down his left arm. Granted, it wasn't the only symptom of a heart attack, but that was all he could remember in that moment. Had he just had a panic attack?

Cognition or a memory of something seeped into his addled mind – *concentrate on the five senses. Ground yourself in what you can see, hear, touch, smell and taste.* He tried, but his brain wouldn't focus. The glimmer of clarity had left him.

And then outside he heard a siren, far off in the distance. He concentrated on it, trying to ascertain if it was coming this way, louder and louder. There was a moment when the scream of the siren and honk of a horn was right outside, and then the sounds were retreating, reducing, becoming quieter and then disappearing again. And with them, Colin's nervous system began to slow and his ragged breathing ease. The tightness in his chest unclenched, the sharp pain under his ribs released and he could take normal breaths again.

Oh god. Okay. You're okay. You're going to be okay. Colin sat inert on the couch, looking around his room.

Slowly the practical part of him began to take shape, as if the focus on a telescope was being turned. At least he hadn't given up work. At least he still had his office and his clients to escape to. His whole world had not imploded – just a sizeable chunk of it had. Phew. Imagine if he was already on the road with Joyce, had taken possession of their horrendously expensive vehicles and had already been in an unfamiliar place. Had his subconscious been trying to warn him of this by being unwilling to fully commit, by leaving him indecisive? The shard of knowledge that Joyce had cancelled the order without discussing it with him reappeared, causing resentment to burn again. But he cut it off. *Least of your concerns, mate.* He let out a long sigh. *Oh, what a mess.* He had to pull himself together, regroup, start out all over again. Alone. Oh god. They'd have to split everything up. Sort out the finances. Again, he thought how grateful he was that he hadn't shut up shop. But he was tired – had been looking forward to having less to occupy his brain that related to other people, even if he hadn't been sure about the grey nomad part. Could he even afford to retire now? Did he want to? All that empty time to fill and keep his mind from wandering.

One of his most frequent pieces of advice to clients was to keep moving, thinking, doing – *something.* But was working the answer? He'd never been entirely sure he was good at what he did. Was he still adequate now, given his age? Yes, he was still capable of listening. But was he quick enough on the uptake these days to actually help? Right now, he had no clear idea of anything. Though, granted, he was very much in the weeds.

Despite checking his watch when he'd left, he now had no concept of how long he'd been gone from the house. Was it safe to go back? That thought caused another ache of sadness to roll through him. Did he want to see Joyce before she left or leave enough time to make sure that didn't happen? At that moment he heard his phone chime with a text message. He reached down to the floor, picked up his discarded coat, and fished the device out of the pocket. He knew it would be from Joyce. He didn't get many texts. Gripped with apprehension, he turned it right way up, put in his code, and clicked the blue logo.

I'm leaving now. It's safe to come home. Love, Joyce.

He stared at the message, trying to analyse it for any hidden meanings. But his brain wouldn't comply.

At least she'd used the word love. Maybe they could at least retain some sort of something when the dust had settled. Surely this wasn't completely the end of his and Joyce's story, which spanned five decades? He really hoped not. The thought of losing his best friend, no, his *only* friend, confidante and companion hurt more than losing his wife, though they were entwined. He didn't have sufficient clarity to explain the difference, just knew there was one. He'd hope for them to cobble something together. He had to hold onto that glimmer of positivity.

He deliberated over whether to respond or not. But then decided that not to was poor manners. And he didn't want to come across as trifling. But he also didn't want to come across as uncaring and glib, nor pile on more guilt. Because, as much as he was simmering with frustration and pain, he did understand that this had not been an easy decision or course of action for Joyce.

He also, despite his own discomfort, held a sense of enormous respect for her for having come to the realisation and then acting on it. Everyone deserved to live their life with authenticity. And Joyce would never have knowingly set out to hurt him. He had to hold onto that.

Thus, it took him five full minutes to construct his reply – typing and deleting and re-typing. Finally, he pressed send:

> Okay. Thanks for letting me know. If you need anything at all just let me know. Keep in touch. Love, Colin.

He stared at the sent message, wondering if he'd left himself open to be potentially exploited. But oh well, it was too late to concern himself with that now. Of course she'd have to keep in touch, to some extent – they'd go through the rigmarole of dissolving their assets and unpicking their long-interwoven lives.

Colin trudged home slowly and once inside placed his things in their usual spots. He stood for a moment listening to the emptiness, trying to gauge if anything felt different to before. He was both relieved and nervous to be home and cocooned. When Joyce had been on her trip, the space she'd vacated had been easy and casual, and had held a tinge of excitement and anticipation of her return with tales of what she'd seen and done. Now, with none of that possibility remaining, the space seemed cloying and oppressive.

He moved through to the kitchen. He was ashamed at his assumption that Joyce's return would reestablish her place in the family, particularly as cook. Colin was further disappointed to realise he'd not considered his dinner anyway and, thus, had not prepared for it. This hit him harder than it ought to have, such was the human unconsciousness's propensity to blow or shrink things out of proportion at inappropriate moments.

As he undid the lid of the tin of baked beans – thankfully a ring-pull that no longer required a can-opener, which he wasn't sure his addled faculties and lack of energy could manage – he thought about the sad irony of where he was at. Eating baked beans alone in the same house as a single man. Very different to when he had done the same as a young man when his parents had been away on a long trip. Back then life had stretched out before him – a full six or seven decades ripe with promise. Now it was a sense of despair that gripped him. If one could just curl up and die without any intervention, he felt he'd be okay with that. Right now, he'd welcome the end; not having to think beyond the here and now. No amount of knowledge or working with people in similar situations seemed of benefit in that moment. Oh, he knew all the right things to say, the suggestions to make, if asked. But right then he didn't want to hear them. Probably wouldn't if anyone offered words of wisdom. He'd lived in this house his entire life and had never wanted to leave. *Will I have to now?* The question sent a shudder of fear racing through him.

As he sat at the table, he wanted to hate Joyce, pity her even. But he couldn't. He loved her. It wasn't really her fault she'd hurt him. Each person owed it to themselves to live their best life. Unfortunately, he was just collateral damage. For her sake, he hoped it would work out with this woman, Carmel. For his sake, he yearned for it not to, for Joyce to come back to him. But no matter how much he wanted that, he didn't want her in pain. He'd seen her through that before with the twins – the most wretched of losses – they'd seen each other through it. It was a unique experience that had bonded them tightly. Or so he'd thought. But of course, it still did – they just weren't in the same room. They each carried the scars wherever they went. Few truly understood. He really hoped Carmel would be empathetic. Had Joyce told her of this enormous private loss?

He dug his spoon into the tin of cold beans, unable to muster the energy to pour them into a bowl and heat them. As he looked at the red sauce and pale chunky beans, his appetite left him. But he raised the spoon to his lips nonetheless, knowing he needed sustenance. As the first spoonful went down, his stomach protested.

Well, here we are again, so much older and hopefully so much wiser this time, old man. One can hope.

He again thought back to the single biggest and most prolonged period of torture and growth in both his and Joyce's lives – had it ever even ended? Probably not. And in that moment, he reminded himself that he'd survived a loss the magnitude of which was unlikely to repeat. And he therefore could get through anything life had to throw at him. It was true, but he didn't have to like it. And it was Sunday evening. How was he going to get up and carry on tomorrow as normal?

Chapter Eighteen

After a sleepless night, it was in a slightly dazed state and with a slower gait that Colin made his way to work, grateful that he had that familiarity and routine to immerse himself in. He was relieved to find his Monday mainly comprised regular easy clients and a few rounds of psychometric testing, none of which was too taxing, and meant he could operate largely on autopilot. Seeing Shirley Royal's name on the list brightened him significantly and gave him the impetus to get through the simple cases scheduled before her. He really didn't know what she was hoping to achieve, or get out of the sessions, but also accepted every person had their own agenda. And, boy, was he looking forward to her presence. Thus, Shirley entering his room was a breath of fresh air so welcome he almost lost his professionalism.

'Hello, Shirley.'

'How's things?' Shirley said, now seated in front of him.

He laughed. 'That's meant to be my bit.'

'Don't mind me overstepping!' He wanted to tell her to overstep all she liked – that it was her session, her money, but it ran the risk of sounding flirty, dare he say, even a bit creepy. Instead, he said, re-mustering his deep, quiet tone, 'What would you like to talk about? How can I help you?'

'I'm not sure you can, as such. I think I just need to vent.'

'Vent away.'

'The world is shit. Humans are arseholes,' Shirley said, holding out her hands in a gesture of helplessness before letting them drop back into her lap. 'Apologies for the language.'

'That's okay. And, for the record, I can't argue with anything you've said so far. Has something in particular happened that you'd like to discuss?'

'I'm not sure, exactly. I'm trying to do all the admin around Norman's departure, beginning with changing the utilities and the like into my name. You'd think it would be an easy process, given people die every day, but I'm not finding it so. Maybe I'm the problem. Anyway, it's made me cranky and ranty! And really missing my Norman. We were a lot of dysfunctional things, but we were very good at getting things off our chests. And we listened to each other; *really* listened. He was a pain in the arse, but he was my pain in the arse. And I'm missing the supporter he was. Fuck. And now I'm going to cry. Damn it.' Colin's heart swelled. He wanted to reach over and clasp her hand. Instead, he pushed the box of tissues on the edge of the desk closer to her. 'Thank you.' She pulled several tissues from the box. 'Didn't come prepared for this,' she muttered, as she dabbed her face and wiped her eyes carefully, without removing her glasses, and then quietly blew her nose.

'Do you have someone else in your life to talk things over with?' he asked.

'I thought I had a decent circle. I'd like to think I've been a good friend to many over the years. But it's when your own chips are down that you see who your true friends are, don't you?' she said sadly, smiling weakly at him. 'I keep myself busy with all sorts of things – dancing, community volunteering, knitting, cards, and most of us catch up socially for coffee or a meal.'

'But …?' Colin prompted.

'Well, it never feels quite right. The connections just aren't really strong enough to completely be yourself. I don't know, it feels too hard to unravel your whole life – I mean, god, Colin, I'm seventy-five, for Christ's sake. There's *a lot*. As the kids would say. Honestly, that's one of the very few bits of modern lingo of which I wholeheartedly agree – *It's a lot!* And no explanation of what *it* is, is needed. Says it all. It's a lot. It's *all* a lot.'

'So, you don't have any old, well-established friendships left? It's hard at our age with friends dying or moving into retirement villages and making new connections, isn't it?'

Shirley nodded. 'Yes, there's a lot of that. And perhaps that's why it feels so hurtful that the ones who remain don't get in touch.'

'I don't quite follow.'

'I'm not surprised – I'm all over the place. My oldest and dearest friend isn't returning my calls or texts. And it's breaking my heart. We … we've been through so much together and been so close. And I have no idea what's happened. I don't know if I've said too many times, "Oh, I'm fine" and she assumes I am, or she's going through something big herself and simply doesn't have the energy or time for me. But wouldn't you think if that were the case, she'd be more inclined to lean on me? There's nothing we can't discuss, probably nothing we haven't, over the years. We've been best friends, or so I thought, for nearly six decades.' Shirley sniffed and then dabbed at her nose.

'I understand how hard that must be. But, I'm afraid, beyond that I don't know what to say.' Colin was surprised to find these words slipping from his lips. How unprofessional. He'd meant to say he understood. Because he really did.

'With all due respect, probably anything you can say I'll have thought myself anyway.'

'I'm sure you have. There won't have been much we haven't seen in our time. Did she come to your husband's funeral, if you had one, or at least offer support then?'

'Yes and no. She sent a lovely card saying to call if I needed anything. But I did. I left a voicemail, which she responded to via text. I just wanted to hear a friendly voice – a shoulder to cry on, so to speak. Honestly, I have to say, Colin, this is almost worse than losing Norman. And magnified because he's not here to provide advice. Or, and I wouldn't have put it past him, to phone and have a quiet word to her himself. I suspect he might have done that once or twice before.'

'So, you've had issues like this before?'

'Not really. Not as prolonged. I don't like to give ultimatums and risk burning a bridge, but this is like death by a thousand cuts. It's gnawing at me something wicked. Any advice?'

'Probably nothing you haven't thought of yourself.'

'Oh, touché.'

'Perhaps let it play out of its own accord? She might come back in due course, reaching out at a time when she needs you. Sadly, as you said when you arrived, humans tend to be very selfish these days.

'Or you can push for some answers – but, as you said, there's a risk. It all depends what is hurting you more, and what you need for your own health. Because, ultimately, we need to put ourselves first in some instances.'

'So, it's as I've thought – I stay silent and suck it up or I ask, push, and risk an answer I don't want?'

'Essentially, yes. I'm afraid so. All human relationships require communication, which I think is like a muscle – or maybe more like a skill – that requires use, or rather, practice. And if unused for a period of time, it can be a bit like driving a car after not doing so for a while. You'll have lost confidence – perhaps both of you have. But hopefully it all comes back quickly, eventually.'

'Hmm.'

Shirley lapsed into silence and Colin waited her out.

'It's the nights that are the worst,' Shirley said. 'The late night – between eleven and time to get up in the morning.'

Oh yes, Colin thought.

'Until then you can keep yourself busy. But the quiet hours, when it was previously just the two of you – they're the hardest.'

Colin nodded.

'Who have you lost, Colin?'

'Say again, I missed that.'

'You're nodding like you know exactly what I mean – and not from a practitioner perspective, from a personal viewpoint, I reckon.'

'Um …'

'There's me overstepping again. Don't answer. It was inappropriate.'

'I appreciate the question, the concern. Actually, my wife recently left me. As in, *left* me, not died,' he said. God, he hated saying the words out loud, and immediately felt his face heat up.

'Oh no. That's tough. Honestly, possibly that's even harder to deal with than a deceased loved one, because you're left with a constant "what if", as in what are they doing? I think it's why my friendship problem hurts so much. It's the human frailty around being left out, not included, when we so need human bonds.

'Also, in my case, with the death of a loved one, I only have to contend with people avoiding me because they don't know what to say. With the breakup of a marriage, one also has to contend with the division of friends. People choose sides; they deny this – but they always do. It's hardest when all your friends are couples you met while together. Sadly, often it comes down to which of the couple reaches out first with the news, and in doing so stakes their claim. Crass sounding, I know, but I've seen it so many times.'

Colin wondered if his face had gone as pale as he feared it might have.

'You're very insightful, Shirley.'

'Ah, well, as I said, I've been around the block a few times. Doesn't seem to have helped, though.' She laughed.

'I know what you mean.'

'You'd think with all the years of wisdom one wouldn't still be feeling and dealing with the same things from our youth.'

'No, it's a bit ironic, isn't it? And I'm meant to be better at navigating it all due to my training,' Colin said.

'Oh well, don't be too hard on yourself. People are still going to war despite the tragic consequences, time after time. Nobody actually learns from history; they just record it.'

'That's true.'

'Humans really are the worst,' Shirley said.

'Unfortunately, I can't disagree with you there.'

'On that note, I'd better be off. My time's up.'

'Oh. So it is.' Colin found his heart sinking.

'Thanks again, Colin.'

'Thank you, Shirley. I'm not sure I was any help.'

'Well, venting is always a help. And better it be to a professional, lest one piss off one's few remaining friends!' Shirley said, shooting him a withering look.

'Yes. Quite. You're welcome any time,' Colin said, though as he said the words, he regretted them. It did seem a little salesy of him. Was he exploiting her? Oh well, she knew it was her own choice whether to book in again. But, oh, he wished she would. She'd cheered him up no end. What a tonic!

Chapter Nineteen

It was Sunday, a whole week since Joyce had left for good. Today she was coming to collect the rest of her things and Colin didn't think he'd been this nervous since his first date with her all those years ago. Though it was a decidedly different bundle of twanging nerves. What hadn't changed was her punctuality. She arrived right on the time she'd told him she'd be there.

They hugged briefly and stiffly at the front door and Colin nodded to the woman standing just behind his wife, *er, estranged wife*, he mentally corrected. He was a little shocked to see a small truck parked at the kerb, two strapping young lads opening the back doors. *Just how much furniture and stuff is she taking?* He couldn't quite remember what was pre- his and Joyce's arrival, and what was already in situ during his parents' day. They'd got rid of some things after their passing, orchestrated by Joyce. He'd lost track of what was what and when. More of the finer details that were often lost on him. He stood aside to admit the women.

Joyce immediately dashed up the hall and disappeared into a room, leaving Carmel standing there with Colin.

'You must be Carmel. It's a pleasure to meet you,' he said, cursing the automatic phrase slipping out.

'Thank you. It's a bit awkward, isn't it?'

'Yes, it is a bit.'

'I can wait outside if you prefer? I would completely understand if you did.'

'No, that's not necessary. It's too cold.' *And it might be an awkward situation, but I can still be a gentleman, or at least decent.* 'Come through to the kitchen and I'll put the kettle on.' He led the way.

'Thank you,' she said, following him. 'Joyce has a list, so it's probably best I stay out of the way. My two sons have come to help. This must be really horrible for you. I truly didn't mean to ruin your marriage.'

'Well, you couldn't have done so if it weren't already vulnerable. And I'd say I have to take some blame – all of it, I suppose – for not knowing the state it was in. We men are rather known for our ineptitude at picking up the subtleties and noting the finer details. It's a complete generalisation but one I clearly fit,' he added sadly.

'She really did – does – love you, you know,' Carmel said.

'Please don't patronise me or try to soften the blow. We wouldn't be here if that were the truth. Cup of tea or coffee?' He went over to the sink, leant on it, and held out the kettle.

'Yes, tea, please.'

'We can at least be civilised. I'm not about to become all beating-chest and possessive. Maybe if I had once …' He shrugged, smiled weakly. He wanted to go back to bed and remain there with the covers pulled over his head until they left.

'Unlikely it would have helped,' Carmel said, smiling gently back. In the silence they could hear Joyce thudding her way quickly through the house, her footsteps heavy but muffled by the carpet over the solid original floorboards.

'She says you're a thoroughly decent fellow.'

'That's nice of her.'

'But, again, not helpful?'

'No, not especially.'

'This is really hard for her, too.'

'I'll bet it is.' He was glad his hands were now busy with getting out the teapot and gathering together the mugs and other tea things on the bench. 'Milk? Sugar?'

'Yes. Both, please. One sugar.'

His grip was tight on each item, clutching onto them for longer than was necessary, relishing their familiarity like they were life buoys or stepping stones from safe place to safe place. What had he been thinking, inviting Carmel in? Damn, adhering to his upbringing and manners. And, more to the point, why had Joyce brought her? Surely, she hadn't brought reinforcements because she'd been concerned about his reaction to her presence? That thought caused him to mis-pour from the kettle over the edge of the teapot. He paused with the kettle raised, contemplating his last thought. Did Joyce really think he'd become difficult, violent – verbally or physically? That made him sad, and disappointed, and a little annoyed. She knew him. But then he softened a bit. There was no way for her to know how he'd react. This was uncharted territory for them. He couldn't recall them even having a shouting match. They'd never disagreed on anything to the extent it required such a fervent reaction. He put the lid on the teapot, grateful for immediately finding the correct point to slip the nub of the lid under to connect the two delicate pieces securely together.

Oh. The strangest thought snuck in and he turned back to look at Carmel in response. Could Joyce have been concerned her resolve might falter once she was back here? Might Carmel be there to make sure she didn't change her mind? Carmel looked at him just then with another sad, sympathetic expression.

'Just letting it steep,' he said, folding his arms. 'I like it strong, if that's okay with you?'

'Perfectly. I'm not too fussy with tea. But coffee, now that's a different matter,' she said, overly passionately. It was clearly forced. Colin felt for her. She was trying. As was he.

'Oh yes. We've never had a coffee machine for fear of disappointment.'

'Oh, I've found the perfect one. Produces a latte almost as good as a decent cafe.'

'Really? Seriously?'

'Yes.'

'Well, then. Maybe I'll get myself one, as an, um, an, um …' *Un-housewarming gift, or was it house-cooling gift?* he thought, but kept the words to himself, unwilling to interrupt their slight rapport. He shrugged helplessly instead.

'I'll send through the details – when we get home.'

'I would appreciate that.' *We. Home.* The words clanged like church bells inside him and it took all his effort to hold in the sigh straining in his aching chest.

'I warn you; it won't be cheap.'

'Quality rarely is.' He finished making the tea. 'Right, here we are, I think that should do the trick.'

He carried the two mugs to the table, placed them down and then sat. 'I'm afraid I don't have any biscuits or cake.' He frowned and looked around while searching his mind for something to offer her. He could slice up some cheese, but there weren't any crackers. 'Unfortunately, you've caught me before my weekly shop,' he lied.

'No problem. We haven't long had breakfast.'

These words and the reminder of no longer having Joyce's presence of a morning, his favourite time of the day, burnt their way through Colin like a trickle of lava.

He swallowed, nodded and sipped on his tea.

'Thanks for agreeing to us coming so early.'

'It's okay.'

'Ah, that's the perfect cup of tea. Thank you.'

'It quite hits the spot, doesn't it?' he said, thinking it was more the action, the physical distraction, and the warming of the hands, rather than the taste that was so fortifying.

'Is it a special blend?'

'I beg your pardon?'

'The tea leaves? I noticed you didn't use tea bags. So …?'

'Oh. No. It's just Dilmah. Or Bushells. I'm not sure which one it currently is – it gets poured into the tin. But it's always the extra strong variety. That does make a difference, though I'm stuffed if I know how it could. You'd think tea leaves are tea leaves and the strength would be with the steeping. But it's not, apparently. Joyce and I did do some googling on the matter, and some testing, many years ago. Not very scientific, but, anyway, we tried. And we came to the conclusion that it was worth the extra cost. Though that information might warrant refreshing now. No doubt the powers that be have found a way to diddle us as part of their shrinkflation or what have you.' He stopped, suddenly aware of his mindless babbling.

'Well, it's a very good cup.'

'Thanks. It's a lovely morning. Bit chilly,' Colin said after a few moments of silence.

'Yes, spring is such a tricky time, temperature wise.'

Colin smiled to himself. Thank goodness for topics such as tea and the weather. 'So, um, do you live far away, Carmel?' Colin ventured. He didn't want to pry, but he did also still care about Joyce and her welfare. Well, he told himself these questions came under that heading.

'Oh. Yes. No. It depends where you start, I suppose,' Carmel said with a laugh, seeming to have been caught off guard by his question. 'I'm down south. Around forty minutes away. Near the beach.'

'Lovely. That must get busy with people in summer, though.'

'Yes, it does a bit. I particularly love it in winter. Walking in the wind with the waves crashing before racing inside to get warm is quite wonderful, and of course less populous.'

'Hmm. Joyce and I loved watching the *Poldark* series.'

'Oh yes, we're watching it now. I didn't see it when it first came around.' Colin felt stung by the comment but immediately pushed it aside.

He wondered if Joyce had told Carmel she loathed the wind and how just watching both the bitterly cold or hot northerly versions made her cranky. Maybe her love for Carmel would see her change her view on that, he thought, a little bitterly. It wasn't his place to educate Carmel. Clearly he'd got things wrong about Joyce, to his detriment.

'So, um, have you had many, er, partners yourself. And, er …'

'No. Just two before Joyce. And, before you ask, one was a man and one a woman.'

Oh, how Colin wanted to pick her brain on this changing from heterosexual to homosexual. If that was still the correct term in relation to two women. Was it ever or did that only relate to men?

'It's nice that same-sex couples can marry now and have the same rights,' he instead mumbled, feeling patronising as he did. Colin stared into his mug and was surprised and disappointed to find it empty.

'Yes.'

'I'm thinking another cup is in order,' he said, getting up. 'How about you?'

'That would be lovely, but I'll just check on Joyce,' Carmel said, getting up. 'And could I use your loo?'

'Of course. Up the hall, first door on your left.' As he said it, Colin wondered if the basin was clean enough. Had he wiped it that morning or not? He couldn't remember, but he did know some standards were slipping with Joyce gone. Not in the kitchen because he'd gone over that quickly, anticipating that Joyce would end up there at some point. It was always the beating heart of their home and they always seemed to gravitate there, alone and when they had company.

'Ask Joyce if she'd like a cup since we've proven we can be civil,' he called, but received no answer, just heard the sound of light footsteps and then the door to the powder room click closed.

He'd just refilled both mugs and placed them on the table when Carmel arrived back and retook her chair. A sudden thought struck Colin when she picked up her mug after thanking him. *That's very trusting of you; I could have poisoned it while you've been away.* He was surprised at his thought. He'd clearly been watching too many murder mysteries or true crime shows of the evenings; or he was feeling more piqued about this situation than he'd like to admit.

'Is she finding everything she wants?' he asked.

'Oh, yes. I hope you won't feel the house is too empty when we leave,' she added in a regretful sounding mutter that trailed off. He did appreciate her humility very much. Again, he thought she seemed a decent woman. Though he had to acknowledge he didn't have much to go on right then, except he did appreciate the fact she wasn't walking around accompanying Joyce and fossicking through everything like a nosy magpie.

'How are the boys with the truck – do they need some refreshments?'

'No. Thank you, though. They're my two sons. And decidedly awkward about this, er, situation.'

'They're clearly good lads, if they're putting any negative feelings aside to help their mum's new ... partner.'

'Yes. They have their moments, believe me. Thank goodness they chose today not to have one – either of them,' she added with a withering look. 'And, please, don't worry, Joyce isn't cleaning you out. She knows most of the furniture belonged to your parents. It's just that Beau, my eldest, is in the process of moving himself, so he already had the rented truck.' She shrugged.

Colin responded with a wave of his hand. He couldn't be worrying about what Joyce was taking, or rather, he was telling himself he couldn't. He'd spent the last couple of days privately counselling himself that it was only stuff and that anything could be replaced, if need be, and that he just wanted this to go smoothly. He didn't really love any of the pieces for their aesthetics; was really only attached out of sentimentality and practicality – each piece had its place and had done for decades. He wasn't a fan of change. Nor was Joyce, or so he'd thought. Clearly something had overridden that recently.

He'd come to the agreement with himself that he wouldn't quibble with Joyce and that he would just have to embrace a bit of change and replace any items he really missed once she had departed with them.

Like the coffee maker Carmel had mentioned. He wondered if he would bother looking into it or not. He rather liked the idea of a shiny new object on the countertop as a bit of a monument to the new status he'd been thrust into. But then was going with the same one as his old wife had with her, er, new wife a good idea? It was a strange situation indeed. Though his new machine wouldn't be theirs. And if it did a good job, no doubt he'd quickly release any thoughts of its connection to Carmel. And rejecting the suggestion might be a case of cutting one's nose off to spite one's face – a relatively innocuous case, sure, but a case nonetheless.

It seemed like half the day had passed, though Colin was surprised only an hour had, when checking his watch as he heard footsteps close to the kitchen door.

'Cup of tea?' he asked as Joyce appeared in the doorway, looking up at her with an expression as inviting as he could muster.

'Oh,' she said.

Colin frowned. What did that mean? He detected disappointment in her tone. Or was it surprise at seeing Carmel settled at the table with him. Or something else? Perhaps Joyce was the one having to fight feelings of possessiveness or concerns around loyalty.

But then his gaze went across to where she was looking – at their large floral teapot. And his heart sank. *Oh bugger.* He wished he'd left it hidden away in the cupboard. But then Joyce had a list, according to Carmel. So it was probably on it. Colin knew he should leap up and offer to rinse it out in readiness, and Joyce was probably expecting him to, but he was frozen. He didn't want to draw attention to it by pouring her a mug of tea from it, either, despite them both looking right at it.

The teapot was the last gift that James and Thomas had given them, not long before their deaths. They'd pooled all their pocket money together to buy the extravagant piece of fine bone china for their eighteenth wedding anniversary. Joyce and Colin had been gobsmacked at their thoughtfulness and how perfect the choice they'd made was. Prior, Colin's parents, and in turn he and Joyce, had always used a plain cream enamel one.

Colin didn't know what to do. He didn't want to fight with Joyce but suspected he would over this. No, he was being overly sentimental. Maybe if he showed just how decent he could be she'd come back to him. *And now you're just being delusional, old fellow.* Thankfully, the small voice in his head was kind and gentle this time. Lately it had had a tendency to be mean and spiteful.

'You take it.' They both said the words at the same time.

'Oh. I see,' Carmel said, only then catching up on the situation. She was now turned towards the countertop where the teapot was currently illuminated by a beam of bright sunlight coming in through the window over the sink.

'No,' Joyce said firmly. 'You keep it. Carmel has a beautiful teapot. And you can only use one at a time,' she offered quietly, and a little sadly, to Colin's ear.

He was victorious but felt anything but. Or rather he did but he was more relieved than joyful in securing his win. He almost issued an open invitation for Joyce to come and visit it. But shut his mouth on the words, telling himself that was utterly ridiculous.

'Actually, no, thank you. I won't have tea, Colin. Thank you, though. You're being very decent about things. And I really appreciate you not making it more difficult than it already is, or could be.' She looked at Carmel who immediately leapt up.

'Ready to go?' Camel asked.

'Yes. Thank you.'

Colin got up and the three of them walked out, him trying to not visibly react to the glaring emptiness of the hall where the stand with mirror, hooks and shelves had been, and where the items stowed on it now lay in a pile on the floor. He knew Joyce would have been careful and placed his things down. But they nonetheless appeared tossed into a heap. It irked him more than it should, the untidiness, and the absence of the perfect piece of furniture and receptacle for capturing his end-of-day chattels.

They were outside, standing awkwardly again, clearly each unsure of how one was meant to bid farewell. Colin had no idea. Hugs, handshakes, fist bumps, a wave? He thrust his hands into his pockets.

'Okay, then,' he said, keen to end the stalemate and disappear back into the house to lick his wounds. He suddenly felt the need to be alone to go through the house and assess the loss of not just his wife but their possessions.

'Oh,' Joyce said, digging into her handbag and then handing him her set of house keys. His hand extended and accepted them, seemingly of its own accord.

'Okay. Thanks.' And as he stood there with the keys warming in his hand, gripped so tightly they cut into his flesh, the two lads leapt, as if being chased, into the cab of the small truck with a wave. And then Joyce and Carmel got into the nearby large SUV wagon, also with a wave, though more tentative than the boys'. Colin felt he had no choice but to raise his own hand in response, despite it being exceedingly heavy all of a sudden. Just like his heart.

He went back inside, quietly closed the front door, and leant against it to look at the pile of detritus on the floor, itching to remove the mess but unsure of where to put it.

He wandered back to the kitchen where he poured another mug of tea from the pot he now wasn't sure he wanted. He should have given it to Joyce and got himself something new to mark his fresh start, he thought as he stared out of the window at the hedge with its beginnings of new unruly growth.

Feeling restless, he added sugar and milk to his tea and then took his mug and strolled through the house to see what was missing.

Other than the hallstand, he wasn't too perturbed by what gaps he found in the décor. Joyce had been efficient, he had to give her that. And fair, he thought, as he idly opened her side of the wardrobe and was both relieved and further saddened to find it empty. He moved around to her side of the bed and checked the drawers. She'd been quiet, too. He was glad they'd never replaced his parents' suite of matching furniture; it meant the room appeared relatively untouched.

He turned his gaze to the tallboy, now absent of the mirror that had belonged to Joyce's grandmother. And then he realised what else was missing in the room. And it caused him to fumble for the bed with his hands behind him and sink down onto it. The collection of framed photos of the boys that he dutifully and lovingly lifted, dusted and replaced weekly, and looked at every time he entered or exited the room, were all gone. He sighed deeply. His chest tightened and then his throat caught and tears sprang into his eyes. He swiped them away with his hand and, with considerable effort, got up. Maybe she'd left him the pictures in the lounge.

She hadn't.

He stood staring at the empty place on the sideboard, hating Joyce and then hating himself for hating her. She had every right to the pictures, but he felt an overwhelming urge to throw his mug at the wall, and was instantly horrified at himself. He didn't want to look behind the solid cupboard doors to see if the photo albums were there. He'd leave that for another day, when he was feeling stronger.

Chapter Twenty

Colin strolled the house again, looking for something to put in the hall for his collection of daily items to congregate a little more tidily, and in the dining room decided on one of the high-backed Edwardian style oak chairs. The large hall dwarfed the piece of furniture, but standing back after hanging his jacket and coat on the small protruding knobs and placing the bowl with keys, wallet and phone on the seat, he accepted it would work for now, and at least stop him having to reach right down to the floor to retrieve and deposit his items each day.

Now what? he wondered as he thought of yet another afternoon alone looming ahead of him. Ordinarily he'd happily settle in and read the last of the paper or finish the crossword. But he was too restless. And without Joyce, it just wasn't the same idyllic experience. He'd tried again yesterday.

Dinner. He really needed to start getting into the swing of things regarding nutrition. He couldn't live on baked beans, eggs on toast or vegemite toast indefinitely. The thought of having to plan meals, buy the ingredients and find the time each evening to put everything together did nothing to improve his low mood. Apparently, some people loved to cook – did it for fun. Right then, he'd rather starve. Yet he was also well aware that sustenance was necessary. Particularly now he had no one to take care of him if he became ill.

Would Joyce come back if something happened to me? Don't be silly. But our vows …? Null and void now, he supposed. No suppose about it – definitely. Carmel was now the recipient of any and all attention from Joyce.

A week of flailing about miserably and simply making do was enough. He had to buck up and get used to it all. Starting with learning to cook. Dinner. What to have? How hard was a roast to do? Surely, he would have done one back during those few times he'd been here on his own. And, he suddenly realised, a roast had always been on Sundays – always. And always a family affair. At home with his parents and then Joyce when they'd been married. Today was Sunday.

With cautious determination in his step, he grabbed his wallet, keys and phone up again from the chair and pulled his light jacket on, checking there was a compact grocery bag in each of his pockets before leaving the house and pulling the door closed. Yes, a walk would do him good. As would the fresh air, he thought, and with a burst of determination he set off.

Outside he deliberated taking the car but didn't think he had the patience to deal with finding a park. Sundays at the shopping centre were usually busy. It was why he and Joyce tended to stay in. Joyce was always organised for a week ahead with a meal plan and ingredients. He wished he'd taken better notice of how she'd done things, and shame rumbled through him as he did. He forced it aside and set off.

Hopefully a walk and the sunshine might see him get a better night's sleep. He wondered when he'd get used to that aspect of Joyce's absence too. And return to sleeping soundly for a decent chunk of the night instead of the current habitual tossing and turning. Though it didn't help that his brain seemed to churn more than it ever had before. He trudged on.

Turning the last corner and seeing the enormous carpark full and the looming structure of the shopping centre made him feel pleased he'd walked, but also pause to steel himself wearily for the onslaught of bustling people pushing and shoving.

Inside the store he picked up a plastic basket, reminding himself not to gather too much because he was walking and already beginning to flag and question his wisdom in coming on foot. He looked around at the fresh fruit and vegetables, realising he hadn't adequately thought this through at all. He should be preparing for the whole week ahead to make his life easier. Should have made a list. Should have brought the car. Joyce always sat down and made a list on Monday mornings over breakfast. Oh dear. He'd gone about this all wrong. Should he get a trolley load and then catch a taxi home? He rubbed his head and looked around, trying to make a decision while looking less incompetent to all those moving swiftly around him.

'Oof,' he grunted in response to being shunted aside by someone pushing past. He moved out of the way, frowning to himself at the curt *tsk* he'd received from the young woman and then her child in duplicate being dragged behind her by the hand. Boy or girl he couldn't tell, not that it mattered. Suddenly he was being jostled from the other direction. He was like the ball in a pinball machine being shunted this way and that. He looked up, ready to apologise, but the person's back was to him. People raced past, here and there, reaching to his left and right, frowning, muttering, hissing their disapproval of him, he presumed, as they went. He was beginning to feel very stressed, so much so he was becoming damp and sweaty. He needed to get out of the way but was too scared to move. Everyone was too close, swarming around him. Beads of sweat must be on his forehead because up there was a bit chilly, thanks no doubt to the wafting of the people racing past dragging the air-conditioned air in their wake.

Come on, old man, pull yourself together.

Seeing a gap between streams of people, he carefully shuffled over to the corner, out of the way. He took several deep breaths and then pulled his folded handkerchief from his pocket and dried his face. *Ah, that's better. Right, now, one thing at a time. Small steps, that's what you're always telling your clients. Focus. Dinner. We're just dealing with tonight for now. We'll bring the car tomorrow and do a proper shop. So, a roast. Which variety?* Joyce always had an order: chicken, beef or lamb – depending on the price – and pork. And then he accepted it didn't matter where they were in the scheme of things. He had a choice. What did he feel like? He searched his faculties, asked his stomach. Chicken. Ooh, yes. But would that require preparation beyond his capabilities? To be fair, all and every species and method of cooking was, but even he knew that a whole chicken required more preparation than a lump of pork, lamb or beef. Did they come with all the organs still inside, or not?

Ooh. Yum. He lifted his nose as someone raced past leaving the scent of cooked BBQ chicken in their wake. Ah, yes, good idea. He headed towards the deli section, suddenly surer of himself.

'Even better,' he murmured, waiting at the counter to be served where displayed in front of him was a fine selection of already cooked roast vegetables. His mouth began to water.

He opted for a full BBQ chicken, rather than a half or a quarter, in order to have sandwiches tomorrow. He congratulated himself for his forethought as he made his way to the checkout with a lighter step. On his way he passed a lot of items that vied for his attention. Some he put his hand out to collect on his way past, feeling much better about things, but then reminded himself of his walk back and the decision he'd already made to return the following day.

Back at home, exhausted and his clothes soggy, Colin checked the time. It was four-thirty pm. He considered the meal now sitting on the bench and decided he may as well eat it while it was fresh. It had cost him plenty; he ought to eat it at its best.

He tipped everything onto a plate. As he began eating, he thought about how he really had to learn to cook. He could now see Joyce's point about the significant price tag attached to convenience. He'd also really better start figuring out the finances. He hated the idea that it all had to be divided into two and banished the thought that he'd have to sell the house as soon as it trundled into his mind – couldn't even contemplate that yet. He'd have to keep working. He probably needed to get some professional advice, but the thought of which industry or what exact job title was involved caused his brain to seize. He hoped he and Joyce could figure it out together and wouldn't need to go the legal route. Though, with someone else on the sidelines, well, on the pitch, in the form of Carmel – as nice as she'd seemed – there was a chance Joyce would be influenced.

He hated to think ill of his Joyce – no longer his – whose very being had once exuded fairness and common sense. But that was the old Joyce, during the well-established life they'd enjoyed together. He didn't know what this one was about at all. Terrible of him to think, but he really hoped Carmel was rich. Not that it made a difference to what Joyce was owed. Oh well, he'd bury his head in the sand about it for a bit longer and enjoy his early dinner.

He rinsed the few dishes and then put the plug in and added detergent. There was no point running the dishwasher. It took a week to sufficiently fill it and he hated the thought of unwashed dishes sitting around for that long in the machine.

As he dried the few things, he wondered if he'd be invited to any more friends' places for a meal, or even receive commiserations. He hadn't received any communication from anyone. He thought about what Shirley Royal had said about people choosing sides. He thought he and Joyce had always consciously had both split parties – or the widowed left behind – on more than one occasion while they'd readjusted to their changed living circumstances, but also couldn't swear to it. They'd also, though not for a long while now, hooked up the trailer and helped plenty of the women move a few things to a new abode.

Lower your expectations, humans are inherently disappointing. People move on, forget things.

He and Joyce never did anything with a view to recompense or quid pro quo. Sadly, he didn't think any of those who'd sought his professional counsel for free over the years during social occasions, or when around for meals etc, would be forthcoming with offers of their own. He could hope, of course. But the last few years they'd seen and regularly commented on how insular everyone tended to be nowadays. God, he missed having her to talk to, to console him, commiserate with, and say, 'Oh well, at least we have each other'.

Oh dear. He really had to pull himself out of this state. Maybe he'd invite some people around himself. He could offer drinks and nibbles. But did he want to put himself under scrutiny and potentially embarrassing questioning? No, best he concern himself with dealing with organising his week of meals and putting together a shopping list – get some sort of culinary routine in place.

Chapter Twenty-one

Colin almost forgot to take the car home from work. He'd only remembered to take it that morning as he'd gathered his things from the chair instead of the hallstand. He was determined to fill the empty cupboards and cook some better meals and stop wasting money.

As he drove to the supermarket, he wondered if Joyce would want the car, but then realised if she had, she'd have taken it when she'd taken everything else yesterday.

Standing behind a large trolley, as much as to provide some protection from other shoppers as an expectation of needing such a large repository, Colin stood beside the red capsicums in the fruit and veg section perusing his list. He'd done his best to group things together on his page and as he now went around collecting his quarry and crossing the items off, he experienced a sense of accomplishment.

But in the next aisle he became stumped and his mood dipped. He'd put all the things that came in glass jars together – gherkins, tomato paste, olive oil, chutney and vegemite. But the supermarket clearly didn't share his way of ordering, he now realised, having got to the end of the aisle without finding everything he'd expected. He'd been hoping to do this efficiently.

'Are you okay – need any help with anything?' He looked up to see a woman with two children of markedly different heights standing quietly beside her trolley.

'Thank you. No. I think I'll be all right. I'm new to this, um, place. Just trying to find my bearings.'

'Oh, well, good luck with that!' she said with a laugh. 'Your first time, you're probably best to go up and down each aisle and figure out where everything is. I've been coming here for years and still I do every aisle in order because it's easier.'

'Right. I see. I've tried to group things logically on my list, but …' He shrugged.

'Yes, only useful when you know the corresponding sections in the shop.'

'Oh dear.'

'Okay. I'd better keep going. All the best.'

'Righto. Cheerio. Thanks so much for stopping.'

After brief deliberation, Colin pushed his trolley forward, resigned to doing a journey up and down each aisle and getting the measure of the place.

It was slow going. But gradually his trolley was filling and the remaining items on his list reducing. And he thought he was even beginning to get an idea of the way things were grouped.

'Hello there again.' Colin recognised the voice and looked up to see the same woman with the two children just up ahead at the fridge containing cheese.

'Hello,' he said.

'How are you doing – finding everything okay?'

'Getting there. Thank you.' Colin returned her beaming smile.

'Don't worry, it does get easier.'

'I'll take your word for that.' He watched as she leant into the back of the fridge and fossicked around before bringing out a container of milk. Just as he was wondering why she hadn't simply taken the one at the front, she answered his unasked question.

'They put the newest at the back. I want my milk to have as much time as possible before expiring, so I get it from the back,' she said.

'Oh. I see. That's a good tip.'

'It's okay, I'm not doing anything dishonest.' She must have mistaken his look of curiosity for condemnation.

'Oh no, I didn't … I was just curious. I'm actually new at the whole grocery shopping thing,' he said, waving an arm around.

'Oh. I see.' The look of sympathy etched in her slight pout suggested she thought him a widower. He was about to correct her but didn't want a further dose of pity. 'They do it with all the stock – put the oldest to the front, that is, unless the shelving person is badly trained, or lazy, or both,' she said with a slightly nervous laugh, he thought.

'That's very useful to know. Thank you so much.'

'My pleasure. Okay. Well, again, all the best. See you again. Most likely. This place feels like my second home, I'm here so much. Not to mention spending the cost of a second mortgage each week. Honestly, I tell you!' She rolled her eyes, shook her head, and then gave her trolley a shove forward. He smiled at the kids as they mimicked their mother.

'Yes. I know what you mean.' Colin didn't think he did, quite, but suspected he was about to. He'd better steel himself for a large total at the checkout. 'See you.'

He finished his lap of the store, checked his list again and headed to the checkout. Thankfully he managed to line up behind the same woman and kids.

'Hi there, um, again,' she said, turning and seeing him as she unloaded her groceries.

'Yes, quite. I promise, I'm not, er, following you.'

'It's okay. I know.' The woman looked into Colin's trolley. 'Another tip I use is to put everything on the conveyer belt in the order you want it packed in. Like cans and bottles first, cold things all together, veg together – the heavier and less fragile items first, like onions and potatoes, so they go in the bottom of the bags. Eggs and the bread always last, so they don't get squashed. It takes some trial and error, but you'll get there.'

'Good thinking. Thanks.' She placed the plastic divider on the belt and he set about unloading his trolley in a logical manner behind it. As he did, he wondered at how he'd got to this age without having learnt the ins and outs of such a big part of everyday life. Though, to be fair, he had been into supermarkets quite a few times, but only to get the odd few items – less than sixteen – and with strict instructions and directions of where they were to be found. During the last few years with smartphones, Joyce had sent him pictures of each thing to make it even easier. He could see now first-hand the downfall of having such an accommodating wife – enabling his woeful ineptitude in the area of domesticity, vacuuming and cleaning notwithstanding.

The same woman waved to him as she loaded her kids and groceries into a large SUV as he pushed his unruly trolley load of bagged groceries towards his car, which turned out to be just a few places along from her. Colin waved back. He felt tired from the mental and physical effort required but a little lighter due to the friendly interaction.

As he got into the car, he for a moment imagined going home and telling Joyce all about his escapade and then laughing together about it. And then his heart sank at the reminder that she was no longer there to share his day with – any part of it. Good or bad. God, he missed her and wished he could be angry at her instead. He experienced a stab of envy towards her at not having to go through all this readjustment. No doubt she was slipping into a comfortable life where they took turns at all this. Maybe Joyce was having to get used to a new supermarket too. Wherever she was. Most likely Carmel was showing her around.

He wondered if he should know where she was – her actual address. No, he thought sadly. There was nothing he needed to send her. If there was any need to advise her of anything, they could email, text or phone. Many separating couples had children – adult or otherwise – to inform the other about. But not them.

He sighed loudly to himself. Well, at least for the next little bit he would be occupied with getting home, unloading the groceries into the house and then the cupboard and fridge and then cooking dinner. Where Joyce had got the energy to do all this week in week out while working was beyond him, he thought, carefully backing out of his park. Hopefully the fact he'd done a big shop was the key, though he felt the stash in the boot didn't equate to the amount having been extracted from his bank account.

Tonight was chops in the pan and veg in the microwave. He thought he could manage that all right – he'd observed Joyce doing it plenty of times. And chops were more forgiving than steak. It wouldn't matter if he overcooked them a little. And, unlike chicken or pork, it wouldn't matter if they were a bit underdone, either. Again, he congratulated himself on his achievement.

After emptying the bags into the kitchen, he looked over at all the cookbooks. He couldn't remember when he'd last seen Joyce with one open, so wasn't surprised they were all still there. He probably should consult them, but which one? A conversation he'd had with Joyce long ago came to him. 'Baking is where you need to be precise – treat it with scientific precision – other cooking, meals and the like, are about love and experimentation, winging it,' she'd said. They'd been sitting here in this kitchen. It was the early days of their marriage. His parents were in the lounge room or their bedroom, keeping out of the way. And he was showing an interest, asking questions and offering to help. She'd batted him away, saying she was fine. It was her happy place. He reckoned he'd stopped enquiring soon afterwards.

Again, shame and regret gathered within him. She'd never ceased asking about his day, or encouraging him to debrief. He'd also stopped asking about her day in the boutique. He'd tried early on but it didn't interest him. He'd liked to think it was her genuine interest in his work that fuelled their conversations. But he now saw his experience should have been enough for him to continue to return the favour. Of all people, he was meant to know the importance of human connectivity and keeping the intimacy alive. He'd failed Joyce. He'd failed them.

Chapter Twenty-two

Colin had texted and tried calling several of his and Joyce's friends during the past few days to meet up for a drink or a meal out at some point but been met with a series of declines or unanswered and unreturned calls. He'd tried not to let it deject him – people were busy – but invariably Shirley Royal's vehement utterances from her last session came back to him. He now completely empathised with her frustration.

Thus, after a week of homemade yet disappointing meals and continued unease with his homelife, this time it took all this strength to not greet the smiling face and friendly presence of the woman in question with a hug. Instead, he kept his hands in his pockets, said hello, and stood back to admit her to his office before closing the door.

'So, what brings you in today?' he said, when Shirley had settled herself into a chair.

'You, actually. Duh, as the kids would say. That's stating the obvious, given whose office I'm in,' she said and shot him a withering look. 'I mean, I'm here for *you*. I can talk about all manner of things and vent, rant and rave, or just gabble away until the cows come home – it is, after all, my dollar we're on. But ...' She clasped her hands tightly in her lap and sat forward in the chair a little, appearing to regard him more seriously. 'It struck me from our last session and conversation that you're going through quite a bit yourself. And, well, this might be completely out of order, but, well, um, Colin, who do you have to talk to? I mean, I've been wondering if you have your own outlet. And it also seemed as if you really knew, from a personal perspective rather than simply a professional empathy that is, about loneliness and significant loss. You also said your wife had recently left you, which is also a big adjustment, so ...'

Oh. Er. Colin blinked as he processed her words and tried to figure out how to react respectfully.

'Oh, I'm being a silly old fool. Of course. You'd have plenty of colleagues. I'm overstepping yet again, and wickedly so this time, aren't I?'

Colin opened his mouth.

Shirley was now blushing and patting her cheeks with her hands. 'Oh dear. I know it's completely inappropriate. It's just that I've learnt not to assume anything. And, well, it's just what you said the other time, or rather *how*.' She shrugged. 'Anyway, forget I said anything. I'll think of something more appropriate to discuss in our time. Just give me a moment.'

'You're quite right, actually, and I really appreciate your kindness in asking,' Colin said. 'Um.'

Shirley looked up at him. He shifted in his chair, examined his hands in his lap. Oh, how he longed to confide in Shirley, to ease his loneliness. Share with *someone*, not keep all this stuff bottled up.

'As I said the last time, Shirley, you're very insightful. You should *be* a therapist, not paying me!'

'We discussed that before – we all need someone to talk to, no matter our age or circumstances.'

They smiled warmly at each other across the desk.

'So, I'm all ears,' she said. 'Unless it really is too untoward or awkward.'

'No. It's not, actually.' Well, it really was, but at that moment Colin didn't care. 'You're very disarming,' he said with a slight laugh, some tension sliding from him. 'And you're right. I think all our friends have abandoned me.'

'Ah. I see. It's par for the course, I'm afraid.'

'I'm not sure if they have chosen Joyce, my wife – my estranged wife – or if they simply think I wouldn't need anyone on account of my profession. Though in some ways, it's probably best – I can do without the humiliation of discussing my situation.'

'Hmm. I understand that, but you can't go cutting your nose off to spite your face. Have you reached out?'

'Yes. And they were all busy with various things. But they were lying, some of them – you know, you can tell. No one committed to getting in touch at a later date or even fobbed me off with proposing something miles out into the future.'

'Oh, yes, a sure sign. That's no different as a widow. People are so predictable.'

'And disappointing,' Colin said.

'Yes, they are. If only they would actually admit to things – their failings – say, "Look, I wouldn't know what to say or the right thing to say". And I'd be, "well, you wouldn't have to say anything – let's go see a movie, sit in silence, listen to music, go see a play, watch TV together … It's the companionship that really matters". Honestly, if a friend said to me "can you come over so I can cry on your shoulder and have you hug me", I'd be fine with that.'

'Exactly.'

'It's that other thing humans are so crap at …'

'What's that?'

'I don't know what you call it, but people seem to think they have to provide answers, solve problems, and if they can't they avoid you entirely.'

'Unwillingness to show their vulnerability, admit to a fault?'

'Yes. And yet it's such a valuable human tonic to help and sometimes — often — to help is just to listen. As I've said before, humans, what a bloody mess. No idea. The things you must see and hear, Colin, I shudder to think.'

'Oh yes. It's a lot.'

They both laughed.

'But seriously, I need to face the reality that Joyce isn't coming back. I've been holding onto hope.'

'Ah, that old chestnut. It's difficult to do when they're dead. Not that I'm suggesting …'

'No. I didn't think you were. And, please, don't diminish what you're going through on my account. I should be happy for her for finding someone else. Quite possibly she's finally living her truth. She's met a woman and fallen in love, apparently.'

'Oh. That *is* a rather bitter pill to swallow.'

'Hmm. I keep wondering to myself if I'd feel any different if she'd run off with another man.'

'And …?'

'I've no idea. I can't seem to come up with an answer.'

'Possibly you're telling yourself it *should* make a difference?'

'Probably.'

'And, you know, we're kind of conditioned to the notion of "if you love them set them free", and I think wanting the best for them falls under that category.'

'Yes. You're right.'

'But you're allowed to also be sad and angry and everything else in between. It's still a betrayal of your wedding vows. I assume, given our similar ages, you had till death do us part in there, too?'

'Oh yes. I need to stop wallowing and embrace bachelorhood. Because she's really not coming back. She came and got some pieces of furniture a week ago, with her new partner, which you'd think would have sealed it for me.'

'And …?'

'She seemed a nice enough woman, too, as far as I could tell. Carmel is her name. She was decently apologetic. And Joyce was so full of life.'

'Which made you feel disappointed in yourself, right, for apparently failing to be the source of the twinkle in her eye?'

'Yes. See, you're very good at this.'

'So, are you now sitting on the floor?'

'What do you mean?'

'You said Joyce and Carmel came to get furniture. I hope you haven't been left with an empty house. I had a friend who got divorced, who said that was one of the worst things – the gaps in the décor, complete with squashed bits of carpet as a stark and permanent reminder of the loss. Filling the first gap with something she loved – just an op shop find, because she didn't have much money – was the thing that saw her turn the corner on getting her life back together. And a new haircut. But that's more a woman thing to do, I think.'

'Oh, I don't know–' Colin patted his short grey hair. 'I could shave it all off and start again. Or grow it long, maybe.'

Shirley laughed. 'I think there are other ways to make a statement or show of getting on with things.'

'Such as?'

'Ooh. Um. Let me think. Well, you could throw a party. I'd bet your friends who've ditched you would come back for that – if only out of curiosity and free booze, if that's what you're after.'

'I'm not sure I want to spend the funds on the possibly disloyal.'

'No, good point. Dinner party for a select few? You could rustle some up, right?'

'Unfortunately, and this I'm mortified to admit, but I can't cook. Joyce did it all. We were a bit old-fashioned, in most regards, in our relationship.'

'Or completely normal for our era. Don't be too hard on yourself.'

'Thanks.'

'My Norman and I were the same. I hope your Joyce didn't resent it as much as I did. Whoops. I shouldn't have said that.'

'Well, I'd hope she'd have said something if she was unhappy. But she really blindsided me with declaring herself a closet lesbian. So, what would I know?'

'Quite.' Shirley giggled. 'Yes, you're really out of the loop. I really shouldn't laugh. It's highly inappropriate of me.'

'Well, it is a rather ludicrous situation I find myself in. I hope one day I can laugh about it.'

'Unlikely. But if you can find it in yourself, I hope it's with Joyce and her new lady friend – partner …'

'Hmm.'

'… Because there's no reason why – once the dust settles and the pain eases – you can't be on good terms. Though that depends on the finances and your attachment to them, I suppose. That always has the capacity to bring people undone. Also, the kids, though that's only when they're still young, really. Do you have children or grandchildren?'

'Yes. Well, no. We had twins. They would have been forty-five this year. But they died in 1995, aged fifteen.'

'Oh no. I'm so sorry to hear that. What are their names?'

'James and Thomas. And thank you for asking.'

'James and Thomas,' Shirley repeated. 'Tell me about them. But only if you want to.'

'Oh. Well, they were great lads. Sensible, on the whole. They had such a special bond, being identical twins. Their attachment was something Joyce and I never truly understood. In some ways it was best they went together. I'm not sure we could have borne the type of grief that sort of separation would have entailed on top of our own.'

'I can only imagine,' Shirley said quietly.

'We didn't want them getting into cars with such inexperienced drivers, but you can't curtail their freedom. They were all so keen to experience new things, escape their old-fogey parents. You have to let them go sometime. So, despite our misgivings, we didn't argue. Every generation goes through it. It didn't help having two kids badgering us at once, nor that they could outthink and outwit us with their twin telepathy,' Colin said with a sigh. 'James was quick on his feet with answers and arguments. He was very logically minded. Unsurprisingly, he was on the debating team. We always thought he'd end up being a really good lawyer. Thomas was more a follower and driven by his heart. Sadly, I'm not sure Thomas was as keen on going to that party as his brother, being the more introverted of the two, but socially they rarely did anything separately. I like to think Thomas might have followed in my footsteps, but it wasn't to be,' he added wistfully.

'Anyway, it's a great comfort to know they went off happily after a hug from both myself and Joyce, and that they didn't engage in drug-taking or underage drinking. Unfortunately, the driver did. He wasn't sloshed, but it was out in the hills where the winding roads combined with speed and overconfidence turned lethal. Nothing more than a tragic accident that changed the lives of far too many families,' he added. *I'm not sure if I'd survive it now, without Joyce by my side*, he thought sadly. 'But we got through it and we're okay,' he added, forcibly dragging himself out of his memories and offering Shirley a smile.

'Ah, the young. They all too often think they're invincible, with their licences in hand and so unaware of the importance of experience and concentration. That's a tough situation. Again, I'm so sorry you went through that and continue to deal with it every day. I don't think anything could compare to that loss.

'I don't know it first-hand but a dear friend went through it. She always said the two hardest things were not speaking her daughter Bonny's name, and friends not sharing their own kids' milestones with her and not realising – selling my friend short – that just because she'd lost her child didn't mean she wasn't happy for her friends and didn't want to hear about their lives. Though, as you've said before, everyone's journey of grief is individual. Maybe another family dealing with the same type of loss might prefer that approach.'

'But then they'd only have to ask your preference.'

'Precisely. People, I tell you,' Shirley added, shaking her head and sighing.

'Exactly. Completely hopeless, as a species. The unnecessary pain we inflict on one another, intentionally or without realising, is astounding.'

'I have to confess; I love the wider animal kingdom for their lack of emotional harm.'

'Except cats,' Colin said. 'They torment mice, just for fun, apparently.'

'Oh yes. You're right. I do love cats, though. Do you have any pets?'

'No. Joyce never liked the idea of them, especially when we were older and planning to become grey nomads. Do you?'

'Yes and no. I foster cats and kittens through a rescue organisation. Best of both worlds – the companionship and snuggles, without the permanent tie.'

'But isn't it hard to say goodbye to them when they leave?'

'Oh yes. But I just tell myself I've done my bit to get them off to bigger and brighter things and I'm making room to get the next lot going. Also, they're each so different in personality, it's quite fun to see who comes along next. The big thing for me is avoiding the need to make the decision to have anyone put to sleep. I've been through it several times. Never again. That's probably the hardest thing I've ever done. Losing Norman has been a doddle compared to looking into the eyes of my darling eighteen-year-old moggie, Pete, trying to work out when he needed to go. I don't think I ever recovered from that.'

'Do you have kids and grandkids?' Colin asked, feeling the need to steer the conversation away into less emotional waters.

'Oh, yes. Two sons. But one is overseas and one lives interstate. Both are a little cold and aloof, like their father, and prone to only getting in touch when they want something or it suits them. I'm afraid we're not what you'd consider one of those close-knit, in each other's business, type of families. I love them, of course I do, but I don't always like them, if you know what I mean?'

'I do.'

'I struggle with people who think the sun shines out of their little darlings – kids and grandkids alike. As you can tell, I'm not a huge fan of humans, full stop. If I'd been born in a different era, when I felt I had a choice, it's likely I wouldn't have had any children.'

'Fair enough.'

'I probably sound like a terribly ungrateful old bag – particularly given your circumstances.'

'Not at all. I like your candour. It's refreshing.'

'Look, enough doom and gloom,' Shirley said, slapping her thighs with her hands. 'You asked for ideas for getting on with things? Or did I imagine that?'

'No, that's right.'

'How about line dancing? I do it sometimes for exercise and to be around people in a purely platonic sense. There's no touching. It's that thing that American people do in lines. Boot scooting. I've been told it's only the lower-class folk that do it, but I don't care. I enjoy it, particularly as there's no hand-holding so no threat of, you know … romance. I'm going tonight, actually. You're welcome to come along for something to do. To kill a couple of hours. I don't think it would be breaching any code of ethics, would it?'

'I don't think so, no. Um …'

'Look, you don't need to answer right now. Think about it. I don't want you to feel put on the spot. I'm going regardless. I can pick you up or meet you there. Here, I'll write down the details.' She leant forward and held out her hand towards the block of sticky notes just out of reach.

Colin pushed the item and a pen towards her and then watched while she wrote, thinking how lucky he was that she'd turned up when she had. What an incredibly special woman.

'There you go. I've put my number down. Feel free to text with your address, if you want to be picked up – or even to coordinate meeting outside the venue. I know how confronting turning up at new places alone can be when you're not used to it.'

'Okay. Thanks. I'll think about it.'

'Please don't feel obligated in any way. No skin off my nose. Well, I'd better go. We've gone overtime.'

Shirley began fossicking in her handbag and Colin realised what she was doing. 'You're absolutely not paying for today,' he said.

'If you're sure? I don't want to muck up your accounting.'

'Don't worry about that. Thank you so much for your company.'

'It's been my pleasure.'

They stood and both seemed to not quite know how to proceed, given their professional relationship had taken a slight detour. And then Colin was being embraced by Shirley for a quick hug.

'Oh,' he said.

'Yes, I'm *royally* overstepping this time,' Shirley said with a laugh and a wink. 'But I just felt the need to do that. Bye,' she added, beaming, and then strode to the door before he could move, opened it, waved and exited with another wave before pulling the door closed carefully behind her with a clunk.

Chapter Twenty-three

Colin was pleased to find the dance venue where he was meeting Shirley to try out boot scooting, was not far away from his home and could be accessed easily by bus – just six stops up the main road he lived a few houses away from.

As he rode the bus – a little too early, thanks to his lack of faith in Adelaide public transport and unwillingness to be either right on time or a little late, such were the other times available – he was also glad he'd made his own way and not accepted Shirley's offer of a ride. He'd thought that suggestion a little odd, considering she didn't know where he lived. Or perhaps, if he'd gone down that path, she'd have revealed she meant collecting him from his work premises. He felt he really should have been offering to collect Shirley, but he didn't want to give the impression he was more invested in things than he was. Anyway, despite being around his age, for all he knew Shirley was fiercely independent and would object to such old-fashioned manners, which he'd heard equated to male chauvinism.

Once online he'd stumbled upon a robust discussion – he couldn't remember where now – about women being cranky at men opening doors. It mystified Colin. When had showing basic manners become equal to putting women down? Oh well, it wasn't something he would be discussing with Shirley tonight. He suspected she might be one who would eschew a man's assistance on all fronts, and none too politely at that. He smiled to himself. He liked her – particularly for her forthrightness. He'd happily take being told off by her for doing something than any quiet seething or expectation of minds being read.

All a mystery, he thought as he pressed the button to signal he required the next stop and checked he had everything – a full water bottle and small hand towel, per Shirley's earlier instructions.

'Thank you,' he called to the driver and raised his hand to wave as the doors opened and he stepped out, propelled by a jolt of nervous excitement and apprehension.

As the bus drove off, he was suddenly unsure if he needed to go left or right for the short walk to the venue. He took a deep breath and then closed his eyes in order to concentrate. At least he knew he didn't have to cross to the other side of the road. He had to remember to do that to go home afterwards, so needed to keep his wits about him else end up wherever the bus did. And then it came to him – it was closer to the city. *No rush*, he told himself. He had ten minutes up his sleeve.

A couple of minutes later he stood outside a nondescript rendered building, which thankfully announced itself as being the right place by way of a poster advertising the boot scooting sessions. People streamed out around him – a heap of kids in leotards, with parents trailing along behind. Then a group of people in cowboy hats and suede leather jackets with fringes, with ornate calf-length boots on their feet, headed on in.

Colin began to feel self-conscious in his plain jeans and striped, long-sleeve button-up shirt. He distracted himself with perusing the other posters behind the glass on the display board. Apparently, it was a dance studio offering all manner of dances – Samba, Waltz ... He was surprised to see what was available. He'd have thought those styles long out of vogue. *Well, there you go*, he was thinking, when he heard a familiar, slightly raised female voice nearby.

'Yoohoo! Colin.' He turned towards it, already grinning in response to the cheerfulness in Shirley's tone.

'You came!'

'I said I would.' Colin thought it said something about the people that Shirley mixed with, or perhaps just society in general, that she sounded so surprised to find him a man of his word. What was the world coming to?

'You found it okay?'

'I did.'

She chuckled. 'I know, silly question. Because here you are! And right on time.'

'No, not so silly. I could have spent hours being lost and only just arrived.'

'That's true. But then I'd expect you to appear harried,' she said, peering at him quizzically. 'And you're not. You look very dapper and calm.'

'Why thank you, ma'am. As do you.'

'So, no thoughts to cancel or regrets for agreeing to do this?' she said, surprising him with a quick hug.

Oomph. The sound escaped. 'No. Not at all. Though I'm a little nervous on account of not knowing exactly what to expect.'

'Don't you worry. I'll take good care of you.'

'I'm depending on it. I have to say, I'm so glad you're not in costume, Shirley. A group of people in cowboy and cowgirl clothing went in before, leaving me concerned about my attire. Not that I own anything remotely suitable in that realm.'

'Each to their own. They must be die-hard boot scooters, or just keen to dress up, since it's a beginners' class. I'm just here for the exercise and companionship. I'm not a big one for dressing up. Oh, except for theme parties. I quite like those, but haven't been to one in aeons. No one seems to be bothered these days.'

'No. There is a lot of thought to go into gathering the pieces and putting a costume together.' Colin thought about some of the rippers he and Joyce had done – bookends, playing cards, farmer and scarecrow and salt and pepper shakers … They'd had great fun over the years, but not done anything like that for ages. He couldn't imagine putting something together without Joyce in charge. And it wouldn't be the same anyway …

'Hmm. Maybe I'll do something like that for my eightieth in a few years. Ooh. Yes.'

'Good for you,' Colin said.

'And you. Because you'll be there. I've decided we're going to be firm friends.'

'Have you?' Colin said with a laugh.

'Yes. I hope you don't mind.'

'Not at all. I'm honoured. I appreciate you taking me under your wing. This old lame duck.'

'Two old lame ducks together. But I'm a bit bossy. So do feel free to put me in my place should the need arise. I'm all for clear and concise and frank communication.'

'Okay. Noted.'

'Shall we?' Shirley indicated the heavy glass door.

'Yep.'

'Right. Follow my lead.'

Colin was surprised to find his hand being clasped and him led by Shirley up the three steps into the building, through a small vestibule and out into a large hall with a timber floor and a stage up the front. The group of costumed people that he recognised from just before, turned around and then rushed over to greet them effusively and introduce themselves.

Colin nodded along to the introductions but at the conclusion could only recall two other names, Rob and Bob – the two who seemed to be running the show.

They all paid with their cards and then they were told that they would be taught the individual steps, then a simple sequence – all without the music, or rather turned down low – to get the hang of things first.

'Let's stay up the back,' Shirley said, leading the way as the group assembled into lines. 'So I don't feel too self-conscious when I muck up the steps.' He appreciated her generosity in referring only to herself. 'And feel free to stop at any point. It can be surprising how much energy it takes – the steps and the concentration.'

'Right.'

It did indeed prove exhausting, and Colin was very glad of the water and small towel he'd brought, which he needed several times to wipe sweat from his brow, under his eyes and from his top lip. The music was accompanied by lots of shouting from Rob calling instructions and regular cries of 'yeeha'. Sometimes hats were raised in unison and gradually Colin got into the swing of things sufficiently to be raising his hand at the appropriate moment.

He couldn't believe so much time had passed when the music was stopped, signalling the end of class, despite knowing they'd already broken for a half-time break for a drink. There was no hanging about. The music machine was unplugged and the cord wrapped around it, and the room began to empty again.

Outside, Colin was pleased for the cool breeze on his skin and the chance to properly catch his breath. He thought they'd be sitting around chatting while they cooled down, but instead had been all but herded out like cattle, which was quite an appropriate analogy, Colin thought as Rob and Bob stood on either side of the door, laden with boxes of stuff ushering everyone out ahead of them and saying 'goodbye, come again', as people filed past.

Shirley and Colin moved away and left the few small groups congregated nearby chatting.

'Wow,' he said, feeling the need to say something after they both paused from taking sips from their water bottles.

'What did you think?'

'Rather fun, thank you.'

'My pleasure. See what I mean about a good workout where you can do as much or as little as you want; same with interacting, or not, with other participants?'

'Yes. They seemed a friendly bunch of people,' Colin said, quietly, so as not to be overheard.

'I agree, it was a great group. It's always Rob and Bob leading things, but sometimes you know people from other sessions – from ages ago or more recently. People come and go. Some come alone while visiting from elsewhere. There's a whole massive community connected online. For instance, you could probably organise to do a class in any major town or city around Australia. Or the world, for that matter.'

'Hmm. Very interesting. I do like that you wouldn't feel too out of place coming alone. Those four stragglers that came in after us I think were each on their own.'

'Yes. I think so too. Right,' Shirley said decisively a few moments later, pushing the top of her water bottle closed rather forcefully, Colin thought.

'I hope you don't mind if I head off, rather than going for a drink or anything. I'm a bit bushed.'

'Oh, no. I mean, yes. No problem at all. I'm a bit the same way. I might seize up at any moment, so I'd better get on home before that happens.'

'Great. I mean, not that you might seize up,' she added with a laugh. 'I'm sure a long hot shower will help. Can I give you a lift? Or did you drive?'

'Neither. Thank you very much for the offer, but I caught the bus. I've just a few stops to go to get home. And there'll be one along shortly.' He checked his watch. 'Actually, I'd better be off. I've got to get across the road.'

'Okay, then. As long as you wouldn't rather a lift?'

'No, I'm perfectly fine. The short strolls will do me good.'

'Yes, well, I hope you haven't given your system too much of a shock. The different muscles and all.'

'I'm sure I'll recover. Okay then …' At that moment Shirley gripped him by the shoulders and hugged him quickly. 'Thank you for coming and keeping me company.'

'The pleasure was all mine, I can assure you. Thank you for the invitation.'

'I'll be in touch,' Shirley said. 'Maybe we'll do this again. Maybe try something else. How about lunch or brunch on the weekend? I'll give you a chance to catch your breath and think about it, though.'

'Sounds good.'

'Cheerio then.'

'Bye, Shirley. Thanks again. Take care.'

'You too.' And then Shirley was striding off down the street, her hand raised in a final wave.

Colin smiled as he checked the road each way for traffic and then crossed as quickly as he could.

On the bus, he was so caught up in his thoughts going over the evening that he almost missed pressing the button to get off at the right stop. Everything looked so different at night compared to daytime. It didn't help that the bus was brightly lit, causing the windows to act as mirrors and the outside environs tricky to see in detail. Thankfully someone else had been on the ball and needed the same stop. It was only at the last moment he recognised where he was and hurried off, calling out 'thank you' as the doors were closing after he'd left the bus.

He put his key in the door and almost forgot himself and called out a cheerful, 'Hello, it's only me,' as he entered the lit hallway, such was his ebullient mood. It was with a surge of disappointment that he remembered the light was only on because he'd left it on.

He threw his jacket onto the back of the chair and emptied his pockets into the bowl, his buoyant spirits leaving him also, a bit like a retreating tide, he thought. Oh well, at least he'd put himself out there and done something different. And it had been fun. And he was weary, so he might actually sleep well for a change.

Chapter Twenty-four

After another week of disappointing fare, created by his own hand, Colin was looking forward to the food side of brunch with Shirley rather more than he ordinarily would have been. He'd put a list together, based on Joyce's creations he'd always enjoyed, and done another grocery run, but was left lamenting his lack of skill and the fact meals just weren't the same when cooked by oneself, to the extent several times he'd pondered the practicalities of searching for a live-in housekeeper. Joyce would be both cheered and horrified, he thought. The fact was, life was much harder alone, particularly coming on the back of a sizeable chunk of one's lifetime being under the care and stewardship of his wife, and, more shameful still, his mother before her. Dorothy Palmer had been equally capable and efficient.

Oh dear. He really had better not invite Shirley too far into his life, lest he inadvertently take similar advantage of her. Though he suspected Shirley would not allow it. Meanwhile, she was very good company and a sound listener with a sensitive and sensible approach.

Standing just inside the door of the cafe he looked around for her while allowing his eyes to adjust to the relative darkness after the bright morning sun he'd just stepped out of. He raised his hand, nodded, smiled and made his way to where her hand was raised in the air signalling her location in the back corner.

'Hello there,' he said, bending to kiss her on the cheek. It was only as he stood back up and grabbed the back of the chair to pull it out that he fully took in what he'd done, as if it were the most natural and expected thing in the world. He blushed a little and cleared his throat quietly. Thankfully Shirley didn't seem to have noticed anything untoward. 'How are you today?' he said.

'Good morning. I'm very well, thank you,' Shirley said, beaming at him. 'How's your weekend been so far?'

He slumped heavily onto the wooden chair and met her gaze. Her eyebrows rose a little higher.

'Honestly? A bit frustrating,' he said.

'Oh? Before we get into that, let's order, I'm a bit beyond peckish.'

'Ooh, that looks good,' Colin said, noticing two plates being carried by containing what looked to be the full breakfast of poached eggs, bacon, toast and several accompaniments.

'Yes. At the risk of being considered a glutton, that's what I've decided on. Life's too short. Long ago I decided there were worse things to be than a little on the heavy side.'

Colin nodded.

Colin was just about to say the meal was his treat, as thanks to Shirley for rescuing him from himself, which he would leave out, when she said, 'I'm ready to order. Is going Dutch – paying for our own, that is – okay with you?'

'Oh. But I was going to offer to …'

'Please, let's not fight over it.'

'Right you are. Dutch is fine with me.'

'Great. Come on, it's up at the counter for ordering. I'll leave my jacket on the chair so we don't lose our table.'

'Good idea.' Colin had almost forgotten he was yet to shed his own outer layer, which he did now, and hung over the back of the chair.

'I hope you didn't think I was too brusque about paying,' Shirley said, as they waited side by side to be served behind several other patrons.

'Oh, you weren't. And it's nice to know where one stands. Though I will say that it does rather go against my usual modus operandi and is therefore a little unsettling. Also, I did want to repay you for getting me out.'

'So, this way we're even,' Shirley said, quite forcefully.

He went after Shirley with his ordering of the same thing – full breakfast with poached eggs and a latte. He wanted to express how much he liked to see a woman with a healthy appetite, but thought better of it. That one was definitely fraught with the possibility of being misconstrued.

'You did well securing us a table, by the looks,' Colin said, when they'd resettled in their chairs, having to lean in to be heard without shouting. The place had really filled up and was quite loud with the dragging of chair feet on the wooden floor, the hum of voices and the scrape and clatter of cutlery.

'Yes. It might be a little loud, though. But it was the only place I could think of. And their food is good. I don't eat out much these days.'

'Me neither. Well, cheers,' Colin said, raising his water glass, 'to brunch out and good company.'

'Indeed. Cheers.' They clinked their solid glasses, before each took a sip.

'So, you were going to tell me something. Starting with honestly … Remember?' Shirley said. At that moment their lattes were delivered, so Colin waited to thank their server before continuing.

'It's not a big thing, perhaps to you, because I can't imagine an area that you would be inept in …'

'I doubt that's the case. Flattery, flattery. But go on.'

'I'm really missing my wife, Joyce.'

'Of course you are. You've lost a big chunk from your everyday world.'

'Yes. It's the area of meals I'm struggling with the most at present. If it weren't for creating potential health issues, and the exorbitant cost, I tell you, I'd still be doing the rounds of the local takeaway establishments. Even probably beyond my immediate neighbourhood!'

'Ah. Well, don't think for a second I'm going to offer to come and take care of you in that fashion!'

'Oh, I wasn't. No.' Colin was a little shocked at Shirley's tone. He found himself blushing in response to the rebuke.

'God, my many apologies. That was a bit harsh of me.' Shirley was a deeper shade of pink in the cheeks too, and now had her hand over her mouth. 'It's just that I'm rather enjoying the freedom from that role these days. I'm a pretty dab hand in the kitchen, if I say so myself, and I enjoy it, on the whole. But I am preferring having just myself to please.'

'Fair enough. And good on you. Well, I'm struggling. I've tried replicating the simplest of recipes or rather *fare* – Joyce wasn't really one for following a recipe. Well, not so much of late.'

'Yes, we all have our favourites on rotation.'

'I can follow a recipe, or so I thought. But everything just seems to be missing her special touch. She always said love is the secret ingredient. I can see now that's so true.'

'Oh yes. More than once I almost selected arsenic as the secret ingredient! Well, I thought about it. Oh, don't look so horrified, Colin, I'm kidding. Well, sort of.'

Colin laughed. There was a cheeky glint in Shirley's eye.

'It's sometimes hard to believe Norman and I survived as long as we did – without either killing each other or one of us leaving. But I think our generation was more about sticking it out, wasn't it?'

'I think so, yes. Speaking of killing each other, I often wonder how Joyce and I would have gone as grey nomads. That was the dream; well, the next phase. Though me not being willing to give up work soon enough was a sticking point. I thought I wanted to. I at least didn't think I *didn't* want to.'

'Maybe that's why you couldn't give up work.'

'I do also feel a certain responsibility to my clients – definitely some of them.'

'I get that, but I'm saying, subconsciously. Perhaps there was a part of you that really didn't want to go caravanning, specifically. I have to say, I can't quite picture you being in charge of all that large equipment, hooking and unhooking. There's quite a bit to it.'

'Yes, you may be right. And I think there was an expectation from Joyce that it was her turn to be taken care of. I fear I'd have let her down on that score.'

'I didn't mean to appear critical.'

'Oh, no, that's okay. I didn't take your comment as criticism – more along the lines of observation. I'm not sure my nerves could handle being out on the road all the time. You hear about so many instances of road-rage.'

'Yes, and there's a particular loathing for caravanners. Not perhaps quite at the level as that for cyclists, but still. Anyway, we can't be all things to all people. You know that. So, what are we going to do about your most pressing deficiency – meals? We can't have you starving, suffering from malnutrition, or your arteries becoming clogged.'

'I don't suppose, being competent yourself, you'd know of any basic cooking schools or books, perhaps?'

'Not really, no.'

'Could I pay you to give me some private lessons?'

'Oh. I'm probably too bossy to be a decent teacher.'

'I find that hard to believe,' Colin said, truthfully. 'And maybe what I need is a firm hand. Oh dear, that sounded rather, er …' He cringed and then shrugged.

Shirley laughed.

Their meals were delivered and they both ploughed in.

'I've had an idea,' Shirley said abruptly, waving her fork above her plate. 'How about I send you some links to some good places online for easy-to-follow recipes with step-by-step instructions?'

'Um. I'm not sure I'd be very good with navigating online. Plus, I'd most likely spill something on the phone or laptop and destroy it. I have a shelf full of cookbooks. Do you recall any titles that might be up my alley?'

'Not off the top of my head. Look, how about I come around to your place and see what you have that might be suitable for getting you started? How about that?'

'Oh yes. Thank you. I'd very much appreciate that.'

'I'm free this afternoon, if you are?'

'Okay. I am, as it happens.'

'Perfect.'

Colin quickly ran through a series of images of the state he'd left the house in. Thankfully he concluded that, while it wasn't in a perfect state of tidiness, he wouldn't be embarrassed.

Chapter Twenty-five

'Well, here we are,' Colin announced, pulling into the driveway.

'Oh wow, it's gorgeous,' Shirley said, and stared up at the 1930s Tudor-style red brick house with her mouth open in awe.

'Thank you. It was my parents'. In another indication of how I became so inept domesticity-wise, I've never really left. Joyce and I stayed on to care for them.'

'I see. It's all making sense.'

Colin wasn't sure what to make of the comment as he couldn't see Shirley's expression. She was busy getting out of the car.

It was only when they were inside the hall that Colin remembered the slightly embarrassing absence of the hallstand and the chair in its stead. Now he felt the need to say something as Shirley appeared to be staring at the chair loaded with items of clothing and bits and pieces.

'Yes, there are a few gaps needing to be filled. Joyce …' He decided there need be no further explanation so closed his mouth and shrugged instead of finishing the sentence.

'Well, it *is* a gorgeous chair. And does the trick.'

'I think so.'

'It's so fabulous to be in a large hall. Modern houses, urgh. So cramped.'

'I must admit I probably take it for granted. The only truly modern dwellings I've been in of late are caravans.'

'Well, trust me when I say everything has shrunk. Some of the new houses I've been in are little more than the proportions of a caravan.'

'Come this way, the kitchen is through here.'

'Can I be nosy and have you give me a bit of a tour? It's such a gorgeous old home. Floorboards. Jarrah. Oh, yum. Proper ones – not that laminate that goes click, click when you walk on it rather than a decent, solid thud.'

'Okay.'

'Oh my god,' Shirley said over and over as Colin took her around.

'It's a little less cluttered than it was,' he said.

'It's fantastic that you've not given in to the developers. I bet they're circling, wanting the block.'

'Yes, they're like vultures. It's to my detriment that I'm so attached, I suppose. It's probably also about my homebodiness – is that even a word?'

'It'll do. I know what you mean.'

'That's probably what's behind my reluctance to embark on the grey nomad life.'

'Possibly. I'm a homebody too. I have to say, I don't miss having a large garden to take care of,' Shirley said as they stood on the verandah at the open French doors leading out from what had been Joyce's sewing room.

'It's not too bad, maintenance wise, but perhaps my regular pottering won't be enough before too long.'

'Oh well, then you can get someone in. You can pretty much pay for anything to be done these days, if you have the means and will. So, you are thinking of retiring? I can imagine you spending your days out here or sitting over there reading the paper. It's the romantic in me. I longed to simply put my feet up upon retirement, but whoever, whatever's, in charge had other ideas. I was given Norman to nurse instead,' she said.

Colin nodded and said, 'What is it you did for work? I don't think you've told me. Or I've been rude and not asked.'

'Nursing. I spent around sixty years nursing, all told.'

'Wow. That's an incredible career. And contribution.'

'No more or less than you.'

'Oh, I don't know about that. I was previously a builder. I guess you could say I came to psychology a bit later. Wise choice, though, as it turns out – with the raising of retirement age.'

'Oh yes. Those in charge have no idea that some jobs are intensely physical.'

'Nursing would have kept you fit, I should imagine.'

'Yes. As I said, I just wanted to sit down for my retirement. Well, at least in my mind. I struggle to sit still, always have. I'd probably be diagnosed with ADHD at school these days. So many seem to be.'

'I could test you – I do those sorts of assessments.'

'No thanks. I'm happy with who and what I am. Mostly.'

'Good for you.'

'Too many little boxes everyone is trying to put everyone and everything into, I think. How about that cup of tea? And I'll look at your cookbooks,' she said, turning around and heading back through the glass doors. Colin closed the doors behind them and led Shirley to the kitchen.

'It's all a bit tired, really,' he said, looking around, trying to picture the cupboards – in gum-leaf-green and pale matt flecked laminate benchtops – through a newcomer's eyes.

'I like it.'

'Cookbooks are up there,' he said, pointing to the cupboard above the fridge. 'There's a step just behind the door there, if necessary.' He filled the kettle. 'Now, just ordinary English breakfast tea, or something else?'

'No, that sounds perfect, thanks,' Shirley muttered, her back to him. He looked over. She was running a finger along the spines of the cookbooks, few of which had been published later than the early nineteen-eighties. 'Here we are. These are good.' Shirley placed on the table a small pile of cookbooks.

Colin looked at them with disinterest. 'I wish we boys had been made to do home economics, or whatever it was called.'

'Well, I wanted to do woodwork, but I wasn't allowed because I wasn't a boy. That still rankles.'

'Hmm. I bet.'

'Not to mention the very few career options we were encouraged to undertake.'

'How about you teach me to cook and my thanks will be a three-course meal cooked by myself for you. Right here, sometime in the not-too-distant future,' Colin said.

'Ooh, that sounds lovely. But you might regret your offer. How about I allow you to rescind at any time? And I feel it my duty to help you become self-sufficient. It'll be nice to have a decent project. Be useful again.'

'Oh, she of little faith,' Colin scoffed. 'I might be quite good when I get going. I'm rather keen on throwing myself into a new hobby.'

'I'm going to have tea and then look into your refrigerator and pantry to see where things stand. You said you shopped yesterday?'

'Yes, and again it was not the fun experience I'd hoped it would be.'

'Well, better get used to it. Unless you want to do home delivery. But that has its downfalls.'

'Hmm.'

'Okay, so what did you have in mind for the mince?' Shirley asked, turning back to Colin from the open fridge.

'Lasagne. It's one of my favourites. Hopefully I have everything that's needed. I have to confess to being a little apprehensive now after failing with the tuna mornay during the week. Silly me thinking that would have been simple.' He looked at Shirley's puckered expression. 'Don't tell me, it *is* easy – one of the easiest?'

'Yes, actually. I learnt to make it at eleven.' She laughed. 'Oh dear, oh dear, Colin. Really, I'm struggling to see how you could not have learnt to cook any *actual* meals.'

'Do eggs count? I can boil and fry an egg. And make a toasted sandwich. And toast. And cook chops in the pan. And steam veggies in the microwave – though they tend to come out either too hard or too mushy. I haven't quite mastered that thing yet. In my defence, I am a very good assistant. I did do plenty of chopping of onions and the like for Joyce.'

'So, you watched?'

'Oh yes.'

'But you didn't take it in?'

'Apparently not, as it turns out. There was me thinking I'd simply buy the ingredients and remember how Joyce put it all together, and voila.' He made a show of spreading his hands, trying to make light of his embarrassed state.

'That's usually how it works. Oh dear. You men and your lack of attention to fine details. As a complete generalisation, of course. With Norman, I'd have to ask him several times to tell me a story or recount a conversation so I'd actually get all of it. It was like pulling teeth sometimes. One of his more endearing qualities was chuckling and saying, "Details, pesky details."'

'If only we still needed to hunt down and procure a beast in the wild. Maybe then we'd do okay. You women were programmed to gather the berries or what have you. So your roles haven't changed quite as much. But us men have been completely dispossessed of our prime function in life.'

'Doesn't stop you all mansplaining everything to the rest of us though, does it?'

'Oh, touché. I'd like to think I don't do much of that. And if you ever catch me, please tell me so.'

'It would give me great pleasure.' Shirley chuckled again.

Colin laughed. 'I sense a keenness to put the male population in its place.'

'Oh yes! Right. Let's teach you how to make lasagne. You can have it for dinner.'

'Oh. Er …'

'What's the problem?'

'I'm rather attached to doing a roast on Sunday. And last week I chickened out. Ha ha. Oh, never mind. It's an in joke that I can't be bothered explaining. You had to be there, I'm afraid. It's meant to be lamb today. There's a leg in there. Could we do both? I do recall Joyce always saying lasagne is better the next day. And I'd like cold meat for sandwiches for the week. You'd be very welcome to stay and join me. Unless you'd rather not spend so long in my company.'

'You do realise you can google everything you need to know?'

'Yes. Probably. Though I suppose that would fall under "men refusing to seek directions or follow them".'

'I'm guessing you've never considered or needed to put a flatpack of furniture together, then?'

'I'm not sure, but I'm guessing not. Because what you just said made no sense at all to me. And I keep forgetting to bring the laptop home from work. Joyce took the tablet computer and I struggle a bit with online searching with my phone.'

'Okay. I'm going to lead by example and you're going to make notes – notes you can follow and in handwriting you can read. Got it?'

'Yes, ma'am.' Colin grinned and almost saluted. He was having enormous fun.

'Lasagne, and then it'll probably be time for the roast to go on.'

'You've been a marvellous help and wonderful company, Shirley, so thank you very much.'

'It's been my pleasure, Colin. I've had a great day, thank you.'

They hadn't long finished eating an early dinner – unsurprisingly, with Shirley's supervision, a great success, much to Colin's delight – and tidied up. Colin stood by while Shirley put her coat on after unhooking it from the chair, picturing, with sadness, Joyce doing just that right there so many times.

'You do realise you need to drive me home?' Shirley said.

'Oh. Yes. I admit I did completely forget.' He hurriedly struggled into his own coat.

'Or I could call a cab?'

'Absolutely not. No, I just got caught up in our day. It completely slipped my mind that we started at brunch. It feels like days ago we were sitting in that noisy cafe.'

'I know what you mean. What sort of hallstand was here? And are you thinking of replacing it?'

'Um. I might do if I saw something that suited. But I've never needed to go furniture shopping so wouldn't know where to look. It was Edwardian in English oak, with a mirror, coat hooks, a shelf, a drawer, a spot for umbrellas and a seat to sit on.'

'Looks like I have another quest on my hands,' Shirley said. 'Goodie. I love shopping for furniture and antiques. It needs to be a feature and suitably welcoming,' she mused aloud.

'So, you don't like my chair?'

'I didn't say that. It's a good temporary measure. So shall I take you to some antique shops next weekend?'

'That sounds lovely. If you're not too sick of me and my overall incompetence.'

'Not at all. You're a fun project, Colin.'

'Glad to be of service,' he said doffing a non-existent hat.

Chapter Twenty-six

The success of the Sunday lamb roast Shirley had supervised and assisted him in cooking had seemed to kickstart a good week for Colin. He'd sent a thank you text message while he'd eaten his sandwich, and another regarding the delicious lasagne on the Monday evening. The deliciousness of that creation had caused him to experience an almost euphoric sense of being invincible. So good was the meal, he'd even taken some for lunch, eschewing his self-imposed rule of not using the office microwave for fear of stinking out the kitchen and offending someone. He'd been a little unsure when it came to the time to heat his meal, but being greeted with the aroma of recently heated curry upon his arrival in the tiny room saw his choice validated.

The rest of the week had progressed smoothly, to the extent he kept marvelling at the effect on life in general that satisfying meals had, something he'd clearly taken for granted until being faced with the alternative. He'd even remembered to bring his laptop home each evening and had become engrossed in, and was now possibly at risk of becoming addicted to, cooking demonstrations and funny videos on YouTube. Several times he'd found himself chuckling with wonder at what the clever inventors of the web would make of their system being used for such frivolous purposes.

Last night he'd painstakingly added ingredients to a bought pizza base, surprised at his level of enjoyment in doing so – almost as enjoyable as eating the finished product, which he'd quietly congratulated himself on. So pleased was he with his efforts, particularly as they'd been completely independent of Shirley's instruction, he was currently researching dough recipes and tips for next time to do it completely from scratch, while eating a leftover slice with a knife and fork for breakfast.

Colin was excited for his day with Shirley on Saturday. He'd have been happy just to sit and wait while she had her hair done, or something as equally humdrum, he enjoyed her buoyant presence so much. But as per her usual service orientation, they were going in search of a replacement hallstand. He was heading off soon to pick her up.

And then an email appeared with a subject heading that caused him to stop mid-chew:

Subject: Notice of eviction from 51 Newland Road.
Dear Colin,
I hope this email finds you well.

Other businesses in the centre have expressed concern around recent events involving you.

Our premises must at all times provide a safe and comfortable environment for tenants and their clients. We feel we can no longer provide this assurance, which places our business at considerable risk legally and financially.

Therefore, it is with regret and disappointment, that we request you vacate your office as soon as possible and no later than 6pm on Friday November 21st. We hope you understand and we do wish you well.

Regards,

Tory Wright

Premises Manager

The Golden Leaf Allied Health Centre

51 Newland Road, Trinity Gardens SA 5068

What? What are they on about? Evicted? His heart began to speed up. He frowned. *Is this because I heated up lasagne this week? Has someone got their knickers in a twist over that? To the extent they'd complain? No, surely not. Anyway, someone did curry before me.*

He read it through again. No, he was sure it couldn't be anything to do with leaving an odour wafting in the kitchen. It fitted the word 'comfortable', he supposed. *But what about safe? What does that mean? Could refer to a host of things, not just physical – mental, emotional … anything. Are they quietly accusing me of being a leery old creep? Oh god.* He couldn't remember the last time he'd seen, let alone spoken to, any of the other tenants. Years ago, there'd been a man running a business specialising in acupuncture and acupressure who Colin had enjoyed chatting with. He'd left after a year saying he didn't fit in. Since then, Colin had kept himself to himself. Was that the reason – he was too much of a mystery, an unknown? Well, they'd only had to ask, make an effort, if they'd wanted to know him better. He'd always respected their space, mainly due to the age gap. Maybe that had been his mistake.

He shook his head, trying to find clarity, but his mind had got stuck on the words *'eviction', 'vacate'* and *'hope you understand'*. *You hope I understand? Well, I don't. Not at all.* He rubbed his face.

How could anything have got to this point without them bringing him in for a discussion? But of course! They'd only ever communicated in writing – email, passive-aggressive notes stuck up here and there. But surely something of this magnitude warranted a face-to-face interaction? Perhaps he intimidated them due to his profession, if not his masculinity. He could see that being the case. Much about the way the younger generations did things perplexed him, so this ponderance was of no help. Should he seek clarification? Should he fight this? And then his slight buoyancy sank again. He was absolutely mortified that his presence or something he'd done, inadvertently or otherwise, had caused enough upset and discomfort to other people that they'd raise it with management behind his back.

Should he seek an explanation? Fight this? And then a new reality dawned. *They don't want you there. Best you suck it up and just leave. Retirement. It'll be fun. You want this. Maybe so, but not in this way. And not now Joyce has left.*

As he glanced at the email again, he noticed the time on the computer. Damn. He had to get going to collect Shirley. A big part of him just wanted to stay home and nurse his wounds and wonder what to do about it. And right then he also felt too ashamed to face Shirley. But she'd seemed to be looking forward to his company while trawling the stores as much as he'd been looking forward to hers, and he couldn't let her down, especially at this late notice, without a lot of questions being asked.

Colin did his best to push the morning's correspondence aside and concentrate on driving carefully.

Once he'd pulled up outside her house and saw Shirley coming out, waving and beaming, he knew having her company was infinitely better than being at home alone with his thoughts. He cajoled his features into a cheery expression.

'Hello there,' Shirley said, getting into the car. She closed the door and looked at him.

'Good morning. How are you?'

'I'm well, thank you. But how are you, that's the question?'

Does she know something? Has the practice put something up online?

'Me? What about me?' he said, stammering slightly.

'You look pale, Colin. Are you coming down with something?'

'Um. I'm a little frazzled this morning, actually, since you ask.'

'Any particular reason?'

'Hmm. Just a work matter, that's all. Come on, let's not let it spoil our day.' He smiled at her and put the car in gear.

'Okay, but if there's anything you want to talk about, I'm all ears.'

'Thank you, but not right at the minute. So, you're happy to navigate? Just tell me where to go.'

'Right you are then. Next left, then after the third street turn right. I'm taking you the back way to avoid the roadworks.'

Colin nodded and looked to the road ahead, his mind drifting back to the email and drowning out Shirley's words.

'Indicator on, turn right at the next one. This one!'

Colin, jolted from his reverie, braked, a little too hard, before turning.

'I didn't mean to raise my voice, but I thought you were going to miss it.'

'That's okay.' What he wanted to do was pull over and put a hand to his chest to still his thumping heart and take several deep breaths. But he kept going. 'No, my apologies. I'm not being very sharp today, am I?'

Colin vaguely thought Shirley had issued the instructions several times at reasonable and regular intervals, but it was all a dull whooshing in his head that felt as if it was full of cotton wool. Everything was muffled and dull and unable to be latched onto with any firmness, except for the few pertinent words from the email lodged in his mind and the rise and fall of the accompanying seesaw of thoughts and feelings: *This is good, old man, you'll have all the time in the world to ... To do what? I enjoy working. And I can't go out like this. I need the money to eventually pay Joyce out. I can't lose the house.*

'And now pull up right here. Colin.'

'What was that?'

'Just here. Stop. Now!'

'Oh.' Colin wrenched the wheel so sharply in his effort to quickly comply he almost hit the kerb. 'Damn it,' he muttered and raised his hand in apology to the several cars behind him as a chorus of honking horns rang out. One continued blasting as they carried on past, the obnoxious sound fading as the car tore off ahead. Colin was more than a little shaken.

'My many apologies,' he said, turning in his seat and glancing at Shirley. 'That was a bit abrupt. Are you okay?'

He now looked around the vicinity of where they were parked and could see nothing resembling antique or second-hand furniture shops. There was a bakery, a supermarket, a health food shop, and a bicycle sales and repairs place.

'Oh, I'm fine. But, clearly, you're not, Colin. Come on, tell me. You really didn't have to come out today if your heart's not in it. I would have understood.'

'I want to. I really do.' *I need to. I'll go mad sitting at home alone with this.* 'So, where's this furniture shop?' He turned to look over his right shoulder back down the street behind them, as much to remove himself from under Shirley's stern glare as anything. When he turned back to face the front, he noticed her arms were folded. She looked towards him, eyebrows raised in question.

'There *is* no place, Colin. I got you to pull over because I'm concerned. I might not know you very well or have done for long, but you are clearly not yourself. So, what's going on? Is it to do with Joyce? You said it's about work – are you having to sell up to buy her out or something? You don't have to tell me, but I have the feeling you need to get something off your chest. You're too distracted. There's no use us doing anything while you're in this state. And you probably shouldn't be driving, either. If you don't want to discuss whatever's on your mind with me, fine, but at least get out and let me drive so I feel safe.'

'Oh god. I'm so sorry, Shirley.'

'Thank you. Apology accepted.'

Colin remained seated. After a moment he sighed and then said, 'I find myself in a quandary.'

'Okay? Would you like to talk about it?'

'I think I have to. You're right. Pretending, well, trying to, clearly isn't working.'

'Would you rather go back home – to your place or mine – or just sit here?' She looked up at the parking sign Colin now realised they were alongside. Thankfully they had two hours and were far enough back from the nearby bus stop. At that moment such a vehicle roared past them loudly. Colin tried to formulate an opening sentence from the jumble of words and thoughts inside him.

'I'm being evicted.'

'From the house, your home? But … *Evicted*?'

'No, my business premises. Apparently, the other tenants don't feel safe or something.'

'What do you mean?'

'I'm not sure. You know as much as I do now. I really don't fit the demographic or the culture. I can only surmise they've decided enough is enough.'

I did notice you and your business are quite different to the others in the centre.'

'Yes, everything about the place has changed over the years.'

'What hasn't? Why can't some things stay the same? But something must have happened ...'

'It's probably best I just accept it.'

'Really? No, sorry, I don't believe that. Otherwise, you wouldn't be so rattled.'

Colin sighed. Shirley made a good point. But he was tired and overwhelmed. If it wasn't the weekend, he might ignore Tory's preferred method of communication and phone the woman. Shirley shifted in her seat beside him.

'Hang on,' she said. 'If something hasn't happened in the office at work, maybe something has happened off in cyberspace. That's practically the young ones' entire world these days. I saw that nasty review and accompanying palaver. It's why I initially came to see you. Has something else of that nature happened?'

'No idea. Joyce took ca– Oh my god.' A thread of memory from somewhere came to him with the clarity of a tumbling, gathering ball of wool.

'What?'

'I'm an old fool.'

Shirley looked at him expectantly.

'I completely forgot about my Facebook page when Joyce left. Haven't even looked at it. She said not to when the review happened. And I now vaguely remember her telling me something about the business just as she left.'

'Oh, Colin. I think we'd better take a look, see if anything's been going on that might have caused someone's ire,' Shirley mumbled as she got out her phone and began typing. As the seconds ticked by, Colin watched her mouth go from relaxed to what resembled a lowercase o and then to an uppercase O accompanied by wide eyes and raised brows.

'There seems to have been a campaign waging in the background. Someone unhappy with their own life for some reason must have commented on that review post, sparking it off again. I think bots get involved too – not actual people, a sort of artificial intelligence – plus real people who look for any opportunity to participate in trolling, and that's how it can appear to take on a life of its own. I don't really understand how it works. And I don't think knowing the ins and outs will help. It looks like they've tagged the other businesses at the centre. There's been a lot of activity. Maybe it's caused cancellations in the real world? Though, and I don't mean to make you feel worse, Colin, the stress from managing their social media would probably be enough to tip them over. You only have Facebook. There are others. And websites ... Oh, fuck!' Shirley brought a hand to her mouth and looked at Colin.

'God, now what have you found?' Colin rubbed his face. He was starting to feel exhausted.

'Um, I hate to tell you this, but there's an online petition with a bunch of signatures.'

'Great,' Colin said with a groan. 'Oh well, at least it probably can't get any worse at this point, can it?'

'No, probably not.'

'How could I have completely missed it all?'

'Be grateful you have, I'd say. I agree, it is unusual. But if you don't have Facebook notifications turned on and you don't look at it online, then how would you know?'

'But wouldn't someone tell me?'

'I guess not, considering you haven't been informed.'

'Yes, good point. Christ. I feel terrible.'

'Hang on. Didn't you experience a decline in bookings at all?'

'No. I didn't. That's a good point. Now *that* would have tipped me off. And I haven't heard a peep via email, either.'

'How very odd. I must say, I was surprised to be able to book in so quickly. I just thought I'd got lucky.'

'Hmm. Though, to be fair, my bookings have always ebbed and flowed.'

'Fair enough.'

'Can't we just delete it all?' He nodded towards Shirley's phone. *Did I ask Joyce that before? If so, what did she say? No idea. Oh dear. What a bloody mess.* His head was spinning. He sighed.

'Not without removing your business page completely. And I don't think that would remove all trace. People have most likely shared screenshots anyway. It might have gone beyond Facebook. There's the petition, too, remember …'

'God, don't remind me. It's all too horrific.' *But thank goodness I have you beside me, Shirley.* 'But I suppose what really matters now is the fact I have to be out before November twenty-one.'

'That's very soon. Can they even do that? Legally? It doesn't sound right to me. Don't you have a lease and they have to give you notice – time to find somewhere else?'

'I imagine they'd be able to claim extenuating circumstances. They'd get around it somehow, legally. If they wanted to. Anyway, I can at least see their point. If there's one bad apple, me, tainting their whole basket – that is, the practice and all its other tenants – well …' He held his hands up to illustrate his point. 'And the last thing I want is to be somewhere I'm not wanted. I know what toxic workplaces do to people. I've had many people in because of it over the years. Oh god. To think that's how they view me – how they've been feeling going to work … I'm absolutely mortified, Shirley.'

'Of course you are. Um, can I see the email – is it on your phone? Not that I don't believe you. It's just it might help me to understand it fully. But only if you're comfortable.'

Colin dug out his phone from his pocket, pulled up the email and handed the device over.

'Oh. I see,' she said, handing his phone back a few moments later. 'Rather to the point – well, not the point by way of explanation, but short and sharp.'

'Exactly.'

'I'm guessing they've had meetings behind your back. They must have done to get to this point. Or maybe the centre has simply made the call. Though, it doesn't really matter, does it?'

'Not really, no. At the risk of repeating myself, I'm absolutely mortified. But I think the most pressing thing is, now what? I feel paralysed. God, how many people have I counselled through changes big and small? You'd think I'd be able to just … Oh, I don't know. I don't know anything right now.' He rubbed his face.

'That's perfectly understandable. You were already dealing with the enormity of Joyce leaving. And just because you know what to do and understand it at an intellectual level doesn't mean you're immune to feeling it emotionally. We've had this discussion before, haven't we? And you know as well as I do that when emotions are involved it can easily become overwhelming. You're dealing with renewed feelings of hurt and rejection, for starters. And more change. It's another massive upheaval, with lots of decisions to be made. The domino effect. It's big. A *lot*, in fact.' She looked at him with raised eyebrows and her head tilted. Colin couldn't help smiling at recognising the catch cry and her efforts to cheer him up.

'Thank you, Shirley.'

'The first thing to do is breathe. Slow, deep breaths. Come on. With me.'

Now Colin wanted to laugh. But she was right. His breathing was sharp and shallow. He needed to slow things down. And then start breaking his looming problem down into manageable parts and deal with each one.

Colin took two more long breaths.

'That's it. In, two, three, hold, two, three, four, five. Out, two, three, four, five.' Beside him Shirley was demonstrating.

Colin took two more long deep breaths.

'There, is that better?'

'Yes. Much. Thank you.'

'Firstly, there are other premises. This you would know in your heart. All over the place there are masses of empty buildings. And you could move the practice to your home. That's what I'd be doing. Well, except for the apparent online vitriol. That might pose a security risk. But no one's calling for you to be burnt at the stake or anything of that nature, as far as I saw, so incorporating measures such as visible cameras might be enough. Mere details to be worked through, I reckon.'

Colin stared at her.

'Don't tell me the thought of running the business from home hasn't crossed your mind before? Because that's what that slightly stunned, perplexed expression on your face is, isn't it?'

'Yes.' He laughed at her observation of his facial features. 'And, no, you're quite right. It hadn't actually occurred to me.' *Why not?* He wondered how he'd go mixing work and homelife to such an extent.

'But you've got the perfect room waiting – the one with the French doors out onto the verandah. I know, that's not the point. Actual premises is not the problem, I don't think. Is it?'

'Isn't it?'

'Well, only you know the answer to that, Colin. But the way I see it, it's the decision of whether you take this as an opportunity to retire or not that is the pertinent question. I'm not really one to believe in signs – being a nurse, I tend to lean more towards the scientific way of things. The less esoteric, if you will. Not that I didn't see some unlikely occurrences. Anyway, I'm going off track. I'm guessing if you're this flummoxed, then you have your answer.'

'I do?'

'Of course you do, Colin. You're just too close to it and getting caught up in the emotion, which is, again, perfectly understandable.

'It is hurtful to be told you're not wanted, whatever the form or circumstance. But clear that away and you have the practical, the logical. Which I know you're very good at sorting through. It's what you do every day.

'So, it's clear to me you're not ready to retire – correct me if I'm wrong – otherwise you'd be expressing some relief at the decision having been made for you. And, in that case, we'd be sitting here discussing the best strategy for how to tell your patients what you'll be doing with all the extra time on your hands, at least the first week or so of it. But the fact is you're clearly not ready to do that, despite probably feeling that you ought to be hanging up the post-it notes, or whatever the equivalent for you is to the doctor and their stethoscope or builder and their nail bag, or whatever. Maybe, just maybe, what you're really wanting is a slight change in direction. Perhaps you'd rather do less in certain areas and more in others.

'If, for instance, you worked from home and thereby reduced your overheads, you might be able to really tailor things. Because, while you're very discreet and professional, I have noticed you don't exactly argue with my dim view on the human population generally. So … well, anyway … You get the picture, I'm sure.'

'Hmm. You make some very good points and give much food for thought, Shirley. And, yes, there are some aspects to my current practice I would happily do without.'

'Like, couples counselling, I'm guessing?'

Colin nodded and even managed a weak smile.

'How did you know that?'

'I might be being ignorant, but in my mind, that would quite possibly involve a lot of one person being there under sufferance, both bickering, and much unspent frustration on the part of the practitioner – i.e. you.'

'You're very perceptive.'

'I am. But on this topic, I have a slightly unfair advantage. I went and googled you and saw the negative review, remember? It was talk of your bluntness spilling over that saw me grace your bookings.'

'Ah, yes, and I'm so glad you did. Speaking of which, if you're thinking of seeing me in a professional capacity again, I'll have to decline your booking. It wouldn't be ethical, now, due to our personal friendship.'

'Of course. The thought had crossed my mind. I wasn't planning to, no, I enjoy your company much more outside of that dreary office! You've quite given me a new lease on life.'

'I feel the same way.' Despite his earlier news and the ramifications hanging over him, Colin indulged in a brief sigh of contentment.

'There, that's better,' Shirley said, smiling over at him. 'And I know exactly how you're probably feeling, actually, being forced out. I've been there. Sort of. Well, no, actually, perhaps not, or even maybe.'

'Make up your mind,' Colin said gently, and laughed.

'Well, I *had* to give up nursing – so there's that similarity. But I also didn't really give it up – it was my choice to devote my time to taking care of Norman. So, I kept nursing, just without being paid for it. And it was very different – I really missed the camaraderie of my colleagues, and the hustle and bustle and variety of tasks and patients at a hospital ... But I was still doing a job I loved. And it wasn't altogether different. There were always grumpy, ungrateful patients, though not all day every day. Oh, the times I wanted to smother the old goat with a pillow, I tell you! Don't worry, I'm joking. Sort of,' she added in a mutter.

'Note to self: don't fall asleep near Shirley Royal.'

'Very funny. But it is good to see your humour shining through again, Colin. You had me worried there for a bit. Are you feeling any better about things?'

'I am a little. Thank you. You're right. I don't want to retire. At least not in this fashion.'

'That's the spirit. Don't let the bastards win – the online ones or the administrative ones. I agree you still have more to give. Because, if you didn't think that, you would have closed up shop when your Joyce put the hard word on you regarding caravanning, not that I'm saying she did. Just a figure of speech.'

'To be honest, I think I might have missed the signs there. The hints which were possibly not much less subtle than a sledgehammer from Joyce's point of view. She'd probably been waging a campaign for several years.'

'Ah, don't be too hard on yourself. In my experience, most humans tend to see or hear what they want to, or not, as the case may be.'

'Indeed.'

'For what it's worth, I think your Joyce would have sat you down and had a serious conversation with you that you had no hope of misunderstanding if it meant that much to her. From what you've told me, she doesn't sound the type to be backwards in coming forwards. And it wasn't like she didn't know you after all those decades together.'

'That's true. You're right there. I'm still sad and disappointed about all that.'

'Of course you are. And you will be for a long time yet. And then, just when you think you're through it, you'll be slapped across the face, or whatever other metaphor you want to insert, by a memory out of the blue and be taken right back to the heart of the pain.

'So, that's cleared up. You're staying on. Next: a premises. I take it you're not going to fight the current people?'

'No. While I don't want to give them the satisfaction of me so easily succumbing to their ganging up on me, I also don't want to cause any of the tenants any further issues. We're all small businesses in there. I'm clearly the problem so ...'

'Well, it's probably mostly the online detractors that are, if that's the reason behind the eviction, but I get your point. How long have you been there?'

'Twenty-two years.'

'Wow. That *is* a long time. No wonder you're feeling so unsettled at the idea of leaving. I don't need to tell you that moving — homes, particularly — is considered one of the three most stressful situations people face, along with divorce and death of a loved one. And you've never moved houses before. So, especially doing it at your age will be doubly confronting. Most people in their twilight years have done it several times by now, and it's still a very stressful experience. Is the furniture at the office yours or does it belong to the building?'

Colin tried to think. 'The couch is mine, and the prints. And my files, of course, and the laptop computer and printer. I could probably live with leaving the couch and prints behind, in the name of having a fresh start. What do you think?'

'Well, that's up to you. The couch is still in quite good nick, from memory. So, it wouldn't be like leaving the manager or staff with a problem to deal with. And if you did want to take it then it'd be easy enough to find someone to help move it. So, what do you think about working out of the house? I can't believe it hasn't crossed your mind before. I thought you'd already have an office set up at home anyway.'

'I made a conscious decision I didn't want to bring my work home – stay present, as we all say these days …'

'That's admirable.'

'And the kitchen or dining table has always sufficed when necessary. That room with the French doors was always Joyce's sewing room.'

'Well, it's yours now.'

'Unless I have to sell the house.' The thought sent a shiver through Colin, just as it did every time it crossed his mind.

'Maybe you can offer Joyce a portion of the business instead – pay her off over time instead of in a lump sum. But that's up to you both. I suppose you don't need to rush into anything if Joyce isn't asking you to.'

'No. I'll ignore it for a bit longer. But now you've got me thinking about workspaces. I think I would like a home office, even if I don't go ahead with having clients there. I'm not entirely sure why. Just because I can, I suppose?'

'That's as good a reason as any, I reckon! I'd love to help you sort out a new office space at your home, if you want.'

'Okay. I have to admit I'm a little excited at having a room of my own. I know, I know, I currently have the whole house. But somehow it still doesn't quite feel entirely mine.'

'Well, maybe a new hallstand of your choosing will help with that.'

'Yes. Will it count still if I end up with something just like what was there before?'

'Of course. I'm sure you and Joyce had very good taste. How about we start with seeing what's around? And for filling a potential office while we're at it?'

'Are you suggesting we let ourselves be guided by signs, Shirley?'

'I certainly am not, Colin Palmer!'

Colin stared her down.

'Okay, maybe, just maybe, I believe in the power of intuition.'

'You have to.'

'Why's that?'

'Because you turned up at my office right when I needed you to. And you were here again today. At another of my lowest moments.'

Chapter Twenty-seven

They got out of the car and made their way slowly around to a shop with two bay windows, separated by a bright blue painted door, which currently stood wide open. In lieu of a business name was the street number and, beneath it, the words 'ANTIQUES, SECOND-HAND FURNITURE, GOODS AND BRIC-A-BRAC' printed in gold lettering.

Shirley wandered away, but Colin was drawn to the nearest of the two windows, which had behind it a complete office setup not too dissimilar to what Colin thought he would like – plain timber desk with drawers down one side, a lamp over a studded leather wing chair and a matching three-seater couch. That style had a name, didn't it? He'd always liked the look, but his parents had a suite with cane sides and upholstered loose cushions that he and Joyce had had re-covered in a sumptuous, patterned velvet fabric.

He'd wanted leather but Joyce didn't – said it would be too cold to sit on, too uncomfortable, and too masculine looking. He'd been disappointed but unable to object as he didn't know otherwise. And anyway, the existing suite was very comfortable — when one stacked cushions up against the timber arms — and held plenty of sentimental value.

Back then he'd just been relieved Joyce hadn't wanted to get rid of all his parents' things, and also that she shared his values of making do with what they had and only replacing things on a needs basis.

It helped that everything was so well made and that his parents had saved and invested in quality. There was no way the modern things would go the distance — that old refrain, nothing is made to last anymore, which from a capitalist business perspective made sense. But from an environmental and waste perspective it was a very disappointing way to go about things.

Again, Colin's mind went to a topic he often pondered — whether humanity's biggest problem was an inability to delay gratification. The constant need of new, shiny, seemingly better, was adjacent, wasn't it? It certainly played a part in the throw-away consumer society they were all forced to be a part of in some way.

He really liked that Shirley had brought him to somewhere where old furniture — hopefully well made — was being given another chance instead of ending up in landfill.

The woman in question appeared beside him.

'Ooh, yes, that's what I was picturing for you and your style of home,' she said.

'Do you think leather would be cold to sit on, or uncomfortable, or difficult to care for?'

'No, no and no. Being natural fabric, rather than synthetic, it will have fabulous insulation properties — warm up quickly in winter and feel cool in summer. Like wool. The chesterfields do get dust trapped around the studs — particularly across the back – but it's nothing a quick vacuum won't sort out. And you just wipe them over with some leather conditioner occasionally and Bob's your uncle. I love how they look as they age. Though the slightly worn appearance isn't for everyone. They don't get dirty marks like other upholstery does. I have a chesterfield suite myself, as it happens.'

Colin nodded. 'Comfortable enough?'

'Oh yes. I think so. A couple of decent feather filled cushions at each end and a throw rug and you'll be blocking out more than one appointment a day for your afternoon nap, I assure you.'

'Joyce was always against leather.' *But you're not here to object now, are you, Joyce? Hmm.*

'Well, this is one area on which your estranged wife and I will have to disagree. Anyway, it's entirely up to you. I like the dark green colour too. I can picture it in the room with all that lovely dark timber you have. And I will say, had Norman had such an objection, it wouldn't have been beyond the realms of possibility that I'd have taken to decking out the whole house in it. Probably before he was even cold, too!'

'At least he wouldn't have known.' Colin laughed.

'Disappointing, but true.' Shirley chuckled. 'Never underestimate an old woman's determination or capacity for crankiness. Anyway, changing the subject. Their prices are very reasonable. Sadly, the young ones don't seem to want the old-style pieces. Plus, they're too bulky for the tiny spaces being built these days and most of our age group are downsizing. Sad, really. But good for us – well, you, since you're in the market.'

'Hmm. I wonder what I'll be up for.'

'Don't forget it'll be tax deductible – that might help, too. But I'm not an accountant.'

'Hmm. Good point.'

'I'll leave you to drool out here alone – I'm heading in. Catch you along the way – there are lots of rooms to explore. Let me know if you want to measure anything – I happen to have a small tape measure on my keyring.'

'Oh, that's clever.'

'Not really, but very useful.'

'I'll be in shortly. I'm just going to take some photos with my phone.'

'Good idea.'

Despite having taken plenty of photos, Colin struggled to leave the view. A part of him wanted to march in and say he wanted to buy all the pieces before someone else did. Another part was unsure. He couldn't recall having to be the sole decision maker before. It was a nice position to be in, but also quite unsettling.

And, yet again, he was reminded of the repercussions of having been enabled by Joyce and his nice stable marriage.

He was also aware he needed, or rather ought, to be sensible – not rush in like a bull at a gate, now he was able to do as he pleased. He again wondered what sort of cost he was facing.

Colin entered the store and, before going any further, checked with the gentleman behind the counter if he minded if he took photos inside the shop. He was cheerfully told, 'No worries at all, go for your life, sing out if you need any help, measurements and the like.'

He enjoyed going at his own pace with no one following him around asking if they could be of any assistance, which always tended to rattle Colin and Joyce and see them ultimately leave the respective store soon afterwards.

In his meandering, he came across several more chesterfield style pieces, though no more in the green colour that had caught his eye outside. Though he didn't mind any of the other colours.

And in the blue was a whole suite – three-seater, two tub chairs and a wingback.

Several times Colin wondered if he was taking too long and where Shirley was, but then reminded himself she'd be sure to come and get him if she'd become bored. As it was, he made his way methodically right through to the back of the shop to find her in the last room, sitting in a rocking chair and making use of its movement.

'I hope I haven't taken too long,' he said.

'No, not at all. I would have said if I was bothered. By anything at any point. How did you go? See anything you like?'

'Yes. The things in the front window. I can't seem to quite get past them. How about you? Are you testing that chair for purchase?'

'Not really. Well, I wasn't. I sat down to look at that.' Colin followed her finger. 'What do you think?'

'What is it?'

'A miniature church.'

'I can see that. But what's it for?' As he said it, he blushed at remembering all the items in his own house he dusted each week. Items that he liked and appreciated, which had no purpose except the purely aesthetic. 'I see now, it's a decorative piece. An ornament.'

'Yes and no. I have a model train set in need of a church. Well, the village it runs through could do with a church. Not that I'm remotely religious. But we've got a butcher, baker, bookshop, pub … You get the picture.'

'Really? Wow, it must be large.'

'Well, it meanders around most of the spare room. So, large-*ish*.'

'Oh, how interesting.' Colin found himself frowning slightly. It seemed a strange thing to have and do.

'Are you unable to picture me playing with a model train set, Colin?'

'I am having trouble getting my head around it, yes. I have no idea why.'

'Oh well, I'm not offended. I was initially a reluctant participant myself. It was Norman's baby, but it became a case of joining in, otherwise spend all my spare time alone. Gradually I gained an appreciation. And, actually, it's really relaxing to sit and watch the dear little thing trundle around. And the gentle click, click sound is very soothing. You wait until you see my train set. You'll not be able to resist having a play with it. You'll be begging for a … Oh my god.'

Colin chuckled.

'No, that was not a euphemism for anything sexual.'

'Hey, I was having no such thoughts,' Colin said, holding his hands up in surrender. He rather liked seeing Shirley blushing and looking a little uncomfortable – didn't think he'd seen that side of her before. She usually appeared so composed and in control.

'Ready to go?'

'Yes. But I want to ask about a few pieces. Do you need a hand getting up from there?'

'No, I'm all good, thank you,' Shirley said, easing herself out of the chair.

'Hello there,' Colin said, back at the counter. 'I'm wondering if you have the measurements of the couch and desk in the window, please.'

'I do. I have them right here. I'll write them on a card, along with the prices for you. They're great, aren't they?'

'They are.'

'The desk is 1920s English oak. And the chesterfield was made in Melbourne. There's also a pair of matching tub chairs. They're in storage in the shed, and are in just as good nick.'

'Oh.'

'Is that disappointment or increased interest?' Shirley said, now beside him.

'I'm not sure,' he said with a laugh. 'I need to go home and think about it and look at the room.'

'Thank you,' Colin said, accepting the card from the man. 'I'm sure I'll be back.'

'All good.'

'Oh. Do you know of someone who can deliver if I go ahead?'

'Oh yes. That's easily sorted. I do free delivery within the metro area.'

'That's very good of you.'

'All part of the service.'

'Great. Thanks. I'll let you know.'

'I'm going to take this,' Shirley said, placing the small church on the counter.

'Fabulous. Isn't it a great piece? A man in Port Adelaide makes them.'

'Really?'

'Yes. I'm not sure if you're aware. It's an ornament, but it's also for a train set. It's the right scale for the HO gauge, which is the most popular.'

'Oh yes. That's what I'm getting it for. That's the size I have.'

'Perfect. He does great trees too.'

'Oh. I wonder if mine are done by him – my husband was the model train buff. I've inherited it.'

'Well, I'm sure he'd appreciate you keeping it going – adding to it, even. I'll write down the guy's web address in case you want to take a look. And pop in regularly – I tend to have a few pieces on hand. We're old friends – met at a model train swap meet many moons ago – two old boys who never quite grew up,' he added, smiling.

'Well, now I'm very keen to see your train, Shirley,' Colin said, becoming a little excited.

'So you've said,' Shirley said with a cheeky glint, and winked.

Colin was relieved the guy behind the counter was looking away right at that moment.

They bid farewell to the man.

'Right, well, I'd like to now go back to your place while I've got the pieces clear in my mind,' Shirley said, as they left the shop.

'Me too. Though I did take plenty of photos. And then you can show me your train set. I'm rather keen to see it.'

'Patience, patience,' Shirley said, nudging him playfully as they made their way back to the car. 'But I'm excited about my little church.'

'It's very cute. I like that you've got a hobby collecting things.'

'Me too. It gives me a mission wherever I go. And it's how I tend to know all the second-hand shops. Though it's always when you're not looking that you find the perfect thing.'

'Listen to you. You keep saying you don't believe in airy-fairy nonsense, yet …'

'Ha. You're right. There's another example. I'm going to have to rethink my philosophies or utterances. Perhaps I don't know myself as well as I thought I did,' Shirley said. 'Or maybe you're having an impact on me.'

'In the very best way, I'm hoping.'

'Of course.'

Chapter Twenty-eight

'Oh yes,' Shirley said, standing beside Colin in what was to be his new home office. 'I reckon the couch along that wall, the desk parallel, over there, and the two tub chairs over there.' She pointed. 'It really is a fabulous room.' Colin, having considered her suggestion thoughtfully and unable to see a better arrangement, nodded.

'I agree. What do you think – the green, blue or brown chesterfield suites?' Colin asked.

'Oh. That's up to you. Which do you prefer? You can paint the room any colour. I think you need to make sure whatever colour leather you choose you can live with it. The small, less expensive things, like paint, curtains and cushions are more easily changed.'

'I'm not so sure the wall paint falls into the "easy to change" category, Shirley. I'm rather averse to climbing ladders these days. And I'm certain I no longer have adequate eyesight to do a decent paint job.'

'I'm not talking about you doing the actual work, Colin. Oh no, much easier to pay someone who has the skills and equipment than trying to cobble things together.'

'Would you know anyone, by chance?'

'I do, actually. My niece – well, she's technically my *great* niece – is a very good painter and decorator – she runs her own small business. Here, I'll show you her Instagram page. She's very talented with putting things together. So many times, she's told me what she's thinking and I've been dubious but when it's done you can't think how it could be any more perfect. Your plain curtains might work okay, but I do think we can do better. You'll see what I mean in a moment. Here it is – look.' Shirley held out her phone for Colin to see.

Colin watched as she flicked through a heap of images, which were lovely but the designs looked very high-end. His excitement began to drift away.

'Wow. Gorgeous. But very–'

'I know what you're going to say – she looks expensive. She's clever like that – great at sourcing bargains – an op-shopper and bargain hunter extraordinaire! She always does a complimentary initial free consultation and quote, so you've got nothing to lose by having her come around.'

'Oh, I like the sound of that.'

'It's entirely up to you, of course. Please don't let me bulldoze you into anything.'

'Oh no, you're not. I'm actually very keen to get her opinion now you've sown the seed.'

'The main problem might be when she could fit you in. That's the trouble with being good at something. I'll at least make contact and get the lay of the land then, shall I?'

'Oh yes, please do.'

Shirley tapped out a text message. 'There. That's sent. Now to wait and see.'

'What would I do without you?'

'Look online or ask friends for a recommendation, I expect.'

'Hmm. I suppose.'

'I just hope she can fit us in soon and I haven't got your hopes up unnecessarily.'

'We'll deal with that then, if that's the way the cookie crumbles. Meanwhile, I do appreciate your dedication to my cause.'

'I happen to think it's a very worthy cause. So, what colour chesterfield are you thinking?'

Colin pondered the matter in silence, looking around the room while he did. The brown was a good idea because it was neutral and would go with anything, wouldn't it? The blue was appealing because it was different. And then he liked the green because he really liked that colour, particularly the deep, rich shade he'd seen.

'If you're having trouble deciding, in these situations I tend to stick with the one I first saw that made my mouth water or heart sing, or whatever, before other options were presented and bamboozled me. You really did like the green. You stood at the window for ages. In my mind, you only considered the blue because it had the tub chairs on display – before you knew the green couch came with matching tubs. And the brown you most likely are gravitating towards because it's sensible – risk-free.'

'Oh, you know me so well, Shirley. I'm going to go with the green. It really did capture my attention.' And, Colin didn't like thinking this, so definitely wasn't going to say it aloud, but the green was a colour Joyce didn't particularly like, so that was another reason to choose it. Or rather, she preferred duller, greyer greens, like that in the kitchen, not the pure glossy forest or emerald shades. This was the first room he had complete say over.

'Fantastic. I suggest you contact the shop and secure them straight away – perhaps text, that way you have it in writing and there can be no confusion later.'

'Good idea,' Colin said, dragging out his phone. 'What about timing of delivery, do you think?'

'If there's a chance you're going to have the room repainted, I reckon hold off and then have everything delivered when that's done. Oh, here's Shelby now, calling me,' Shirley said, holding up her phone.

'While you take your call, I'll secure the furniture and then put the kettle on,' he said.

'Good idea. Thanks. Darling girl, how's things?' he heard Shirley say as he left the room.

On his trip down the hall, Colin decided he was going to throw caution to the wind and have Shelby do the full treatment on his room. Joyce apparently had a fabulous new life; he at least deserved a fabulous new office space! And the more he thought about Shirley's words and enthusiasm, the more he wanted it to be for clients as well.

At the table, with the kettle roaring to life behind him, Colin constructed what he hoped was a clear message with all the pertinent information for the furniture purchase. He asked if it was okay to wait a few weeks for delivery. If it was a problem, or the time stretched out too far due to Shelby's availability, he'd revise things then – perhaps have it delivered into the garage if necessary. He typed out, but then deleted, an explanation about having some work done on the room first, and instead concluded with requesting preferred payment arrangements and timing, signed off with his name and pressed send before he could get caught up in a long, drawn-out bout of editing.

He hadn't quite realised just how keen on the particular pieces he was until he received almost immediate confirmation that the items were still available and had now been placed on hold for him and a surge of relief passed through him. He was also pleased to read all other details had been verified: holding back delivery for a few weeks was fine and payment was required in full at any time prior to delivery and could be either made in-person at the shop or by direct deposit, the details of which were included. Colin was very impressed with the man's service.

He was just pouring the tea when Shirley came in.

'She's actually not far away, and has the time to drop in, so should be here in twenty-five minutes.'

'Oh wow. That's great.'

'Yes, it was a surprise to me. How did you go with the shop?'

'All good. Everything is officially mine. Well, on hold for me. I'm yet to pay – will do a payment online between now and the delivery date.'

'Brilliant. How exciting!'

'Yes. I have to admit I'm quite thrilled by it all. Though also a little daunted.'

'Of course you are. If it's about the money, I get it, I'm careful too. And don't worry. Shelby's used to clients querying costs and working to tight budgets. She'll go through everything clearly and if you have any issues, just say. She's very forthright and down to earth, you'll see, so don't hold back on asking any questions you have.'

Just go with it, old man. One step at a time.

Colin nodded and concentrated on his tea.

They stood leaning against the bench, sipping from their mugs, and then Shirley turned to look out the window.

'Would you like me to source a gardener?' Shirley said.

'Is that a dig about the roses needing deadheading?'

'No. It's fine. I just see how big your garden is.'

'Do you have a nephew or another niece who's a gardener or landscaper?'

'I do, as it happens. We're a practical, hands-on family,' Shirley said with a laugh. She looked at Colin with raised eyebrows.

'I quite like spending time out there trimming it, when I can find the necessary motivation. Thanks for the offer, and it's certainly something to think about, but how about we focus on the office for now?'

'Fair enough. It's not like it's going anywhere.'

'No, that's true.'

'You might find one thing done – the office – triggers the energy to tackle all sorts of other jobs. I tend to find a cascade of impetus occurs.' She looked thoughtful. 'I can help you with it too, if you like. I'm pretty good with the secateurs. Except, of course, if it's one of those things you want to and need to do yourself.'

'Yes, it probably is actually. I'm not entirely sure at this point, to be honest. I've always done it.'

'Fair enough. I understand. Bit like me and Christmas lunch. I've always made Christmas lunch – turkey, roast pork, all the trimmings, pudding … Woe betide anyone who tried to help! Yes, I know, perhaps this is one of those reasons why the kids live elsewhere with their partners.'

Colin didn't know how to respond to that.

'And the joke's on Norman for dying and leaving his trains for me to play with. He'd have a conniption to know I've become a town planner and rearranged everything, poor fellow. So, yes, I know we all have our quirks.'

Colin really liked how well she knew herself and was unapologetic about who she was and her foibles. He wished he had her confidence. Maybe it would rub off on him. He could hope. And he had, after all, just ordered a bold green leather suite of furniture.

'Here she is. That was quick,' Shirley said as the doorbell rang. They both headed out to greet Shirley's niece.

'What a gorgeous house! Great bones!' Shelby said when Shirley had made the introductions.

'Thanks,' Colin said, feeling pleased with her appraisal but not knowing what else to say.

'It's a much-loved family home. As you can see, Colin is also in need of a hallstand. We were off to look for one but got sidetracked,' Shirley said as Shelby looked around the mainly empty space.

'Okay. I'll think about if I've seen anything suitable and where, and let you know.'

'Thank you. I'd appreciate that. Though the office is now the priority. Come on through, it's this way.'

'Great,' she said.

They moved to the door into the room in question.

'Isn't it fabulous?' Shirley said. 'It's going to be a home office. Colin's a psychologist, so it *could* become his main business premises too–'

'I've decided. I *will* be working from here.'

'Oh, that's great. Good for you!' Shirley said.

'Right, so it needs to be welcoming and comfortable for clients as well as for you to spend time in alone,' Shelby said thoughtfully. 'Got it.'

'Actually, do you have any contacts in the area of security, Shelby?' Shirley asked.

'I sure do. Several. Do you have a particular concern?' Shelby looked at Colin, who cringed.

'It's a bit embarrassing, actually. I've been evicted from my current premises, um, due to a bit of an online campaign that's, er, apparently affected the other tenants. I think. It's a bit of a long story.'

'Oh no. How awful. I hope you're okay. The stuff online can be brutal and very traumatic, even without going viral.'

'Thank you. I'm fine. Luckily, or unluckily – whichever way you look at it – it seems I completely missed the whole thing. I'm really not much into all the online stuff. My w– My approach is to bury my head in the sand and hope it blows over or blows itself out. Honestly, its machinations are all a bit beyond my old analogue brain. Perhaps if I'd seen it earlier and tried to delete, but …' Colin let it go and shrugged.

'I doubt it would have helped. People are so quick to take screenshots now, there's really no point trying to delete them.'

'That's what I said,' Shirley cut in.

'I think all you can do is wait it out and hope for the best. That would be my approach, for what it's worth. So, you need to make sure you're going to be safe if you bring the business home, right?' Shelby said.

'Exactly.'

'There'll be a solution. I'm sure of it. There's so much great affordable tech these days. I'll keep it in mind, but let me think about in here first.'

'Brilliant. Thanks.' Colin felt the tightness inside him begin to uncoil. He moved over to the French doors and opened them in order for Shelby to see the whole room.

'He's got a full suite of dark green chesterfield furniture and an English oak desk coming from the place in Kensington with the two bay windows – we've just been there,' Shirley said. 'Show her the pictures you took, Colin.'

Colin went back over to the women and opened up his phone.

'Oh. Okay. Perfect. That'll go brilliantly in here with the dark timber. What about floor covering? I'm not saying there's anything wrong with bare floors – they're gorgeous, especially being original and in such great nick. It's just that rolling an office chair on floorboards might be quite loud and also can be a bit dangerous. Plus, a rug will dampen the sound generally and make it feel cosier.'

'I see. That makes sense,' Colin said.

'What do you like, Colin?' Shelby asked.

'How about one of those white ones with the thick tufts? I don't recall the name of it.'

'Do you mean shagpile?' Shelby said.

'That's the one. What about that? Or not?' he added, frowning, having just noticed Shirley wrinkling her nose with clear distaste before turning her face away.

'It's your office, you can have anything you want,' Shelby said.

'But …?' Colin looked from Shelby to Shirley.

'Well, you probably won't be able to roll an office chair over shagpile,' Shelby said.

'Oh. Of course. Good point. I hadn't thought about that. See, I don't know this stuff.'

'Well, that's what I'm here for,' Shelby said with a kind smile. Colin was grateful to her for not treating him like the clueless idiot he clearly was in this situation.

'Also, if you ever decide to get a robovac to make life easier, it'll probably get stuck,' Shirley chimed in.

'I see. Yes, perhaps it would be best if I leave it up to you, Shelby, with your input, Shirley. What do you think?'

'That's perfectly fine with me.'

'Definitely. How about a handmade or machine-made Persian style rug?' Shirley said.

'Yes, or go plain with a looped jute – or other natural fibre – for adding a bit more of a modern touch. Actually, show me those pictures again. Are the colours true, do you think?'

'Yes, pretty close, I reckon,' Shirley said, peering in.

Colin looked on, trying to follow the conversation.

'I have a couple of rugs for sale. I often buy bits and pieces to keep on hand for clients,' she explained to Colin. 'And I'm always combing op shops and second-hand stores. It's an addiction. Perhaps I need to see you about my problem,' she added with a laugh.

'It's not a problem, it's a business that you're doing very well at,' Shirley said.

'Well, I hope you say that when I ask if I can stack some stuff in your spare room under your train set because I've run out of space in my unit.'

'Okay, well, *then* you might need to come and see Colin about dealing with your addiction.'

'Maybe we can do a barter arrangement for the labour,' Colin said, joining the banter. But he instantly regretted his choice of words, which most likely had him coming across as a cheapskate.

'I'd be happy with that. Whatever works. Now, this lovely space …' Shelby pulled a notebook and tape measure from her bag and began taking measurements and making notes, Shirley beating Colin and hurrying over to hold the end of the tape several times when it kinked and twisted in the wrong direction.

'Please don't think my budget is minuscule,' he said, feeling the need to say something while he stood watching on as the women moved about the room. 'I'm just not sure how much one ought to be allocating for such a project.'

'No worries. I'll put together an itemised quote so you can decide if you want to leave anything out.'

'What do you think about window coverings?' Shirley said.

'I'm all for drapes. It will depend on which rug we go with – plain for the windows if going patterned on the floor, or floral and colourful if having a plain floor covering. Don't worry, when I say floral, it doesn't need to be too feminine or fussy. There are a lot of modern large floral prints now and geometric abstracts that look a little floral due to their repetitive pattern. I've got some samples in my car.'

'Now, walls. Any idea about paint colours – neutral or are we going bold?'

'Um.' Colin thought for a moment. 'I'm not sure about actual colour – happy to be guided on that – but I think I'm rather keen to be bold for a change.'

'Listen to you, Colin, you brave thing!' Shirley said.

'I tell you what, if you decide after, say, a week or so that you really don't like the colour, I'll change it free of charge. How about that?'

'That's very generous of you, Shelby. Thank you. I'm sure it won't come to that. I'm all in, as they say.'

'Brilliant, Colin. What direction are you thinking, Shelby?'

'I think let's try matching the couch. Green is a refreshing, natural colour that evokes feelings of harmony and balance. Blue is also good, but since you've got the green leather sorted, let's go with that.' Colin watched as she pulled from her bag a thin but long book containing masses of paint colours, which she began flicking through. 'Ah, here we are. Colin, how about this?'

'Yes. It's lovely.' Colin thought the colour very nice, but he turned around trying to picture a whole wall in it and couldn't.

'I think it'll work with either the plain rug or patterned one I have in mind,' Shelby said.

'I have no idea what goes with what. Honestly, I'm happy to trust you and be surprised. You haven't said anything to this point that concerns me, so I have no doubt I'll be absolutely thrilled with the result.'

'Great. I think I have a good grasp on what will suit you, but rest assured, Colin, I'd never leave you with a room you're not completely satisfied with,' Shelby said.

Colin returned Shelby's warm smile, feeling absolutely no qualms.

'Good on you, Colin, just roll with it,' Shirley said, also smiling broadly.

Again, Colin experienced a surge of excitement, and gratitude.

'Do you need the furniture here in order to choose your colours and curtain ideas, or are the photos enough, Shelby?' Colin now asked. 'I'm just thinking of the logistics. I suppose I could get everything delivered out to the verandah and cover it up. But I'm not sure about moving it in, so would have to get someone to help. Unless you have a team?'

'No, it's just me, but I do have plenty of reputable people I can get hold of, if necessary. Anyway, you said the furniture's at the Kensington place, Auntie Shirley? That makes life easier. I've bought a lot from him over the years. Steve's great to deal with. I'm sure he'll be fine with bringing it once we've done the room and then placing everything exactly where we want. I can take care of arranging that.

'Now I've been in here a while, I'm definitely leaning more towards a plain rug for the floor – it's the cheaper option too – and patterned curtains. I'll just pop out and get my sample book. Back in a sec. Can I get to my car from here?' Shelby said, pointing to the French doors.

'Oh yes. Just go around the corner and through the picket gate, rather than traipsing through the house,' Colin said.

'Isn't she fabulous?' Shirley said when she and Colin were alone again.

'She sure is. Very reassuring.'

'What fun!'

'Yes, I have to admit to feeling quite pleased at the prospect of my new office.'

'It's going to be awesome. And you're going to love it, I just know it.'

Colin smiled. Inside he glowed. Shirley's enthusiasm was contagious. At this point he didn't even care what this was costing him.

'What a great spot. It gave me a different perspective coming back around. I love the French doors. It really is perfect for clients coming here – nice and easy to access, and private. The garden is beautiful and welcoming. Only thing I'd do outside is put a water feature – for the soothing sound of water – in a spot where you can hear it inside. Anyway, just another thought I had. But it's pretty special just the way it is,' Shelby said as she re-entered the room, large folder of fabric samples in her arms that she was already flicking through. 'Here. This one. This is what I'm thinking for drapes,' she finally said, tilting the book towards Colin and Shirley.

'Ooh yes. That's lovely,' Shirley said.

'It's very nice,' Colin said.

'See what I mean about it sort of looking floral but it's actually an abstract geometric print?'

'Yes. I do see what you mean.'

'And definitely not too fussy. Strong, bold, gives a no-nonsense and reliable air, which is just what you want,' Shirley said.

'Listen to you, Auntie Shirley. Exactly right. So, Colin, try and picture walls in this green colour, a plain, pale beige rug – with edges of your dark timber floor visible – curtains around the doors and the window in this, and then the green couch there and tub chairs there. Desk over there,' Shelby said, thoughtfully, clearly ticking things off in her mind while pointing. Colin watched her finger, nodding. It all made sense and he was surprised at how well he could now picture it in his mind.

'And he'll need a small coffee or occasional table – two actually – for a box of tissues and glass of water,' Shirley said.

'Oh yes,' Shelby said, 'good point. I might have the perfect thing in my collection. Or we can go and do another day looking.'

'We'd want round, wouldn't we?' Shirley said.

'I think so. And definitely timber – either dark or light will work, but not stained too red. What are you doing for file storage?'

'Oh. I haven't given it any thought,' Colin said, frowning.

'I think a cupboard – like a sideboard style, lower, for under the window there. In oak, to go with the desk, would be perfect,' Shelby said.

'Ooh, yes,' Shirley said.

'Sounds good to me.'

Shelby took additional measurements and wrote them down, along with some more notes. 'Okay, that's me for now,' she finally said, closing her book. 'I'll get a quote to you this afternoon. Actually, on second thoughts, it'll be tomorrow. Any questions before then?'

Colin searched his brain and initially came up empty. *Oh god, of course!* 'When could you do it – the work, the painting, get the curtains made, have everything up and running?' he asked.

'I did warn Colin you'd most likely be booked out for some time,' Shirley said.

'It's a small job – the painting will only take a day. Not much prep is needed. We might have to wait on the curtains, we'll see, but it's no problem for me to come back and hang them later. But for painting, and everything else, how about next weekend? Is that too short notice?'

'Not for me. But I don't want to put you out,' Colin said.

'Oh no. You wouldn't be. I wouldn't suggest it if it was. I've actually had a client postpone. That's why I can fit you in. After that I'll be tied up until after Christmas, barring any other changes. Just make sure you're happy with my quote and then decide. I don't want you feeling put on the spot. Auntie Shirley, no pressuring the poor fellow.'

'All right, all right. That'll be enough out of you, young lady.'

Colin watched on, enjoying immensely their banter and good-natured ribbing.

'Okay? All clear?' Shelby said, looking at Colin.

'Perfectly. Thank you.'

'I'd better run. It's been so great to meet you, Colin. It really is a gorgeous space.'

'And it's going to be even more stunning when you've worked your magic,' Shirley chimed in.

'Well, that's up to Colin. Seriously, there's no pressure and no hard feelings if you decide not to go ahead, for any reason.'

'I appreciate you saying, Shelby, thank you,' Colin said.

'Oh, I almost forgot. Do you want me to have someone contact you to discuss security options? Again, no pressure – from me or him. Aaron's his name. He's a good guy with a wealth of knowledge, and also does free quotes.'

'Oh, yes, please. I'd be very interested in meeting with him if you can arrange it. Or you can send me his details and I can do it?'

'That's okay. I'm happy to call him. Great, well, I'll be in touch very soon.'

'Bye for now.'

And then she was heading out the glass doors with a final wave of her hand.

'Wow,' Colin said in response to Shelby's effervescence, departure, ideas, and everything about the last half an hour.

'Isn't she great?'

'She sure is.'

'I'm sure the quote will be very reasonable, too.'

'Everything about her seemed to be that way, so I'm sure it'll be fine. At this point I'd say yes to pretty much anything she said. What a lovely young human – and clearly very talented. I can see why you're exuding all the proud auntie vibes.'

'Oh, you've no idea, Colin. If you knew where she'd come from, what she's had to overcome. She's not had it easy, let's just leave it at that, and yet she's remained a beautiful and very kind soul.'

'What a perfect day.'

'It sure has been. Well, except for the eviction.'

'Don't remind me.' Colin was surprised to find he really had forgotten it and now he'd been reminded of it, it didn't hold anywhere near the same power.

Chapter Twenty-nine

Despite not having to be out of his rented office for another two weeks, Colin was a little apprehensive when approaching the door from the carpark on Monday morning. He half expected to have been locked out, or find the security code had changed without him being notified.

As he successfully unlocked his own office door and turned the light on, he laughed to himself at having his distrust and pessimism proven unfounded – he'd entered and no alarms were currently blaring. As it was, he was experiencing both relief at his admittance but also a sense of slight disappointment.

Two weeks was a long time to spend here now he knew of the animosity towards him. But he had to. The other tenants had always ignored him, or barely glanced his way or only offered a grunt in acknowledgement when in close proximity. He just hoped it continued that way and there was no additional noticeable tension in the air. If only his new office at home could have been done yesterday. He was excited to see what Shelby would do.

Meanwhile, he had an email to respond to, notifying the centre he would be leaving without a fight, already drafted and only needing him to press send, an office to sort through, and bits and pieces to pack up in among a full schedule of clients.

He read through his short response:

Subject: Notice of eviction from 51 Newland Road.
Dear Tory,
Thank you for your email.

I agree it's an unfortunate situation we find ourselves in. Please accept my sincere apologies for any inconvenience and upset caused to you and the other tenants. I understand and accept your position and will therefore vacate my office space on or before 6pm on Friday November 21st.

I wish you all well in your endeavours.
Yours sincerely,
Colin Palmer
Clinical Psychologist
The Golden Leaf Allied Health Centre
51 Newland Road, Trinity Gardens SA 5068

Colin read through the message. He still felt the itch to defend himself, seek clarification, and explain he'd known nothing about the online carry-on, if need be, as well as also trying to adequately express his level of mortification on the matter. But he also agreed with Shirley that there was no point in going into things any further and the best thing to do was to simply show his respect and capitulation, and express his agreement with the terms set out in Tory's email. Thus, he pressed send and prepared to get on with his day, which involved really nailing down the new direction for his business and preparing for it. He hadn't felt this enthused for ages.

He'd spent the evening before roughly crunching the numbers, becoming more and more excited, and had decided he could definitely, financially, do without the couples counselling. Thank goodness for that!

He was also keen to stop doing psychometric testing at the corporate level when the last bookings were out of the way. He'd happily keep on with private clients needing testing and career advice. He'd never really thought about it before, but now, with his salubrious new workspace in mind – and he just knew it was going to be fabulous – he wondered how much influence these current drab surrounds might have had on test participants' results. On all clients, for that matter … *Hmm*. Oh well, he couldn't dwell on that now. He was making the change, and that was what was important. And he was feeling so optimistic about it he was sure he'd attract the sort of clients he enjoyed working with more and closing down these parts of his business was going to be fine. His mind went to his client Andrea Carlton and how valued she'd made him feel. Maybe he was a better psychologist than he gave himself credit for. Shirley had said as much, hadn't she?

And Colin was sure he'd be even better if he wasn't so worn down by having to listen to ridiculous couples bickering, and administering so many tests that he didn't fully support.

Given the increasing prevalence of people seeking help generally, and the volume of victims of domestic abuse and narcissists – which was often tied up together – he'd have a much more fulfilling work life. In his positive state he was certain plenty more clients would come. If they didn't, he could look into advertising, which he'd never done before. He saw lots of ads online whenever he was on YouTube or browsing.

He could look into that right now … *No, stay on track.* He had to write the wording for the website, do the same for the

Facebook page. Maybe he'd get over his fear of that and embrace it, utilise it properly ... He also had to write to all his corporate clients explaining the situation. Oh, and advise everyone of his new address. He'd better start by making a list of things to work through slowly. Yes, one step at a time, bite-sized pieces ... At the top should probably be updating his address details with everyone who had it. He quickly wrote down the items that had already come to him.

He paused and frowned at the haphazard nature of the items, and then sighed. There was so much to consider and learn, across a variety of areas: website, social media ... The automated booking and integrated finance system ran smoothly in the background, but Joyce had spent ages with online tutorials and the helpdesk when setting it up, so he'd better get up to speed with that too.

It was overwhelming and wearing just thinking about it all. Where was Joyce when he needed her? She'd have everything done in a flash, would no doubt put an efficient system immediately in place or pluck one out of nowhere.

The thoughts pulled him up. He sighed again and rubbed his face. He'd really had it good with not having to deal with all of this tiresome and tiring admin.

But that hadn't always been the case, had it? When had their roles changed so much? He'd once been the authority figure in the household and not only in his mind — Joyce had said so back in the early days. But somewhere along the way Joyce had taken over that role. When? Had it been after losing the twins? Had she needed someone else to mother? Perhaps. Memory pulled.

Ah. That was when he'd also embarked on studying, on top of working, and she'd taken over paying the bills and had begun helping him with research. He'd always thought the new shared interest had helped them through their grief. But perhaps he'd just dropped the ball and indulged in some weaponised incompetence. *That is the term, isn't it? Oh. It had been Joyce who'd mentioned it. Is that a hint I missed?* She'd done all the background work for setting up the business and handled the finances and bookings before the fantastic automated systems they now used which, thankfully, were both simple enough even he handled them without issue. Though he hadn't had any tech problems to sort out since she'd been gone ...

Oh. She'd indicated she'd been missing working and feeling useful, hadn't she? Maybe he could employ her as his administration assistant – and actually pay her. *No.* No doubt any lingering voids created by retirement would have been fulfilled or washed away by her new and blossoming relationship with Carmel.

Anyway, oh dear, poor Joyce. Most likely she'd not actually run *to* Carmel but *away* from him. He longed to apologise to her. Maybe one day he'd have the chance to, and perhaps somehow make amends, though he had no idea what that might look like.

But right now, he wanted to make some headway before his new private client by the name of Cameron Doyle arrived a bit later. He at least wanted to send the emails withdrawing his testing services from his corporate clients before he had a chance to have any wobbles on that decision.

Oh, I can do a proforma and just add the details. Yes, that will save some effort. Smart thinking. Go, Colin, he thought gleefully, conjuring an image of his cheerful and wholeheartedly supportive new friend Shirley, and smiling himself in response.

Colin found his mind drifting to their conversation about the twins' deaths. Shirley's understanding had meant so much to him, and had cemented their friendship. Humans tended to behave awkwardly around death. Or perhaps it was just Westerners. He'd never looked into the customs of other regions or cultures. But the immediate loss all too often saw the deceaseds' names banished, as if mentioning them might bring up the pain, make the grief sadder and harder. But those who hadn't lost didn't know how the silencing deepened the well of pain. That had certainly been his and Joyce's experience. They had regularly discussed this fact and taken great care to keep talking about James and Thomas, particularly being mindful of using their names – having to consciously do so in the first days, weeks and months. Gradually it had become commonplace. And it had proven so incongruous to others that they'd been greeted with strange looks, as if their grief had consumed their mental faculties. So many of their friends must have endured miscarriages and not let on, such had been the times. He knew the self-silencing added immeasurably to pain, thanks to those he treated decades on who came to him often only able to speak the names of the lost to someone who wouldn't shut them down or tell them enough time had passed – that enough was enough. *Concentrate on the children you have. Don't dwell on the past, the negatives. Move on.* But how could anyone know the enduring loss and reminder for the living as each milestone and achievement was checked off – the exhaustion of living in a world where you had to put your own pain aside in order to make those around you more comfortable?

When it came to dealing with grief out in the wild, it really was hard not to despair of the human race. Hell, only recently were employers beginning to start to accept that a pet was a family member, and worthy of a day away from the office at times of illness and bereavement. The failings didn't bear thinking about; it risked being dragged into a quagmire of despair one was unable to climb back out of again. At least he was doing his bit to help those who sought him out and he was determined to do an even better job going forward.

Colin felt good about the amount of headway he'd made when he finished up his current task and prepared for Cameron's arrival. He'd felt so energised he'd been unable to fall asleep for his usual nap, instead using the time to separate his long list of things to do into smaller separate groupings.

'Come on in and take a seat. Anywhere you like,' Colin said, standing back, offering the nervous, frowning man a reassuring smile.

Cameron plonked himself down on the couch and remained rigid and upright, fiddling with his sunglasses in his lap, feet close together, knees touching. His eyes seemed to dart around the room, taking in his surroundings. *Is he frightened? On drugs? Suffering PTSD? A victim of abuse?* Colin wondered as he waited for the appropriate moment to speak and gave the fellow a chance to relax. Though current indications were that relaxation was doubtful. Colin silently cleared his throat and mentally steeled himself to do his best for the man and also not take on the energy himself. The older he got, the harder that was becoming. It didn't help that he no longer had Joyce to decompress with. Maybe working from home with different and plusher surrounds would help with this too.

'Now, how can I be of assistance, Cameron?' he asked, deciding to take charge.

'Are you a no-nonsense type of bloke?'

'I have been known to be, yes,' Colin said, again trying to reassure him with another smile and hoping he wasn't instead coming across creepy. It could be a fine line. 'Firstly, take a couple of deep breaths. Try to relax. You don't want to break them,' he said, nodding at the sunglasses. Colin watched the white-knuckle grip on the item in question ease a little.

'Oh yes. Shit. I'm a bit tightly wound,' Cameron said with a tight, awkward laugh, which came out more like a cross between a croak and a gasp. 'Best I put them down here,' he said, leaning forward and placing the sunglasses on the arm of the couch. Sorry, I'm a bit of a mess,' he said, running both hands over his face and through his hair.

I'm leaning towards him being the victim of abuse. Physical or emotional? Emotional, I reckon.

'Have some water.' Colin now watched the young man pick up the glass with a hand so shaky he had to add his other. He gulped the water so forcefully Colin was waiting for him to start choking and spluttering.

'Okay. That's better. Thanks,' he said after returning the glass to its coaster.

'I'm glad. Now, tell me how I can help.'

'I really hope you can. It's my wife – well, I suppose, technically my *estranged* wife, as of several hours ago. She moved out.' He harumphed with resignation, or bewilderment, or perhaps even satisfaction – Colin couldn't tell which. 'She's been having an affair.'

Ah, Colin thought, but remained silent, choosing to nod instead.

'But here's the thing. She denies it, despite me last night actually reading the texts on her phone and her confirming it. But this morning she reckons she didn't say anything of the sort and that there are no such text messages on her phone. Plus, she refuses to let me look again. And, here's another thing, neither of us had been drinking or doing drugs – or anything that would explain such a confusing situation. I feel like I'm losing my mind.' Again he rubbed his face with his hands before pushing them through his hair.

Hmm. Not drugs or too much alcohol ... Gaslighting?

'Have you forgotten other things?'

'Well, yes. Or no. Sorry. She says I have. But I'm sure I haven't.'

'Such as?'

'She told me she was home by eleven the other night. I'd gone to bed early and then got up to get a drink of water and she wasn't in bed and I checked the driveway and her car wasn't there. We had a huge argument about it. But I looked at the time because I was worried about her.'

My money's on you being gaslit and her being a narcissist. Go on, prove me wrong.

'I see,' Colin said. 'Have you experienced any other issues of a similar nature – not relating to your wife? Such as at work or out with friends?'

'No. I'm an IT executive. I'm focussed. Well, not right now, because of this.' He waved a hand. 'But up until very recently, I've felt fine, at least with regards to work.'

'Has your wife lied in the past?'

'Not that I'm aware of. Oh. Um. Well, just the odd little thing, now I think of it. A bit of money was missing from the bank account and, when I enquired, she told me it was for one of our subscriptions. But it's for a subscription I paid myself the week before. I put it down to her being cagey because she was buying me a gift for my birthday, which wasn't far away, but we don't really do gifts and nothing materialised. So now I guess it was something for the bloke she denies having an affair with. What a mess. I just can't wrap my head around it. Everything feels out of whack. Fuzzy. They're the two main things I can pinpoint. We used to be able to communicate quite well. Or so I thought – I don't know anything right now.'

'Hmm. How long have you been together?'

'Eight months. I know, it doesn't sound like long. It's a whirlwind situation. Maybe that's why it feels so devastating.

You know. I'm not the best-looking bloke. And when a woman shows interest, call me shallow, but I grab her with both hands. She's absolutely stunning. Look.' He held out his phone where an image of a bikini-clad younger woman was smiling at the camera, head tilted.

Colin opened his mouth to speak, but before he could say a word, Cameron ploughed on.

'You'll probably think me terrible, but what single man is going to turn down a beautiful woman showing him attention? I mean, you hear some shocking stories about online dating and catfishing these days. But this wasn't like that at all. I was getting lunch at a bakery and we got chatting. And, as they say, the rest is history. Absolutely stunning. I wouldn't have had the guts to ask her out, so it's lucky she took charge. And, yes, I've always had low self-esteem. I think.

'Anyway, I can't believe after less than a year, she's doing this. I mean, one thing to decide you don't like me, for whatever reason, but an affair? And there's no need to be so cruel. I don't really want to get into the details of that now, but I might have turfed her out myself if I wasn't such a wimp. Anyway, I thought it was blokes who were the main cheaters. And then why deny it?'

'Cameron, you asked for no-nonsense?'

'Yes. Lay it on me, because I'm losing my mind here.'

'Right. Well, I suspect you've been a victim of love-bombing.'

'Is that as self-explanatory as I'm thinking – like, being over the top with love and affection and gifts and stuff?'

'That's right. And you just said she was cruel, so much so you might have asked her to leave you?'

'Yes. Picking fights, mimicking me, belittling me. Sorry, I can't think of anything specific. I'd rather not go into it, if you don't mind.'

'That's okay, I get the picture.'

'Do you? There's an actual picture – this is a *thing*?'

'Well, without knowing your wife, I can only speculate, of course. But I suspect there's every likelihood of you being the victim of a narcissistic abuse cycle. Or she might be a psychopath.'

'God. Isn't that what serial killers are? Don't answer that, I don't want to know. My head's spinning enough as it is. I've heard of narcissism in relation to bigwigs in the corporate world. Some blokes seem to wear the title as some sort of badge of honour – I don't get that. So, abuse, as in domestic abuse?'

'Yes. It can be. It's a covert and insidious form of domestic violence.'

'Okay, but why?'

'I don't know. Perhaps she's stringing you both along for some reason. Money?'

'Well, I don't have a lot spare. She knows that. I've been up front about everything right from the start.'

'Unfortunately, there might be no reason at all that's obvious – other than that they choose to manipulate and torment their victims. Not unlike a domestic cat preying on a mouse or bird it doesn't need or intend to eat – it's sport.'

'Oh god. I guess that would explain the mixed messages and confusion.'

'It sure would.'

'So, is what I'm saying making sense to you?'

'Oh yes. Perfectly. I've seen it plenty of times.' *Sadly, our conversation could be part of a case study in a textbook.*

'Well, thank Christ for that. You said it's a cycle – if it is what you say it is?'

'That's right.'

'So, what happens next? And, more importantly, what do I do?'

'Well, another phase, that doesn't always get enacted, is hoovering. It involves trying to win you back – sucking you back in, if you will. The term is in reference to the well-known brand name of vacuum cleaner, the Hoover.'

'And, then, if that happens the cycle starts again, right?'

'Exactly.'

'I'm exhausted just thinking about it.'

'I imagine your whole life is exhausting with trying to navigate it – all the wondering, second-guessing, confusion.'

'You're right about that.'

'So, what do I do now?'

'If your wife still has keys, I suggest you change the locks and cease contact with her. It sounds drastic, but you're vulnerable to her charms. You've been there before. It will just continue until you break the cycle.'

'Yes, I can see that.'

'You said before you've always had low self-esteem?'

'That's right. For as long as I can remember.'

'Well, if you'd like to work on building your sense of worth, that would be a good place to start. It's actually one of the traits a narcissist looks for in a victim.'

'So if I'm not weak, I can't be lured in, is that it?'

'I didn't say you're weak. And I don't think that at all. You're showing considerable strength and courage in being here today and talking about all this.'

'Okay. My dad always said I was weak as piss. So, you can help with making me feel better about myself?'

'Absolutely.'

'I'd really like that. Maybe then I'll meet the right person.'

'Don't get ahead of yourself. One step at a time.' *If I'm right, you've got a lot of work and healing to do.* 'But I think that's a good place to end today. It's a lot for you to get your head around.'

'Yes. But I do feel so much better for having voiced it. And knowing it's a *thing* and not just me losing my mind. Thank you so much, Colin.'

'It's been my pleasure, Cameron.'

'I'm definitely coming back – I'll book in again online. You've been great. And already a big help.'

'I look forward to helping you sort through some things. One thing, though, I'm moving premises in a couple of weeks. Not far away. All the details will be on the booking app. I'm just mentioning it since you're here,' Colin said as he processed Cameron's payment.

'Righto. Thanks for that. See you later, then.'

'Goodbye, Cameron. Take good care.'

Colin sat back down behind his desk and returned to his to-do list and thoughts of his new streamlined business. Once he got settled in his home office, should he think about setting up some in-person group sessions for the likes of Andrea, Cameron and his other clients dealing with similar issues? It was certainly something worth thinking about.

Chapter Thirty

The rest of the week passed uneventfully for Colin and then, true to her word, Shelby had spent the weekend in Colin's new office, the project coming together on time and on budget. It was late Sunday afternoon and she'd just left. Colin was now seated at his newly placed timber desk and Shirley was on the chesterfield couch nearby. He sighed contentedly. The result was even more stunning than he'd envisaged.

He now had one week left at the old premises and couldn't wait to leave, having laid eyes on several other tenants in the building and experienced averted gazes or people who moved quickly away without a word. It gave him a whole new perspective on the clients who came to him about toxic workplaces and bosses, of which there were many.

'So, how do you feel? What do you think?' Shirley asked Colin.

'Amazing. I have to be honest; I wasn't entirely sure how I'd like a room with all green walls, but it's great. And I do feel both relaxed and focussed. Shelby was so right about the colour choice in terms of aesthetics and from a therapy point of view. What do you think?'

'Oh, yes, absolutely. I love it! I agree, it's sumptuous and tranquil, and I feel very comfortable. Your other space was okay, but not a patch on this. What's your favourite thing, do you think?'

Colin didn't need to look around the room again. 'Of course, I love everything, but that.' He pointed up to the abstract multicoloured oil painting with its thick textured paint and heavy gold frame, titled 'Wildflowers'. 'I have to admit, when Shelby said she'd found the perfect piece of art for that wall, and it was an abstract, I was dubious,' he said, spreading his hands out wide.

'Well, well done for just trusting her.'

'Yes, I'm not sure what I had in mind – sharp edges or really bright colours – but that ties in beautifully with the green and multiple colours in the curtains. I see now how every single thing is connected or relates *somehow*. It's quite incredible. How about you – what do you like the most?'

'If I really have to choose, then it's the lino-cut prints up there.' She turned and pointed to the wall behind the chesterfield couch where a series of four small black and white prints of old buildings hung in dark grey frames.

'Yes, they're marvellous.'

'Honestly, it's not just the room that's been renovated, I feel completely rejuvenated and excited for the future,' Colin said.

'That's great, Colin. I'm really pleased for you.'

'Thank you so much, Shirley.'

'Oh, I didn't do much.'

'But you did. I'd probably still be worrying about the eviction email without your guidance.'

'Ah, you'd have figured it out. But thank you for your acknowledgement. It means a lot. I hadn't quite realised how much I need to feel useful on a practical level – somewhere to direct my bossiness. And thank you for trusting Shelby. She loved doing it too.'

'She's clearly a lot more talented than simply the painting side of things. It's amazing how quickly she can pull things together.'

'Yes, especially the curtains getting made. I was sure that would prove an impossibility. Oh, it's all so lovely! It makes my mouth water. You know what the next thing is, don't you?'

'What's that?' Colin looked around. He was genuinely baffled.

'We need to hunt for the perfect water feature.'

'Yes, though I bet Shelby stumbles across one first. It was genius to take the outdoor setting from the front garden and put it out there under the verandah, rather than suggesting buying more seating. Overall, it's not been as expensive as I'd feared. And worth every cent. Now, as a thank you to you for everything, how do you feel about me cooking you dinner tonight? Are you free and would you like to stay on? Or go and come back?'

Colin became a little flustered. He wasn't sure why – perhaps it was the daunting task of cooking for someone else competent in that area, particularly while under scrutiny.

'Oh, you don't need to cook for me, Colin, though I'd like it very much. But no pressure.'

'I know it's Sunday, but I'm doing a beef curry, if that's of any consequence – either way.'

'My, you are changing, Colin! I must admit I do like the idea of being cooked for.'

'Yes, I'm becoming positively recalcitrant!' he said with a laugh. 'So …?'

'I accept your very kind invitation, thank you, Colin.' Shirley checked her watch. 'I'll stay on, if that's not going to discombobulate you too much while cooking. You can put me to work as your sous chef.'

'Great, well, I'm going to head to the kitchen and get started. I want it to simmer for a few hours. Would you like to join me or stay here enjoying the new room?'

'I'll come and keep you company, as lovely as it is here. I could do with a cup of tea.'

'Good idea.' They got up and made their way out.

'I'm so pleased Shelby found the hallstand, too. It's perfect,' Shirley said, pausing in the hall to look over at the piece of Edwardian oak furniture, which looked to Colin as if it might have been made for the space. He thought he might even prefer it to what had been there before, but what he liked best was that the high-back chair had been returned to its place at the dining table and all was back in order.

The hallstand had come from the same place as everything else. Shelby had gone to double-check the colour of the lounge suite before choosing the paint and new stock from an auction house had arrived and she'd put a hold on it straight away, along with two small round occasional tables for his office that could be stacked together if necessary to save space. It had all worked out so perfectly with the furniture being able to be delivered at once – all coordinated by Shelby.

Colin had a new pep in his step and a warmer feel about humanity in general as a result. It was really heartening to see a dynamic, capable young person at work when there was so much in the media and online – and, to a lesser extent, in his own office – about young people's sense of entitlement and reluctance towards kindness and generosity. If more like Shelby were in charge of wider society there might be a chance of halting the downward slide of humanity he feared was almost at the point of no return.

'It rather shows up how tired the rest of the house is, though, doesn't it, having the fresh paint and the colour and everything,' Colin said, looking around as they made their way.

'It doesn't look too bad to me,' Shirley said, now looking around. 'Are you thinking you want to repaint the whole house? Change more curtains?'

'Hmm.' Now in the kitchen, Colin gazed about with new focus. It did seem drab. They hadn't repainted for years because of the upheaval involved and the issue with finding people who wouldn't rip off a senior. He and Joyce had muttered many a time that they should do it themselves, but had never quite got there.

Like many, they'd done a few rounds of painting themselves. But they'd both lost a lot of mobility in the last ten years compared to the decade before that.

'It's more that it was such a refreshingly stress-free experience having Shelby take care of things,' he said. 'It makes the world of difference. And I'm suddenly feeling I'd like more colour in my life.'

'Ha! We've created a monster.'

'Maybe. Or perhaps just woken one up.'

'Well, I'd say don't rush into anything. Repainting the whole house will require a bit of turmoil. Yes, Shelby can get someone in to help her move everything, but it's still going to be messy for a while. The question is if you want that when you're starting working from home.'

'That's a very good point, thank you. It could be unsettling for clients too. You're right.' Colin felt a little deflated.

'But I do understand that you'd want to get it all out of the way. Ongoing maintenance is exhausting. It's taxing on several levels.'

'I'm going to put all that out of my mind for now,' he said, getting a clean apron out of the drawer and putting it on.

'Cute pinny,' Shirley said, grinning.

'Thanks. Yes, I'm yet to get one for myself. Though the frilly ones do the trick, so there doesn't seem much point in getting rid of them just because men aren't meant to appreciate or be dressed in ruffles.'

'You're forgetting the sleeves in … is it Elizabethan times? Oh, and ruffs, of course – around the neck.'

'That's true. So there. Frills it is. I will embrace them!'

'Good for you!'

Colin consulted his printed-out recipe for his upcoming curry and went to the fridge where he got the ingredients out and dumped his armload onto the table.

'Give me something to do,' Shirley said. 'And an apron, please, if you have another.'

'Here we are,' he said, retrieving another apron and handing it to Shirley who stood to put it on.

'Two onions, finely chopped,' Colin read from the recipe and placed them on a board along with a large knife in front of Shirley who was now reseated at the table. 'Are you okay doing onions?'

'No problem. I might get a bit weepy, but that's okay. I'm glad to see you keep them in the fridge. It helps with the tears. Or so I've heard or read somewhere. It could be a myth.'

'I don't know why we keep them in the fridge – we always have, to the best of my knowledge. And then it's two large carrots.'

'You know, I think that same green wall colour would be lovely in here. Or a similar depth or tone but in cobalt blue. Actually, any of the colours in your beautiful teapot would work, I reckon,' Shirley said, nodding towards the object in question as she began skinning the onions.

'You're probably right. I'm trying not to think about it now,' he said with a laugh, as he got out the frying pan and placed it on the stovetop.

The onions were starting to sizzle and Shirley was chopping up the pumpkin when the doorbell rang.

'Expecting anyone?' Shirley said.

'No. Unless Shelby has forgotten something, though I don't know what that would be,' Colin said, setting down the wooden spoon. He didn't feel right about leaving Shirley to keep an eye on things when she was the guest and he the chef, so he pushed the pan off the heat before undoing his apron and hanging it over the nearest chair and heading out to see who was there. As he went, he reminded himself Aaron was coming around late Wednesday afternoon to discuss the security bits and bobs, and possibly do the work, time permitting.

Colin was surprised to open the door to find Joyce on the doorstep and was unable to keep it from his voice. He noticed she held a cardboard box.

'Joyce! Hello.'

'Hello, Colin.'

'Come in. Um, I'm in the middle of cooking, so I'd better keep an eye on things.'

'I can't stay. Oh, that's lovely,' she said, now inside and looking at the hallstand.

'Thanks,' he said, and hurried back to the kitchen, leaving Joyce to follow.

'And do I smell fresh paint?' Joyce was looking around her as she walked. 'Oh. Hello there,' she said, noticing Shirley at the stove, stirring the onions.

'Hello. Colin, I just thought I'd check they weren't sticking – in case the pan kept the heat.' Colin looked at Joyce and Shirley, who seemed to be sizing each other up. 'Thanks for that. Shirley, this is Joyce. Joyce, Shirley.'

'Hello,' they said in unison.

'We've not long since had a cuppa, if you'd like one, Joyce?' Shirley said.

'No thanks. I won't stay. I just wanted to drop this off.' She placed the box on the table.

'What is it?' Colin asked.

'Just some photos. I'll leave you to it; you're clearly busy.'

'Not too busy to stop.'

'I've actually got Carmel in the car. So …'

'You have to at least see Colin's new home office – it's just finished today, so we're quite excited, aren't we?' Shirley said.

'Yes. It's really something.' Colin was glad Shirley was taking charge of the conversation because he was a little stuck for words and what to do. Suddenly it seemed very foreign to have Joyce in the kitchen – almost like the first time he'd brought her home. A similar level of discomfort and nervousness was there, but the years had dulled the feeling, keeping it more grounded. He was experiencing a strange sense of guilt around appearing so carefree and also from the desire to show her he was fine without her.

'Come on, you have to see it.' Shirley wiped her hands on her apron and moved past Colin. He wondered if, like him, she was struggling to stop her eyebrows from raising and fighting to keep her expression neutral as she moved past him, leading Joyce out. What were Joyce's thoughts about Shirley looking so comfortable in the house, and particularly in Joyce's domain? he wondered as he followed them.

'You cook now?' Joyce said, pausing and turning back to look at Colin.

'Yes.' Colin bit back the rise of anger and the retort it brought to his tongue: *'I have to — you left me, remember?'*

'And why are you doing a home office?'

'Oh, well ...'

'Here we are,' Shirley said, opening the door and stepping into the room.

'Wow.'

Colin wondered if Joyce was perturbed at him having taken over her sewing room and was ready to reply with, *'Well, you aren't using it,'* if necessary.

'So are you an interior designer, Shirley?'

'Oh no. Not me. My niece, Shelby, is responsible for this. What do you think?'

'It's very nice. So why the move here — it looks like you'll be consulting from here, Colin, the way it's set up.'

'That's right. I got, um, evicted from the, er, other building.'

'Oh. Was it because of how much the demographic and culture over there had changed?'

'Yes, it was something like that.' *You left, Joyce, you don't get to know the ins and outs of everything now.*

'Well, you can't hope to please everyone all of the time,' Joyce said.

Colin wondered if she hated the room and this was her way of being polite. A part of him wanted her approval. Another part wanted her to be dismissive so he could be annoyed with her for more than leaving him. But as it was, he was exasperated with himself for allowing her to unsettle him to such an extent, and for the anger to be not forthcoming. In its stead was a rush of warmth and, dare he say it — think it — love for Joyce and sympathy for her current discomfiture.

'Well done, Colin, it looks great. I'd really better keep going. It was lovely to meet you, Shirley,' Joyce said, moving around them towards the door again.

'Likewise. Bye,' Shirley said.

Colin walked Joyce to the front door and then shifted on his feet while wondering if he should hug her or not. It also crossed his mind to mention their financial situation. But that wouldn't be right or fair in front of Shirley, particularly when Joyce seemed so unsettled right then. He thrust his hands into his pockets and nodded.

'Well, okay. Bye. And thanks very much for the photos,' he added, just remembering the reason for Joyce's presence.

'My pleasure. See you. Take care.'

'You too.'

As he made his way down the hall again, Colin wondered if he'd done the right thing or not. Shirley was at the stove again, tending to the onions. She turned to him.

'Apologies if I overstepped. I fear I might have. I just sensed you were a little discombobulated,' she said.

'I was a bit. So, thanks. And, no, you didn't overstep. Not at all. It was a strange situation. I suddenly felt like a shy teenager again.'

'Understandable, given the circumstances.'

'The sad thing is how uncomfortable it was. After all the decades we've spent together, and now … to be like that in each other's presence …'

'You'll get the hang of it. These things just take time.'

'Hmm. It might have helped if she could have stayed for a cuppa. And Carmel, too, for that matter.'

'Yes. Unfortunately, I feel it might have occurred if I hadn't been here.'

'It was Joyce who turned up unannounced. And, by the looks, was taken aback that I've got on with my life – am not a shell of a man, curled up sobbing in the corner.'

'As if, Colin.'

'Well, thanks to you.'

'What has she brought?'

'Photos, apparently,' he said, opening the flaps of the small box and peering inside. 'Oh. Well, that's very good of her. I wonder why ...' He brought out a stack of framed photographs, which he recognised as the ones from the tallboy in the bedroom and the top of the sideboard in the lounge. But there was something different about them. Why had Joyce returned them?

'What is it? Is that the twins, James and Thomas?'

'Yes.' Colin went through the photos, holding them up for Shirley to see.

'Good-looking young people. Great photos.'

'I wish you'd met them. They were great kids.'

'I'll bet they were.'

Colin retracted any uncharitable thoughts he may have held towards Joyce just before. 'Oh. She's actually replaced the images. And the frames, by the looks. These aren't the frames we had.' *That's good of her, I suppose. Though I quite liked the other ones. She could have at least asked my preference.*

'They're very nice.'

'They are.'

'Good quality, too, by the looks.'

'Oh, and there's a disk,' he said, noticing it in the bottom of the box. He held it up and turned it over. 'What's this, do you think?'

'A digital copy? Did she take any albums of photos?'

'I'm not sure. I'm ashamed to admit I haven't mustered the fortitude to check that particular cupboard.'

'I can relate to that. It wouldn't achieve anything – just relief at finding them there and perhaps guilt that Joyce didn't take them or disappointment and anger at finding them not there,' Shirley said, and shrugged.

Colin nodded.

'I'd love to watch it – see the photos sometime.'

'Okay. I'll just put these out of the way and get back to the dinner. But first I'll just send her a thank you text.'

'Good idea.'

'It was very kind of her,' he muttered, picking up his phone from the charger. 'I wonder if she wanted something else – to talk to me or something. It just seems odd she couldn't have left them on the step while I was at work,' he mused as he typed.

Thank you for the photos. Love, Colin.

He deliberated over deleting *love* but instead added **much appreciated. Take care** before it and pressed send before he could rethink the whole thing and get caught up going back and forth for ages.

'Perhaps she didn't want to risk the box being stolen. Maybe now was when she was in the area.'

'You're saying don't read too much into the delivery?'

'I think so. But you know Joyce. I don't. At least you've texted a thank you, so you've indicated the lines of communication are still open. Now, if there's any problem or something she *did* want to discuss, then she'll feel free to.'

'Yes, all good points. Right, curry. Where were we?' he said, more to himself, and returned to the recipe beside the stove.

'I must say, I do like seeing a man slaving over a hot stove for me,' Shirley said.

'Well, hold your applause for the finished product. It might yet be inedible.'

'Unlikely. But duly noted. How are you going with today's crossword? I see a few gaps. Can I help, or are you precious about them?'

'No. I'd be glad of the assistance.'

'Right. Let's see ...'

Three hours later they had a completed crossword and bowls of curry, rice and green vegetables in front of them. Colin was proud of his accomplishment – well, visually. They were yet to dive in. He waited expectantly for Shirley to begin, watching carefully for her immediate reaction. He was disappointed by how much he longed for her approval. But thankfully he received it.

'Yum, Colin, it's very good. And, no, I'm not just saying that,' she said.

'Not too hot, not too runny?'

'No. And no. Perfect. Now stop fishing for compliments and eat,' she added gently. They exchanged smiles.

'Thanks for staying.'

'Thanks for the invitation and the meal.'

God, it's good to have easy company in the kitchen again.

Chapter Thirty-one

Colin checked the clock. It was almost time to vacate. He looked around his office of the past twenty-two years for the last time. He'd brought the car the previous couple of days to remove his files and anything else he'd accumulated, and now the drawers and cupboard stood open and the desk clear.

He acknowledged his conflicting feelings and reminded himself to focus on the part that was embarking on an exciting new phase. But still it was with a slightly heavy heart that he pushed back the chair and rose. He grabbed his bag, jacket and hat, gave the room one final glance, and left, locking the door behind him. He walked down the empty hall with its doors on each side labelled with the various names and occupations of his fellow tenants to the reception desk. Tory, the practice manager of the last several years, looked up and enquired with her eyebrows.

'I'm off,' he said. 'Thanks for everything.' It took him considerable effort and control to inject some cheer into his tone and features. 'Here are my keys,' he said. When Tory didn't put her hand out for them, he placed them on the top of the counter.

'Okay. Thanks.' If she'd been on the landline phone or computer, he might have expected this level of disinterest, brusqueness, but she'd been filing her nails.

'Right. Well. Bye then.'

'See you. All the best.' These final three words were the only indication to Colin that she was acknowledging, or perhaps even realising, this was the final time he was there and the keys not just those used by the public to access the toilet facilities.

'You too,' he added. *I guess that's that then, Colin.*

He pushed the heavy glass door open and then stopped short. There in the brilliant sunshine was Shirley, leaning against his car, smiling at him. His heart soared, so much so he felt a lump rising towards his throat, which he forced back down.

'There you are,' she said. 'I thought I was going to miss you.'

'Oh, it's so good to see you,' he said, hugging her. He never wanted to let go, but tore himself away before it might become strange and his feelings transparent.

'I know you didn't want a fuss. But I thought … Oh, I don't know what I thought.'

'I'm very glad you're here.'

'Are you okay? You appear quite glum.'

'I'll be fine, thanks. Just a moment of disappointment and self-pity. It wasn't as if I was expecting a party or a signed card or anything …' He shrugged.

'Ah, yet another reminder of the disappointment of humans and the direction of society. Well, their loss. I care, and appreciate you,' she said, sliding her hand under his elbow. 'You're going to love everything about your new direction and working from home. I just know it!'

Colin smiled at Shirley and reached over and patted her hand. 'Thank you, Shirley.' *You're the best.*

'So, where's your box?'

'My what?' he said, looking around.

'Your plain cardboard archive box. Every depiction of someone leaving a job – through resignation, retirement or being fired – on TV or the movies, has them carrying an archive box out the door.'

Colin laughed. 'You're right. Sorry to disappoint. I took everything home gradually over the last few days. I'm not even sure why I brought the car today. I didn't need to.'

Shirley eased away from him and said, 'Lucky for you, I come prepared.'

Colin watched, intrigued, as she reached into her car.

'What's this for?' he asked, accepting the box being pushed towards him.

'Stand there by the door to the building with your box, and I'll take a photo. Come on, humour me. You'll regret it if you don't at least mark this with a photo. Okay, that's a little strong. You won't. But I do think it's a good idea.' Colin did as he was told.

'Smile. You look like you were fired.'

'I sort of was, Shirley.'

'Okay. Fair enough. Right, well, um …'

Colin looked on as she tapped her lip with her finger thoughtfully.

'I know! Smile like you've just told them to fuck off or have left a bucket full of confetti on the top of the door ready to fall on someone's head when they open it.'

'Damn. Why didn't I think of that?' Colin grinned.

'I brought some if you want to,' she said, with raised eyebrows and a mischievous glint before returning her attention to taking the photos.

'It's too late for the confetti – I've given the keys back, and locked the door.'

'Oh. Bugger.'

'Did you really bring confetti?'

'I might have.'

Colin laughed.

'No, don't be ridiculous. That would be juvenile.'

'I have to admit to feeling just a touch disappointed.'

'Unfortunately, I bet the person who cleans is not one of the people to whom we'd want to be directing our ire.'

'Good point. I'm so glad you're here, Shirley. Thank you.'

'The pleasure is all mine. I left work unexpectedly – to care for Norman, as you know – and I too slipped away without any acknowledgement or supposed care from the powers that be. So, despite any flippancy on my part, I do know how much it might be hurting, even when you think it shouldn't.'

Colin nodded. 'You're an absolute gem.'

'Now, we need to celebrate or at least mark this momentous occasion somehow. The options are: One, drinks and/or dinner out, anywhere of your choosing. Or option two, homemade spaghetti bolognaise and garlic bread at my place, where I might even let you play with the train – no inuendo intended.'

Colin chuckled again. 'Ooh, yes, please, option two sounds perfect. You are wonderful.'

'I try. Next question. Your car or mine, or both?'

'Um.' Colin thought about it. He suspected he might become very tired very soon. And he didn't want to drink too much lest he become too melancholy. 'I'm happy to drive my car to your home. So I guess that's both cars?'

'Okay, then. Follow me. And no, before you ask, you absolutely do not need to stop on the way and get anything.' And then Shirley was kissing him on the cheek before going around to her car and getting in.

Colin tossed the empty box onto the passenger seat, got in and sat looking up at the building as he turned the car on. *Well, thanks for your service all these years. I hope your next tenant is a good one.* As he checked the mirrors before carefully reversing, he wondered if they'd already filled the spot. It would make him feel much better about things if that had been the real reason for him being pushed out – perhaps one of the other tenants wanted a friend or colleague to move in.

Shirley got through the first set of traffic lights just a few hundred metres out of the carpark and he got caught. With her out of sight, when the lights turned green, he took the opportunity to pull into a florist, which appeared just about to close. Buckets of flowers were starting to be taken inside though the sandwich board was still up on the pavement. Regardless of what Shirley had said, he was not turning up empty handed unless he absolutely had to. In the store, he looked around for the brightest arrangement.

'There you are. I was beginning to think you'd got lost,' Shirley said when Colin knocked on the door.

'No, all good. These are for you,' he said, holding out the flowers.

'Ooh. Thank you. They're gorgeous. You shouldn't have, but I love them. Gerberas. So cheerful. So that's what you got up to.'

'Now, do you want your box back?'

'My what?'

'The cardboard box you gave me,' he said, indicating over his shoulder towards his car.

'Oh no. That's my very expensive farewell gift to you,' she said, grinning. 'I'm sure you'll find a spot for it. If I need it, I'll know where it is. Come on in.'

'Hello there.' Colin looked down at the tabby cat strolling down the hall. 'Did you get a cat, or is it visiting?'

'Tabby – yes, I know, very original – meet Colin. Colin, Tabby. She's a foster, along with her kittens. They arrived a couple of days ago.'

'It's a pleasure to meet you, Tabby.'

'You're not allergic, are you?'

'No. Not that I'm aware of.'

'I've plenty of antihistamine tablets on hand if necessary. Just say the word ... Well, that's you accepted,' Shirley said, as Tabby rubbed on Colin's leg and then twined between his feet in a figure of eight.

'Ooh. Aren't you lovely?' he said to Tabby who was looking up at him. She blinked slowly. He leant down to run his hand over her back. 'You're very soft.' She presented her head and he scratched her ears. 'What a sweetheart,' he cooed.

'She's a good mum, too, aren't you, Tabby? Ooh, yes you are.'

Colin smiled as the cat walked off with a definite strut to her gait, her tail waving high in the air above her.

'Oh. Wow. Kittens *and* trains. All my Christmases have come at once,' Colin said.

'I'm thinking I might have to pack the train away before they get big enough to climb. Meanwhile, I'm keeping the door shut so madam here doesn't cause a derailment or tip the church over, or what have you. Come on, miss, you have to stay out. Quick, while I fend her off.'

Colin squeezed past, smiling while Shirley held the cat back with her foot.

'Tabby, are you sure your kittens don't need you? There's a good girl.' Colin enjoyed watching the interaction.

'Do you have to do much with the kittens?'

'Not this lot, because they have their mum. No bottle feeding, which is good – though very rewarding.'

'I bet.'

'Basically, when it's Mum and bubs, they take care of themselves. I just feed Mum and she takes care of them.'

'I'm very keen to see them.'

'Well, careful, because they are very cute.'

'Okay, thanks, I'll bear that in mind,' he said, grinning.

'But first, voila, the trainset,' she said, turning on the light and illuminating the previously quite dark space. The train started with a whir and a metallic clatter.

'Oh, wow.' Colin watched the line of carriages chug their way along a track spanning several levels. Lights came on and went out at intervals, the train disappeared into tunnels covered in green imitation grass and reappeared, its light shining brightly on the front, and travelled over bridges that traversed simulated waterways and parts of the village. He struggled to know where to look. 'It's fantastic.' Colin couldn't remember the last time he'd been so enthralled with a moving object.

'Isn't it?'

'It's beautiful, Shirley. A real work of art. Utterly magical. And the church is wonderful. I see what you mean about soothing and mesmerising.'

'Take a seat,' Shirley said, nodding to the two high stools at the corner of the large board holding everything up at table height.

He settled himself. The level of detail was incredible.

'Oh. I've just seen the post office, complete with flagpole.'

'Yes. The flag's deliberately at half-mast. I did that the day Norman died. I haven't quite brought myself to put it back up. And the world is in such a poor state, a flag at half-mast permanently feels kind of apt.'

'Yes. I agree with you there.'

'I have to admit, having Tabby and her kittens is great as both a distraction and a focus. I wasn't planning to do more fostering for a while, but I got a frantic call. They're desperate. I couldn't refuse.'

'I'm sure Tabby appreciates your dedication.'

'I'm not so sure about that, Colin. Have you met many cats? Law unto themselves, contrary creatures. But that's one of the main things I love about them – their nonchalant, dismissive attitude. Well, those that aren't skittish anyway. You know, one of the best things is seeing them go from wary to demanding.'

'What's that saying there is – cats have masters?'

'No. It's dogs have masters, cats have staff. And it's so true. I love their independent and feisty nature. They're each so different.'

'I don't know much at all about any animals, particularly domestic dogs and cats.'

'Well, we'll have to change that. Anyway, how about a drink to celebrate your last day? Or simply because it's Friday … whatever?'

'Yes, please, but I'm happy to wait for a bit. I'm rather enjoying watching the train.'

'Oh, we don't have to leave. That's Norman's well-stocked bar behind you, complete with fridge. I can offer red and white wine, scotch, Baileys Irish Cream, sherry, gin and tonic.'

'Wow. Thanks, Norman. Well in that case, I'd love a Baileys. I haven't had one for many years.'

'Thank goodness we had in here set up so well and we could each sneak off and be alone at times,' Shirley said, heading over to the bar.

'I could sit here all night,' Colin said with a long, contented sigh as the train passed by.

'Here we are. Hold mine, please, while I get settled,' Shirley said a few moments later, handing him two glasses before settling herself on the stool next to him.

They clinked glasses, said cheers at the same time, and then took their first sip.

'Ooh, goodness, that rather hits the spot. Don't let me have another, else I'll be over the limit for driving,' he said.

'Right you are. I'd better feed you before too long, too.'

They sat side by side watching the train in silence, enjoying their drinks for a few minutes.

'Come on, bring your drink and come and see the kittens. And then I'll do the finishing touches on dinner.'

'Yes, before I embarrass myself and nod off. You might need to nudge me at some point.'

'Noted. I'll be gentle. I'm not surprised you're exhausted, though. As you well know, most changes and goodbyes are a wild mix of swirling emotions, no matter the circumstances. And you have had a lot to think about of late. You'll probably need a particularly restful weekend.'

Colin followed Shirley out, glancing at his feet to make sure Tabby didn't slip past him into the room. But she was nowhere in sight.

In the laundry, they found the cat stretched out in a bed with five kittens feeding from her.

'There you are. Who's a good mum? Let's come back after we've eaten,' Shirley said quietly. 'Leave her to feed in peace.'

'Gosh. How cute are they?' Colin said, as they made their way down the short hall to the kitchen.

'Another drink?' Shirley asked when they'd enjoyed the spaghetti bolognaise, with pasta that Colin couldn't believe had been homemade. He looked forward to a lesson in how to do that one day.

'No, I'd better not, thanks.'

'Go and sit in the lounge and put your feet up while I organise dessert.'

'Can I help?'

'No. Thanks, but it's your night.'

'That's very unnecessary, but I really do appreciate all the attention.' *More than you'll ever know.* Despite starting to flag physically, Colin was feeling decidedly chipper.

'I'm glad.'

Colin was slightly startled when Tabby leapt up onto the couch beside him. She sat upright, staring at him. 'Is Tabby expecting me to do something? She's on the couch staring at me.'

Shirley moved around the corner and looked. 'I think that's her polite way of asking if you'd like her company. She's quite the well-mannered madam – and quite human at times.'

'Oh.' He stretched his fingers out for Tabby to sniff. With no idea about cats and not much more about dogs, beyond approaching them slowly with an outstretched hand to sniff, he was a little trepidatious. He'd seen enough cat videos online to know one of the creature's paws could come flying out, with claws extended, with little to no notice. What he always found incredible was how a moment later the cat would appear as if nothing had happened, or worse, be apparently extra loving and affectionate. Very unnerving. Although, he was also aware editing of the videos could well be involved.

He smiled as Tabby pushed her head under his hand and moved it back and forth. He wriggled his fingers and gently rubbed her head.

'Are you doing okay over there?' Shirley enquired.

'I think so. It looks like she wants me to scratch the top of her head. Oh.' Colin raised his hands as the cat began prodding at his thigh.

'What?'

'She's poking me. Is she sizing me up, sharpening her claws on me – like a knife?' He let out a tight laugh. Shirley appeared again.

'That's you having been accepted. She's making you comfortable.' Colin ran his fingers through the cat's fur, stroking her over and over. Any lingering tension from the day seemed to drain away as he did. Tabby moved towards him, put her two front paws on his thighs and arched her back.

'Aww, she's a darling.' He could now hear her purring. 'Who's a lovely girl?'

'You are definitely being claimed. Well, your lap is,' Shirley said with a laugh. And then Colin knew what she meant because right then Tabby moved across him so she had all four paws on his lap. And then, *plop*, she was sinking down onto him and curling up with a loud harrumph of what he could only deduce was satisfaction and contentment.

'I apologise in advance for the cat fur you're about to be covered in.'

'Oh well, there are worse things. Are you a busy mum in need of a break?' he said to Tabby, stroking her. He let out a long sigh in response to feeling the thrum of her deep purr vibrating on his thighs. He thought he'd been relaxed before, but now experienced the uncoiling of all his muscles. He thought if he didn't have the couch for support, he might have slid down onto the floor as a pile of jelly.

'Is it a dessert we can have over here, Shirley? Because I fear I'm now rather stuck.'

'Ha! I see what you mean. You absolutely cannot move now until she gets up. There's no way you can disturb that picture of contentment.'

'I've no desire to. She's so warm and soft and vibrate-y. It's all very soothing.'

'Careful. You sound like you're being converted.'

'I might well be. As I've told you, I'm not against pets per se. It's more the work involved and the tie.'

'I hear you on them being a tie. It depends how often you go away and need to make arrangements. Of course, they're not all as lovely as Tabby there, but with both fostering and adopting a rescue, I think you get enough recompense from knowing you're helping. Honestly, I get a lot more out of it than they do, the little darlings.'

Colin stroked Tabby and his mind began to wander to his big quiet house, which was sometimes lonely now Joyce had left. And now he was going to be there all during the day as well. Would a cat strolling about be a lovely addition? The idea was certainly growing on him.

'I bet your clients would love, and would benefit from, the presence of a cat. And your situation is perfect now you'll be working from home.' *And there she is, reading my mind again. I agree, Shirley.*

'Hmm.'

'Ignore me. I'm honestly not meaning to pressure you.'

'You're not making it easy, are you, Miss Tabby? Nor you, Shirley. I'm beginning to feel set up.'

'I can see how you would. But, I promise, that wasn't my intention. I really did just want to make your last day at the office memorable and uplift your spirits if they happened to be low.'

'Oh, you've done that, in spades.'

'And, anyway, Tabby only arrived the other day, and, as I said, out of desperation.'

'Well, I'm glad you're here, Miss Tabby. You're lovely and have been the icing on the cake.' At that moment Colin was surprised to find the cat stand up, yawn, stretch by arching her back, and then hop off, landing on the floor with a gentle thud.

'Oh. I see. Is your work here done, Miss?' He watched as she sauntered off towards Shirley, with her tail straight up, with a little hook at the tip and hips swaying.

'Hello there,' he heard Shirley say. 'Are you hungry?'

'Aww, she talks too,' he said, as he heard a gentle meow.

'She's a clever girl,' Shirley said. 'Rarely makes any noise – only when it's necessary, apparently.' Colin listened to the sounds going on in the kitchen and a few moments later Shirley appeared, carrying bowls with spoons in them.

'Here we are, homemade chocolate, strawberry and vanilla ice-cream. I assume you like ice-cream. I forgot to ask.'

'I do, very much, thank you. Did you say it's homemade?'

'I did indeed.'

'Is there no end to your talents?'

'Well, I'm not sure it's the best version going around. It got a little hard – hence taking a while to get it into bowls.'

'I've never considered how to do it – wouldn't even know where to start.'

'Having a machine to churn it and cool it at the same time is the game changer. Norman loved his ice-cream. It was one of the few things he could cope with when he was sick, so I started making it. I hadn't used the machine since he died. I'd forgotten how much I enjoy doing it.'

'Well, it's very good. Yum.' Colin sighed contentedly again. 'What a lovely end to an otherwise odd and unsettling day. Shirley, do you think you'll adopt Tabby when she's ready? Because, if not, I think I might like to.'

'Oh, Colin, you old softie.'

'Guilty as charged. She's rather captured my heart. And I think she could also be a great asset for the home practice.'

'That's fantastic news.'

'As long as you're sure I'm not stepping on your toes.'

'No, absolutely not. I'd say if that were the case. Knowing the gorgeous girl has a loving and safe and happy home will be enough for me. Maybe I'll keep one of her kittens, we'll see …'

'I might need to prevail upon you to give me some pointers in the area of cat ownership, since I have zero experience, if that's okay.'

'Of course. I'd be delighted.'

Colin looked over at Shirley who was grinning like the proverbial Cheshire cat. He grinned back while thinking how lucky he was to have a friend like her.

Not long after finishing dessert, Colin hit a wall – or maybe it was the sugar coma after Shirley's delightful ice-cream. He said goodbye to Tabby, who was back in with her kittens, bid farewell to Shirley, and left.

Arriving home, Colin was struck by how quiet and slightly gloomy it was entering the empty house after such a lovely, vibrant evening. He pictured Tabby rushing up to greet him and his mood instantly lifted again. In his mind's eye, he could also see how her strolling into the office, while clients were there, might have its benefits too. And also serve as an advertisement for gaining more foster carers and pet adoptions. He liked that idea – that additional way to help.

Chapter Thirty-two

It was well after his last session for the day and Colin was leaning back in his chair luxuriating in satisfaction over his new workspace and the fact it had been so well received by his first few clients. Never before had anyone commented on how calm the room in which they'd sat had felt. And there had been visible signs of tension unwinding – shoulders relaxing, less wringing of hands and scrunching of tissues so tightly as clients spoke and he listened. Even he found he didn't want to leave. At the other place, he'd watched the clock and left right on time. Though that had also been his commitment to Joyce. So much had happened in a short amount of time. It made his head whirl when he thought about it. But not all of it had been bad, even the online stuff. He did owe that whole fiasco some gratitude, because without it he wouldn't be here now in his new setup.

Though, as much as he loved it, the weight of behind-the-scenes administration, particularly concern over what he'd do if the automated and tech systems fell down, hung heavy. He'd done some online tutorials and understood plenty more than he had previously, but while he knew there was enough help available, particularly via the helpdesk, which he knew Joyce thought very highly of, he'd rather just not have to have that side of things on his mind at all. He'd toyed with looking into getting a virtual assistant – hadn't even known they were a thing until very recently – but trusting a stranger with the inner workings of his business, especially the finances, was a major block for him. His thoughts always came back to the fact he knew the perfect person already. Joyce. Several times he thought he'd even take up the corporate work again if he needed to in order to pay her a decent wage. But no matter how often he looked at his phone and pondered calling her to ask, he hadn't been able to bring himself to. She had her own life now and while his pride wasn't as big a hurdle as it might have been previously, he didn't think he could, or had the right to, even ask her opinion on the matter.

He was dragged reluctantly from his meandering thoughts by the sound of the doorbell at the main door. It sounded odd to his ear now he'd been hearing the electronic sound of the new system installed at the side gate by Aaron, the security guy. *Access to the practice is via the back, people, per the signage posted.* He got up and headed out to see who was calling.

He looked through the old-fashioned peephole. *Oh.*

'Joyce. Hi.' Colin took in her appearance. Her face was red, eyes puffy, cheeks streaked. 'Whatever is the matter? What's happened?' He'd tried to wait for her to tell him but she'd opened her mouth twice and only managed to gasp, as if she was out of breath.

'Oh, Colin,' she finally managed, 'I didn't know where else to go, what to do.' He felt as if they'd been standing there with the open doorway between them for minutes but, in reality, it had probably only been a few seconds. Joyce's swollen eyes began to leak again.

'Can I come in?'

'Yes. Of course. Come, come,' he said, standing aside and waving a hand to usher her in. He opened his arms and she leant into him. He stroked her hair as his heart tumbled over from the elation of Joyce being in his arms to the disappointment that this would be fleeting because she'd chosen to leave and he shouldn't be setting himself up to be hurt all over again.

'Has something happened with Carmel?' *They've split up? Is Joyce coming back to me? Do I want that?* All these thoughts raced through him and then collided with a jolt at Joyce's next words.

'Carmel's dead.'

Colin wasn't sure he'd heard correctly as Joyce's face was still buried in his chest.

'What?'

'And her kids have frozen me out. Oh, Colin, it's all such a mess.'

'Hang on a second. Did you say Carmel has died?'

Joyce nodded. And then she uttered a strangled, gurgling sob and burst into a new bout of tears. She became more animated, her chest heaving, her mouth and throat gasping for air.

'Just breathe, Joyce. Breathe … Slow it down … Come on … You're okay …' He stroked her hair rhythmically.

He was relieved when his words seemed to seep through to Joyce and her panic began to subside. As she eased herself away, sniffing, he dug into his pocket for his handkerchief, which he handed to her.

'Thanks,' she said. The action of dabbing her face with the soft cloth and blowing her nose seemed to serve to calm her considerably.

Now he felt he had her attention, Colin asked, 'Would you like a cup of tea?'

'Yes, please. I'm really sorry to do this to you. Are you busy?'

'Joyce.' He placed his hands on her shoulders and looked into her eyes. 'I'm never too busy for you. And you don't need to apologise. I said when you left you could call on me if you ever needed anything. I meant it and always will, regardless of our marital status.'

'Thank you. I really appreciate it. I'm sorry I'm so overwrought.'

'It's perfectly understandable in the circumstances. Now, would you like to sit in my office or in the kitchen?'

'Kitchen? Would that be okay?'

'Of course. Come on, then.' He put an arm around her and shepherded her through to the kitchen.

'Shirley's not here?'

'No.' *Why would you think Shirley would be here?*

They sat in silence while Colin prepared the tea. He thought, as he did so, he ought to be putting a kettle in his office and offering clients tea. He always had water available, but it was tea that was known to be helpful in pretty much every conceivable situation – to fortify, console, calm, rehydrate ... It was suitable in hot weather and cold.

'Here we are.' He sat down opposite Joyce and wrapped his hands around his own mug, noting that they were back in their respective chairs from before Joyce's leaving.

'Thank you. That's much better,' Joyce finally said.

Again, Colin felt as if he'd been waiting her out for ages, but in reality only for a few seconds. She kept both hands around her mug as she raised it to her lips, and even then it still wobbled.

'Oh, Colin,' she said again. She took a deep breath and let it out slowly. 'I feel completely wretched. I know it hasn't been long, but I loved her. I really did.'

'I know.' It was like a dagger to his heart. But he reminded himself that just because she loved Carmel didn't mean she'd stopped loving him — though it was definitely different.

'Sorry. This must be really hard for you.'

He waved her words away. 'I'm fine. Don't worry about me. You're who's important right now. So, what happened? And if you don't want to talk about it, that's fine too.'

'You're a good man, Colin Palmer.'

There are plenty online who'd disagree with you. He deliberated over saying the words. Toyed with *I try*, too. But settled for a gentle smile. As much as he wanted to see her smile, be the one to put it on her face, it wasn't fair. Nothing in this moment was about him or, at least, it shouldn't be.

'She had a heart attack at home. After lunch. We were clearing up and she complained of heartburn, became short of breath, mumbled something about being light-headed and woozy, and then collapsed on the floor. I started CPR but then remembered to call an ambulance. And … God, that awful moment where you can't be doing both — dialling and doing chest compressions — seemed like hours. You've no idea.'

Colin nodded. He did know. She was forgetting his father dying at home all those years ago. His heart went out to Joyce. It was traumatising, frightening. She ran her hands up over her face, pushing her hair away as if feeling sweat on her face, as she probably would have at the time.

'The ambulance people were amazing and very prompt. Anyway, they worked on her for ages. But …' A new rush of tears began to fill her eyes and then spill over. 'I guess I should be grateful,' she added, dabbing at her tears.

'You shouldn't *be* anything. You be whatever you are and need to be,' Colin said quietly.

Joyce nodded.

'When did it happen?'

'Yesterday.'

'Oh god, Joyce, how truly awful.'

'I didn't know where else to go,' she now said in barely a whisper. 'I feel so lost. It doesn't seem right to be in the house. Her boys and their families descended and took over. I felt quite pushed out. Like I was the maid. I've been thanked for all the cups of tea and sandwiches I've made and handed around. But, oh, I can't explain it … It's like …' She shrugged.

'It's like in their eyes you don't exist?'

'Yes. Her ex-husband – the kids' father – is there, too.'

'Oh. Oh, Joyce.'

'I know I wasn't on the scene long, but our love was real.'

Colin nodded, lost for words.

'I had to get out of there. I didn't really want to because at least they couldn't completely ignore me. But it almost destroyed me. And I kept thinking "Carmel wouldn't want this. She would hate the way you're treating me". But I couldn't risk staying and potentially saying something like that. They're grieving. I wanted to be part of that – they're all good people – but they don't want or need me. I do understand. It just hurts too, you know?'

'I do. Grief brings up a maelstrom of conflicted emotions, thoughts, actions – none of them pleasant. Would you like to come home? Stay here for a bit?'

'Could I? I know it's a big ask.'

'Not that big,' he said, smiling kindly. 'Now is not the time to worry about any optics. You need to do what's right for you.'

'Well, I really appreciate your generosity, Colin.'

'Right. So, you can have the bed and I'll take the couch.'

'Oh, that's not fair. There's the twins' room. Have you done anything with that?'

'No. Why would I?'

'I don't know. You've done a new office.'

'I wouldn't touch their room without you, Joyce, regardless of our status. Never.'

'I appreciate that.'

For thirty years he'd opened the door, dusted the surfaces inside, dragged the vacuum around and back out again, before closing the door behind him. And not once had he wondered if he should be getting rid of their things. He didn't think Joyce had ever gone in there, but for all he knew she'd sat in there all day reading while she'd been retired and he'd been still working.

'I made pumpkin soup last night. It's what I'm having for dinner, if you'd like some. There's plenty.'

'This is a different side to you, Colin.'

'Yes. I'm quite enjoying it. Within reason. I'm not sure I'll be entering anything into the Royal Adelaide Show, but it's early days.'

'I'd love some, thanks. I can't remember when I last ate. I'm not really hungry, but I probably should have something.'

'Yes, you'll need your strength. Do you know when the funeral will be?'

'Saturday. Eleven am.'

Oh. Colin wasn't sure he'd ever heard of funerals being held on weekends, but that didn't mean it didn't happen.

'They seemed in such a rush to arrange things. I mean, Colin, poor Carmel was barely cold and they were … Oh, I don't know. I just felt they were being insensitive. But Carmel was practical, and could be quite blunt when it suited her, so probably would have said something like "Why wait, I'm not going to get any more or less dead. Dead is dead". Oh my god. Her colour. It was like ash. I'd forgotten that from the twins. And your father, of course.'

'Hmm.'

'I'm not involved in the service.'

'Do you want to be?'

'Say a eulogy, you mean?'

'Yes. Speak about her, suggest some music …'

'Not really. You know how I feel about public speaking and being the centre of attention. Though I fear I will be to some extent anyway. I feel like such a silly old fool.'

Colin wanted to utter his precious phrase, *'But you're my silly old fool'*, but he couldn't. She wasn't his. Not anymore, current circumstances and impending re-cohabitation notwithstanding.

'But you want to attend?'

'Yes. Definitely. Well, I *don't*. I'd rather she was alive.'

'I know what you mean. Don't forget you'll still be in shock, most likely. As will the family. It's a very fraught situation.'

'Can I ask you a favour, Colin?'

'Anything.'

'Will you come with me?'

'Of course. What about practicalities – your belongings in the house? Do you want to collect them, make sure they're not claimed?'

'Oh no, that won't be an issue. They hated my things – the kids, the ex-husband, commented on them. Carmel was very much a white minimalist.'

'A what now?'

'Everything was stark white and only just a few essential pieces dotted about. You know – it's the style of decorating.'

'Oh yes. Now I know what you mean. She seemed fine with you taking your things to her home that day she was here, though.'

'She was. She was very welcoming and accommodating. She really loved me. She was wonderful. Oh, Colin, I'm so sad.'

'Of course you are. It's heartbreaking. I just wish I could help.'

'Your kindness is a huge help. Everything. You don't know how generous you're being – when I ... I ... I know I broke your heart. So, you have every right to ...'

Colin wanted to say, *'Who do you think I am? As if I'd turn you away'*. But the reality was he might have done a few short weeks ago when his anger had been at its highest. Now he was steadier on his feet – his emotions evening out, his independence ensured – he knew he'd get through it again, so he could do this.

He wondered for the umpteenth time where all their old friends were. But then remonstrated with himself for his thoughts on behalf of Joyce. This situation was very new, and evolving. She'd come straight to him and not one of their many supposed friends. That warmed the cockles of his heart.

'Right. Soup. Toast?'

'Yes, please.'

As Colin prepared their meal, he thought how odd were their changed roles and how satisfying it felt to be able to do this for Joyce.

'That's very good soup, thank you.'

'It's roasting it first, along with whole cloves of garlic, apparently, that gives it the perfect flavour.'

'Yes. That's how I did it. I'm not going to be ruining things with you and Shirley, am I?'

'Oh no. We're not an item or anything like that. Just friends.'

Chapter Thirty-three

'How are you feeling this morning?' Colin asked when Joyce came into the kitchen looking bleary-eyed and dishevelled, still wearing the same clothes as the night before. They'd retired early, Joyce requesting Colin share the bed and hold her. He'd felt unable to refuse, despite his misgivings. He'd intended to make his way to the couch later – in either his office or the lounge – but each time he'd moved, Joyce had reached for him. He wasn't aware if she knew it was him she held or thought it was Carmel, but accepted it didn't matter. Not long ago he'd slipped out, grateful she was getting some sleep after much tossing and turning.

'I don't know, to be honest.'

'Fair enough. I've just had toast. Would you like some?'

'Yes, please.' He placed a mug of tea in front of her. 'Thank you, Colin, for everything.'

He nodded. 'I really wish you weren't going through this.'

'Me too.'

Colin rubbed his eyes, which were gritty and burning from not enough sleep. 'Did you get much sleep?'

'I must have got some. I hope I didn't disturb you too much.'

'I'm okay.' He retrieved the toast, put it on a plate, added a knife and placed it in front of Joyce.

'Do you have much work on today?' she asked, picking up the knife.

'Yes, quite a reasonable list,' he said, sitting down again.

'That's good, I take it?'

'Yes. Do you have any plans?'

'I suppose I need to go to the house and at least get my clothes.'

'Do you want me to go with you?'

'I don't know. I could really do with the company, but I don't want to inflame the situation back there further by appearing to arrive with reinforcements. But I am a little concerned about what I'd be walking into.'

'Would you like me to go and buy you some things instead?'

'Hmm. Avoiding it isn't the right thing, is it?'

Colin shrugged. 'That's up to you. I can't really answer that.'

'Thanks for the offer.'

Colin cast his mind over his bookings for the day, trying to see a large enough window during which he could duck out to the shops, and also if there was a client he could put off without causing too much drama. Not that he wanted to. He was still settling into the swing of things here. But he also needed to be there for Joyce.

And then he had an idea. Shirley. Could he ask Shirley to help – to take Joyce under her wing? Would that be out of line?

'What are you going to do in the longer term, I mean, beyond just today?' He hated how blunt and potentially cold he was coming across and could only hope Joyce would take it for what it was: his need to be organised.

'I don't know, Colin.'

'Do you want to move back home – here – on a more permanent basis, well, for a few weeks to see how you go?'

'Could I? Would that be too ... I don't know ...' She shrugged, letting the rest of the sentence remain unsaid.

'One thing to be aware of, and it might see you change your mind, I've decided to adopt a cat. Tabby, she's called. She's currently being fostered, along with her kittens, and will be ready to come to me in about a week or so.'

'Oh.'

'Is that an objection? Because–' *It's too bad if it is. I'm firm on this.*

'Oh no. Not at all. It, *she*, will probably be a good distraction for me. Carmel had two cats, actually, and I took quite a liking to them. They're those sphynx-looking type with no hair and wrinkly skin – an acquired taste, aesthetically speaking, but they had lovely temperaments. They were like sage little old men. I think I'd rather like the idea of a furry creature wandering around for additional company. And anyway, I know that I'll be the interloper. I do really appreciate you putting yourself out like this, particularly when you've probably adjusted to having the place to yourself, and started to heal from my rejection.'

'It's okay, Joyce. What matters right now is your wellbeing.'

He was well aware of the high proportion of older women on their own becoming homeless due to their particularly vulnerable state, with the current cost-of-living and rental crises. If she wasn't saying it, he thought she must at least be thinking it. This was the least he could do. So much for living in a first world country. *The lucky country, my arse,* he thought.

'If you stay, or rather, move back in, I think we'd better have separate rooms. I'm not sure why,' Colin added, in order to soften things.

'I understand. I agree, it's probably for the best.'

'So that only leaves the twins' room,' he said quietly.

'Yes. I'm aware of that.'

'And …?'

'Maybe it's time.'

They fell silent; both had their heads down staring into their mugs. What went through Colin's mind then was: *Thank goodness I don't have to be the one to do it – make the decision to take that final step.* He sighed. He hoped it would be an easier process than he feared – that the room and its memories might have lost some of its power in the years it had remained locked up as a time capsule containing their fifteen years of joy as parents and a reminder of the exact moment between happiness and trauma.

'What about the rest of your things – the furniture et cetera?' Colin said.

'A part of me wants to just leave it all, walk away and not ever go back.'

'But that wouldn't be fair to them or you. You took your things because you wanted them. I think you'd eventually regret not doing that this time. Though I do understand that it might be difficult.'

'They're only things at the end of the day, Colin.'

'But they're your things, and they hold a lot of sentimentality for you.'

'Can we afford to hold onto sentimentality at our age?'

'I don't see why not. How about holding off any decisions until after the funeral? The dust may have settled enough by then for you to be received in a better light. Or for you to feel more comfortable going to the house. Remember, a lot can change over these first hours and days.'

'You're right. Thank you.'

'Do you want me to see if Shirley can come around and keep you company – take you shopping for some new clothes to wear in the interim?'

'Thank you, but I'm cramping your style enough as it is. I don't want to impose on anyone else, if I can help it. I feel a little better after a cup of tea and the toast. I'll head out when the shops open, let you work unhindered, and get enough things to go on with to see me through to after the funeral. Is it okay if I take the car?'

'Of course. And that sounds like a good plan. Do you have plenty of money?'

'I'm fine. You'll see I've taken another thousand dollars from the travel fund. Thank you for not closing me out of the accounts.'

'All the money is equally yours.'

'I know, but I still think it's very good of you. And, now, well, I've no idea how things will stand going forward on that front.'

'Let's not think about that right now. One thing at a time. And you're sure you don't want me to ask Shirley if–'

'Yes. Please, I'm not a child. I don't need minding. Well, okay, I sort of do, to some extent. But not by someone I barely know.'

'But she's a retired nurse, she'll be–'

'Colin, I know it makes sense to you. But I really don't have the energy to be with someone I don't know, having to mind my Ps and Qs. I know you'll say she won't care, is very understanding and down to earth. But still, I appreciate you being here for me. Can we please leave it at that? For now, at least.'

'Yes. Of course.'

'Sorry for snapping.'

'It's okay. I understand.' He pushed back his chair and got up. 'I'm going to clean my teeth and go to my office. Please feel free to help yourself to anything. If you want to wash out your things and put on some of my clothes, then do so. You know where everything is, not that I'm telling you that you smell or look untidy or anything of that nature.'

Colin desperately wanted to leave. He could all but feel his feet were on a slippery slope heading towards his mouth.

'Thank you. But please don't feel chased away.'

'It's fine. I have some work to catch up on,' he said, putting his breakfast things in the sink and leaving the kitchen with a wave, thinking as he went, thank Christ he had his office to retreat into. And then, he wondered, how often had Joyce gone to the sewing room to escape him? Had she even been into sewing in the first place, or had she just needed somewhere to go and something to do in there that could be justified? Oh dear. Maybe he'd never known her, or them, as well as he thought he had. Hopefully Joyce would assume his client had turned up before she headed out, so she wouldn't disturb him.

'Do you need me to get any groceries while I'm out?' she called.

'No, thanks. Everything is under control in that department.' Irritability rose in Colin at having his routine potentially derailed.

Colin had just said goodbye to his second client for the day – grateful that he was still able to ease into his new space with a private personality test and subsequent discussion about suitable careers afterwards. He'd heard Joyce leave and was yet to hear the car return. He was surprised at how much he objected to having his new homelife invaded, and shocked at how quickly and steadfastly he'd become used to, and protective of, his solitude. He was further surprised to see his phone announcing Shirley was calling – without a sound because it was on silent mode.

'Hi, Shirley, how's things?'

'Hello. I wasn't sure if I'd get you. I was ready to leave a message.' She sounded breathless.

'I'm between clients.'

'How's it going – your first few days settling into the new setup?'

'Good. Good. But are you okay? You sound a bit croaky.'

'Yes, I'm upset.'

'Oh? What's happened?'

'An old colleague and dear friend of mine has died, Lulu.'

'Oh no. That's awful. Please accept my sincere condolences.' *Goodness, first Joyce and now Shirley?*

His mind strayed to a client from many years ago who swore that all bad things came in groups of three. He'd had to admit along the way that it did indeed appear to often be the case.

'Is there anything I can do?'

'Well, I'm calling to ask a favour.'

'Okay. Ask away.'

'Would you accompany me to the funeral? It's on Saturday, so won't impact your work. I know I've become used to going everywhere on my own, but I fear a funeral, particularly the first after Norman's, might just bring me undone. So, it would be a huge help to have you beside me – and also drive, if that would be okay?'

'Of course. It would be my pleasure. Well, not my pleasure, but well, you know what I mean. Hang on, this coming Saturday?'

'Yes. It starts at eleven.'

'Oh no.'

'What?'

'I have a prior engagement that I really can't get out of. Oh god. I'm so sorry.'

Colin hated that he was lying to Shirley, even just by omission, but it struck him that Joyce might not like him spreading her news by giving Shirley specifics. So, he remained silent, feeling uncomfortable, and thinking it strange that both funerals were at the unusual time. But he quickly let that go. There were probably a thousand funerals going on around the country at that exact time slot.

'It's okay. I can't say I'm not disappointed. But I do understand.' Colin was grateful she didn't press for details of what he had on. At that moment he heard the chime of the new camera doorbell system at the side gate. He glanced at his computer monitor to double-check it was indeed his next client who had arrived, and pressed the button to unlock the gate.

'I'm really sorry to do this to you, Shirley, but my next appointment is here. I'll talk to you later?'

'Okay. Bye for now.'

He opened his mouth to apologise again, but she'd already hung up. Colin stared at the phone feeling deflated. Of all the people to have to let down. But he couldn't dwell on it, he had to snap into work mode.

He took several deep breaths, mentally changed gears into his professional persona, plastered a warm smile on his face and hoisted himself out of his chair and went to open the French doors.

Chapter Thirty-four

'Hello, Andrea,' Colin said, letting the young woman in.

'Hi. Great new digs,' she said, looking around.

'Thank you. Did you find me okay?'

'I did. No problem at all. Wow, I really like it in here,' Andrea said, now settled on the couch, though sitting upright this time. She appeared much calmer than she had in previous sessions but was still a little fidgety, Colin thought.

'I'm glad. So, how are you? And how can I help you today?' He'd been surprised but also pleased to see her name in the bookings.

'I think I really just need to vent.'

'That's okay. This is a safe space.'

'Well, my mother and I had a big blow-up. I know it's been a long time coming. There's only so long you can hold your tongue and ignore the ridiculousness, I suppose.' She waved a hand.

Colin nodded and watched as she twisted her mouth this way and that, as if trying to find the right words or order her thoughts. After what seemed ages, and just as he was getting ready to prompt her, she resumed speaking.

'Right, so I had a few pieces of my work, my photography, in an exhibition and there was an opening event and an award ceremony.' Colin thought he knew exactly where this was going and how it would end up.

'So, you know how I'm never good enough …?'

'Yes, you've said you feel that way.'

'… And my photography is considered a pipedream by my mother, and anything in the arts isn't considered a *real* job? I told you that too, didn't I?' Andrea rolled her eyes.

'You did.' *Mostly.*

'Anyway, I won an award; actually quite a significant one.'

'Oh wow. Congratulations. That's fantastic. I'm thrilled for you.'

'Thanks.'

Colin's heart went out to the young woman. The victims of narcissists, from his experience in treating them, were mostly unable to celebrate their achievements due to being trained to not become too big-headed. They couldn't win; if they did achieve something, and merely mentioned it in line with trying to prove their worth to their tormentor – which was perfectly natural – they'd then likely be either dismissed, or someone else would be held up as an example of doing better. One-upmanship by proxy. It was always a no-win situation. He'd been told by other clients in a similar boat that it felt as if nothing – no hobby, no success – was ever truly their own and subsequently, over time, they'd learnt not to want to achieve anything. A normal and healthy sense of pride was not allowed.

'So, guess who was lining up to have photos with the award-winning photographer, all smiles, going on about how proud she was?'

'I see,' Colin said.

'Yep. Exactly. I just wanted to cry. There was media there and she insisted on the longest interview. It's not the journos' fault, she kept edging her way in. It was horrible. And, oh, yes, I get my talent from her, apparently. She's never so much as picked up a camera, let alone focussed a lens or changed a setting.'

Now Colin saw the glistening signs of tears in Andrea's eyes.

'Finally, I do something for me. And become good at it. And she makes it all about her. I'm angry. And frustrated. And really, really sad.

'Anyway, I called her on it. As we were leaving. Told her a few home truths of how she makes me feel, blah, blah, blah and gave her the opportunity to apologise. I hoped she would, despite what I've read online about that. More fool me, I suppose. Anyway, as I said, big blow-up – but also very controlled on her part, you know? She'd never raise her voice in public or make what one would consider a spectacle. And I'm well-trained enough not to either …'

Colin nodded.

'So, while it was big for us, two people who don't show emotion – one because they can't and the other because they shouldn't – no one probably noticed. But I've never really talked back or stood up for myself before. But she took no notice of me. Didn't react to anything except to look at me like I was a piece of dog shit she'd stepped in and calmly tell me to stop being so melodramatic and attention-seeking. And, yet again, I was told I was being too sensitive. And, yes, as could have been predicted, I was then warned not to let my award go to my head and become too full of my own self-importance.'

Colin nodded. This all could have come out of a textbook.

'It's the frustration due to what I now know is gaslighting and invalidation. It does my head in.'

Colin nodded again.

'Anyway, I haven't spoken to her since and I don't intend to again. It's too exhausting. It's like living in the twilight zone or constantly banging your head against a brick wall. Enough is enough. I gave her the chance to make amends, take responsibility, and she didn't. So, that's that. I'm not even angry anymore, just done.' She swiped tears away. 'It shouldn't be like this, should it?'

'No. It should not.'

'I am so glad I know – and thank you for opening my eyes to it all – but in some ways I kind of wish I didn't.'

'That makes perfect sense to me.'

'Because now I've poked the bear hard enough. And, I'm a little ashamed about this, but I did raise my voice a bit and tell her I don't want to speak to her ever again. I know, not helpful. I'm annoyed at myself for getting to that point – letting her get under my skin, particularly now I know so much more. And now I'm worried about what she's going to do. Because I've read about how once they can no longer control you, they start a smear campaign and influence how others see you – in a negative light, obviously. I'm already seeing it, I think.

'An old friend who was visiting from overseas, who I knew was seeing my mother and who I was booked to have lunch with, cancelled at short notice due to supposedly feeling unwell. But then she was all over Facebook at the time when we were meant to be catching up. Out and about looking as healthy as can be. It sounds paranoid and insecure of me – hell, I am insecure! But I can't help wondering what my mother said to her about me.'

'What do you think she said? Because you've obviously given it some thought.'

'Oh, yes. The great curse of the overthinker. You know me so well.' Again, Andrea rolled her eyes. 'I think she will have told

Jane, my friend, that I consider myself too famous or important or whatever – too good for anyone from my old life, or something along those lines. Or maybe she simply told Jane I didn't have time, now I was so … whatever … and was only being polite, so Jane would cancel to save me doing it. All of the above, probably.'

'I think you're likely to be right.'

'I'm so disappointed in Jane for listening, if that's the case. Why wouldn't she have asked me? Why take my mother's word for it? I know – you don't need to answer that – because she's a fantastic manipulator.'

Colin nodded again.

'I can't consider her a friend now, Jane, can I? My mother has probably recruited her to her side to be one of her flying monkeys, right? Oh god, so much to navigate, it's too much like school days. Gah.'

'Yes, that's quite possibly how it is. At least you're aware. Honestly, I think that's really the only solace you can take from it.'

'I'm starting to realise I don't really have any friends left that I can trust. Even the one I'm staying with – Tabatha – looks at me sideways when I talk about this stuff. It's like she doesn't believe me.'

'I'm afraid that's very normal too.'

'Thank goodness I have you. You might be the only one I can talk about all this with who understands, or at least doesn't dismiss my experience and feelings.'

Colin's mind again went to setting up group sessions for abuse survivors. It was on his list to look into. He was still settling in here and didn't want to rush into such an important initiative and run the risk of it going wrong or him letting anyone down. Meanwhile, oh, how he wished he could introduce Andrea to Cameron, his client with the narcissist estranged wife – not for any potential love matching, but so neither were alone. It was a pity Shirley wasn't nearer Andrea's age, and he didn't know any other young ones she would benefit from spending time with, if he could manage to orchestrate such an introduction without overstepping and/or offending anyone.

'I'm so glad you didn't retire, didn't let the trolls win. You've been such a source of strength for me.'

'I'm pleased to hear it, Andrea. And thank you for saying.'

Oh. A thought struck him. *Shirley.* 'Have you considered doing voluntary work? I know you'd be very busy, but I was just thinking. I have a friend who is involved with animal rescue and rehoming. And I'm sure they must need a cohort of decent photographers who can present the animals at their best online. Perhaps that might be a way for you to meet some kinder people. It was just a thought. Please don't feel compelled to even consider it.'

'Oh. I hadn't thought about that sort of volunteering – that organisations would need my sort of skills for their social media and so forth. Hmm. It's certainly something to think about. Yes, please ask your friend to contact me, or feel free to pass on my details. I can always see how I feel then. Here, I'll give you my card.' She fossicked in her handbag and then handed Colin a business card, which was plain purple and white with elegant black glossy raised lettering.

'Well, that looks like my time is up,' she said with a long sigh. 'Honestly, at the risk of sounding, oh, I don't know what, I really enjoy seeing you. You make such a difference. You're worth your weight in gold,' she said, digging in her handbag for her credit card and then holding it out to Colin.

'Thank you for saying, Andrea,' he said, smiling warmly at her. 'You're going to be okay.'

'I know. Thanks largely to you. I know it's going to take quite a while and a lot of soul-searching, though.'

'Just be kind to Andrea, take it slowly and stay strong.'

Andrea nodded as she tucked her credit card away again and then accepted her receipt.

They both got up and made their way to the French doors.

'Bye, see you again soon,' she said, and departed with a wave.

Chapter Thirty-five

Colin wandered out to the kitchen for lunch, listening as he did for Joyce's whereabouts, hoping he had the house to himself, and then remonstrating with himself for his selfish, uncharitable thought.

'Joyce, are you in?' He didn't think he'd heard her come back, but he'd been focussed on his client and the house being solid brick meant you rarely heard other people wandering around beyond a closed door, unless their footsteps were unusually heavy or they trod on one of the few creaky floorboards.

'I'm in here.'

Colin cocked his head and made his way down the hall towards where he thought her voice had come from. He paused at the doorway to the master bedroom and peered in. Empty. He carried on. The laundry? Ah, but … He paused at seeing the door to the twins' room was open. Inside, Joyce was stretched out on Thomas's single bed.

'Hi,' she said. He tried not to smile at her appearance in his winter flannelette pyjamas. He wanted to comment, too, but thought better of it.

'How are you doing? Silly question. Are you okay, in the general scheme of things?' he asked.

'I think so. Are you sure you'd be okay changing this room – me making use of it?'

'Yes. If it's what you want.'

Colin didn't really remember having had any objections at all, ever. He'd never had need or a use for another room, or hadn't thought so. But he'd been guided by Joyce all those years ago and beyond. She'd been adamant about leaving the room untouched until she was ready, but had never told him she'd reached that state.

'I'm just trying to get a feel for it,' Joyce said, looking around, 'you know, to see how I'd go being in here.'

'If it's too much, I could put a camp bed in my office or sleep on the couch.' The sofa was certainly proving comfortable enough for his afternoon nap. 'And … how do you feel in here?'

'All right. At peace.'

Colin nodded.

'I think it's time.'

'Fair enough.' He sat down on James's bed, which was parallel to Thomas's, separated by a small cupboard at the head end, and mirrored Joyce with taking the space in.

The posters might have been worth something if they hadn't been held up with Blu-tack and sticky tape by their corners.

In the next moment Joyce was up and beginning to carefully unstick the images of musicians Danni and Kylie Minogue, basketballer Andrew Gaze, and the Adelaide Crows Australian Rules Football team, and laying them on the end of the bed she'd just vacated.

For the first time Colin noticed a cardboard box on the floor and a couple of flattened ones leaning against the wall. Slowly, Joyce began putting each piece of the twins' lives into the box.

Colin could almost hear the music now, and would have given everything to be in the position to tell the boys to turn the sound down. He thought about asking Joyce if she'd come across their music CDs yet. He wondered what CD had been left in the ghetto blaster up on the shelf, and couldn't believe in all these years he'd never thought to lift the lid and look. A new ache settled upon him. No, he couldn't ask Joyce, who was closer, to check and turn that on while they worked. It would certainly bring them both undone. And that wouldn't be helpful right now.

'Is there anything you want to keep, Colin?' Joyce asked, pausing.

Colin pursed his lips and frowned. *Yes, everything.* Suddenly he wasn't sure about this course of action. He'd thought he was ready ...

'I'm not actually turfing anything yet – just making space for myself. That box there is for anything you want to keep out and go through.' She pointed. 'Everything else I'm going to put in the garage for now. Except their clothes – they can go to the op shop right away, unless you have any objections.'

'No. That all sounds fine with me. Um.' Colin looked around the room and his eyes settled on the bookshelf where a stack of boardgames sat. 'How about keeping those out – the games?'

'Good idea. I read online that boardgames are making a comeback.'

'Did they ever go away? Maybe we just stopped playing ...' *Because they were connected to the twins.*

'You're probably right. Anyway, I agree to keeping them out. Then maybe we'll give them a shot again at some point. Also, their music. I don't think I can today, but I do sort of feel the urge to listen to their music again.'

Again, Colin nodded. 'How did you go this morning – get everything you need okay?' he said quickly before tension had a chance to catch hold too firmly. He thought it odd she was in neither yesterday's clothes or anything new.

'Yes, thanks. I've put the new things on to wash.' She must have read his mind, because she said the words at exactly the same time Colin remembered she always washed new clothes before wearing them. 'I'll certainly have enough now to go on with and get me to the funeral. Then I am hoping you're right and I can talk to Carmel's family and formulate a plan. Are you still okay if I move back?'

'Yes. I am.' He wanted to say, *'No. Not really. I'm still hurt by your actions. But I care too much to make it a hill to die on and kick you when you're down.'*

'Well, I really appreciate it. I had a quick look at rental properties online and the prices are horrific. And, to be honest, Colin, I don't think I'd like to be completely on my own right now.'

'You don't need to be. Not right now. But let's get one thing straight. You're not to take back up where you left off with doing all the meals and other domestic duties you did. I don't want you feeling you owe me and doing all that for that reason.'

'I actually rather like cooking, Colin.'

'Be that as it may, I feel I've essentially let myself down with taking such a back seat all those years.'

'Um, well, I hope I haven't overstepped, because I put your clothes on to wash, too – thought I might as well fill the machine. Okay?'

'That's fine with me. Thank you.' Colin felt a little sad about the clear disconnect they were experiencing and how they were treading around each other like new acquaintances.

'Also, Colin, do let me know if you need me to make myself scarce at any time.'

'Whatever do you mean?'

'Well, if you're entertaining your friend Shirley, for instance.'

'Joyce, I'm sure I've already said we're just friends. I'm serious.'

'But is that friends with benefits? That's the question.'

Colin frowned. There was something odd about what she was saying. Or, rather, the tone attached – an inflection – to the word *benefits*. He didn't understand it at all.

'What do you mean? "Benefits?" All friends have benefits. Shirley's been a great comfort.'

'I bet she has.'

'Spit it out, Joyce. You've lost me. Clearly there's something you're angling towards that I'm missing.'

'Well, all the young ones talk about *friends with benefits*.'

'Do they?'

'Yes.'

'And what's that when it's at home?'

'Sex, Colin. Friends with benefits is what the young ones refer to as friends who are not dating but have sex sometimes. No feelings involved beyond friendship. All fun, no responsibility. Apparently.'

'I see. Well, you're barking up the wrong tree, Joyce. I'm not having sex with Shirley and have no intention of doing so. And I'm positive Shirley is of the same opinion. We're simply two old people supporting each other through choppy lonely waters and enjoying some companionship. She's recently widowed herself. Okay?' He wanted to say, *'You don't get to come in here and pull the jealousy card.'* He might have if it weren't for the fact Joyce was grieving. And feeling very unsettled and vulnerable. Insecurity and pain caused people to lash out in any number of ways. So, he remained silent.

'Okay.' Joyce stood up again and resumed her methodical emptying of the room.

'Would you like some help?'

'No, thank you.'

'How about lunch? I'm making a tomato and cheese sandwich.'

'Sounds perfect. Would it be an imposition to bring it up here? I'd like to keep on, if that's all right.'

'Perfectly. And, no, no imposition. I'll be back soon.'

'You're welcome to bring yours and keep me company while we eat, if you like. But, up to you.'

'I'll be back in a bit.'

Colin left on a lighter step than when he'd arrived. He'd seen a few glimpses of the old Joyce shining through, he thought.

Chapter Thirty-six

Colin was unusually nervous as he waited for Joyce to get ready for Carmel's funeral. He was currently pacing his office in between checking his watch. He wasn't sure why he was feeling so antsy – it wasn't as if they were running late or Joyce was prone to delaying them. He just wanted it to be over. He felt bad about letting Shirley down and anxious about the scrutiny of Carmel's family. He wasn't sure what to put that down to, other than feeling on edge about keeping his thoughts to himself while protecting and supporting Joyce. He, on the one hand, appreciated they were grieving and understood their behaviour in shutting out Carmel's new partner. But he could also see the pain it was causing Joyce, who was being very stoic.

He'd hoped one of them might have reached out directly to her. Instead, she'd been left to check Facebook for any updates on proceedings. Or rather he had been left to. Joyce didn't want to look.

She'd weakened the other day, only to discover someone had gone through Carmel's Facebook profile and taken out all of the posts of her declaring her love for Joyce, including photos of them together – effectively eliminating her from their mother's life. Colin might not have believed Joyce had it not been for the fact she'd accidentally taken a heap of screenshots while trying to turn her phone off or do something else with it weeks ago. He'd been uncomfortable traipsing through their life together.

He thought one good thing about it was that at least Joyce knew where she stood heading into today. He had to give her considerable respect for going through with this, though they weren't there yet. He might not have attended if he were in the same position, though their age group did tend to go to funerals despite the discomfort in doing so. He wondered if it was indeed generational. Perhaps people these days tended more towards private cremations and the scattering of ashes, given the cost of things. Regardless, here they were about to head off. He gave a final sigh and left the room to wait in the hall.

'It's time to go, Joyce,' he called.

'Coming.' She appeared, smoothing her dress self-consciously and then her hair.

'Are you okay?'

'No.'

'It's not too late to change your mind.'

'I haven't. I'm going, if only to make them see they might be able to erase me from Carmel's online life, but they can't in her real one.'

He nodded. 'Ready?'

'As much as I can be.'

'You look very nice, by the way.'

'Thank you, Colin. As do you. And, just in case I haven't already said, and/or I get snippy later, I really do appreciate you doing this with me.'

'It's my pleasure, Joyce. And if you need anything at all – including leaving in a hurry – then just ask, or pull my sleeve, or whatever. He'd wanted them to have a signal phrase for each of them to utter in case of the need for a swift exit but neither of them could come up with anything suitable. And they weren't in the right frame of mind to joke about silly options.

'After you,' he said, opening the front door.

They drove in silence for the entire twenty-five-minute journey, which was well known to both of them.

Colin was glad their arrival timed perfectly with a group walking through the cemetery's gate. He didn't know if the mass of people of all ages were there for Carmel's service or another. He paused to double-check the signage and then took Joyce's hand, gave it a squeeze, and began leading her towards the chapel.

Along the way he glanced across at Joyce who offered him a grateful grimace. He gave her hand another squeeze.

'Colin?' He turned at hearing his name called in a familiar voice. *Shirley?*

'It *is* you,' she said, hurrying over and pecking him on the cheek. He let go of Joyce's hand to hug her. 'What are you doing here?'

'Carmel's funeral – Joyce's um …' He couldn't make himself say the words *'new partner'*.

The women nodded their acknowledgement and mumbled a greeting.

'Sadly, it seems a popular activity. Is yours a graveside service?' he asked, looking around. There was only the one chapel, but possibly there were plenty of other places for a smaller service. And of course there was always the graveside option. He had no idea how many the cemetery could handle at one time.

'Oh! My Lulu is your Carmel,' Shirley said to Joyce. 'Sorry, not mine as in–' she hurried on but then broke off.

Colin was grateful for the clarification on Joyce's behalf. He'd just seen her drawn face fall even more after the initial surprise. Now some colour had returned. He'd leant around in case he might have to catch her. She'd seemed momentarily so unsettled.

'There's Adelaide being true to form with having only one degree of separation. I stopped being surprised aeons ago. Anyway, we worked together for many years. Sadly, we'd lost touch a bit in the last couple of years.'

'Oh! You're *Shirley* – Shirley the nurse. The ...'

'Yes. The bossy one. That's what you were going to say, wasn't it?' she said with raised eyebrows.

Joyce nodded, her expression now sheepish.

'Don't worry, I am. That's me. No apologies.'

Colin experienced a wave of admiration for Shirley. God, he wished his client Andrea could meet her – or, better yet, be taken under her wing.

'I'm really sorry for your loss – of your husband and also now your dear friend, Shirley,' Joyce said. 'How truly awful.'

'Yes. It is. Thank you. And my heartfelt condolences to you for your loss and situation, Joyce.'

Colin watched as the women smiled sadly at each other. And then Shirley pulled Joyce into a tight embrace. He really was glad she was there, as she was undoubtedly much better at all this than him. He preferred the slightly hands-off position of being the professional observer.

'Are you doing okay?' Shirley asked Joyce when they'd parted. 'I mean, absurd question, really ... Actually, shouldn't you be already in there, being as you're immediate family?'

Colin realised a new batch of tears was rushing out from behind Joyce's sunglasses, and put his arm around her shoulder.

'She's rather been frozen out,' Colin explained to Shirley in a hushed voice as people pushed past them.

'Oh no. I'm really sorry to hear that.'

'Are you speaking?' Colin asked before the atmosphere had a chance to become awkward.

'I'll say something off the cuff if the opportunity arises. So, I'd better head in. Coming? Oh, Colin. I'm so glad you're here,' she said, hugging him quickly again.

'And I'm pleased to not be letting you down after all.'

'Come on, then, you can go in the middle and escort us womenfolk,' Shirley said. Colin allowed himself to be positioned with Shirley on his left and Joyce on his right. Shirley threaded her arm through his and he took Joyce's hand again. Colin was now grateful for Shirley taking charge.

'Okay?' he said to Joyce, giving her hand another squeeze.

'Yes.'

He thought she seemed a little better, stronger, than prior to Shirley's arrival on the scene, fresh bouts of tears notwithstanding, but it could just be her heightened colour in response to the surprise and raucous nature of his new friend.

'I'll just stay on the aisle in case,' Shirley whispered, stepping back to let Joyce and then Colin slide into the pew with just enough spots left for the three of them.

As he sat, again between Shirley and Joyce, Colin thought if they were of the impression he was the one providing the support, they'd be mistaken.

He felt greatly fortified for having them sitting close, their bodies touching like pillars either side of him. He wasn't at all a fan of funerals – no one was, he figured. But these situations always brought up his previous experiences. His parents and the twins, mainly. Images and emotions bounced around in his mind, jerking at his heart strings, swelling everything inside him painfully when it was quiet and the organ or string quartet was playing while people congregated. Thus, he was feeling decidedly anxious. And sad. He could only imagine how Joyce was doing beside him.

While getting settled he'd let go of her hand. Now he longed to pick it up again – as much for himself as for her. But Joyce was busy wringing both of her hands together and squishing a wad of damp tissues. He didn't feel he could clasp her hand now, otherwise it would appear he was doing so merely to stop her activity, as one would do with a fidgeting child. And he wasn't about to do that. One of Joyce's knees was jiggling, too, and again he wanted to put his hand on it. But that didn't feel quite the right thing to do either. So he slipped his hands in the gap between his legs and hoped this would be a quick service. Thankfully there was enough chill in the air for the building full of people to not be too stuffy.

As he watched the large screen up front with rolling images of Carmel's life and family he wondered, despite already knowing the answer, if there would be any of Joyce. He'd just spotted some of a much younger Shirley Royal in her nurse's uniform. He wondered if Joyce was keenly looking for herself too and was about to receive a new painful reminder. Humans were so good at setting themselves up in this way. Probably because it helped to hurt. She shouldn't be surprised, yet she'd still be disappointed. He could only hope the feelings would keep her on track to process her grief.

'You have me, Joyce,' he wanted to say. But he couldn't. He was no consolation prize. He didn't know if she even still loved

him, even in a different way. Like he did her. It didn't matter, he told himself, she'd chosen him for this. And he was sure it wasn't because of his professional standing.

The service was a blur for Colin. He'd tried to listen to Shirley's piece after she'd jumped up and moved out into the aisle, jolting him from his vacant state, but his mind had faded out soon after she'd begun speaking. He did become aware of a few titters of laughter around him a couple of times, so clearly it had gone okay. He was pleased and relieved on Shirley's behalf.

'Phew. Thank goodness that's over,' she said, easing herself back into the tight space beside him and the pew's end timber.

'Well done,' he said, offering her a gentle smile and patting her leg. He had enormous respect for people who didn't love public speaking yet were prepared to leave their comfort zone and do so. He hadn't picked Shirley as someone who would have any qualms in this area, but knowing she did enamoured him of her even more.

At that moment he felt Joyce's hand reach across him and also pat Shirley's leg. And then Joyce was leaning and whispering.

'Very well done,' she said.

'Thank you,' Shirley replied with a grateful smile, giving Joyce's hand a squeeze. Colin was delighted the women were getting along so well.

After what seemed a very long time and also hardly any time at all, such had been Colin's mental meandering, they rose along with everyone else and began filing out. In the sunshine, Colin eased away from the congregating people swarming around the immediate family. Joyce moved with him. Shirley was still coming out of the chapel, having stopped to speak to some people. He felt his hand being clasped, and responded by giving Joyce's a squeeze.

'Still doing okay?' he asked. She nodded. 'Do you want to go over and speak to the boys? I can go with you.'

'No. Better not.' Though from her tone he knew she really wanted to, or at least thought she ought to. He'd ask if she wanted to write them a note later instead. There were masses of people here. Plenty might not have the opportunity to speak to Carmel's remaining close family members.

He felt sad for Joyce all over again. She really wasn't just one of the many, or rather, shouldn't be considered as such.

He suddenly couldn't remember if refreshments had been mentioned as being on offer or not. Tea and biscuits tended to be available afterwards, at a minimum. Given the timing today, he'd have thought sandwiches, or other style of light lunch, not beyond the realms of possibility. His mouth began to water in response to his thought. He tried to scroll back to just before they'd left the chapel for a memory of having heard an invitation. Perhaps it was a select few, and they'd been quietly and privately invited. If so, best he and Joyce didn't know about it.

'Okay?' Colin now said to Shirley, who had arrived beside him, and was looking a little flustered.

'You did very well, Shirley,' Joyce said again.

'Thanks, Joyce, I appreciate you saying. Just between us, I'm not at all a fan of speaking in public or being up front and under scrutiny. But it's over now. Are you going to stay on for refreshments?'

'Oh. I missed that. Is it for all and sundry or by invitation, just close family and friends?'

'No. Everyone. They announced it right at the end.'

'I'd probably better not,' Joyce said. 'Colin? I'm in your hands.'

'Well, Joyce, it's really up to you. How about you, Shirley?'

'I don't need to stay. Too many people for my liking. Lulu would understand, as would Carmel,' she added with a gentle laugh.

'How did you get here? Would you like a ride home? Or back to ours for some lunch?'

'I caught a cab. So, yes, I'd really love a ride, thank you. And, actually, I'd also appreciate the company, so lunch would be fabulous. Thank you, Colin.' She smiled at him and he thought she looked very relieved, which gave him an extra glow.

'So, ready to go?' Colin asked, keen to get back to the sanctuary of the car and then his home.

'I need the loo first,' Joyce said, looking around.

'It's over there. Come on, I'll go too,' Shirley said. Colin moved over to beneath a nearby tree to wait.

'I'll be right here,' he called. He pondered ducking off to visit the twins' resting place, but didn't want the women coming back to find him gone. Also, he'd probably had quite enough emotional tension for one outing.

'Colin? Isn't it?'

'Yes.' Colin looked up to find Carmel's ex-husband striding towards him, recognisable due to the images he'd seen online and his close proximity to Carmel's adult sons and their families and the funeral director and celebrant at various times when Colin had looked up.

'Stefan – Carmel's ex-husband,' he said, holding out his hand to be taken up by Colin, which he did. 'Thanks for coming.'

Colin nodded. 'My condolences for your loss.'

'Thank you.'

'Are you going to be home tomorrow?'

'Um. Yes. Why do you ask?' At the same time a series of questions made their way through Colin's mind: *Bit familiar, aren't you? And how do you know where I live? What could you possibly want with me? Professionally or personally? He said home not in or at work, didn't he?* Colin cursed his lack of focus, which almost caused him to miss the next bit – the pertinent piece of information, as it turned out.

'The boys, Beau and Gareth, will be returning Joyce's things. How does ten am work for you?'

Golly. That's a bit harsh, don't you think? I really hope your insensitivity is due to your grief and discomfort. Poor Joyce.

'Er. Okay. Yes, that's fine. Thank you.' He felt he should be objecting or in some way standing up for Joyce in this situation, but didn't see how. And wasn't given any time to anyway because Stefan was now nodding and speaking again.

'Very good. Bye then. Thanks again for coming,' he said.

Left alone again, waiting for Joyce and Shirley to return, Colin wondered if he ought to tell Joyce or not about the furniture being returned tomorrow. He looked around to see if she might be in close enough proximity to have witnessed the brief interaction. She wasn't, as far as Colin could tell. He was still deliberating when Shirley and Joyce reappeared a few moments later. He smiled at them. He'd worry about this new conundrum later.

'Home?' he said.

'Yes, please,' Joyce said.

Colin had to hold himself back from hurrying, deliberately walking slowly back to the car. He was so grateful to close the car door behind him that he let out a loud harumph.

'Exactly,' Joyce said. 'I'm glad that's over. No offence, Carmel,' she added in a mutter.

'Yes. I concur. All very harrowing,' Shirley added.

Colin started the car, turned the air conditioner higher to

counteract the heat after the vehicle had been sitting in the sun for the last while, and carefully backed out of the parking space.

As he set off, he was appreciative for the silent journey, the atmosphere of which was that bit lighter than earlier. However, inside he churned with what to do about the furniture delivery tomorrow. He went through the options – tell Joyce. Don't tell Joyce and see if he could get Shirley to take her out so she wasn't there. Lie – never a good thing. And when Joyce found out, which she would next time she peered into the garage to put something in one of the large bins, she might react badly to the deception. Or not even the deception, but be upset simply because of what she was going through. No, it was really best he ripped that sticky plaster off now, got it out in the open now. Hopefully the journey home in the enclosed car would help Joyce deal with the shock. Shirley's presence would certainly help. Yes, better for all of them.

'Joyce,' he said when they were stopped at the next red traffic light, turning to face her. 'There's something you need to know. Carmel's ex-husband, Stefan, came over while you were in the toilet. They're bringing back your things tomorrow morning at ten am. Apologies for my bluntness, but I've chewed it over and decided soonest was preferable to later for you to know,' he said.

Joyce nodded slowly several times. He could practically hear her cogs turning and was tense as he waited for the outcome.

'Right,' she finally said. 'I appreciate you telling me.'

'How do you feel about it?' he asked, instantly regretting his professional persona slipping through.

'Okay. It's good that I won't have to deal with it, I suppose. That's something. Beyond that, I'd rather not think about it right now, thank you.'

Colin nodded and accelerated as the light turned green, and carefully released his tension with a long quiet breath out.

'It's not like I don't know how they feel,' Joyce continued. 'At least this way there's not any awkwardness. In light of that, I might make myself scarce and have you deal with them, if that would be okay?'

'Yes. That's perfectly fine.' He glanced in the rear-vision mirror and caught Shirley's eye. Her expression seemed neutral, so he had no idea what she was thinking, if anything.

'If you'd rather not be there at all, we can go out together – I could collect you or you could meet me somewhere,' Shirley said.

'Thank you, Shirley, that's very kind. I'll think about it.'

Colin again surged with warmth for Shirley.

Back home, Colin went to wash his hands in preparation for making lunch and the women continued on through to the kitchen.

As he made his way down the hall, he cocked his head at hearing their amicable chatter – Joyce asking Shirley if she wanted a cup of tea and Shirley replying yes, please, she was parched. He smiled to himself and sent yet another silent wave of gratitude for Shirley being there to help run interference.

Chapter Thirty-seven

Two weeks had passed since Carmel's funeral and Colin and Joyce had settled into an easy rhythm, though one that was different to previously; there was now a slightly stilted reverence between them. Thankfully, Shirley had become firm friends with them both, her bond with Joyce cemented when she'd taken Joyce out shopping the day Carmel's sons had brought her effects back; the sewing cabinet and hallstand in the garage and upholstered armchair and other smaller pieces of furniture in what was now her bedroom.

She'd pushed the twins' beds together to make a king-size bed and had gone with Shirley to purchase a topper to soften the join, new linen and so forth.

Joyce was keen to do away with the powder-blue walls and repaint the room, but Shelby as yet had been too busy to even come around and discuss the small project. In the interim, Shirley and Joyce had selected colours from the new bedspread and had stuck up sample swatches to be contemplated. The fact they seemed to be vacillating between blues, greens, pinks and purples told Colin it was probably best Shelby had been unavailable to date.

Tabby had arrived a week ago and was proving to be wonderful company. She strolled around the house as if she'd been there forever and was mistress of all she surveyed. But she seemed to have a particular knack of knowing exactly when Joyce, in her grieving state, needed her presence. Oftentimes Colin would be passing Joyce's bedroom to find the cat curled up on the end of the bed or nestled close to Joyce when she was there.

The feline in question was currently sitting upright beside him on his green leather couch, peering at the camera and putting on a good show of being a veteran model while photographer Andrea, Colin's client, snapped away with her camera.

'When I suggested animal organisations could probably use your talents, Andrea, I didn't think this would be the outcome,' he said jovially.

'Ah, you're loving it, Mr P. Just a couple more. Turn to your right a tad. That's it. And, anyway, it's win-win – you get some good shots for your website and your socials, and the rescue gets more publicity. And, let's face it, you need to improve your image after the last few months!' She grinned.

Colin smiled. The young woman was such a wonderfully vibrant presence. He tried not to think about all she'd been through and what was ahead of her.

'There. That's it. See, not so hard, is it?'

'All right. No. No, it's not. I have to admit. You make it fun, Andrea.'

'That's what we like to hear. And, Tabby, could you look any more photogenic? Don't let it go to your head – either of you – but the photos are *stunning*. She really does go beautifully with your couch, and it brings out the green in her eyes.'

'I heartily agree, Andrea,' Shirley said from the doorway where she stood with Joyce beside her.

'It suits you, Colin,' Joyce said.

'What does, Joyce?'

'The whole setup there. I wish Shelby would become available and do me a room,' she added, pouting.

'Now there's no need to get competitive,' he said good-naturedly.

Colin wondered if Joyce wanted to stay on permanently. He didn't mind the idea, but would like to know where her head was at on the matter. Though he wasn't about to ask. Nor had he broached the idea of her coming back to the business as a proper partner or paid employee. He itched to, but it was too soon. He thought she was doing rather well with not being in tears most of the time at this point.

It had idly crossed his mind several times that a granny flat in the back yard might be in order so Joyce had somewhere to sew without commandeering the dining-room table, which, if left covered with stuff for days on end, would do his head in.

And when thinking of small spaces his mind had gone to caravans – the subject of which, or rather specifically the grey nomad lifestyle, hadn't come up again.

The other day he'd chuckled to himself at the irony of thinking about a caravan permanently in the back yard, to the extent Joyce and Shirley had looked up from the paper where they'd been doing the crossword at the kitchen table. He hadn't dared share what had been causing his amusement – had placed that in the too soon basket. But the thought of a space in the back yard had remained, popping into his mind with regularity. Maybe a cute retro van on blocks ...

'Right, that's you done, Mr P.'

Colin nodded and vacated his seat.

'Just a couple of you now, Shirley, if you wouldn't mind, for the fostering part of the next newsletter. The team was adamant, so I'm not taking no.'

'Okay. Where do you want me?'

'On the couch. Thanks. To start with. See if Miss Tabby would be amenable to a cuddle.' No sooner had the words been spoken and Shirley, now seated where Colin had been, reached out to attempt to scoop the cat up, and the creature in question took it upon herself to climb into Shirley's lap.

'There's a good, clever kitty,' Shirley said. 'I swear, she must have done this before.'

'Or maybe she just loves the limelight,' Joyce added.

'I don't know much about her other than the fact she was surrendered and was too distressed to stay in the shelter,' Shirley said.

'If it's because of the rental crisis, I'll be livid,' Joyce said.

'Well, be livid, because that's the reason the majority of dogs and cats are needing homes at the moment. That and the cost-of-living crisis, which are two sides of the same coin, really.'

'There, that's the money shot,' Andrea said. 'Gosh, that was quick. And easy. Thank you, Shirley. And you, Tabby.' And with that, the cat hopped off the couch and strolled out of the room. Andrea set about packing away her equipment.

'Thanks so much for all your hard work, Andrea,' Colin said.

'It's been my pleasure. Thank you, for allowing me to make use of your gorgeous space.'

'I have to admit I didn't mind it one bit in the end. To start with, I was a little uneasy. But I have to say, you do put your subjects at ease beautifully.'

'Thank you for saying,' Andrea said.

'I'd like to pick your brain on something, if you wouldn't mind, Andrea,' Joyce said.

'Oh?' Andea paused with her packing of her gear.

'No rush. When you're finished here. But you're artistic. How are you with choosing paint colours?'

'Oh, um. I'm happy to give it a shot,' Andrea said, zipping up her bag and placing it by the door.

'Brilliant, right this way.'

'Also, I'm putting on a roast soon for an early dinner,' Colin said. 'Would you like to stay, Andrea? It's roast pork, if that's of any consequence. Also, I wouldn't mind breaking out the Cluedo or Scrabble – before dinner and/or afterwards – if anyone's interested. Joyce and I were doing some cleaning out and came across them recently after many years …'

'Oh, yum. I'd love to stay, Mr P, thank you. And, yes, Cluedo and Scrabble are my favourites – though I haven't played either for a long time. What fun!'

'Great. Shirley, you're staying, too?'

'Yes, please.'

'And Joyce? Just checking.'

'Absolutely. Thank you, Colin.'

'Well, I'll get on. You girls go and sort out Joyce's colours.'

Colin smiled as he heard them traipse up the hall.

In the kitchen he started preparing everything for dinner, and while he did, he marvelled at how unfazed he was about cooking for company now. Though he did also know that with Joyce and Shirley in the house to call on there was little chance of getting into trouble in the kitchen.

Tonight's pork was a trial run for Christmas Day, just over a week away. They'd discussed their disappointment at how no one had been in touch – not one of their old friends – since either Joyce's permanent leaving of Colin or her sudden loss of Carmel, despite them both leaving several messages via each of the available means.

Shirley, in the same boat and facing her first Christmas without Norman, had suggested they come to her place. But Colin had offered to both host and cater, hoping over time their gathering would grow to include others who might be orphaned, or feeling so, and fill the twelve seats around the dining room table. And it had a little. Andrea had already accepted, and had also quietly enquired if she could bring a friend – not a romantic friend, but a guy called Cameron she'd met at her new volunteering gig who was going through a tough patch. Colin hadn't quite known how to enquire if it was the same Cameron he'd met professionally but Shirley had cut in and said Colin already knew Cameron because it was she who'd sent him his way, having met him and hit it off while they were both volunteering at the rescue centre.

Dinner having been a success, the small group was now seated around the kitchen table with the game of Scrabble well under way. While Andrea and Joyce were studying their tiles and the board and pondering their next moves, Colin, smiling with contentment, took the opportunity to look around the little group. In doing so, he caught Shirley's eye. She winked at him, which he returned, and then their chests rose and fell in unison as they each sighed.

Acknowledgements

Thank you to Sue Brockhoff, Laurie Ormond, Jo Munroe, Victoria Struthers, and everyone at Harlequin and HarperCollins Australia for turning my manuscripts into beautiful books and for continuing to make my dreams come true.

Thank you to Abigail Nathan for the editorial expertise and guidance to bring out the best in my writing and this story.

Thank you to the media outlets, bloggers, reviewers, librarians, booksellers and readers for all the amazing support. It really does mean so much to me to hear of people enjoying my stories and connecting with my characters.

Thank you to my dear friends who provide so much love, support and encouragement – especially Mel Sabeeney, Bernadette Foley, WTC and LMR.

And, above all, enormous thanks to my wonderful partner and best friend Phillip for making everything so much better. I am truly blessed to have you in my life.

talk about it

Let's talk about books.

Join the conversation:

@harlequinaustralia

@hqanz

@harlequinaus

harpercollins.com.au/hq

If you love reading and want to know about our authors and titles, then let's talk about it.